Sign up for our newsletter to hear
about new and upcoming releases.

www.ylva-publishing.com

Other Books by C. Fonseca

Food for Love
Where the Light Plays

tracing INVISIBLE THREADS

C. FONSECA

Dedication

To my family and friends. This has surely been one of the strangest and most testing times of our lives as the COVID-19 pandemic physically isolated us from one another. I'm grateful to have had this project to keep me focussed, and not allow my thoughts to drag me down, dwelling on how much I miss each and every one of you.

For Jane, who has the patience of a saint and whose devilish sense of humour got me through…everything.

Acknowledgements

I love exploring ideas and writing about my corner of the world, here in Australia. To do this accurately and beyond my lived experience, I need a lot of help.

Heartfelt thanks to my beta readers Elke, Paula and Lariane for their advice and pertinent direction. To Carol who invited me to her Chewton cottage, to dream, soak in the beauty and listen to the birds. Much appreciation to Jules who drove me around the goldfields area of Castlemaine and filled me in on local knowledge. Who'd have thought Prue's search for her ancestors would trigger my interest in Chinese immigration to Australia? At the beginning of my research, Kathryn and I had hours of fun on our jaunt to State Library Victoria rediscovering the beauty and mystery of this gloriously refurbished Melbourne icon. The trip in the lift up to the Dome was a highlight that day! Thanks also to Anna for ignoring us while Jane and I enacted scenes and argued over the tiniest of details of the story.

Hats off to State Library Victoria, who during the global pandemic has re-invented itself through social media platforms and other forms of remote communication. I am one of the millions who would have been lost without their ability to adapt. The Library's resources provided invaluable insights and entertainment as I researched this novel.

My gratitude to Marita Dyson, from Melbourne band The Orbweavers, who allowed me to include her as a character in my story, and reference one of their incredibly moving songs throughout the pages.

I am indebted to my publisher, Astrid, and the Ylva Team for all their hard work. Special thanks to my editors, especially Hayley, whose gentle prodding teased all those extra emotions and feelings out of me.

Thank you to my readers: writing this story took me on an amazing journey, and I hope you enjoy reading *Tracing Invisible Threads* as much as I loved writing it.

The two main locations featured in *Tracing Invisible Threads* are set on the traditional lands of the Kulin nation and the lands of Dja Dja Wurrung people, and I acknowledge them as the traditional owners. I pay my respects to their elders, past and present, and recognise their connection to country and community.

This book would have never been finished without Jane. To my darling, thank you.

An invisible thread connects those who are destined
to meet, regardless of time, place, and circumstance.
The thread may stretch or tangle.
But it will never break.

Chinese proverb

Chapter 1

East wind

Waterloo Television Studios, London.

ELEANOR DRUMMED HER FINGERS ON her thigh. She glanced at her watch for the umpteenth time, looking up with a start as the program assistant stuck her head around the open door. "Ms Heysen," she said, elongating her name with a thick Scottish accent. "Two minutes, and we'll move you behind the set."

"Here we go." Eleanor jumped to her feet and spun around, her black leather sneakers making a squeaky sound on the polished tiled floor. Something sharp dug into her back, so she reached behind her and lifted the lightweight suit jacket, where the techie had tucked the battery pack into her matching heather-grey trousers. She adjusted the pack, rolled her head from side to side and followed the assistant who set off at a cracking pace.

Through the gap between the drop curtains, she spied the host, Ian Sinclair, with his well-coiffed hair, flashy silver suit, and burgundy bow tie. He was charming the audience with his signature pre-show banter. Eleanor placed a shaking hand over her racing heart.

To calm herself and give her courage, Eleanor twirled the emerald-green bead bracelet around her left wrist. It was a gift from Aunt Helen after Eleanor had landed her first paid job with a small Fleet Street publication. The beads were pale, semi-transparent, and shimmered with hues of green and yellow. She hadn't wanted to accept such a generous gift, but Helen had wrapped her in a warm hug and told her she'd bought it in a backstreet market on her first photographic assignment in Beijing. Recalling Helen's earthy, hearty laugh and sparkling blue eyes as she had clasped it around Eleanor's wrist, Eleanor felt a sad smile tug at the corner of her mouth.

The audience erupted with a round of applause, and the assistant nudged Eleanor forward. She squared her shoulders, stepped between the curtains and on to the stage.

She blinked a few times. *God*, the lights were bright. When her eyes refocussed, Eleanor was comforted to find the set was way smaller and less intimidating in real life than on the TV. She clenched her fists to stop them from trembling, remembered the assistant's detailed instructions and strode to the sofa, where the chat show host greeted her with a toothy grin and a firm handshake.

"Sit yourself down, Eleanor Heysen." Ian gestured with a flamboyant arm wave. She carefully perched on the edge of the canary yellow sofa—that resembled a relic from the 1970s—while Ian took a seat behind his desk. In his trademark smooth drawl, he said, "To be honest, we don't need an excuse to highlight exceptional female talent, but since it's International Women's Day, we will make sure to. Eleanor, thank you for joining me today." He paused as the audience cheered and clapped. "We are here to honour and celebrate women and their achievements and you are my lucky, lucky, lucky first guest."

Lucky, lucky, lucky. Well, that's what Renate, her publisher had told her and of course she was right. Eleanor took a deep breath. Even though she'd dug in her heels at first, refusing Renate's suggestion, here she was. The show was a perfect opportunity to promote her book.

"You have gone from newspapers and magazines, to major photojournalism projects, to capturing the human condition in ways that are compassionate and at times jaw-dropping." Ian clapped his hands in the air, and his audience joined in. "In recent years, you've travelled widely, doing a lot of humanitarian work covering inequality, cultural diversity, and gender imbalance. Thank you for taking time out of your busy schedule to be with us today."

"Thank you for inviting me." Eleanor smiled, shifting her gaze away from the large screen at the back of the set that showed her iconic 2008 photograph of Nelson Mandela chatting with England's newest princess. It had been taken in Hyde Park at a concert celebrating his ninetieth birthday.

"Oh, it's a pleasure." Ian picked up a remote control device from his desk. "Of course, you are recognised for your individual style of photography and not your gender, but in this industry...well, all things are not equal." He regarded her directly. "How do you feel about being labelled a *female* documentary photographer?"

"I'm sure my colleagues would agree it will be progress when we are simply known as photographers." Eleanor quickly scanned the audience. "But I am a woman, and I am a photographer."

"Too true," Ian said, bobbing his head up and down. "Very true."

Eleanor reached for her water glass and took a large gulp. She'd half expected that question.

"Let's look at some of your career highlights, shall we?" He swivelled around to face the screen and pushed a button to start the slide show.

While random images flashed across the display, Ian rattled on about her accomplishments, asking her questions, sometimes waiting until the audience quietened. Eleanor wriggled back on the sofa and placed her hands on her knees. She was chuffed at Ian's generously flattering remarks. It was pleasing to discover that he had a genuine interest in her work.

"One last picture. I hope you don't mind, but it shows that being a photographer with a social conscience is damned hard, and sometimes harrowing." He pushed a button on the remote, freezing a large black and white photograph of Eleanor on the screen. *Hell.* Her stomach churned as she recalled the time and place. Unsurprisingly she looked a wreck. It was a photograph she hadn't seen before and never wanted to see again.

"Whoever turned the camera on you at that moment certainly captured a maelstrom of emotions." He rubbed his goatee beard between his thumb and forefinger, clearly waiting for Eleanor's response.

Eleanor winced. With no small effort, she kept her voice calm and her hands steady. "Yes, they did."

Pictures of her had surfaced before, especially in the good old days when the paparazzi would snap shots of Eleanor with her celebrity girlfriend. Why would anyone bother taking a photograph of her now? She no longer had the celebrity girlfriend, and she was just a photographer doing her job.

"Where were you at the time, Eleanor?"

"São Paulo, Brazil."

Eleanor pulled at her shirt collar, as though the intense heat had drifted all the way from that tiny airless shanty into the air-conditioned Waterloo Studio. The enormous image showed her insect-bitten, blotchy face, the sweat dripping off her forehead nearly blinding her. She looked totally haggard, almost dwarfed by the camera she had her hands wrapped around.

"What was going on?" Ian asked.

She lowered her eyes away from the screen, swallowing the lump rising in her throat. "It was the funeral of a fourteen-year-old girl who'd died during childbirth in the favela slums. Fernanda," Eleanor whispered, almost reverently. "Her name was Fernanda. I was on assignment covering the government's campaign to reduce teenage pregnancy. It was actually backfiring and the situation was only getting worse. I spent two weeks in the favela, photographing young pregnant girls in the community. Fernanda went into premature labour and died as a result of multiple complications."

"Horrific circumstances. It's not surprising you look so distraught in the photo," he said, his voice laced with concern.

Eleanor forced herself to look back at the huge projected image again. Someone had obviously sold it to the press. Eleanor appeared fragile, bedraggled, and distressed. It truly captured her state of mind then, and now. Raw and exposed.

"You're thirty-six years old, Eleanor. You've been covering traumatic events for over ten years. How have you been affected by this?" Ian asked.

Eleanor shrugged. *Anyone could see. It was pretty obvious in that photo.* "It's my job. I'm a storyteller and documentarian, and sometimes the stories I cover take me into heart-breaking situations." She lowered her eyes, staring down at her hands. When she looked up again, thankfully the image had gone, and the spotlight had shifted back to the host. "It's not always like that. Sometimes the occasion is joyful."

"Thank God for that," Ian said, walking around his desk and picking up a copy of her brand-new, hardback, publication. "If anyone was born to be a photographer, Eleanor Heysen was. I promise you; her poetic images will trigger a tingling feeling, proving beauty can be found in the most unexpected places, and this extraordinary book of Eleanor's photographs, *Treading Lightly,* can be bought at all the best bookshops right now." He waved the book in the air. "*All* the money will go to organisations around the globe whose main focus is to save lives and improve the quality of life for women and girls."

"It's a cause that is close to my heart. I hope the sales will make a difference." Eleanor smiled. She was proud of the book. It was dedicated to Aunt Helen. A small step towards forgiving herself for letting Helen down.

Off camera, a man, probably the producer made a wind-up gesture with his hand signalling the segment was coming to an end.

Ian wrapped up, strode across to Eleanor, and shook her hand firmly. "Good luck on your journeys. Come back and visit us sometime." Covering his microphone, he whispered, "I've received two in-ear prompts that someone has been calling, urgently trying to get hold of you." He gestured to a stagehand, hovering nearby. "Tom, take Eleanor back to the dressing room, now."

Eleanor followed Tom backstage. Who was trying to get hold of her so urgently? A weight seemed to press on her chest as she thought of the possible reasons behind the calls.

"Tom, do you know who rang?" Eleanor called out.

He stopped and turned around. "Someone from Melbourne, Australia."

She gulped. Had something terrible happened back home?

At the end of the corridor, Tom pulled out a set of keys and unlocked the dressing room door. He pointed to the black antique telephone hanging on the wall. "Go ahead and use that if you want. They'll put a call through. I hope everything is okay."

After Tom left, shutting the door behind him, Eleanor grabbed her rucksack and pulled out her phone—which she'd flicked to silent. A list of notifications dropped down. Three missed calls and a message from her brother. *Oh, God.* It had to be something serious.

What on earth could be wrong? She scrolled through the call log. The one from her mother was just over an hour ago. The other two from Leo were more recent—so was the text:

Eleanor call me ASAP. Dad's in hospital.

Her heart began to pound in her chest. All manner of horrifying scenarios flashed through Eleanor's mind. Had he been in an accident? He did love driving fast and pushing the boundaries of his classic old sports car on the open road. *Please. Please, let him be okay.*

Eleanor's fingers trembled as she called her brother.

Chapter 2

High stakes

Five days later. Melbourne, Australia.

ELEANOR APPROACHED THE ROOM AT the end of a long hospital corridor and read the name plate—Harold Heysen. Even though Leo had told her what to expect and had assured her their father was making good progress, as she stepped inside his brightly lit room, Eleanor had to lean against the doorframe to steady herself.

Her strong, dependable dad lay propped up on a raft of pillows. His body barely made an impression under the starched white sheets covering him, and his face was gaunt and pale. It was the first time in her life she'd witnessed her father looking so frail and her heart ached for him.

Reassured by the soft continuous beep-beep-beep of his heart-rate monitor and the steady rise and fall of his chest, Eleanor moved quietly into the spacious, boutique-hotel styled room to stand beside his bed. Tears welled up, and she sighed deeply, reaching for his hand.

He grabbed her fingers. "Well, that was a huge sigh," her father croaked. "It must be jet lag."

Eleanor smiled. *He knows it's me.* The fear and foreboding that had followed her all the way from London gave way to an enormous sense of relief.

"I thought I was dreaming that there was an angel beside my bed." He squeezed her hand again and gave her a sleepy half-smile. "And here you are. My angel. I didn't mean to scare you, Nell."

A tear slipped down Eleanor's cheek, and she wiped it away with her free hand. "Daddy," she whispered.

"My God, you're more beautiful than any angel I could imagine." He winked. "You look like Sarah when she was your age, apart from your short snazzy hairstyle."

Eleanor leaned forward to kiss his forehead. "Thank you, Dad."

It wasn't the first time he'd mentioned she resembled her mother. She supposed they did share some physical similarities, like their light-olive skin tone and dark brown eyes. However, he knew as well as Eleanor that their temperaments were very different.

Her father cleared his throat. "Apart from obviously needing a good rest, you're still my little Nell."

She pulled back, just far enough to gaze into his soft blue eyes. "I'm so glad to see you at last. We sat in the plane for two hours in Singapore sweltering in the heat." Her voice cracked, and a few more tears escaped, landing on her father's chest. "I'm so sorry…" She'd been worried sick from the moment she'd spoken to Leo five days ago. It seemed as if weeks had passed since she'd first received his text. Her exhaustion from fear and lack of sleep was catching up with her—it was not like Eleanor to cry openly in front of her father.

"All that matters it that you're safely here now." He tightened his grip on her hand and gave a strained chuckle. "And I'm here. More importantly, the doc tells me, in due course, I will be just fine." He let go of her hand and patted the bed cover. "Sit up here."

"I don't think the scary nurse who glared at me from the desk in the corridor would approve." Eleanor dragged a heavy upholstered chair close to the state-of-the-art hospital bed and sat down.

"She's a softie. Alice is an extremely competent and compassionate nurse. Everyone here knows I've been waiting for you to arrive." He craned his neck to peer at the wires and monitoring equipment behind the bed. "Don't let all this paraphernalia frighten you. It'll be gone in a couple more days."

Eleanor leaned over to brush her hand lightly across her father's broad shoulder. "That's good to know," she said. "I would have come straight from the airport, but Leo, not so tactfully, suggested it would be better if I showered and changed first. He said something about socks and armpits." Imitating what Leo had done, she pinched her nose.

Her father grinned. "Good idea. They are very particular here about clean socks and the liberal use of deodorant."

Eleanor laughed. "Good thing I took Leo's advice." She lowered her eyes, wondering if it would be all right to ask her father about his heart attack. She looked up, and he gazed at her questioningly.

"What is it, Nell?"

"Tell me what happened, please. When did you realise something was seriously wrong? Had you been feeling unwell? Leo said you told Mum it was indigestion when she asked why you were rubbing your chest after dinner that night."

"Hmm. Up 'till then, I hadn't noticed any symptoms. It did seem a bit like indigestion. You know that feeling after you've eaten a big roast, followed by pavlova?"

Eleanor shook her head. "Actually, no. It's years since I've had a Sunday roast. As for pavlova, now you *are* making me drool. I doubt Mum has time to bake these days like she did when Leo and I were kids." It had been a long time since Eleanor had tucked into a wedge of her mother's crispy pavlova with its gooey marshmallow-like centre.

He scratched his forehead. "If your mother has her way, I'll never eat pav again. From now on, I've got to limit red meat, cream, butter, and salt. All the good stuff. And then once I've recovered from the surgery, there's cardio rehab twice a week to rebuild my fitness."

Eleanor squeezed her misty eyes shut. While working across the world, she'd suffered nightmares about being unable to get home if anything happened to her family. She opened her eyes and looked at her father. Thankfully the nightmares had not turned into reality. Eleanor was home and her father was alive. "I'm here to help with things like that. I'll be able to take you to rehab."

"Thanks, love. That will take some pressure off your mother." He sighed. "I'll be happy when I can get behind the wheel again and drive myself around, that's for sure."

"Of course, you will." Eleanor smiled encouragingly, although Leo had mentioned their father would not be able to zoom around in his classic sports car for at least a couple of months.

Her father got a faraway look in his eyes. "I've never experienced anything like it before. As if some monstrous beast was sitting on my chest." He squeezed his eyes closed. "Then I heard this strange voice saying something like, "Just relax, Harold. You're having a heart attack."

Eleanor squeezed his hand. "I'm so sorry, Dad. That must have been terrifying. The main thing is that the surgery was successful and you'll be home soon. Then I can fuss over you, take you to rehab, and feed you poached fish on a bed of lettuce."

He scowled. "That will be stretching your culinary skills to the max, sweetheart."

Eleanor giggled and lowered her head in agreement. "I'm afraid my cooking hasn't improved—probably because I don't spend much time in the kitchen."

A beaming smile lit up her father's face. "I just remembered about your TV show. Leo downloaded the footage from your television debut, but I haven't seen it yet. We can watch it together when I get home." Pride glowed in his eyes.

"Jeez. The Ian Sinclair Show seems as if it was months ago. I haven't even had a chance to see the recording myself," Eleanor said. "It'll be fun to watch it with you at home."

Home. Eleanor hadn't realised how good that could sound. She'd return home at least once a year to catch up with family and recharge, but there was never enough time, and the pressure of getting back to work usually sat heavily on her shoulders. Eleanor sighed. Jet lag and exhaustion was a bummer—she was on the verge of tears again. How long could she stay in Melbourne this time, before she had to head back overseas?

"Are you all right, Nell?"

"Yes, I am, Dad." She shook the thoughts away. There'd be time enough to worry about that later.

He squinted at the bedside clock. "Sarah had to pick up some papers at the office, but she'll be back soon. Your mother has been so excited about having you home, too. Have you spoken to her yet?"

"Not since the plane landed."

"Sarah wouldn't have told you about Helen's trunk then," he said.

"What trunk?"

"Would you believe the Chinese government returned Helen's personal effects?"

Eleanor leaned forward in her chair. "Finally. I made that special trip to Beijing two years ago after the promised ten-year anniversary release date, but the government refused to hand over her things. They were *still* questioning Helen's motives for going to Chengdu at the time of the earthquake."

He shook his head. "Bloody red tape. Accusing Helen of being a spy."

"Totally ludicrous." Eleanor had been powerless, unable to slice through the excessive bureaucracy and gain possession of her aunt's belongings. "I don't suppose anyone's had an opportunity to look in the trunk?" Eleanor smiled eagerly. She couldn't believe she was finally going to get the chance to see what Helen was working on when she died.

The sound of the heart-rate monitor changed, and her father's fingers tightened around her forearm.

Eleanor looked up hurriedly to see his strained face. "Are you okay, Dad?" She took his hand, her eyes darting towards the door. "Should I get someone?"

He squeezed her fingers and shook his head. "I'm okay, Nell. Once I'm home, we can go through the trunk together."

Eleanor caught her lower lip between her teeth. "Don't worry. I can sort through Aunt Helen's belongings—"

"It is wonderful that you are home, Ms Heysen, but it's time for me to check your father," Alice said, wheeling a medicine trolley to the end of the bed. Eleanor hadn't even noticed her come in. "Mr Heysen has been eagerly awaiting your arrival. We've heard so much about you. Welcome back." She skirted the bed, leaned over, and pressed the monitor screen.

"Thank you, Alice." Eleanor let go of her father's hand and jumped to her feet. "I'd better go and let you take a nap before Mum gets back." She stifled a yawn behind her hand. "Love you, Dad."

"Love you, too, Nell," he said softly and laid his head back against the pillows.

"Seems like the both of you need a rest." Alice gave Eleanor a wry smile. "See you again, Ms Heysen."

Eleanor rubbed her eyes. Now that she'd finally seen her father and knew he was doing okay, the idea of stretching out on a bed sounded like heaven. She knew she'd bounce back after a few hours of sleep, but now, her body ached and keeping her eyelids open was near impossible. She wanted nothing more than to climb into bed. That was if she could stop herself from opening Helen's trunk first.

Chapter 3

Winds and dragons

The tram came to a shuddering halt at the crowded La Trobe Street stop, and Eleanor braced herself against a metal pole before being caught in the slipstream as everyone headed for the exit, only to be slowed down by the crowd of people trying to get on. The CBD was simply mad at peak hour. She breathed a sigh of relief when she jumped out of the tram and caught sight of the State Library Victoria, with its sturdy portico supported by eight lofty Corinthian columns.

Eleanor glimpsed a flash of bright blue enamel through the top of her partly open canvas rucksack and hurriedly re-tightened the drawstring. She lifted the rucksack onto her shoulders and readjusted its leather straps. It was heavy, but not any more weighty than usual. The burden of the box's contents and honouring Helen's memory far exceeded its actual weight.

It was almost two weeks since Eleanor had found out about Aunt Helen's trunk. She'd spent nearly all of her time with her father since she'd got home to Melbourne. Her dad insisted that no one fussed over him, but of course she did, and they'd fallen into a comfortable routine. Apart from driving him to various medical appointments around town, they'd spend the morning together discussing politics or world events, teasing each other about their differing taste in music, and just hanging out. It warmed her heart to be able to spend so much time with her father again.

This was her first foray into the city. Inside her jacket pocket was the map of the library her father had insisted on printing for her. She took it out and quickly looked over it to check her bearings before glancing at her watch. Ten minutes was more than enough time to find her way around the building, into the Russell Street Welcome Zone, and to the gallery foyer.

She was pleased with herself. Eleanor had timed it perfectly for her appointment with Katherine Kent, her mother's friend and the manager of collections.

The library was in the final phase of major renovations, and as she strode past the temporarily closed main entrance, Eleanor gazed nostalgically across the expansive forecourt lawn. She'd spent many stolen moments sprawled on the lush grass daydreaming or perched on one of the well-worn stone steps far away from the pompous, stuffy Law Library in the Supreme Court Building—where, as a law student she was supposed to be.

It was here that she'd explored the world through stories, atlases and maps, exhibitions, photographs, and travel journals that had piqued her curiosity for faraway people and places.

She reached inside her jacket to tug on the strap of the Leica camera that hung from her shoulder. She patted it lovingly. After her meeting, she hoped to have time to take a few shots before racing home again. Her camera of choice today was fitted with a crisp 50mm Summilux lens. Perfect for shooting in the low-light conditions of the domed nineteenth-century building.

Checking out her reflection in the sliding glass doors at the library entrance, Eleanor pulled at her short hair and straightened her collar. "You'll do."

She entered the East Wing directly into a bright white-walled foyer. Tantalizing aromas from the ultra-modern coffee bar tickled her nose. "Hmm...Melbourne coffee."

There was no smell of musty old library books here. The lounge space was filled with a sprawl of people in armchairs, while others sat at long work desks and stared at their screens. One wall was flanked by a larger than life mural depicting giant pages of books, where colourful illustrations appeared to leap off the pages. *Brilliant.*

Eleanor growled, instinctively reaching for her rucksack, clutching it to her side as a dozen or so schoolgirls barrelled past, almost knocking her off her feet. The worn canvas bag essentially carried her life's necessities when she traversed the globe, and it had suffered a lot of abuse over the years. She pulled it against her chest, took a deep breath, and sighed as the children—giggling and whispering—and their minder moved down the stairs and out into the sunlit street.

On her last assignment in West Africa, Eleanor had witnessed first-hand how some rural communities placed little value on educating girls. It incensed her that many females had hardly any opportunity for even basic schooling and the tiniest possible chance in the world of learning to read and write. She glanced at the people around her. *Most of us here take our privileges for granted, not realising how lucky we are.*

With her rucksack hoisted safely on her shoulder, Eleanor strode past the security guard, along the corridor, and towards the designated meeting place. If she didn't get a move on, she'd be late for her appointment, and she hated tardiness, especially in herself.

Alexa pushed up the bridge of her thick-framed glasses and held the leather-encased, velvet-lined image at eye level. The precious daguerreotype measured a mere two and three quarter by three and a quarter inches, and its imperfections and quirks hinted at its history. The portrait, a silver-plated copper image, portrayed a woman holding a tiny infant and was dated 1854, making it very rare. The delicate plate couldn't be used to make copies. It was too fragile and easy to damage. A one-off.

It was crazy to think that using her smartphone, Alexa could in mere seconds, capture and manipulate an image and beam it to the world across social media.

Alexa lifted the daguerreotype into a cotton-lined box, carefully closed the lid, and held the box in the palm of her hand. "Creating you was a lot more complex." She caressed it with her blue-gloved finger. "So, where will you be in a hundred years?" Alexa mused, then scowled. "Tucked away on a tiny piece of the library's eleven kilometres of shelving. But *I* won't forget you."

"Are you talking to the objects again?" Jac Dupont walked into the lab, pointed at the box, and rested her hand on Alexa's shoulder. "Those images can't talk back. They've been dead a long time."

"Phew. I'm actually relieved to put it away safely," Alexa said with a sigh and placed her chin on her friend's wrist. "Hi, Jac. You're right about the dead not speaking. It's one of the post-mortem portraits. You can hardly tell the baby's dead in the mother's arms."

"Creepy. One of the shadier sides of Victorian photography." Jac squeezed Alexa's shoulder, then removed her hand. "My teams had a hell of a time preparing the two hundred drawings and paintings for this installation. Good reason for us to get out of here tonight and celebrate." She twirled around on the tips of her patent-leather flats. "The gang's heading for cocktails and nibbles in an hour or so. Can I count you in?"

Alexa pursed her lips. "I'd like to join you, but I have to return this to storage and then keep an appointment." She checked the wall clock. "Oh damn..." She placed the archival box onto a trolley, threw her coat and bag over her shoulder, and tucked the folder Katherine had left on her desk under her arm. "I have to get this all the way to storage then sprint to the Cowan Gallery to greet my visitor." She swore under her breath.

Jac wrinkled her nose. "Meet us afterwards then. Come on. It's Friday," she said. "Isn't it a strange time for a meeting?"

"It wasn't arranged by me. Katherine was summoned to an emergency meeting with the Chief. She couldn't contact the woman, who's the daughter of her old school friend or something. I'm just the fill-in meet and greet."

"What's it about?" Jac asked. "Maybe a new acquisition?"

"Hopefully. Katherine promised we'd help with identification." Alexa retrieved the folder from under her arm and read the label on the front cover. "The historical slides are part of the estate of Eleanor Heysen's aunt. She's the one I'm meeting today. Eleanor, I mean. They may relate to Chinese/Australian migration."

"Well, that could be fascinating." Jac crossed her arms matter-of-factly. "Who was her aunt?"

"There is a tragic side to the story. She was a journalist who went missing after the 2008 earthquake in Sichuan."

Jac rubbed her temples. "The one that killed nearly seventy thousand people. The Great Sichuan Earthquake?"

"Uh-huh...and where thousands more were unaccounted for." Alexa shuddered and stared down at her hands, unable to comprehend the scale of such a devastating tragedy.

"My brother and I were travelling in Tibet at the time." Jac shook her head. "There was a lot of political unrest, and then the earthquake happened in China. I remember an Australian National Press photojournalist based in London disappeared somewhere near Chengdu."

"Hmm…interesting. I wonder if the journalist's disappearance was linked to the political turmoil." Alexa checked the wall clock again. "Oh no, the story of my life. I'm running late." She glanced at the large two-tiered trolley with the tiny box containing the daguerreotype sitting on the top shelf. She rolled it towards the exit. There was no way she'd run with the precious cargo. "Be a darling and lock up here for me. I may see you later."

Jac called out after her, "Hey, I think the photojournalist's name was Helen."

"Oh, really?" Alexa raised her voice just a little as she manoeuvred the trolley towards the hallway. "I'll let you know how it goes with Eleanor."

The trolley's wheels vibrated and echoed through the subterranean maze of corridors and passageways as Alexa walked as fast as she could.

Eleanor shifted her weight restlessly from one leg to the other. Katherine Kent was nearly fifteen minutes late. Either that, or Eleanor had gotten the time wrong. It had been years since she'd met her mother's friend, but she couldn't recall Katherine as someone who would be late.

Walking over to a wooden bench close to the librarian's desk, Eleanor removed the rucksack from her shoulders, figuring she might as well sit down if she was going to have a long wait. She dropped heavily onto the bench, drew up her legs, sat cross-legged, and pulled the rucksack with Aunt Helen's precious contents into her lap.

At this end of the gallery, she was well positioned to observe the library patrons getting on with their business, without being too noticeable. What were those two men doing, with their arms folded, heads down on a desk? Were they asleep or praying? Or the young mother with her toddler balanced on the edge of her knee who typed on her keyboard with her free hand?

Eleanor reached inside her jacket. With the camera's silent shutter, she could blend into the scene, focus, and shoot. It was slim and compact enough that she could remain inconspicuous even in a busy public space. She'd learnt many invaluable photographic techniques from her aunt, but most importantly, Helen had taught her how to view her subjects with an artist's eye.

Eleanor discreetly drew the Leica onto the rucksack, her thumb perfectly positioned to press the button. Sometimes photographing perfectly mundane, everyday moments could bring unexpected joy.

"I am *so* sorry I'm late."

At the sound of a woman's deep and melodious voice, Eleanor turned. "Katherine," she said, smoothly tucking the camera back into her jacket. Their gazes met, and she smiled sheepishly. This was, unquestionably, not her mother's old school friend.

"I do apologise, Ms Heysen." The woman held out her hand. "I'm Alexa Bellamy. Katherine Kent was called away at the last moment. An emergency meeting." Her gaze swept back and forth across the foyer, glossy deep brown hair swinging over her shoulders, brushing the surface of her crisp, black-as-midnight shirt. "You're probably aware the library has been undergoing a major refurbishment."

A faint flush heated Eleanor's skin, working its way from her neck to her cheeks. Alexa Bellamy. There she stood, her tall and graceful figure quirkily fitted out in a collared, wide-cuffed shirt and flared houndstooth-weave trousers, as if she was ready for a photo shoot. *Alexa*. Sounded like elixir, a magical potion.

"Ms. *Heysen*?"

Eleanor inclined her head to meet intense hazel eyes. "Hello, Alexa." She reached out and grasped Alexa's hand in a brief, firm handshake before tucking her own hand into her jacket pocket. "Please, call me Eleanor."

"I am really sorry to have kept you waiting, Eleanor."

Alexa's lush brows curved above eyes that twinkled under the suspended gallery lighting. A starburst of hazel-green and grey-blue hues. Eleanor found it hard to look away.

"Katherine sends her apologies." Alexa's lips turned up in a slight smile.

Eleanor traced her finger over the outline of her phone that sat snugly in the back pocket of her jeans. She hadn't received a message from her mother's friend. "You're definitely not Katherine."

Alexa cleared her throat. "No." Those same perfect brows slanted in a frown, and she folded her hands primly in front of her. "I work in Pictorial

Collections. I'm a historian, photo archivist, and librarian. Katherine asked me to assist you in her absence."

Eleanor swallowed. "My turn to apologise. I was taken by surprise."

"Really? Oh, I'm sorry I'm not who you were expecting."

The tone of her voice and her languid yet striking posture exuded confidence. Let's face it, Alexa Bellamy did not fit the stereotype of the demure, introverted librarian often portrayed in pop culture. Not at all. In fact, she smashed it. "I'm not sorry," Eleanor muttered, giving Alexa a wide grin to prove just how not sorry she was.

She lowered her gaze to the polished floorboards, giving herself a moment before finally looking up to meet Alexa's alluring gaze again. "It's been a long time since I was here. I didn't expect to like the changes, but I do. It's awesome." She was relieved to see Alexa's gentle smile. "I can't believe there are students sitting in the entrance welcome zone loudly discussing assignments. And people playing computer games. Actually, there isn't a book in sight." Eleanor didn't usually ramble. She stopped herself, hoping Alexa hadn't noticed.

"That's because it's not a lending library. You'll have noticed all the guards. You can't borrow our books to take them out, but they can be read and researched in one of the study spaces and reading rooms."

"Oh, of course. I knew that." Eleanor rubbed the back of her neck. *Why am I acting like a fool?* Reaching around for her rucksack, she said, "I have Aunt Helen's slides with me. Do you want to see them now?"

"Well, that is why you're here, Eleanor," Alexa said with a twinkle in her eyes. "I have a viewing room booked for us in the South-East Wing. Follow me."

Alexa set off at a brisk walking pace, and Eleanor hurried after her. They weaved in between and around people, out of the gallery foyer, and through a vast room with curved architraves and a high glass-panelled roof. Eleanor was happy that the skirting mezzanine balcony was still lined with wooden shelving and rows upon rows of books, just as it had been when she was a student.

At the far end of the room, they stopped at a barely noticeable doorway tucked behind a neatly stacked bookshelf. Eleanor didn't know what caused the fluttering in her stomach, but when Alexa had to lean across her to swipe the magnetic card that hung from a lanyard around her neck across a small metal pad, she held her breath. The metal door slid open with a soft *whoosh*, revealing an unexpectedly light-filled hallway flanked on both sides by wooden doors, all firmly closed. Talk about a rabbit warren. It would be easy to get lost here.

"It's all very mysterious," Eleanor whispered as Alexa stopped outside one of the doors and turned the handle. The lofty room with sand-coloured walls contained an oversized timber desk, two upholstered chairs, and a grey metal locker.

Alexa arched one perfect eyebrow. "Come inside."

Eleanor passed through the narrow entrance close enough that her arm brushed lightly against Alexa's. She inhaled deeply. Alexa's scent was reminiscent of a Marrakesh garden. Warm and subtly sensuous. Eleanor felt the sudden urge to run away right now, except that she'd never find her way out of the library.

Almost as if Alexa could read Eleanor's mind, she shut the door behind her with a soft clunk. She placed the folder that had been tucked under her arm onto the desk and set her leather satchel down beside it. "I think the mystery has only just begun." She gestured to the rucksack in Eleanor's hands. "Should we get right to it then?"

"Yes." Eleanor nodded. The slides were a precious link to Helen and even though she was excited at the prospect of learning more about them, a small part of her was reluctant to hand them over to a stranger. "Yes," she repeated, more firmly. "This is what my aunt wanted."

Chapter 4

Throw the dice

Alexa reached for her satchel and retrieved her trusty tool kit, bouncing lightly on her toes. She loved this part of her job. The beginning of a journey, the anticipation, the not knowing what would be revealed always sent tingles down her spine. She unrolled a rectangle of Polyfelt liner onto the desk and laid out one pair of blue powderless nitrile gloves, one pair of white cotton gloves, a roll of acid-free measuring paper tape, a pair of tweezers, a magnifying eyepiece, and a flat dust brush. She rubbed her hands together in satisfaction once everything was in its place.

She looked up to find Eleanor clutching her bag to her chest, peering at her from where she'd remained by the door. Her reticence was intriguing. Eleanor was strikingly good looking too, with broody eyes and clear, light-olive skin. Alexa gave a barely audible sigh.

"Let's see what you've got." Alexa patted the top of the desk. Okay, the art of subtlety was not her strong point. She needed to work on that, but Eleanor had *on edge* written all over her and Alexa had to put her at ease. "Excuse my rudeness. Please sit down."

Eleanor placed her well-worn bag on the floor beside the desk and sat in the office chair. She flicked her short, wavy hair back with a brush of her hand. Was this a nervous habit? In the glow of the pendant light, her hair was enriched to warm honey brown.

"Would you like to show me what you have?" Alexa asked.

There was a hint of apprehension in Eleanor's eyes as she gazed at Alexa. "Yes, of course. As you said, that *is* why I'm here."

Alexa blinked, pulled the chair closer to the desk, and sat down. *Yes, that is why she's here. It isn't a date.*

Eleanor leaned over and loosened the leather cord at the top of the bag. With two hands, she reached inside and slowly pulled out a large, heavily decorated rectangular box, teal blue in colour. "Where shall I put it?"

"Right here." Alexa pointed to a clear space on the desk.

"This is just how we received the slides," Eleanor said. "They were in this box, in a trunk with my Aunt Helen's belongings." She smoothed both hands over the lacquered lid, then placed them on either side of the container. Her knuckles were white from the pressure and she seemed reluctant to let go.

Alexa reached out to squeeze Eleanor's hand, noticing slender fingers and well-manicured nails, then stopped herself, realising how inappropriate the gesture would be. "I can't imagine how difficult it's been for you and your family."

"It was some time ago," Eleanor said in a matter-of-fact tone. But there was no hiding the sadness in her soulful brown eyes.

"Grief has no expiration date." Alexa picked up the nitrile gloves, blew into them, and slid them on, taking a moment to compose her thoughts and still her heavy heart. After two years the burden of Alexa's own grief was no less painful. She pulled back her shoulders. "May I?"

Eleanor's brows narrowed. "Yes," she said with a slight nod.

"The box is gorgeous," Alexa said. "Blue enamel with Chinese temple and dragon ornamentations." She lifted it with her gloved hands, surprised by the weight, and rotated it slowly. "And it's heavy. Actually, it has five dragons. On the top and on the four sides. The clasp looks to be hand-fashioned copper, and look…" Alexa raised the dragon box so they could both see the base. "…there's an identifying tag."

Eleanor lifted herself out of the chair and pushed herself forward, leaning across the desk. "I don't suppose you can interpret these symbols?"

She edged close enough for Alexa to breathe in the fragrant warmth of her skin. "Umm…no." She let out a slow, controlled breath. "Let's leave that to our experts. We have an excellent Collections and Research team." She pointed again to the tag. "But I've seen this kind of Chinese symbol before. The reign mark is written in vertical columns and usually depicts the dynasty, country of origin, and signature of the craftsperson."

Eleanor sat down. "Okay."

"It's exquisite." Alexa touched the copper clasp on the front. It was easy to get distracted by the beauty of the box, its bright colours and artwork. But it was not her area of expertise. "Let's get to the reason you're here, shall we?"

The hinge was stiff and made a hollow tinkle as Alexa opened it. Within the box's red velvet lining lay a discoloured muslin bundle about seven inches long and four inches wide. She lifted out the bundle, noting its weight and laid it on the Polyfelt liner.

A careful search inside the blue dragon box revealed that the lower section of the red velvet was loose. She picked up her tweezers and gently lifted the lining. Alexa cracked a smile. "My goodness. What have we here? There's a secret compartment, Eleanor."

"What do you mean? I didn't see anything."

Controlling the slight tremor of her fingers, Alexa cautiously lifted out a brownish coloured envelope as anticipation made her heart beat faster. "This must have been tucked in here for safe keeping." She drew apart the sides of the envelope and peeked inside. "Looks like a very old photograph. From the reddish tint, it is possibly an albumen print."

Eleanor leaned across the table. "What can you see?"

Alexa allowed the print to gently slide onto the liner. Although the image showed signs of abrasion with minor wear at the corners, it was in amazingly good condition, and she couldn't hold back a smile. "It is rare to find a print of this age." She picked up the eyepiece, whistling though her teeth. "I'll have a closer look."

She peered through the magnifying eyepiece and gasped in recognition at the pocket-sized building with its scrolled gable above the arched doorway. "I know that building; it's Chewton Town Hall. Looks like a family standing on the steps. The gentleman appears to be Chinese, and the European woman has her arms around two small children."

"Chewton?"

"My mother has…I mean, I have a cottage in Chewton."

"That's amazing." Eleanor tapped her forehead with her hand and shook her head.

Alexa could only blink. *Yeah, absolutely. A weird coincidence.*

"Remind me, where is Chewton?"

"It's part of greater Castlemaine. Are you familiar with the area?"

Eleanor nodded. "I think it's close to Bendigo, but I haven't been there since I was in school."

"Well, it hasn't changed that much," Alexa said. "I like to think the town has its own unique historical identity. It was a thriving city during the gold-rush years. Over twenty-five thousand diggers moved to Chewton, which was then known as Forest Creek—including many Chinese." She hesitated. "Eleanor, this is so fragile, we'll put it aside for now and look at the other treasures." She was itching to know what lay within the muslin bundle.

Alexa placed her gloved hand on the dragon box. "This and its contents are quite a load to carry around in your bag."

Eleanor folded her arms across her chest. "I'm a photographer. I'm used to lugging my gear around."

"Is that why you're wearing a camera under your bomber jacket?"

She flicked her fringe off her face and gave Alexa a fixed stare. "I know the rules. I wouldn't have thought of using it back here without asking." She shrugged out of her jacket and draped it on the back of the desk chair to reveal an orange V-necked T-shirt and a very sleek, sexy black camera.

"Nice camera," Alexa said. *Nice body, too.* She wished she'd had time to do a thorough background check on Eleanor Heysen and her aunt. She'd correct that mistake as soon as possible. Alexa was curious to learn more about the women, especially the good-looking one sitting right in front of her.

Eleanor removed the camera from around her neck and lowered it slowly into her bag. "I couldn't resist unwrapping the cloth bundle when I found it." She sighed.

"I don't blame you." Alexa wiggled her gloved fingers and extended her hand to pick up the bundle. Eleanor appeared uptight, as though she'd done something wrong. Alexa grinned at her to ease the tension and reassure her. "Hey, this is yours. We'll take a look and then you can decide how you'd like to proceed. It's up to you, really." Alexa waited until Eleanor nodded her permission.

"Go ahead. The glass plate negatives look really old and fragile. When I realised what they were, I decided I'd better not take them out of their padded envelopes." A small frown still creased Eleanor's brow.

Alexa almost squealed with excitement. "Did you just say glass plate negatives?"

Eleanor looked bemused. "Yes, I told you, I looked inside the box."

This was Alexa's area of expertise, her passion. If Eleanor was correct about the negatives, it was a very rare find. Alexa sucked in a breath as her heart raced. "Okay," she said, shakily. "You've done the right thing, keeping them protected. If these are *glass* plate negatives, they are extremely vulnerable to light and air…and can easily fracture."

After carefully untying the material, she exposed a slim wooden receptacle. She slowly turned it over in her hands. "I wonder what secrets this will tell us."

"I was itching to have a proper look," Eleanor said. "But it was too risky."

Alexa picked up the box with two hands and gently placed it in front of Eleanor.

"Turn it upright," Eleanor said. "It has a hinged lid and wooden slots inside for the slides."

Alexa nodded and turned it in all directions as she inspected it closely. "No markings, no inventory numbers or identification notes, but, thankfully, it was very well protected." She opened the lid, pulled out a support, and put it on the liner. Using her bent nose tweezers, she carefully removed the envelope from inside.

"Crikey." Alexa pointed at red markings in the centre of the envelope, nearly leaping out of her chair. "That's a Norlane and Bolton stamp."

Eleanor tilted her head to one side. "Who are they? Are they the photographers?"

"Yes. We have many images of theirs. I've researched and worked on their collection for years. Oh, look, there's a handwritten date. See these tiny numbers here?" Alexa pointed to the corner of the envelope. "It's smudged, but I can make out 1872."

Eleanor's eyes grew wide. "1872. That's nearly a hundred and fifty years ago."

Alexa steadied her hands. With the tweezers, she peeled back the stained, fragile paper, revealing a glass plate, incredibly thin, with an almost pristine negative image. She picked it up with one hand, careful to make contact with the sides only, and held it above the bright white liner surface, squinting to see it better. "I can just make out what appears to be two children. One in long shorts, shirt, and cap and the other in a tunic dress and bonnet. They're standing on some steps in front of a building. There's a sign above them, but I can't read it. Could be a schoolhouse."

Eleanor rubbed the back of her neck. "That's interesting. Let's look at the others."

Alexa lowered the glass negative to the liner and glanced up to find Eleanor staring at her expectantly. "These are special and awfully fragile. No doubt about it," she said. "Let's leave the rest to the experts. You can trust us, Eleanor. This..." She waved her hand over the small collection. "It could be historically unique." Curiosity gnawed at Alexa's insides; however, she repackaged the negative and replaced it into its housing. She had to follow protocol.

"It was Aunt Helen's wish to have them identified. It's just that I was hoping..." Eleanor lowered her eyes and placed her hand on the dragon box. "If they are historical images from Australia, could the Library look into it further, investigate why they were in China? I hoped that looking at the negatives today would give us a hint."

Alexa raised an eyebrow. "A hint to what?"

"A clue to why my aunt had them in China," Eleanor said. "She'd written in her notebook that she intended to bring them here, to the Library. But she didn't say why."

"If you're prepared to leave these in our care for the time being, we'll investigate and compile a full report of our findings." Alexa was at pains to reassure Eleanor that she understood how important her deceased aunt's slides were to her family. "I can assure you we follow the strictest handling and documentation procedures. They will first go into Quarantine, then on to Preservation."

Eleanor slumped back in her chair. "I suppose that's fine. Sounds like you've got a plan." There was a hint of a smile as she spoke, "I expect next time, I'll be meeting with Katherine?"

Not if I can help it. Alexa eyed the dragon box eagerly but was careful to keep her voice controlled. "We'll see how it goes," she said smoothly, getting to her feet. "Katherine has so many meetings these days, you may have to make do with me." Katherine had assigned her this project today, and Alexa would fight tooth and nail to secure it. The Norlane and Bolton stamp on the envelope could very well mean the slides were connected to one of the Library's significant collections. The Lehmann Collection included such detailed images depicting life during the Victorian gold rush, and Alexa buzzed with excitement at the thought of having new material to investigate. On days like this, Alexa really did love her job. She held out her hand.

"Working with you will be just fine," Eleanor said. With a handshake faster than the speed of light, Eleanor's fingers brushed Alexa's, leaving a trail of sparks that had Alexa wondering if Eleanor also felt them.

"Good, then I'll see you soon." Alexa put her hand to her mouth to hide her silly grin.

Chapter 5

Red lantern

Eleanor opened the heavy oak front door and could tell that her mother was not home by the wall of sound that greeted her. Ear-piercing music. She smiled fondly at the thought of her father enjoying his favourite bands at full volume while he had the house to himself.

She dropped her jacket and bag into a winged armchair near the cedar staircase and headed past the dining room to the study. A few hours ago, Eleanor had left the house a bundle of nerves, but Alexa Bellamy had put her at ease with her professionalism. And, damn it, the pictorial historian had a killer smile. Eleanor rolled her eyes at the direction her mind was travelling.

Knocking on the study's half-closed door was pointless; there was no way her father would hear her with the sounds of Australian '60s beat music blaring through his fancy sound system. Even so, she rapped loudly out of habit—after all, this was his sanctum.

She pushed through the door, expecting to find her father sitting behind his mahogany desk. A stack of open books lay across the desk's leather topped surface, but the high-back rolling chair was empty. Over the din, she could hear a sharp tap-tap-tapping. "Dad? Dad, where are you?"

The music suddenly stopped. "Nell, is that you?"

She peered around the carved screen into the alcove where her father stored his cherished collection of records and audio equipment. "Oh, you're in here. Are you okay?"

He laughed. "Yes, of course. I'm fine."

"Really? Because that music was so loud it could burst my eardrums."

He gave her a beaming smile and chuckled.

"Why are you laughing?" She couldn't help but smile; it was good to see him more like his old self.

Her father picked up the ebony cane that lay beside him and tapped it on the wooden floorboards. "Because I'm happy to see my darling daughter, and I believe you meant that as a joke?" He ambled towards his desk.

She leaned towards him and laid an affectionate kiss on his unshaven cheek. "Is Mum home?" she asked, even though she knew the answer.

"Obviously not." He steadied himself, resting a hand on the desk before slowly sitting down. "It's another late evening at the office."

"Again?" Eleanor grumbled. She shook her head and moved to the window seat overlooking the garden.

Rays of evening light fell across the stone wall surrounding an azure swimming pool. She never tired of her parents' stunning garden. Today it was filled with the brilliant colours and sweet fragrances of early spring. Eleanor gazed at the vanilla-scented wisteria, still in bud, scrambling along the pool house.

As the days grew longer and warmer, she'd be able to savour the blush-pink blooms and heady citrus perfume of the daphne bushes, which, along with the wisteria's aroma would float in the breeze and tease her senses. This was her favourite time of year in Melbourne, before it got too hot.

"Don't be hard on your mother, Nell. She lost almost two whole weeks' work sitting by my bedside in the hospital, and now the two of you are waiting on me hand and foot since I came home," he said. "It's not Sarah's fault I can't pull my weight at the firm. There's a lot going on."

"I know, Dad, but you've had a triple bypass."

"Sarah was here when I most needed her and so was your brother. And then you came back. I'm a lucky man." He blew her a kiss across the table.

Eleanor feigned catching it and pressed it to her forehead, but she was still sceptical that her mother couldn't make at least a little more time for her family.

"You know your mother's doing what's necessary for our clients, and for us. Anyway, Joel is around here somewhere. Thanks to you, I can ring for help on this gadget." He pointed to the smartwatch she'd bought him when he'd flatly refused to wear a MediAlert pendant around his neck. "Had a visit from the doctor today, and he's pleased with my progress."

"That's great, Dad. Really good news." Eleanor gazed upward, thanking whomever was watching over her father, and the medical staff who'd saved his life. He'd had a tough two days last week before his medication had been adjusted. Even her mother had stayed home.

"Okay. That's enough about me." He shifted about in his chair until he was comfortable. "I want to hear all about your trip to see Katherine. Did she shed any light on Helen's treasures?"

"Unfortunately, she couldn't meet me."

"Oh? That was a waste of your time."

"Far from it, Dad. I ended up having a pretty good afternoon." Eleanor briefly closed her eyes. "Where do I start? You know I always loved spending time at the library, but honestly, with all the renovations, it's even more extraordinary." She leaned forward and launched into what had transpired that afternoon. "I was on the edge of my seat when Alexa, err… Ms Bellamy, lifted the red velvet lining with nifty little tweezers and exposed a secret compartment." Eleanor took a quick gulp of air. "Can you believe it? There was a really old print hidden inside, in nearly perfect condition!"

Her father chuckled. "Tell me more."

Eleanor continued to explain nearly every aspect of her visit, only omitting how much Alexa Bellamy had captured her attention.

"Well, Ms Bellamy seems to have made a good impression on you. Does she think the images are of historical significance?"

"Yes, she does." Eleanor grinned at her father. "I'd say she definitely took a keen interest. It seems they were the work of Australian photographers in the 1870s. Alexa had no explanation for why they were in China, but I left them with the library for further investigation."

"That's probably for the best. I was hoping they'd be able to tell us at least something about why Helen had them. I trust they'll keep us informed?"

"They have thorough procedures and policies. It may take some time, but I'm reasonably satisfied that Ms Bellamy is proficient in her job and will keep us in the loop." Eleanor reached into her back pocket, pulled out a folded piece of paper, and handed it to her father. "Here, you'll want to check this out. It's the temporary loan documentation."

"Good, I'll look at it after dinner." He rubbed his forehead and slumped slightly in the chair. "Thank you for making time for this. I'm so glad you're home." Eleanor was surprised to see that tears threatened at the corner of his eyes.

She gazed at her father with concern. Usually stoic, the illness had changed him. Softened him, somehow. Away from the firm, he'd lost the tough corporate image. She'd always been his little Nell, but now the fierce need to protect him brought tears to her own eyes.

"So am I," she whispered.

Her father cleared his throat.

A thick hard-covered book lay at the corner of his desk beside a copy of Eleanor's recent publication, and he pulled Aunt Helen's book towards him, holding it against his chest. "Helen would have turned sixty-five this Christmas. Being seven years older, and a selfish prat, I didn't have much time for her when she was growing up," he said sadly, placing the book back on the desk. "I remember a little red-headed whippersnapper with pigtails who complained about being born on Christmas Day." He laughed quietly. "She carried that Kodak Instamatic our parents gave her for her eighth birthday everywhere."

Eleanor leaned across the desk and squeezed her father's hand. "I wonder what happened to the Instamatic. Helen used to talk a lot about popping in a film cartridge and heading out for a photo shoot as a kid. I know she'd rather have had Grandpa's Leica camera, though."

"You're right, she would have. But he would have never parted with it then. It was his pride and joy."

Now, the Leica was Eleanor's pride and joy.

"Unlike me, you inherited his passion for photography." He tapped his hand on Eleanor's book. "Your grandfather saw that in you, and it made him happy; after all he gave you his precious camera when he could no longer use it. Helen and your grandfather would be proud of you."

Eleanor lifted her aunt's book off the desk. Published posthumously in 2009, it represented her life's work as a documentary photographer. The weight felt good in her hands. Real. It was a constant inspiration for Eleanor and a tangible link to Helen.

She flicked through the pages until she found what she was looking for, the photograph of Helen with her arm firmly around Eleanor's shoulder.

Along with two hundred thousand campaigners, they were in Edinburgh, Scotland on part of the Long Walk for Justice. Trailing Helen as she covered the 2005 G8 Rally against poverty had been an incredible experience and one Eleanor would never forget.

"That's a cracker of a photo, isn't it?" Undisguised pride shone in her father's eyes. "Wasn't it the first time you went on assignment with Helen?"

Eleanor smiled, tracing her finger over the black and white photograph. "Just as her shadow, really. It was a frenetic few days chasing after Helen and her journo friends as they covered the many events amongst the huge crowds of people," she said. "It was exhausting and scary at times, but I loved it, and definitely earned my dram of whiskey every night. I learnt so much from Helen. She was an expert at contrasting stillness and motion—isolating her subject in a crowd." Eleanor closed the book, gently placing it on the desk, and rested her cheek in her hand.

"Will you be in for dinner, sweetheart?" Her father laid his hand on her forearm.

She lifted her head to meet his gaze. "Yes. If that's okay. Are you expecting Mum?"

"Afraid it will be just the two of us tonight. Sarah's tied up with a civil proceeding rising out of a regulatory investigation. As I said, she'll be having a late night."

"Okay then." Eleanor shrugged, fighting the urge to roll her eyes. What else was new? "Would you like me to cook you something?"

"I believe Joel has everything under control." Her father clutched his chest. "A man in my condition must be careful."

She laughed. "I know how to open a can of baked beans."

"Please pour yourself a whiskey. Unfortunately, I can't have one." He sighed dramatically.

She appreciated his self-mocking humour and winked. "I couldn't, Dad."

"Why not? I'll sit here and sulk." He grinned. "Go on. The Balvenie Tun was a gift from a satisfied customer. Someone may as well enjoy it."

"It would taste a lot better if you'd join me. So, let's wait until you can," she said thoughtfully. "I'll take my gear to the studio and freshen up and change. But you can tempt me with a glass of wine at dinner." She tapped her watch and feigned a royal accent. "What time do we dine, Father?"

"Seven thirty. And there's no need to talk posh." He slipped his fingers around hers and squeezed lightly. "I hope you have enough room in the studio. I expect you are more comfortable there, out of Sarah's way."

She swallowed her irritation and ignored his reference to her absent mother. "Don't be ridiculous, Dad. You saw my digs in London; I shared the same amount of space with three others. I love the studio, especially with the darkroom set-up, and it's so peaceful."

"If you change your mind, there's plenty of room inside this commodious pile."

"Thanks, Dad," she said. "It's perfect." And it was. Eleanor hummed happily to herself.

The studio apartment at the rear of her parents' estate was a sanctuary. At thirty-six, having lived independently for years, Eleanor really appreciated having her own space.

"Off you go. You have about half an hour before we are summoned to dinner." He extracted a remote control device from his cardigan pocket. "Ellington or Bach?" He pressed a button on the remote, and the room was filled with the richly textured sounds of jazz. "Easy choice," he called after her.

Eleanor blew her father a kiss and skipped out of the room. She grabbed her belongings and took a shortcut through the living room onto the patio and across the inner courtyard to the studio. She removed her camera from the rucksack and took the stairs two at a time to the first-floor bedroom.

Eleanor was relieved her father appeared happy she'd left Helen's slides in the care of Alexa and the library. During their meeting, she'd been impressed by the professionalism of the photo archivist, librarian, and historian. But just in case her judgement had been impaired by Alexa's charm, she wanted to check Alexa's qualifications. The slides were too important to her to be left in the care of someone who wouldn't look after them properly.

It took all of sixty seconds to sit at the desk, power up her laptop, and type, *Alexa Bellamy, State Library Victoria* into the search engine. As she scrolled the webpage listing Alexa's university achievements, academic papers, and the library's in-house videos, Eleanor's admiration only grew. "Alexa Bellamy." She smiled. "I like that name; it kinda rolls off the tongue."

Chapter 6

All green

THE *PETER...PETER...PETER* OF A JACKY Winter bird—calling from where it clung to a low branch of iridescent yellow, flowering gum—caught Alexa's attention. The small grey-brown flycatcher was swinging its tail from side to side, probably looking for a mate.

She raised her coffee mug. Alexa hoped the little bird had better luck with relationships than she did. He deserved success because, unlike Alexa, he was putting in a lot of effort with his song and dance routine.

Light poured through the open French-styled doors of the 1850s miner's cottage. Reclining in her favourite wicker chair with her laptop balanced on her knees, Alexa picked up the thick slice of toasted sourdough baguette from her plate on the side table, sinking her teeth into the chewy, tender centre and creamy, locally cultured butter. The rays of sun were warm against her legs, bare below the mid-thigh hem of her cargo shorts, tempting notions of gardening and planting those punnets of heritage tomato seedlings she'd brought with her.

She'd arrived at the cottage late yesterday evening, parked her car in the carport just in case it rained, unpacked, and gone straight to bed.

This morning, she'd woken up with the incredibly attractive photographer on her mind. Eleanor had wanted to know about the images—where they were taken, and more importantly, why they were in her aunt's trunk. Alexa could definitely assist with the first request, but the second was more of a conundrum. Hopefully she and the library resources could help Eleanor shed light on that mystery.

Eleanor had a reserved manner and had given away very little about herself during their brief meeting. It wasn't just her good looks that piqued Alexa's interest. She had an air of mystery about her that Alexa just couldn't help but want to figure out. Although she'd intended to do a quick search online, as was her habit, one web page led to another. Eleanor's images had featured in prestigious magazines; she'd won several awards; her first book had recently been published. "Wow." Before Alexa knew it, just one more minute had turned into an hour. *You did say you were a photographer. You just left out all the most interesting bits.*

Alexa closed her laptop. She yawned, stretched like a lazy cat, pulled herself out of the low chair, and gathered her breakfast dishes, placing them in the sink. She glanced through the open French doors, ready to begin digging in the dirt and nurturing the plants the way her mum used to. Wearing a long-sleeved cotton shirt over her tank top, a wide-brimmed hat and sunglasses, she headed out into the brilliant, mid-morning sunshine.

Alexa strode down the slate path which led to a small red shed, its roof laden with moss, at the end of the cottage garden. She eyed the comfortingly large amount of firewood stockpiled under its eave. The bespoke outbuilding, designed by her mother, held all the implements she'd need to plant the seedlings.

The garden was a chaotic mix of fruit and native trees, shrubs, honeysuckle, salad greens, vegetables, and a vast array of herbs. Her mother had taken a rather higgledy-piggledy approach when she'd planted it, and Alexa treasured every square inch of her legacy. She sighed heavily as she gazed across the small field of lavender where she and her grandmother had scattered Eloise Bellamy's ashes.

Eleven months ago, on the first anniversary of her mother's death, she'd finally summoned the courage to sort through her belongings. It was hard to be in the cottage without her mum's physical presence; every corner was filled with reminders of her life. Framed photographs, art and knick-knacks from her travels, and her precious collection of botanical books. Through every doorway, Alexa expected to see her mother, brewing a pot of lemon verbena tea in the kitchen, or painting at her easel on the patio.

Alexa often referred to her mother's gardening journal, filled with roughly drawn maps and handwritten notes on the dozens of flowers, vegetables, and medicinal herbs she'd planted. As she dug a trough for the tomato seedlings, Alexa was thankful for the mountains of soil and compost her mother had trucked in to enrich the barren, stony plot.

She dropped one seedling after the other along the trench and covered their roots with soil. Although her grandmother had encouraged Alexa to make Gold-Dust Cottage her own, she'd kept most of the furniture, all of the books, and her mother's flower paintings. The cottage was Alexa's hideaway, and apart from a new watering system, she hadn't changed the garden much at all, wanting to preserve this piece of her mum.

"Alexa!" a sharp voice called. The bark of a dog and the clip clap of approaching footsteps across the cottage's floorboards brought her out of her daydream.

"I'm out here," she called back. On her knees, she leaned back and braced herself as the Staffordshire terrier barrelled towards her. "Whoa, Daisy," she cried, holding out her hands in front of her. The puppy flopped onto her back and Alexa tickled her tummy. Daisy wriggled with delight. "Hello, darling Daisy, it's good to see you, my little petal. Where are your mamas?"

"We've arrived." Kelly came through the back door and into the garden, sporting oversized dark glasses and a big grin.

Alexa smiled. She wasn't surprised to see Kelly's sturdy athletic frame clothed in her signature khaki shirt and trousers—minus the wide-brim hat that usually kept her wiry spiralling curls in check.

"Ah, we thought you'd be out here. It's such a spectacular morning." Kelly lifted her arms to the sky and bowed as though in homage to the sun. "You should have ventured with us to the Res." She picked up Daisy with an easy swoop of one hand and tucked her under her arm. "You'd have enjoyed the swim, Alexa."

Alexa got to her feet and dusted the earth from her hands. "You're crazy. Too cold for me this early in spring." She looked around. "Where's Louise?"

"Putting some things in your fridge, probably reorganising your kitchen." Kelly laughed and jumped as Louise, who'd appeared by her side, lightly punched her on the arm.

"I was just putting the dessert in the fridge," Louise said. She walked up to Alexa, balanced on the tip of her toes, and gave her a hug.

Alexa wrapped an arm around Louise's waist and leaned down to brush her friend's forehead with a kiss. "Great to see you, Lou. Thank you for the dessert, but you shouldn't have. I asked *you* over for lunch," she said. "How late is it? Time seems to have got away yet again."

"Is that so?" Kelly winked at Alexa and gently placed the struggling pup onto a patch of grass. "Daisy, you've wet my clothes with your dirty feet." She pulled at her damp shirt.

Louise groaned. "Oh no, I'm so sorry. I told Kelly not to let Daisy go through the house."

Kelly stepped up beside Louise and placed an arm around her wife's shoulder. "She took off before I could stop her. The front door was open."

"Don't worry about Daisy's footprints. It'll be cleaned up in a flash," Alexa said. "Now, about lunch. It won't take long to put together. There are drinks in the fridge. Make yourselves comfortable on the patio." She waved her hands in front of her friends. "I'll have a quick wash and change."

"I brought some Pale Ale," Kelly said. "Would you like one?"

"I'm right for now, thanks." Alexa turned to Louise. "What dessert did you bring?"

"Rhubarb Crumble and coconut custard," she replied.

"Yum, that sounds a treat." Alexa swooned at the thought.

"We've got loads growing in the garden."

"Not custard. She means rhubarb." Kelly smirked. "Not that you need to worry, bean-pole. We can walk it off after lunch."

Alexa frowned. There was only one person who was allowed to use her nickname from school, and that was Louise. Kelly did tend to take liberties.

"I'm looking forward to lunch," Kelly said. "What are we having?"

"Ignore Kelly. She wasn't impressed with the Green Goddess smoothie we had for breakfast."

Kelly winced. "It was more like green slime."

"Don't worry. No slime, but your food intolerances have all been taken into account," Alexa said and walked into the cottage, contemplating what she was going to feed her friends. She slapped her forehead. As usual she'd forgotten the time and wasn't prepared.

With the ingredients in her veggie patch and those she'd picked up on her way through Woodend yesterday, she decided on the spot to throw together a salad of grilled halloumi and couscous with tomatoes, leafy greens, and herbs. She hummed contentedly as she spotted the remaining three-quarter loaf of sourdough on the kitchen sideboard. "All sorted. She'll be right."

"That was delicious." Alexa scooped the remnants of crumble onto her spoon. "You said it was Kelly's grandma's recipe?" She popped the last crumbs into her mouth, savouring every last bit.

"My mother's crumble and Kelly's mum's Tongan coconut custard. She taught me how to make it when we visited her in Auckland."

The sun had moved behind the gumtrees, shadowing the patio where Alexa sat with Louise, enjoying her cup of tea.

"You managed to rustle something together quickly. I gather you'd forgotten we'd been invited for lunch." Louise grinned.

"Of course, I remembered." Alexa hid a smirk behind her hand. They both knew she hadn't exactly forgotten; she'd just been oblivious to the time.

They'd been friends since secondary school, when outgoing Alexa had befriended petite, sweet-natured Louise. She'd been in a loving partnership with Kelly for over a decade. Even though they were proof that it could happen, Alexa couldn't imagine it happening to her anytime soon. In her immediate family, love often led to heartache, so Alexa would rather maintain her uncomplicated single status than take any risks. She admired Louise and Kelly. They were one of the few couples in her life that had stayed together long-term—and were happy.

"Your mum must be smiling down on you," Louise said. "Look at the great job you've done maintaining her garden."

"Thanks. It is nice to cook for others using stuff from the veggie patch. The garden supplies more than Granny and I can ever eat." Alexa propped her feet on the upturned wooden crate, closed her eyes and let out a deep sigh. "We should have joined Kelly and Daisy on their walk."

"Hmm. Do you think so?" Louise groaned contentedly. "You realise, Kel volunteered to take Daisy for another walk to get out of doing the dishes."

"Smart girl." Alexa laughed. "She seems more relaxed since she changed jobs."

"Thank goodness." Louise gave her a dimpled grin. "I'm fond of her new ranger uniform."

"If she's happy, then you're happy, too," Alexa said in a playful sing-song voice.

"Speaking of happiness, it's a shame things didn't work out with Tara. What happened to her? It was turning into a long-term relationship," Louise said with a sarcastic smile, tapping Alexa on the knee. "Lasted for nearly two months, didn't it?"

Alexa rolled her eyes. "Can you believe it—she didn't like Bruce? It was mutual; he didn't like her either."

"How so?"

"Bruce bit her nipple."

Louise clutched her breast. "What? Shock, horror. When did this happen?"

"He was staying with me at the loft while Granny was away. Tara was on his side of the bed." Alexa folded her arms across her chest. "It wasn't working anyway. She wanted more of me than I was prepared to give. You know what I mean, the clingy type." It wouldn't have been fair to string Tara along when Alexa knew she couldn't give her what she wanted. Commitment.

"Oh, Alexa. I suppose you tried to send her packing even before breakfast?"

Alexa examined her fingernails. She should trim them soon. Thinking about that was easier than thinking about Louise's question and its implications.

"No comeback? I hope that when the right woman comes along, you'll actually recognise her." Louise flipped her blonde ponytail over her shoulder. "And you'll want to make her breakfast."

Alexa squirmed in her seat as they fell silent. She didn't enjoy being reminded of her inadequacies. Alexa had no idea if she could change, or if she wanted to. She might be kidding herself, but why create complications when her current laid-back dating style suited her perfectly?

"Okay," Louise piped up, startling Alexa. "Tell me more about the photographer you met at work."

"I was hoping you'd be able to tell *me* something." Alexa smiled, relieved at the change of topic. She'd messaged Louise asking her if she knew of Eleanor, or her aunt.

"Yes. I looked them up. They both have impressive bios," Louise said with a bright smile. "I thought I recognised the name. One of my students based their masters on Helen Heysen's work."

"Really?" Alexa gently prodded her friend's forearm. "That's interesting."

"Uh-huh. Eleanor's aunt was well respected in her field, and Eleanor herself has won a few awards of her own," Louise said. "And you didn't have a clue, did you?"

"No, I didn't know anything about Eleanor before we met, but Jac knew who her aunt was. Eleanor comes from a Melbourne dynasty of corporate lawyers."

"Yeah, I read that. I wonder what Eleanor's family thought when she graduated with honours and didn't practice law." Louise reached into her pocket and pulled out her phone. After a moment of tapping on the screen, she held it up to Alexa. "She takes a rather good photo."

Alexa bit her lip. "Yes, as you said, she's won awards."

"Awards for her good looks?" Louise arched an eyebrow.

"She seemed strangely defensive when I met her. But I guess she's seen a lot and been in some pretty tough situations." Alexa ignored Louise's comment, but it was true. There was no denying the fact that Eleanor Heysen was extremely good looking.

"That's the life of a documentary photographer. How old is she?"

"Only thirty-six."

"I wonder what she's doing back here?"

"I have no idea," Alexa replied. "We should have information on the glass plate negatives fairly soon. I'm hoping to call her back to the library by the end of next week." Fingers crossed Katherine would give her the project.

"What did I miss? Who are you hoping to call by the end of next week?" Kelly strode towards them from around the side of the house with Daisy padding slowly behind.

Louise held up her phone to face Kelly. "Her."

"Her." Kelly moved closer to peer at the screen. "Now, where have I seen that woman? And why have you got a photo of *her* on your phone?"

"She came in to see Alexa at the library yesterday with some old photographic slides," Louise said. "How do you know Eleanor Heysen?"

Kelly waved her finger in the air. "Ahh, that's who she is. I met Eleanor a few years ago at an exhibition. She was swanning about with the Melbourne art set on the arm of that Aussie actor." She scratched her forehead. "What's her name?"

"Mia Conti," Alexa said staring at the screen. While researching Eleanor, she'd found lots of stuff about the couple. She'd been amazed that Eleanor had made such a name for herself and mixed in such glamorous circles. "You've actually met Eleanor Heysen?"

Kelly nodded. "They'd been touted as a couple on social media and then there they were, seen with my very own eyes in a St. Kilda gallery."

"I remember you were thrilled about meeting Mia Conti and her girlfriend," Louise said with a smirk.

Alexa turned to Kelly. "I read that they'd split two years ago."

"Yep. Mia's been working in Hollywood for a bit. She's with an American now. At the time, I remember thinking Eleanor was pretty gorgeous. She and Mia looked fantastic together," Kelly said with a dreamy eyed expression.

"My wife is so star-struck. Aren't you, honey?" Louise asked fondly. "More importantly, Alexa, what was your overall impression of her?"

Alexa took a deep breath and shrugged. "Eleanor was only with me for an hour. She was okay. I was suitably impressed," she replied laconically, even though just the thought of Eleanor made the back of her neck tingle.

Kelly reached over and held her hand out for Louise's phone. "Can I take another look?" She scrolled through the pictures, rocking back and forth on her heels, occasionally squinting at Alexa.

"What?" Alexa asked, even though she had a pretty good idea what Kelly was thinking.

"You thought she was okay?" Kelly beamed at Alexa. "Great, because really, she looks like she could be your type."

"I don't have a type," Alexa snapped.

Louise and Kelly stared at each other, turned to Alexa, and grinned.

"A bit broody, slightly dishevelled hair, big brown eyes," Louise began, bowing to Kelly to continue.

"Lean, fit, tall…gorgeous."

"I disagree." Alexa shook her head and scrambled to her feet, determined to hide her embarrassment from her friends. She held her hand to the top of Kelly's head. "She's more your height, actually, about five centimetres shorter than me."

Alexa squeezed her eyes shut and held out her arms, soaking in the warmth of the afternoon sun. One of her friends nudged her playfully on the shoulder, and she was aware of their friendly laughter, but her mind had already drifted back to *...lean, fit...gorgeous...* Alexa smiled to herself as she thought of spending more time with Eleanor.

Chapter 7

Triple knitting

Each time Eleanor returned to Melbourne, she noticed how the central streetscape changed. The buildings grew taller, the spaces between them smaller, like crowded plants pushing upwards reaching for air, reaching for the sky. Her hometown was now in the league of some of the most modern cities of the world. Thankfully, it had retained many impressive heritage buildings within the inner-city matrix.

Today, as she walked along crowded pavements, through secret laneways and into the central market, as always, her camera hung around her neck, tucked inside her jacket.

Watching natural light play across the buildings, reflecting off the glass and onto people in the street, Eleanor was struck by the contrasts and similarities of the organic human form caught in everyday activities and the geometric shapes in the architecture around her.

A silvery shimmer drew Eleanor's attention, and she spied two ladies of advanced years, with snowy white hair sheltering under a plane tree. The shopping trolleys tucked beside each woman overflowed with packages. Dappled light lit their smiling faces. Eleanor's camera was ready with the aperture and shutter speed set and the lens focussed to affinity. She unzipped her jacket and pulled out the Leica, knowing she would have to act quickly as the mood could change in a flash of a second.

Positioning herself behind a tall A-framed signboard, she lifted the camera to her eye. As the taller of the two women reached inside her trolley and plucked out two bananas, handing one to her companion, Eleanor pressed the shutter button, capturing a continuous series of images.

She glanced down at the screen and smiled in satisfaction at the pictures. Moody, gentle—almost mystical monochromes. Beyond the details of the women's faces, their wrinkles and slightly bent bodies, their vitality shone. Using a shallow depth of field, Eleanor had created an intimate portrait with a streaky, blurred background of the pedestrians hurrying by, bringing the women into sharp focus. She'd followed her instinct and it had paid off.

When she turned back towards the couple, they were nowhere in sight. The moment had passed, gone forever. Now, light filtering between the large leaves of the towering plane tree lit the empty pavement.

Eleanor secured the camera back inside her jacket and kept walking towards the library. She didn't have a definitive answer when people asked, "What made you the photographer you are today?" The obvious answer was Helen, but that didn't tell the whole story. Since Eleanor was a child, she'd loved capturing a moment in time with her camera. There had always been something that stirred her very bones and called her to document the world around her. She just wasn't very good at explaining that to people.

At the library entrance, there was an elderly woman standing all alone at the bottom of the stairs, gazing upwards. She was stylish in a deep red jacket and skirt, holding a cane in her right hand and a large upholstered bag in the other. Eleanor's fingers tingled. *That would make a great shot.* Just as she retrieved her camera, the woman turned, caught her gaze, and gave her a tentative smile. Eleanor grinned back in return. *Too late.*

She slid the camera back inside her jacket and took a couple of steps until she stood beside the eye-catching woman. Photographing the older generation—emphasising their resilience—was a concept she'd like to develop further.

"May I be of assistance?" Eleanor asked. "These stairs are steep. Would you like to take my arm? We can go up together."

"Oh dear, my driver usually helps me, but the traffic is atrocious this afternoon. Patrick is going around in circles." The woman gazed at her with piercing dark brown eyes. Eleanor pulled back her shoulders, stood to attention, and almost saluted. After a moment's intense scrutiny, the woman said, "You look safe enough. I will take up your offer, young lady."

Eleanor supressed a laugh; she wasn't used to elderly women checking her out and she wasn't often described as a young lady. "Your bag looks rather heavy. Would you like me to carry it for you?"

"Fruit cake." The woman giggled.

Now she's calling me a fruit cake. "Maybe I am a little eccentric, but I've never been called a fruit cake before," Eleanor said with a friendly smile.

The woman's face lit up, her eyes twinkling. She handed over the bag. "It's a cake for my granddaughter. It weighs a tonne." She chuckled. "The secret is in the candied peel."

"Sounds delicious." Eleanor gripped the bag securely in one hand and offered her arm. "Shall we go?"

"Onward and upward."

Eleanor pressed her lips firmly together. She didn't want to ask outright, but why was this sweet old lady on the library steps by herself? The woman had a fierce grip and allowed Eleanor to escort her to the landing.

"Let me catch my breath, and I'll relieve you of my bag." She puffed slightly but otherwise seemed okay. "My dear, introductions are in order. Mrs Grace West." She squeezed Eleanor's forearm even tighter. "And you are?"

Eleanor winced subtly. "It is a pleasure to meet you, Mrs West. I am Eleanor Heysen."

"Eleanor. What a lovely name." She released Eleanor's arm and looked about her.

"Where are you meeting your granddaughter? I have time to help you."

"Oh, you are a darling," Mrs West said. "She should be here right now, but she does have a habit of letting time get away from her."

Eleanor shook her head. "Don't you find that annoying?" *She* did, but sometimes you just had to be patient.

"Afternoon, Granny. I'm sorry, but time got away."

Eleanor looked on in amazement, with her mouth half open as a familiar figure planted a kiss on Mrs West's cheek. Low and behold, if it wasn't Alexa Bellamy.

Mrs West caught Eleanor's gaze and winked, as if to say, 'I told you she'd be late.'

"Patrick called from the car and explained he was having trouble finding a park. He's worried you are wandering around outside, waiting for him." Alexa frowned.

"I was fortunate this young woman came to my assistance."

"Which young woman?" Alexa turned suddenly and tilted her head to one side, giving Eleanor a questioning look. "It's you!"

"Hi, Alexa."

Mrs West looked from Eleanor to her granddaughter and back again. "Well, how delightful. You two know each other."

"So, Alexa is your granddaughter?" Eleanor turned to her with a grin.

"Eleanor, what are you doing here already? I'm sure Katherine said two o'clock."

"I'm early," she explained sheepishly. "I came to the library to look at some books."

Alexa raised her eyebrows. "You're in the right place for that."

Eleanor slipped her hands into her pockets to stop herself from fidgeting. "I should get on with it. Alexa, I'll see you at two o'clock then." She turned back to the elderly lady. "It was a pleasure to meet you, Mrs West. I hope your granddaughter enjoys her gift."

Alexa uncrossed her arms and held out her hand to Eleanor. "She was lucky you came along. Thank you for helping Granny."

Eleanor stared at Alexa for a moment before she reached out and took her hand. Her fingers were soft, but her handshake firm. She looked down at her own hand, held warmly in Alexa's grasp, and gave a little shiver of pleasure. She remembered her earlier phone conversation with Katherine Kent, who'd conveyed that Alexa Bellamy would be taking over, much to Eleanor's delight, and assured her she was in good hands.

"Eleanor," Mrs West said, stepping closer. "Have you had lunch?"

Eleanor reluctantly let go of Alexa and glanced down into Mrs West's keen brown eyes. "No, I planned to grab a sandwich in the coffee shop."

Mrs West waved her cane in the air dismissively. "Alexa, you won't mind if Eleanor joins us for lunch, will you, dear?"

"Oh, I couldn't intrude, Mrs West." She flicked a concerned glance in Alexa's direction to gauge her reaction.

Alexa shrugged.

"You are not intruding. And none of this Mrs West. Please call me Grace," she said. "I visit Alexa during her lunch break twice a month after my Mahjong morning. It will be a pleasant change for the both of us."

Eleanor rubbed at her temple and looked at Alexa, who smiled. She let out a sigh of relief.

"It's true. She's an ace at rolling a dice and creating winning sequences of tiles. Granny organises a regular game at an aged care home." Alexa accepted the bag her grandmother passed her, bent forward, and plonked it on the tiled floor. "Gosh. What have you got in here? If I didn't know you'd just arrived, I'd think you'd stashed away a few heavy volumes."

Grace leaned lightly into Eleanor's side and giggled. "*Fruit cake.*"

"I don't know what you two are conspiring about, but please, Eleanor, join us. We can head up to my office later." She picked up the weighty bag with ease and shifted it from one hand to the other. "Granny's obviously taken a shine to you."

Grace beamed. "Make my day and join us," she whispered to Eleanor.

"How could I refuse such a persuasive offer?" Eleanor smiled. "Thank you. I'd love to."

With her grandmother there, it was a perfect opportunity to learn more about Alexa Bellamy. The thought of getting to know her better sent a frisson of anticipation through Eleanor.

Alexa gave her grandmother an affectionate grin. She loved that Gran made the effort once a fortnight to have lunch together in the city. Today, she'd cleverly coerced Eleanor into joining them.

Granny sipped delicately on her apple juice and placed the glass on the table. "We don't always meet here for our lunch date, do we, Alexa?" She folded her napkin and tucked it under her empty plate.

Actually, this had been their regular lunch spot for over a year, because it was so convenient for Alexa.

"Don't get me wrong, Eleanor," Granny continued. "I'm not complaining. The food is passable, but its fare is more suitable for the student crowd."

"Yet, I see you've managed to eat every last bite of your frittata, Gran." Alexa tapped the empty plate, once again tickled by her grandmother's whimsical nature. Turning to Eleanor, she said, "It's actually the limited lunch menu here that Granny isn't fond of."

"All they serve is standard fare." Gran scowled. "I much prefer the food at Grossi-Florentino."

"That restaurant was a favourite with my parents." Eleanor's mouth lifted with a charming grin. "They took me there for my sixteenth birthday. I especially remember the cassata cake with candied fruits."

Alexa watched in amused silence as her grandmother and Eleanor chatted as if they'd known each other for years. Eleanor was noticeably more relaxed than the first time Alexa had met her, and Gran was clearly enamoured with Eleanor.

Alexa pondered Eleanor as a sixteen-year-old. Had she always had an athletic build? Did she wear her hair wavy and cropped, even then? Looking across the table, Alexa sighed dreamily. Eleanor's fitted black T-shirt showed off her finely muscled arms. Alexa could certainly appreciate her agile body and the near-perfect symmetry of her face, and those arresting brown eyes. What stories lay within their soulful look?

Eleanor shifted in her chair and her gaze fixed on Alexa. Her mouth widened, the corners lifting upward—her white teeth glistening in the light streaming in from the window. Alexa's face grew warm under Eleanor's undisguised scrutiny.

"So, you've only been back for a short time?" Gran leaned forward in her chair. "It must be such a relief that your father is on the mend."

So, that explains why Eleanor is back in Melbourne, but for how long? Alexa felt a slight pang of disappointment at the thought that Eleanor might be leaving soon.

"Yes, three weeks," Eleanor said. "He's not entirely himself, but he is doing really well."

"Will he be able to return to work?"

"Not for at least a few months." Eleanor cupped her chin in her hand. "His doctor warned him about returning too soon and risking a setback."

"I expect you'll stay a while then?" Gran asked, stealing the question that had been preying on Alexa's mind.

"Until he's tired of me fussing over him and I'm totally satisfied he's out of danger." Eleanor shrugged. "I'd love to hear about your Mahjong tournament, Grace."

The pair bantered back and forth on the topic of Mahjong, until Alexa got tired of being the third wheel. Was Eleanor interested in the game or was she just being polite? Alexa arranged her cutlery neatly on her plate and pushed it aside.

"Gran." She placed an arm lightly around grandmother's shoulder. "Eleanor's mother is a friend of my boss, Katherine Kent. Eleanor came into the library last week with some extraordinary old slides from the mid-1800s."

Her grandmother looked at Eleanor for an explanation. "Oh," she said. "You must tell me more."

Eleanor reached into her bag and extracted a file that had been folded in half. "Alexa e-mailed me the preliminary report. I have it here." She glanced tentatively at Alexa across the table, as though silently seeking permission. "Thank you." She looked down at the file held together with a red ribbon. "I made a few notes…for our meeting." Her dark lashes fluttered; a hint of shyness surfaced whenever she spoke to Alexa. Surely, it wasn't a reaction to Alexa. She must still be anxious about her aunt's slides.

"I hope you don't mind that Katherine handed the project over to me. We are pleased that you've left your slides with us for now. What did you think of our findings so far?" Alexa rubbed her hands together. "I don't know about you, but I'm excited."

Gran placed a hand on Eleanor's forearm. "Alexa is the expert on old pictures, you know."

"Yes, I know your granddaughter is the Pictorial Collections Manager. And highly regarded according to Katherine." Eleanor squeezed Gran's hand, then lifted her head and looked directly at Alexa, her eyes bright with interest.

"I'm just part of the team." Alexa felt the heat rise in her cheeks. Why did Eleanor's small praise make her feel a little giddy?

"Nonsense," her grandmother declared. "You spent years at university, have your master's in history, and started your PhD."

Eleanor gave Gran a warm smile. "You must be so proud of her."

"I am." Gran beamed with pride. "Alexa Primrose Bellamy."

"Primrose?"

"What can I say? My mother was a florist," Alexa explained.

Eleanor leaned towards her and said, "Primrose, the symbol of beauty and youth."

"How on earth do you know that?" Alexa stared wide-eyed at Eleanor.

The warmth of Eleanor's sparkling grin disarmed Alexa. She undid the top button of her shirt and looked away. "Thanks for embarrassing me, Gran."

They all fell silent for a few moments. Alexa pondered what else her grandmother planned to reveal.

Eleanor reached for her file, untied the ribbon, and flattened the pile of papers. "I can't believe the slides are the missing part of a collection you already have at the library," she said, looking very pleased.

Turning to her grandmother with an excited grin, Alexa said, "Granny, we found out they are from the Lehmann Collection. I told you about this project when I first started working on it. One thousand, seven hundred glass plate negatives from the 1870s. Do you remember, they were discovered in a garden shed?"

Gran raised her chin. "Wasn't Lehmann the chap who found the huge gold nugget?"

Eleanor's eyes widened. "A huge gold nugget. Who was he?"

"A German prospector who made his fortune in the goldfields. He's the one who commissioned touring photographers Norlane and Bolton to photograph his family and members of the goldfield communities," Alexa said. "As you can imagine, it's a significant record of life in the 1800s."

Eleanor cleared a space on the table and tidily spread out the photocopied slide images and the notes Alexa had e-mailed her.

Alexa leaned forward, pointing to the corner of the top image. "See this number, Gran?"

"Bring it closer, Alexa." Her grandmother lifted the spectacles that hung around her neck on a delicate chain. "I'm intrigued."

"Of course. Look here." Alexa held the image steadily in front of her grandmother. "The number 1062/1705 identifies the slide's sequence, proving it is part of the Lehmann Collection."

Gran patted Eleanor on the forearm. "You had the winning hand. Well done. What is this picture?"

"It looks like a medicine cabinet to me." Eleanor pointed at the wooden box in the image.

Alexa nodded. "And the man sitting beside it is probably a Chinese herbalist. They were prevalent in the goldfield towns."

Her grandmother covered her mouth with her hand. The colour had drained from her face.

Panic tightened Alexa's chest. "Are you all right, Gran?" she asked, keeping her voice as calm as she could.

Gran patted her stomach and let out a loud groan. "Oh dear, that meal most surely contained gluten, I can tell. I'm getting a queasy feeling. You must complain to the kitchen, Alexa."

"Oh, Granny," Alexa said with a relieved smile, "we did check with the waiter, and he asked the chef. They assured us your meal was entirely gluten-free. In any case, you aren't gluten intolerant. You've just been funny about it since you saw that healthy cooking show on television."

"Well, then. I must be intolerant to something else," her grandmother said with an indignant pout and pushed the paper back in front of Eleanor. She gave Alexa a stern look and drained her remaining fruit juice. She placed the glass down with a thud. "Gluten is linked to many stomach conditions, and I'd rather be safe than sorry."

Alexa scrunched her forehead, considering her grandmother's retort. She couldn't think of a reason for her strange behaviour, but she was sure it had something to do with the image of the Chinese herbalist and not the perceived gluten in the food.

"Can I do anything?" Eleanor asked, looking alarmed. "Shall I get you another drink?"

Gran shook her head and gave Eleanor a bright smile. "No, dear. I'm feeling slightly better already. But thank you for being concerned." She glanced down at the elegant gold watch on her wrist. "Alexa, you need to call Patrick and tell him I'm ready to go home." She placed her glasses into her bag. "Anyway, isn't it time you two conducted your meeting?"

Alexa was reluctant to let her grandmother leave, but she knew she wouldn't budge about the real reason for her outburst, especially in front of Eleanor. "Indeed, you're right," Alexa said. "Thank you for the cake, Gran. It must have a kilo or more of fruit. I'll have to watch how much I eat."

Her grandmother dismissed her with a wave of her hand. "Fiddlesticks. You are just like your dear mother. Slender as a reed," she said and turned to Eleanor. "Maybe you would like some of my fruit cake? Absolutely gluten-free."

At the mention of her mother, Alexa lowered her head and toyed with the treasured ring she wore on her right index finger. The vibrant gold-flecked, green-hued ring had been given to her mother, on Alexa's birth. The ring was an heirloom from Gran's side of the family. "It's the colour of your eyes, my darling girl," her mother used to say, "It will be yours when I'm gone." She missed her mother so very much. Her heart ached at her loss, every single day.

Alexa looked up to find Eleanor and Gran chatting quietly. Her grandmother sat, as always, with a ramrod straight back, her head held proudly. Occasionally, she'd pat her snow-white hair and lean her delicate frame ever so slightly toward Eleanor, her dark eyes blinking mischievously as they spoke. Alexa sighed. Gran seemed absolutely fine.

She gave a little wave to attract their attention and reached into her blazer pocket for her phone. "Excuse me, I'll just check if Patrick is close by."

Eleanor steadied the back of Gran's chair and held out an arm to help her stand. So, Eleanor was incredibly attentive *and* sweet. Alexa couldn't help but smile. Eleanor's movements were smooth, and she wore her arty T-shirt, jeans, and leather ankle boots like a chic but dishevelled rock star. *Cool and sexy.* Obviously, Eleanor would be here in Melbourne until her father recovered, and Alexa was open to a brief encounter of the no-strings-attached kind. Kelly was right. Eleanor was high on the scale of Alexa's type. Alexa hoped the attraction was mutual.

Gran looked delighted as she held onto Eleanor's arm. "Such impeccable manners. If only I was fifty years younger." She almost swooned.

Oh, Granny, you've still got the moves. There's a thing or two I can learn from you. Alexa wished she could be as spontaneous as her grandmother.

A faint blush darkened Eleanor's cheeks, as if she could read Alexa's thoughts.

A short time later, Eleanor and Alexa delivered Grace into the safe hands of Patrick. Grace referred to him as *her* long-time driver, as though he was exclusively at her disposal; however, Alexa whispered to Eleanor that he was an ex-taxi, now Uber driver with a soft spot for her grandmother. Eleanor could understand that. In a short time, she had already established a fondness for Grace and a respect for her feistiness. She'd enjoyed witnessing a flash of that spark in Alexa.

Alexa took the back-of-house stairs two at a time, and Eleanor followed closely behind, the leather soles of her shoes striking the marble stair treads, the noise bouncing off the stone walls.

As she reached the top of the stairwell, she stopped to get her breath and to take in the sight of Alexa leaning on the balustrade on the second-floor landing with a pleased look on her face. Eleanor gazed admiringly up at Alexa who raised an eyebrow in a nonchalant, almost cheeky way. Her two-button blazer, crisp white shirt, and striped trousers were purposeful clothes; however, worn with white leather sneakers and jet-black shoelaces, the look was avant-garde. With her height and terrific figure, Eleanor imagined Alexa would look stunning in just about anything.

"Sorry there are so many stairs, but they're the quickest way up to the Collections offices, and we avoid the crowded lifts," Alexa said.

Eleanor climbed the few stairs until she stood beside Alexa. "No problem. Actually, I prefer stairs. In fact, they're safer in a disaster situation." Embarrassed by Alexa's concerned frown, she smiled and said, "Lead on," to lighten the moment.

"We're just down the corridor to the right and through a couple more doors," Alexa said. Much to Eleanor's amusement, Alexa set off again at a cracking pace.

"It's very hard to get my bearings." Eleanor lengthened her stride and caught up with Alexa. "Which way is Swanston Street?"

Alexa pointed to the left and grinned. "That way. The building is a rabbit warren. It's actually a requirement of employment here to know the wall-follower maze-solving algorithm."

Eleanor gave a shake of her head. "And what is that?"

Alexa stopped outside a glass sliding door, card in hand. "You keep your hand on the left or right wall, following that wall until you find your way out." She swiped the card across the reader and waved for Eleanor to enter.

"Or in?"

"Yes. Or in." Alexa strode into the room and gestured for Eleanor to pull up a chair at the desk.

They both sat down facing one another. Alexa unlocked the desk drawer, pulled out an official-looking ring binder and lay it between them on the desk. Eleanor was pleased to see HEYSEN printed in bold letters on the cover of the thick folder.

"My grandmother was quite taken with you." Alexa's eyes twinkled. "Thanks for having lunch with us."

"Thank you, for letting me crash your lunch date." Eleanor looked up and met her gaze. "Grace is pretty remarkable."

"She is indeed, and strong willed and independent." Alexa gave a wry smile and opened the folder.

"I hope I'm as sprightly when I'm her age." When Grace had declared she was in her ninety-first year, Eleanor had been gobsmacked.

Alexa's whole face lit up. "I'm sure you have questions. Should we go through the report on each image together?" She laid out the papers in a neat row facing Eleanor. "Our team are experts, accustomed to handling glass plate negatives and we're delighted by the quality of the images retrieved from your aunt's slides."

"Do you know how these five negatives became separated from the others in the collection? Why was there one print with them? Have you any ideas, now that you've had a chance to examine them? And why did they end up in China with Aunt Helen?"

"That's a lot of questions." Alexa reached into the top pocket of her blazer and pulled out a pair of chunky, black-rimmed glasses. "Perhaps the notebooks you found in your aunt's trunk with the Chinese dragon box will give us some clues."

Eleanor shook her head, her heart sinking in disappointment. "Unfortunately, the only information pertaining to the slides was that she wanted us to hand them over to the library for identification. There was nothing about where they came from or why they were in China."

"Strange," Alexa said. "Your aunt was on assignment there at the time of the Sichuan earthquake, wasn't she?"

"Yes, she was covering the effect of the Chinese government spend on infrastructure for the Summer Olympics. Hundreds of farming communities were displaced." Eleanor lowered her eyes. With trembling lips, she said, "Helen wanted me to meet her in Beijing."

"Oh."

"I had a lot going on. I didn't go." Eleanor stuffed her clenched fists into her jacket pockets. *Why does that shitty feeling never go away?* "Helen was last seen at a Chengdu school. We don't know why she was there, so far from Beijing."

"Chengdu was the city closest to the epicentre of the earthquake," Alexa said.

Eleanor looked up and caught a glimpse of sadness in Alexa's eyes. She swallowed hard to suppress the pain. "Helen wrote in one of the notebooks that she was looking forward to me joining her in Beijing. She wanted to take me on a photoshoot to the Great Wall. I didn't go," she repeated.

"I'm sorry," Alexa said in a soothing tone.

Eleanor tried her best to blink unshed tears out of her eyes. "Can we have a look at the images now, please?"

"Yes. Let's have a look." Alexa put on her glasses and tapped a neatly trimmed fingernail on the image to the left. "This print of the family in front of Chewton Town Hall has been identified. It is also one of the five glass plate negatives. The subjects are Mister Yang Jun Lye, his European wife, Mabel, and their children, Arthur and Margaret."

"Really? What have you learnt about them?" Eleanor breathed a sigh of relief. Thankfully they'd moved on from the subject of Aunt Helen's disappearance.

"They were residents of the town. There are two other pictures identifying them in the Lehmann Collection. Yang Jun Lye was a miner who also worked as an assistant to the photographer Robert Norlane," Alexa said. "His wife, Mabel Yang, was the personal maid to Mrs Lehmann."

"But how on earth did these slides get to China?" Eleanor raised her hands in exasperation. "They are fragile, and it would have been a long and bumpy journey by sea and land from Victoria all the way to China."

"Many of the miners returned to their families there," Alexa explained. "However, some stayed and, like Yang, married European women and started families here."

Eleanor nodded. "Well that makes sense."

Focusing on the next image, Alexa said, "This is a worker's cottage in Chewton—remember, it was known as Forest Creek back then—where the Yang family lived." She pointed at the next image. "And here are the children in front of what we've positively identified as a schoolhouse. If you look closely, you can see part of a sign, just covered behind the child's outstretched arm."

"This one looks like Mabel, with what appears to be a gold nugget in the palm of her hand. Look at the size of it." Eleanor glanced up from the paper she held and caught Alexa watching her over the top of her glasses. "Imagine what that was worth."

"We estimate the nugget weighed over five hundred grams. Pretty handy find, I'd say." Alexa wiggled her eyebrows and placed the last sheet on top of the pile. "We have not determined the name of the man in this slide, but as you can see, he is sitting in front of a dispensary with the large herbalist box. The folding doors of the box are open, and you can see the contents."

"Hmm..." At the library café, Eleanor had thought Grace's reaction to this picture was peculiar, but she decided not to raise the subject now.

"It would appear the glass plate negatives are related to the family's life in Australia," Alexa said. "It is possible they were given to someone returning to China—to take to Yang's family..." She tapped her pencil on the desk. "...as evidence of his prosperity in his new homeland."

Eleanor rested her chin in her hand and said reflectively, "Maybe, the Yang relatives entrusted Helen with the slides in China because she was an Australian journalist." It was a shot in the dark, but it could be true.

"That's right," Alexa said.

Eleanor picked up one of the prints and studied it. "These are remarkably sharp considering they're copies taken from the slides."

"Our tech guru has offered to explain to you how he performed the magic using his *super* scanner."

"Are you sure? I'd love that," Eleanor said quickly, sitting upright in her chair. "I'm curious about the process."

"Seeing as you're a professional photographer, Katherine has wheeled and dealed to get special dispensation for you to spend time with the tech team. But don't worry, I told her you're probably too busy," Alexa said with a straight face, although her eyes twinkled with obvious amusement.

"Are you serious? That would be brilliant." Eleanor covered her mouth with her hand. She was sure she wore a big goofy grin. Alexa and her colleagues were going out of their way to be helpful.

"Okay, I'll set it up." Alexa's mischievous smile was reminiscent of Grace.

"Thank you." Eleanor glanced down at the photograph of the unknown Chinese herbalist, recalling Grace's reaction again with a frown. "Was it my imagination, or did your grandmother get upset when she saw this picture? Or was she really unwell from the gluten in the food?"

Alexa leaned forward in the chair and pressed her fingers against her forehead. "Gran has recently been obsessed about gluten. It's just one of her quaint idiosyncrasies. But I agree, she was distressed about something."

"It was as though the frittata incident was being used as a diversion. The picture had her flustered. Why would that be?"

"I have absolutely no idea," Alexa replied with a shrug.

Eleanor was puzzled by Grace's behaviour and was keen to know more about what caused her surprising reaction. Alexa's grandmother was a fascinating woman. It occurred to Eleanor again that she would make a perfect subject. She'd always been passionate about taking photographs that conveyed deep emotions, and she wanted to capture the story behind the wrinkles around Grace's laughing brown eyes—the window to her soul—that belied her ninety-one years.

"You got on well with my grandmother," Alexa said, as if reading Eleanor's thoughts. "I could have vanished, and the two of you would have barely noticed."

"You're wrong. I am aware of your every move." She glanced at the ceiling. *Did I really say that?* Heat rose from the tip of her toes to the top of her head. "I mean, I was. No, I mean, I am," she choked out. Eleanor took a moment to compose herself. "Grace interests me, and I would really like to photograph her. With her consent, of course."

Alexa tilted her head to one side, and she twirled a strand of dark lustrous hair through her fingers. "Did you ask her?"

"No, I haven't," Eleanor said. "I have an idea for a project exploring older people, especially women—their daily lives, their attitudes to life." Eleanor surprised herself. She didn't find it easy to talk about her work, especially while still in the conceptual phase. The idea had been mulling around in her subconscious for a while, and meeting Grace West today confirmed it was a subject she planned to pursue. "It may not come to anything, but I'd still like to photograph your grandmother."

Alexa blinked, and her face took on a serious expression. She nodded for Eleanor to continue.

"Some people are convinced that their age makes them unworthy of being photographed. I want to change that. People of advanced years have so much wisdom, so much to teach us. They deserve to have their own particular stories portrayed." Eleanor stopped. She was getting carried away. "I'm sorry, just tell me to shut up." She laughed.

Alexa lowered her glasses, leant forward in her chair, and gave Eleanor what could only be described as a tender smile. "I can hear the passion in your voice. It's refreshing."

Suddenly shy, Eleanor shrugged. "I am lucky to do what I love."

"You are," Alexa said quickly. She gathered the papers together and placed them into the ring binder. "I think you should ask Gran. I'm sure she wouldn't mind."

Eleanor whipped her phone from her satchel. "I'd be really grateful if you'd give me her telephone number."

"I will, but it would be much better if you asked in person."

Eleanor stared quizzically.

"I'm having lunch at Gran's this Saturday," Alexa elaborated. "Why don't you join us?" Eleanor detected a hint of a challenge in Alexa's sparkling eyes.

She blinked in surprise. "Lunch? Really? Twice in one week?"

"Uh-huh. Yes, I'm positive. Gran would love to get to know you better, and I would love to see her reaction when you ask her to pose for you." Alexa stood up, reached into the inside of her blazer, and pulled out a small pocket watch on a silver fob.

"I will definitely ask her then." Eleanor pointed at the watch, with amused admiration. "That's awesome."

"Thank you." Alexa held up the antique silver watch by its chain and let it swing.

Eleanor liked Alexa's air of confidence, almost impudence.

"I bought it at The Mill Market in Castlemaine. I'd been looking for one just like this forever. My trousers are from the vintage bazaar, too. I love it there. It's like a step back in time. A great place for a bargain." She checked her watch again and tucked it back into her pocket. "I am sorry, but I have another appointment, Eleanor." She smiled hopefully. "I'll give you my number, so you can text or call if you're free on Saturday."

"Absolutely." Eleanor held up her phone and entered the digits as Alexa rattled off the numbers. "Got it." She smiled sheepishly. What an unexpected bonus; now, she had a direct line to Alexa.

"I have yours on file." Alexa patted the folder. "If I don't hear from you about lunch, I'll let you know when Katherine has things arranged for you to hang out with Digital Imaging."

The low enticing pitch of Alexa's voice caused Eleanor to take a deep breath, and she simply nodded.

Alexa walked to the door and held it open.

"Oh, I'm making you late for your appointment," Eleanor said, scrambling to her feet. She collected her bag and jacket from the back of the chair. "I really appreciate you taking the time to go through the report, and I look forward to you keeping me up to date with new information. It's exciting to be involved, even in a small way." She almost held out her hand but changed her mind and slipped it in her pocket. When she looked up, and their gazes met, Alexa's eyes shone with what looked like interest. Eleanor gulped. "I'd better get going. Thank you; it's been great."

"Very well then. I look forward to seeing you soon," Alexa said with a matching bright smile. "Let me know about Saturday."

"I will," Eleanor said. "After you."

They walked silently, side by side, along the corridor. Alexa was no doubt already focussed on her next appointment, and Eleanor had plenty to think about herself. Her mind was still reeling after everything that had happened in such a short period of time.

Alexa tugged on her sleeve. "Here we are. This will beam us down to the ground floor," she said, stopping at the lift. Alexa pressed the button, they stepped inside, and the lift began its descent.

Eleanor leaned against the back wall and stared at her shoes.

"Oh, no," Alexa cried out.

"What is it?" Eleanor looked up, alarmed.

"I just remembered you don't like lifts." Alexa reached for the control buttons with panic in her eyes.

"Wait." Eleanor grabbed Alexa's wrist. "It's not that I'm afraid. I just choose not to use them, if possible." It was thoughtful of Alexa to remember Eleanor's aversion to lifts. "I've never much liked them. Apart from being dangerous in disasters, being trapped in one during an Athens heatwave for over an hour with a woman who vomited was unpleasant."

"To say the least. You poor thing." Alexa turned her palm upwards, slid her hand into Eleanor's, and gently squeezed her fingers.

Eleanor's gaze dropped down to their joined hands. She savoured the warmth and reassuring strength of Alexa's grip. Her palm tingled.

"All good, then?" Alexa smiled, a brilliant smile, and Eleanor noticed, not for the first time, the perfect shape of Alexa's full lips.

Startled by the loud *ping* of the lift reaching its destination, they drew apart. Eleanor was surprised to feel a twinge of regret at the sudden distance between them. She could think of worse things than being trapped in a confined space with Alexa Bellamy.

Chapter 8

Earth's grace

"I'm just an old lady—why do you want to photograph me?" Alexa's grandmother held up her small glass of champagne and chuckled.

"The first time I saw you at the library, I was struck by your determination to carry that large bag up the stairs. Even from a distance I noticed the twinkle in your eyes and was drawn to you." Eleanor raised her glass, and Alexa smiled at her explanation. "Your face is so expressive and full of life. You're the perfect subject."

"I'll drink to that," Gran said, taking a sip of her drink. "Please don't make me look like an old fool. Even though I can be."

Alexa spluttered. "Oh, Granny." She was filled with admiration for her grandmother, even if Gran had a tendency to play down her worth.

Eleanor narrowed her brow. "Actually, the relationship between the subject and photographer is a creative collaboration. I'm the one looking through the lens, but you're taking a risk by revealing yourself and trusting me," Eleanor said earnestly. "I'd seek your permission to publish any images of you. You can trust me, Grace."

Alexa leaned towards Eleanor. "What happens when you're in the field? Surely, you can't always get permission?"

Eleanor's brown eyes took on a serious expression. "Speaking for myself, I follow a code of ethics. Before I accept an assignment, I thoroughly check the agency or publication's credentials. Things can go wrong—but not if I can help it."

Alexa admired Eleanor's passion and sincerity. Was she really only thirty-six years old? Alexa smiled ruefully to herself, at nearly forty-one, suddenly finding herself lacking. As a historian, she was knowledgeable about a lot of things and could recite nuggets of information with ease; however, her own *lived* experience of other countries and cultures was limited.

Gran placed her glass on the table. "You've more than proven your ability," she said to Eleanor. "Alexa didn't tell me much, but I looked you up on the Google." When Eleanor's eyes widened, Gran tapped the table with her hand, her wedding ring making a clunking sound. "Don't look surprised, dear. I am computer literate. I surf the *Net* too. You, Eleanor Heysen, have achieved a lot already. I'm prepared to give you a go."

"I really appreciate your confidence in me. Maybe, *by the time I'm ninety-nine, I'll get it right*," Eleanor said with a cheeky grin.

Alexa blinked and watched her grandmother's jaw drop. Eleanor had recited Granny's by-line from the magazine column she'd written in the 1950s and 1960s. "Looks like you're not the only one who's been surfing the internet," Alexa said, impressed that Eleanor had researched her potential subject.

"Oh, my word." Gran gasped. "Fancy you unearthing that after all this time. Uncle Oswald gave me a job with his magazine when my darling Gerald passed away. I needed something to keep me busy and an income as well."

"You managed to bring up Mum on your own and write a successful column for over ten years," Alexa said proudly. "*Life with Grace* was ahead of its time."

"It was a challenge being a woman working in publishing." Her grandmother clasped her hands together. "Some of the stories I could tell you, Eleanor."

"That's another reason I'm keen to photograph you, Grace, and if you allow me, I'd love to take the pictures here. In this house filled with your treasures and memories." Eleanor made eye contact and Alexa gave her an encouraging wink. Eleanor pushed up the sleeves of her checked shirt and folded her arms in a self-assured manner.

Eleanor stood up and walked over to the fireplace where framed photographs and several small objects were displayed on the mantlepiece. She peered at Gran's peculiar little blue glass bottle filled with tiny dried flowers poking out of its narrow neck. Was she gathering inspiration for the photo shoot?

"Of course, I've lived here for a long time and accumulated a lot of trinkets," Gran said, leaning forward in her chair, and Eleanor walked over to stand beside her. "Father gave Gerald and me the down payment for this house just before our daughter, Eloise, was born. We had dreams for at least three or four children, then," she said sadly. "This house was much too large for a widow with one child. But I couldn't leave then, and I can't leave now. I'm attached to the place; it's my home." She sat back in her armchair and raised her chin. "I'm independent here."

Even though her grandmother had Patrick and other trusted home-help, Alexa couldn't help but feel concerned that she lived alone. Gran *was* fiercely independent and there was no point interfering; she was determined to stay put as long as possible. That didn't mean Alexa didn't worry about her physical safety, though, and the ever-growing threat of internet and telephone scams.

"Girls, I'm going to sit here with Bruce and have a short rest." Gran called out for her handsome orange cat and he sauntered in, plonking himself on her lap. "Alexa, please show Eleanor the rest of the house so she can plan our photo shoot."

Alexa was proud, and not surprised, that her grandmother was jumping in with both feet, accepting Eleanor's challenge. "Okay, Granny. I'm all but finished here. Thank you for preparing lunch for us." Alexa put away the last of the dishes in the china cabinet and turned the small brass key, locking it firmly.

"Your chicken noodle soup was really delicious. Thank you, Grace," Eleanor said. "Enjoy your nap with Bruce."

"You're welcome. Once upon a time, I made the chewy egg noodles myself. The store-bought ones just aren't the same, but I do still enjoy cooking, and it's always lovely to have company." She gave them a little wave and patted Bruce until he purred loudly. "We're all set. Off you go. I'll close my eyes for twenty minutes."

"We'll try and be as quiet as mice," Alexa said. "Follow me, Eleanor. I'll show you around, but I'm not taking you up to the attic. It's full of dusty relics and rodents. You can hear them scuffling around at night."

"I heard that," Granny said dozily. "And you're right. You don't want to go up there."

Alexa shook her head vigorously. "No problem, Gran. I'm sure Eleanor doesn't want to crawl amongst your ancient things covered in mountains of dust anyway."

The attic had always been out of bounds when Alexa was a child, and so naturally, she'd romanticised about what her grandmother had hidden up there. She'd imagined boxes of love letters from her grandfather, Gran's secret old diaries, and funny out-of-date hats and clothes.

At age ten, her curiosity finally got the better of her, and she'd lifted the large key from the biscuit jar and sneaked to the back of the house. Granny had been occupied, serving afternoon tea to Sister Mary Rose, when Alexa, torch in hand, had unlocked the door and climbed the wooden stairs.

She'd entered the spooky roof space, walked headfirst into a thick net of spiders' webs, panicked, and tripped on an unseen object, falling into a heavy layer of dust. Insects scurried, and rodents scattered. Alexa had run, vowing never to return again.

From that day on, sleepovers here had never been the same. Alexa would lie awake imagining rats chewing through piles of cardboard boxes or birds flapping in the roof space. Even now, the mere thought of creepy crawlies inhabiting the attic made the hairs on the back of her neck stand up.

"This is a fascinating house." Eleanor stopped at the beginning of the long hallway where a red patterned runner brightened the floor, and the walls held a collage of framed photographs. "Are these all of your family?"

"Mostly, and some of Gran's friends," Alexa said. "I've been helping her with the restoration and display." She joined Eleanor, pointing to a dark wood-framed image. "This is my mother, Eloise Beth Bellamy. She died suddenly from a ruptured aneurysm."

"Oh, Alexa, I'm so sorry." Eleanor's voice cracked.

A surge of pain welled up inside Alexa, and she tried her best to push it away. "It was two years ago. One moment she was here—so full of energy and life." She tried to quell the emotion in her voice. "And then she was gone."

"I'm so sorry," Eleanor repeated, placing her hand on Alexa's forearm. "She was beautiful, Alexa. Would you like to tell me about her?"

Staring at the image of her mother in her florist shop surrounded by blooms of every shape and colour, Alexa swallowed the lump in her throat. Her mother's hour-glass figure was concealed behind her customary uniform of tan leather bib apron, chino pants, and grey utility shirt. Her chestnut brown hair held back by a leaf green headband. Alexa reached out and touched the smiling face in the picture. "I was surrounded by flowers from birth. We lived above Mum's North Fitzroy flower shop. After school, I'd sit in the back of the shop, amongst the pots, doing my homework."

"Is that one of your favourite memories, being in the flower shop with your mum?"

"Yes." Alexa sighed, placing her hand on her chest. Just *one* of her favourite memories. There were so many and yet there would never be enough.

"You must miss her very much," Eleanor said softly. "In this picture, it looks like the two of you were selling flowers from the back of a donkey-drawn cart." She pointed at Alexa's skinny legs in the photo. "You were leggy, much taller than your mother."

Alexa squinted at the picture. "That was in 1997. It was a fundraiser for the Abbotsford Convent. Mum was part of the coalition formed to fight a property developer who wanted to buy the land and build a huge number of apartments." She pointed to the placard she and her mother were holding which read: *Daffodils against demolition.* I'd just turned eighteen in that picture, but I was already taller than Mum before my thirteenth birthday. She took after Gran."

Eleanor took a step closer, as if measuring her height against Alexa.

"You know, my place is a hop, skip, and a jump from the convent. If you're interested in going there, give me a ring; we could meet up for coffee." Alexa tried to sound casual, as though it wasn't important, but she realised she actually wanted to spend more time with Eleanor, and not just for the pursuit of physical pleasure. She was drawn to people who were out of the ordinary and Eleanor, in her quiet way, hinted at mystery. She was a highly accomplished woman, yet humble—not to mention, effortlessly sexy. Alexa's heart skipped a beat.

"I may just do that," Eleanor replied with a slow smile before turning her attention back to the wall of photographs. "Tell me more about these."

Was that a flush in Eleanor's cheeks? Maybe she is interested in more than photographing my grandmother.

Alexa leaned against the wainscoting on the opposite wall, while Eleanor continued studying the pictures.

"Who are these distinguished-looking people?"

Sliding in beside Eleanor, Alexa peered at the photo. "That's Granny's mother Elizabeth and her three brothers," Alexa replied. "They do look rather stiff and formal, don't they? Those beards on the men make them look like hipsters. They were the Hamptons."

"Are there any photographs of your dad?"

"Definitely not here." She scoffed at the idea. "My father is not in Gran's good *grace* or favour."

"Oh."

"He's been absent the majority of my life," Alexa said in as dispassionate a voice as she could. She'd learnt as a young child to hide the distress caused by his absenteeism. "After my parents divorced, he took his new wife back to Dampier where he'd grown up."

"In Western Australia?"

"Yep. Way across the other side of the country."

"Do you see him very often?" Eleanor asked, curiosity resonating in her tone.

Alexa shook her head. "I used to visit Pop Bellamy occasionally, but since he passed away, I've had no reason to go there. I did shadow one of my stepbrother's Facebook pages for a while. But I got sick of seeing Stephen Bellamy Junior's happy family posts. So, I quit it."

"I'm so sorry, Alexa. That must have been really tough." Eleanor placed a hand on Alexa's shoulder and gave it a comforting squeeze.

"It's been tough on my step siblings. The old man divorced their mother, too. If anything, he is consistent." Alexa waved her hand in dismissal.

Eleanor looked at her sharply. "Okay," she said. Clearly getting the message that the subject of Steven Bellamy was closed, she turned once again to the photographs on the wall. "Are there any photos of Grace's father here?"

"No. It upsets her when I ask about facts and photos of my great-grandfather, William. He passed away before I was born. Granny said there was a fire and whatever photos might have existed were lost. My grandmother is the only person I can ask, and she won't talk about it except to say he was a lovely man." Alexa crossed her arms in front of her chest. "I know it seems incongruous, but I am not ready to pursue it yet. Not without Granny's blessing."

"In your line of work, you'd have access to hundreds of images and heaps of information. There may be records in the library."

"Yes, I know. Please drop it, Eleanor. I know there are *millions* of images in the archives." Alexa took a few deep breaths. In a gentler tone, she said, "Once I start searching, I'll be like an echidna. I won't stop digging."

Eleanor grinned. "I have trouble picturing you as a spiny insectivorous mammal with a long snout and claws."

"Funny." Alexa nudged Eleanor's arm. She strolled the rest of the corridor, contemplating the gap in her family history. "I just can't bear to upset Granny," she said, half to herself. Alexa turned to find Eleanor following her slowly, while she studied the remaining pictures.

"If you were to find photographs of Grace's father, she may feel like sharing stories about him."

Alexa scowled and shook her head. Eleanor was scratching at a sore spot.

"Okay, okay. I get it," Eleanor said, turning back to the pictures with a fond smile. "I like how you've displayed the photographs. Precious possessions, displayed properly, not shoved into storage boxes or albums in an attic." She stopped near a photograph of Alexa, taken by her mother on their holiday together in the South of France. "I particularly like this one of you, with the sun hitting the lens so it creates a halo around your head; the vineyards behind you turning splendid shades of gold."

"Oh, you are poetic." Was Eleanor a Renaissance woman, gifted with many talents? Spontaneously, Alexa squeezed Eleanor's shoulder, boldly running her hand over her bicep. She teased the skin of Eleanor's forearm with her fingers and lingered on her finely boned wrist. "Have you always been known as Eleanor? Or do you have a nickname?"

Eleanor blinked rapidly. "Pretty much. Dad likes to call me Nell," she stammered.

"And what do you like?" Alexa gently brushed Eleanor's closed fist with her thumb.

"Eleanor." She flipped over her hand and held on to Alexa's fingers. "Nell makes me feel like I'm five years old," she said with a gleam in her eyes.

Alexa laughed. "We can't have that, can we, *Eleanor*?" For a few moments they smiled, staring at one another.

Unnerved by the sudden tug of attraction that flickered between them—the unmistakable gravitational pull, Alexa let go of Eleanor's hand. "Do you want to see the rest of the house? Where would you like to start?"

Eleanor's eyes widened, and she took a step back. "What's that scuffling I can hear? How about the attic?"

Alexa looked up at the ceiling, dragging her gaze away from Eleanor's big brown eyes. "No, way." Alexa wagged her finger playfully before beckoning for Eleanor to follow her down the hall. "Come on, I'll show you where I used to hide and spy on the neighbours."

Chapter 9

Prevailing wind

"Mother. Give me a break." Eleanor raised her voice as much as she dared. Her father was taking an afternoon nap, and, although there was little chance he would hear them in the studio, she didn't want to risk causing him distress.

"But I don't understand why you are spending so much time fussing with Helen's slides."

"I'm only following my aunt's wishes," Eleanor said in a controlled voice.

She studied her mother carefully; her arms were crossed, and a crease etched her forehead. Eleanor couldn't understand why her mother was being so unreasonable. Sarah Heysen, the principal of the family's law firm, was known to dislike showy emotions. Eleanor stared, bewildered by her mother's extraordinary behaviour, but even though she was losing her cool, Eleanor knew that she shouldn't forget her mother was a formidable litigator.

"Yes, it was Helen's wish that we hand them over to the Library. It's done now. Can't we leave it at that?" Her mother ran her hands down the sides of her crisp black pencil skirt.

Eleanor took a deep calming breath and released it slowly. "In her notebook, Helen only wrote she wanted the slides to go to the state library, sure, but I know she'd be pleased that I'm taking it further. I'm an investigative photographer just like she was. By learning more about the slides, I may discover something about Helen's disappearance."

Her mother stared stonily at her for a moment. "Don't forget, I'm the one who arranged your meeting with Katherine."

"Thank you for that," Eleanor said softly.

"However, now that you've carried out Helen's wishes, Eleanor, we need to put Helen to rest so you can move on to more important things...like what are you doing with your life? After all, it has been over eleven years." She strode up to Eleanor, interrogating her with the intensity of her gaze.

Eleanor's body tensed, and she flinched at her mother's tone. "I've only just got home."

"And soon, you'll take off again."

Eleanor hesitated, hating the inevitable trajectory of their argument. "I've had to give up my room at the flat in London because I didn't know when I'd be back there." She shrugged her shoulders. "Who knows? I don't know how long I'll stay in Melbourne. All I know is I won't accept any overseas assignments until Dad gets better."

Her mother had her arms folded tightly across her chest as she began to pace up and down the length of the studio. "Then you'll be offered work in some godforsaken place, and off you'll go. There are plenty of reasons why you shouldn't go back into those danger zones."

"It isn't always dangerous," Eleanor retorted. Sometimes it was necessary to take calculated risks to capture the true story.

"What about when you were stuck in the middle of that battle in Mosul, for five days?"

"I was documenting an archaeologist who was helping with the rebuild of her bombed city." Eleanor wanted to appease her mother, but in reality, she had been in very real danger. She recalled the pile of dead bodies visible in the open trunk of a battered car, causing a wave of nausea to rise in her throat. Eleanor swallowed hard. "It was a photographic assignment."

"Or the time in Sri Lanka when you went missing during the floods and landslides? We didn't know if *you* were alive or dead."

"As you know, I was following a group of human rights lawyers. We were caught in the middle of a natural disaster." Eleanor ran her hand through her hair. Why did it always feel as if she was having to justify her career choice to her mother? "It was my ethical duty. I had to stay to document the plight of all those suffering people."

"So far, you've been lucky." Sarah's voice lowered. "Helen wasn't."

"It's not about luck, Mum." Eleanor hung her head, avoiding her mother's scrutinising gaze. "If I hadn't been selfish eleven years ago, so hell-bent on making a name for myself in the London scene, I would have done what Helen asked and met her in Beijing. It may have stopped her from going to Chengdu."

Her mother groaned and said in a choked voice, "More likely, you would have followed her to Chengdu and died as well."

Eleanor stared at her mother. Her words held some truth. She could have died as well, and that would have only doubled the tragedy for her family. But that wasn't the way Eleanor saw things. If she'd gone to Beijing, Helen wouldn't have gone to Chengdu.

"Yours is a precarious profession, Eleanor."

"I don't know why we're even having this argument. I agree with you; it can be. Perhaps I do need a change of direction, after the things I've seen…" she said tiredly. "But I will always be a documentary photographer—wherever I am. I want to continue to open people's eyes and make a difference." Eleanor knew her mother was only arguing with her right now to try and persuade her yet again to switch to the legal profession. *Why doesn't she just let it go?*

"You can't pretend that you're unaffected by your work. That photograph of you in Brazil on Ian Sinclair's TV show was an eye opener for us, and I could tell it was for you as well."

"I'm home *now*." Eleanor put her head in her hands. "Can't you be happy with that?"

"Are you telling me you're going to stay home and settle down?" Her mother threw herself back onto the sofa and stared at her, as though cross-examining a witness. "With a partner and children?"

"I didn't say that exactly." Eleanor dropped into the opposite chair.

"Hey, what's all the ruckus? I could hear your voices from across the courtyard." The resounding deep voice of Eleanor's brother cut through the tension in the room.

Relieved, Eleanor jumped to her feet and threw herself into his arms. "Leo. I'm so glad you're here."

Leo pulled her close until her forehead rested against his chest. "Eleanor, it's good to see you, too." He kissed the top of her head, held her at arm's length, and searched her face—no doubt seeing how exasperated she was.

"Hey, is everything okay? It's only been a couple of weeks since I saw you." Leo tore his gaze away from her to look over his shoulder. "Hello, Mum."

"Nice you could join us, Leo." Their mother stood and walked towards the door. "I'll check on dinner and let the two of you catch up." She gave Eleanor a conciliatory smile, turned, and closed the door softly behind her.

"What's going on?" Leo asked. "I know Dad's doing okay. I just checked on him. Did Mum do something to upset you?"

Eleanor shook her head. "Just the usual. I shouldn't let her get to me," she said resignedly. "How are you, Leo? How was work?"

Leo tugged her hand and pulled her onto the sofa beside him. "You know how it is, the customary hard slog." He sighed. "Things were hectic in Darwin. Thankfully, I'm back now and can help out again with Dad." He scrubbed at his trim beard that was speckled with grey. "I'm really sorry I shot off up north virtually as soon as you arrived back in the country, but once Dad was out of danger and I knew you were with him, I couldn't put off the trip. How are you coping?"

"We've been fine, but it is nice to have you back." Eleanor smiled. She hoped that having Leo around would lighten the intensity between her and her mother. After living away from her parents for most of her adult life, even though she wanted to be here, being in such close proximity with them was a challenge.

"It was such a relief you got home from London so quickly," Leo said earnestly. "Thank goodness you weren't in some remote location where we couldn't get hold of you."

"When I heard about Dad, I was desperate to get on the first plane out of there."

"You did. And here you are." Leo put his arm around her shoulder.

Resting her head against the back of the sofa, she relaxed. Eleanor was grateful that Leo didn't judge her. Unlike their mother, he'd supported her career choice and always came to her defence. She'd missed the easy-going connection with her brother.

Leo leaned forward and rubbed the back of his neck. "It weighs on me that I can't do more to help Mum. She is carrying the burden, running Miller Legal without Dad. I know it's her family dynasty, etc. etc., but they're a team."

"They are, Leo, but just because you are a lawyer and Dad can't work at the moment, it doesn't mean you have to join the family firm. You've never practised commercial or corporate law. Why would you want to start now?"

"You're right, Mum hasn't asked for help, but I am a lawyer, and it does put me under pressure." He hung his head.

"Didn't you recently get a promotion?"

He nodded. "It's a long-winded title. Legal Officer for Domestic and Family Violence Reform."

"Heavy stuff. I'm so proud of you. Congratulations."

"Let's hope I can make a difference." He sighed.

Eleanor smiled in recognition of their shared goal—to make a difference. "Don't worry, Leo. I doubt either of them expect you to drop what you're doing and work at the firm." It was all very well saying that to Leo, but Eleanor still felt the pressure of her mother's expectations and judging by the look on his face, Leo wasn't convinced either. He must be worried about their father's ability to return to work, if he was questioning his career path. Should Eleanor be worried? She'd assumed that their father would make a full recovery. She needed to hang on to that hope.

"Now that you've spent time with Dad, how do you think he's doing, really?" Leo asked.

"There was that problem with his medication last week, but as you know, that's sorted," she reassured him. "He tires easily of course, but overall I think he's doing really well."

"Must be because you're home, Eleanor."

"It's certainly not my cooking!"

Her phone buzzed, and she looked across to the table where it lay.

"That will be Mum, summoning us for dinner." Leo chuckled, slapped his knees, and jumped to attention. He grabbed Eleanor's hand, and pulled her to her feet. "Hey, as I came into the studio, I heard her say you were settling down with a partner and children. Who is this woman?" He scanned the room like a sea captain searching for land. "And where are the children?"

"Leo." She shook her head, groaning. "Don't you start, please. There is no one."

"Well, that's a shame. You know Mum would love to introduce you to eligible girls. A judge or partner from a good law firm—from a 'nice' family of course." He mimicked their mother's voice and shook a finger at her.

Eleanor put her hands on her hips. "You should have gone on the stage; you sound just like Mum."

Leo's phone rang, and he reached into his jacket pocket and answered the call. "Yes, Mum." He gave Eleanor a cheeky grin. "We won't be long."

"Drop the girlfriend rubbish. I don't want you to encourage her." On her way to the door, Eleanor pinched his cheek, playfully. "Anyway, what's your excuse?"

"Okay, I hear you. But I really don't have the time. Yet." He drew the corner of his mouth down and wiped at pretend tears. "But you, dear sister, don't have a woman because you're looking for perfection."

This time, she punched him on the arm. "Aren't we all?"

Chapter 10

Twofold fortune

ALEXA ROLLED DOWN THE WINDOW and waved her arm madly to catch Eleanor's attention as she alighted the tram, peering in all directions. Her rain jacket was reminiscent of the deepest green of summer leaves and, with an oversized daypack slung over a shoulder and a vivid red umbrella tucked under her arm, Eleanor looked like a vibrant twinkle on an overcast day. Her smile, now aimed toward Alexa, was quite dazzling as she strolled towards the car.

Why all the rain gear? Alexa stuck her head out the window and glanced skywards. It was scattered with clouds and patches of blue. She'd checked the weather forecast, and there was only a slight chance of showers today.

Stretching across to unlock the passenger side door, Alexa pushed it open with a shove.

Eleanor crouched down and leaned into the car. "Hi, Alexa."

"Hello, Eleanor. I could have picked you up from your parents and saved you the tram ride."

"Oh, no. I love trams, especially the old W-class rattlers on this line. Anyway, it would have added an extra twenty minutes to your journey." A flickering grin crossed her lips. "I've been known to hop on the City Circle tourist loop just for fun." She rustled her hand through her slightly dishevelled hair.

Alexa's heart skipped a beat as she caught a hint of Eleanor's light citrusy fragrance. If there was such a thing as bottled sunshine, today, it was Eleanor.

"Really? You surprise me." Alexa looked at her curiously and returned the smile.

"Actually, *you* surprise me," Eleanor said. "For some reason, I had you pegged as driving a hybrid car. Clean and green, more of a modern machine." She tapped the bonnet. "This is cool. I can't wait for a ride in this set of wheels."

"You'd better get in, then," Alexa declared.

"Thanks. I will." Eleanor offloaded her backpack and shrugged out of her coat.

Alexa turned and pointed to the back seat. "Toss your things in here. I'm sorry the coupé's a bit tight for space."

Eleanor carefully arranged her backpack, folded coat, and umbrella on the rear seat. "You actually drive a vintage car. I'm envious." She slid into the front bucket seat and settled back against the headrest. "Wow. Is it from the sixties?"

"It is. An Italian-designed original French classic built in 1962." Alexa fondly patted the dashboard. "Eleanor, I'd like you to meet Farina."

Eleanor uttered a soft, husky laugh and buckled herself in. She slowly stroked the soft tan leather armrest. "Hello, Farina. Dad would love you. What kind of car is this?"

Alexa reached for the gearshift and slipped it into reverse. She put her arm across the seat and looked behind her. "A Pininfarina-designed, Peugeot 404 Coupé," she said proudly and eased the car back, shifting into drive and looking into the rear vision mirror before moving easily into the traffic. "Off we go."

Eleanor pushed up the sleeves of her black and white long-sleeved T-shirt. "I was really surprised and very happy you rang yesterday. Thanks for offering to show me around Castlemaine and Chewton. Let's hope we find the locations where the glass plate negatives were made."

"You're welcome. I've been looking forward to spending the day with you." Alexa kept her tone light. She'd thought about Eleanor often, maybe too often, and when Eleanor had accepted the offer to drive out to the country, Alexa had smiled like a Cheshire cat.

"It's always nice to get out of town," Eleanor said. The leather squeaked as she settled into the car seat.

"Your jeans are almost the same shade as Farina." Alexa nodded towards Eleanor's dark blue jeans. "It's called *Bleu Foncé*."

"Is that so? Now I feel suitably dressed for our drive. How long will it take to get to Castlemaine? What have you got planned for us?"

Alexa grinned at the excited tone in Eleanor's voice. "The traffic is reasonably light for a Saturday. It will take about an hour and twenty once we get on the Calder Freeway." Alexa raised her eyes to the electric clock on the instrument panel and back to the road in front. "We'll get there in time to explore the Heritage Park before we grab something to eat in Castlemaine after that."

"Okay, that sounds like a plan." Eleanor tilted her head. "Why are we starting at the park?"

"Well, it was the heart of the Victorian goldfields from the 1850s. I've sketched out a map for a three-kilometre walk, to give you a feel of the place. Our tour will include an ancient riverbed, mine shafts, and the Garfield Waterwheel built around that time. Then, we can explore Chewton, where at least two or more of the slides were made. The archival box in the back contains the high-quality images." She glanced quickly over her shoulder. Knowing the box was on the rear seat gave her a sense of accomplishment. The tech team had done a stellar job reproducing the images, and Alexa looked forward to hunting down their locations with Eleanor. "The details are incredible."

"Fantastic. I can't wait to get my hands on them." Eleanor playfully wiggled her fingers in the air.

"Clean hands," Alexa said in a mock stern voice.

Eleanor angled her body towards Alexa, and gave her a sweet smile. "I'm lucky that my personal guide knows the area and has a master's in Australian History to boot. Believe me, it's the best offer I've had in ages."

"Hard to believe," Alexa muttered and laughed to herself. Did Eleanor intend the double meaning about tour guides and potential dates? Surely Eleanor was kidding when it came to dating. With her dreamy eyes and sultry lips combined with a natural wit and understated charm, she must get plenty of offers. How many of those offers did she accept?

Eleanor made no comment; instead she ran her hands slowly over the leather dashboard. "Oops," she cried as the glove box popped open. "Sorry, I couldn't resist." She peered inside. "Hey, there are actually gloves in here, brown suede, and a torch and… Oh dear, I shouldn't be rummaging in your glove box."

Alexa laughed out loud. She appreciated the emerging light-hearted, fun side of Eleanor.

Once she'd navigated her way through the hectic city traffic and turned onto the freeway, Alexa hummed, tapping a tune on the steering wheel, very pleased to be driving with Eleanor beside her. She loved her vintage car despite its idiosyncrasies. On the open road, Farina was silky smooth, so quiet the motor almost purred.

"Look at those clouds building over the Macedon Ranges." Eleanor pointed out the window. "Blue-black and silver-edged, with those celestial rays of sun beaming down on the hills."

"That's a picturesque description," Alexa said, taking a quick look towards the Ranges. They didn't look like rain clouds. *They'd better not be.*

"It may not come to anything." Eleanor rolled down the window, the wind changing the shades of her hair as it curled and moved. "The air is warm, and it's so atmospheric. Beautiful."

"Yes, it surely is." Alexa's gaze briefly rested on her passenger before returning to the road. *And so are you.* How had she ever thought Eleanor was aloof when they'd first met in the library? She'd never expected to be charmed by Eleanor so easily, or even find her such enjoyable company. It was shaping up to be a fun day.

With her right hand loosely gripping the leather steering wheel, Alexa reached for the column shift as they approached a bend. After half a kilometre when the road straightened, she revved the engine and accelerated, enjoying the smoothness of the ride. Close to a hundred kilometres an hour, Farina's engine emitted a low hum as they rolled past paddocks strewn with granite boulders and dotted with fluffy white sheep.

"That dramatic skyline makes an incredible backdrop to the red hills." Eleanor turned around, reached into the back seat, and pulled something from her daypack. She placed a scratched red camera case in her lap, cradling it in her hands.

"Ah, I wondered how long it would take." Alexa was amazed Eleanor had restrained herself this long.

Eleanor took out an antique-looking metal camera, half encased in worn leather. "Do you mind?"

"No, not at all. As long as you don't point it at me." Alexa slowed down to allow a car to pass. The passenger flashed a grin and gave them a thumbs-up. 'Nice wheels,' he mouthed as the car sped past. She turned her head and winked at Eleanor.

With her hands on the steering wheel, Alexa leaned back and stretched out her arms. She tilted her head towards the camera. "Does that thing actually work? It looks older than both of us."

Eleanor held up the camera. "You're not the only one into vintage. My grandfather bought this in the fifties. Of course, it not only works, but it's built to last. I have no doubt that my grandkids will be using it. The Leica M3 is the epitome of vintage style. Even though it's old and fully manual, it is still one of the best cameras. It's magic."

"I'll take your word for it." Alexa stole a glance at the camera, narrowing her eyes at all its shiny buttons, dials, and winding thingamajigs. "It does look special, but complicated. There's a lookout up ahead. Why don't we pull off there, and you can show me how it works?"

"I'd like that." Eleanor turned her radiant smile towards her. Alexa would have liked to grab her phone and capture that moment, if she hadn't been driving.

Eleanor's earlier comment about grandchildren was intriguing. Did that mean she wanted kids of her own? Alexa hadn't even entertained the idea of a steady relationship, let alone children.

"All good then." Alexa smiled. She manoeuvred the car through rolling hills and valleys, pine groves, and eucalyptus forests dotted with pretty vineyards with fresh spring growth and livestock grazing in lush pasture. She was spending the day with Eleanor, on their way to the heritage goldfields region. If this was cloud nine, Alexa was floating way up there. She rolled her shoulders and let them fall. Time to be in the moment and enjoy the rest of the ride.

For over an hour, Eleanor did her best to keep up with Alexa, who scrambled like a mountain goat over the rocky terrain of the Forest Creek Diggings site.

At the top of a small hill, Alexa pointed down into the valley. "It's hard to tell from here, but that's a historical cemetery. Want to take a look?"

Eleanor raised her arms in the air. "You've brought me all the way to the mountain top, just so we can go down again?"

"Hardly a mountain. Come on, it's all part of your education." Alexa laughed, and took off without a backward glance.

They wandered amongst crumbling old gravestones and stopped beside a large headstone commemorating the gold-rush pioneers.

Eleanor crouched down to read the inscription. She nearly fell backwards. "Over two hundred children were buried here. Why so many?" she asked.

"It was a gruelling life." Alexa shrugged. "Whole families lived in one-room shanties. Dysentery and other contagious diseases swept through the diggings due to poor sanitation and contamination of the rivers."

Eleanor could only nod. She had seen for herself the appalling conditions in many countries where she'd worked on assignment. It was an outrage—far too many people were still dying from bad sanitation.

Reaching gratefully for her water flask, she lifted it to her lips and looked across to find Alexa watching her. Eleanor pulled at her collar. Did she look as hot and sweaty as she felt?

"Thirsty?" Alexa licked her own lips.

Eleanor swallowed hard and held up her flask. "Want some?"

"Thanks, but I have mine right here." Alexa leaned down and picked up a bright purple bottle with a flower decal plastered over it. "At least the weather's cooled down a bit," she said before taking a large swig. She'd rolled up the pant legs of her denim dungarees, showing off bright-coloured socks and toned calves. Pretty cute, Eleanor considered, but not in a puppy dog way.

"I was a bit worried when you went off track and took me along the riverbed to those old mine shafts." Eleanor had been alarmed to find that many of the huge holes in the ground were not fenced off. "I wouldn't want to wander around here on my own—but you're clearly familiar with this area."

Alexa laughed, her voice throaty and low. "We were never far from the trail."

Eleanor watched her draw another healthy swig of water, flip down the top, and place the bottle in her satchel. Alexa set off again and gestured for

Eleanor to follow her between some large boulders and into an unsignposted wooded area.

"Take a look at this," Alexa called after a few minutes. "Here's the gravestone of one of the only female gold miners—a widowed Englishwoman who travelled to Australia in 1851, with eleven children, to make her fortune. Sadly, she and three of her daughters didn't survive the hardships of the diggings and were buried here."

Eleanor shivered, imagining they'd walked over many unmarked graves, and wondered how many ghosts roamed the forest. She stopped to lean against a knobby ironbark tree trunk, took another swig, and let the cool water wash away the layer of dust from her throat. She wiped a stray drop from her lips with the back of her hand.

"Your work's taken you all over the world," Alexa said. "Surely, you must be used to travelling off the beaten path?"

"Only when I've planned the route and I'm the one in charge." Eleanor shoved her hands into her trouser pockets, glanced up, and was captivated by Alexa's bright smile and those vivid hazel-green eyes. She reached for her camera, tempted to record this moment, but instead—recalling Alexa's reluctance at being photographed—turned and scanned the forest backdrop.

Despite not being in charge in this situation, Eleanor didn't give a toss. It was a nice change to be led around by a knowledgeable woman, an expert in the goldfield's history, who had taken time to plan ahead.

"Once you've finished taking photos here, a little further on is the Garfield Waterwheel. It's a huge stone relic looming out of the trees that once had a towering wooden wheel providing power to the mine for gold extraction." Alexa kicked the toe of her burgundy boot into the dust. "But you must be tired of all this by now. How about we leave visiting that for later and head back to Castlemaine for lunch?"

"I would really like to see it, and I'm not tired of you talking, but I am a little peckish," Eleanor admitted.

Alexa stared at the sky with her hands on her hips, a scowl on her face. "Look, you can see the change of weather coming over the hills. The clouds are getting darker and heavier, and the wind is picking up."

"What do you suggest? Shall we take shelter inside an old mine shaft?" Eleanor giggled behind her hand.

Alexa arched an eyebrow. "No way. Fingers crossed the rain holds off. Let's get going."

"I was joking." Eleanor patted her abdomen. "You may have heard strange noises. It's my stomach rumbling."

"Oh, is that what it is? I thought it was a bunch of ravenous possums scrambling around in the bush," Alexa said with a straight face.

"Now that my hunger is satisfied, can we take a look in that?" Eleanor tapped the lid of the black archival box that was on the seat between them. "I can't wait any longer."

"Righto, let's get started." Alexa rubbed her hands together and placed the box in the middle of the cleared table.

Eleanor wriggled her chair closer to Alexa's and eagerly looked on as Alexa set each of the prints out in front of them. Leaning in together, heads almost touching, they poured over the high-resolution prints.

"Look at the incredible tonal range here." Eleanor pointed to the picture of the herbalist's box. "Such gloriously intricate details. I can clearly make out the symbols on the bottle labels." She frowned.

"What is it?" Alexa's eyes widened.

"It doesn't matter how long I stare at these; I'm no closer to understanding why Helen had the slides." Eleanor let out a long sigh.

"Not yet, no. Small steps, Eleanor," Alexa said. "I have a plan to identify the locations. We can get started if you like." She brushed her fingers over Eleanor's forearm. Her touch was slow and tender. "Is that okay? You never know what we'll discover around the corner."

Eleanor nodded and closed her eyes, comforted by the warmth of Alexa's skin against hers. Although she had a sizable online fan base and thousands of Instagram followers, the opportunity to develop a real, in-the-flesh friendship with Alexa was very appealing. The last few weeks had been especially tough, and Eleanor did feel lonely sometimes.

Soon after, they were parked across the road from a two-storeyed red brick, vine-covered façade. "This is the place I was telling you about," Alexa said. "It must have been a grand home back then. It's still impressive and really does look like the house Mabel is standing in front of holding the gold nugget." She opened the car door and gestured towards the building. "Come on, let's take a closer look."

Alexa had done her homework. Of course, she had. This time, for the sake of practicality, Eleanor grabbed her digital camera while Alexa examined the image of Mabel she'd lifted from the archival box. Eleanor's fingers itched to raise her camera and snap a series of photographs of Alexa, but she wouldn't do it without her consent. Maybe Alexa would agree if she had a good reason.

"So, Alexa, hmm…you said you didn't want me to take your photograph, but for the purpose of recreating the image, would you pose as Mabel in front of the doorway?" Eleanor leaned down and scooped up an egg-sized rock. "Here, you can hold this gold nugget in the palm of your hand."

Alexa looked up and quirked an eyebrow. "Perhaps. But why? I'm not entirely convinced by that nugget."

Eleanor laughed. "If you stand in the exact same spot as Mabel, we can determine the dimensions of the doorway, configuration of the brickwork, and height of the entrance steps."

"I'm way taller than Mabel. I can tell from the family photo she wasn't much taller than her young children."

Eleanor placed one hand on her hip. "Well, that's easily taken care of. Why don't you kneel down?"

Alexa handed the picture to Eleanor and turned her palm upwards. "Give me the *nugget* and tell me exactly where to stand," she said. "We'll have to pretend I'm short."

"Thank you." Eleanor grinned. She handed her the rock, examined the photograph, and pointed just to the left of the wooden door. "Right there, but come forward a foot."

Alexa took her position, shading her eyes with her hand. "Hey, that's a different camera."

"Just a more modern variety of grandfather's," Eleanor said. "It's a digital."

"Why do you have a piece of tape on the front? Is it broken?"

"No. It's not broken. I have the badge covered because thieves tend to target expensive brands."

Alexa smirked. "I've read your profile, so even with the disguise, I'm guessing it's a Leica?"

Eleanor stared in surprise. "You read my profile?"

"Sure I did."

Eleanor fiddled with the camera strap around her neck. Fair enough. As soon as she'd met Alexa, she couldn't wait to check out her profile, either. She'd enjoyed Alexa's contributions to the state library's online memory bank, especially her talk on the transgressive behaviour of 'dog-earing' books. She smiled to herself. Alexa could probably make any subject engrossing. "Okay, are we going to get this done before those clouds move in?"

Alexa gave her a little wave with her fingers. "Hurry up, then."

"Just give me a second." Eleanor looked through the viewfinder and set the focus. "I'm ready. At least you don't have to stand like a statue for two minutes like they did in the 1800s."

Alexa shook her hips and smoothed down her make-believe starched dress. She struck an austere pose, with the 'nugget' held in the palm of her hand, and Eleanor quickly held down the shutter button, not wanting to miss Alexa's endearing performance.

When Alexa stood still, Eleanor took a series of pictures, from a tight shot of Alexa framed in front of the doorway to a wider shot to show her height in relation to the front of the house, even though Alexa would have towered over Mabel.

After she was finished, Eleanor checked the screen and started flicking through the images. She chuckled to herself. The ones of Alexa play-acting were priceless.

"Can I move yet?"

Eleanor lowered the camera and smiled. "Sorry. Yes, come and have a look. We'll pick up finer details on the computer, but I'm pretty sure this is the same building."

Alexa moved beside her and peered at the screen. She nudged Eleanor lightly in the ribs. "You'd better delete those first ones."

"I don't think so," Eleanor exclaimed happily. She pulled Alexa closer and zoomed in on the next image. "Look at the intricate pattern of the cast-iron lacework at the top of the veranda posts."

Alexa rested her chin on Eleanor's shoulder. The intimacy of the gesture sent a wave of pleasure all the way to Eleanor's toes. It wasn't just positively identifying the location of the first image that had her pulse racing.

"And the patterns on the brickwork are identical." Alexa raised her head, took a small sideward step, and turned to Eleanor.

Eleanor met her gaze and held it. Disarmed by their shared private moment, she tried to speak, coughed, and cleared her throat. "Yes, that's right," she said eventually.

Alexa tossed the rock she was still holding up in the air and did a little dance around Eleanor, jiggling the pretend skirt once again.

"You're crazy." Eleanor laughed; she couldn't help herself. "I can almost imagine you in Mabel's dress."

Alexa's eyebrows shot up. "*In* Mabel's dress?"

"You know what I mean. *Wearing* her dress." Eleanor looked down at her feet to hide her blush. "Mabel's dress on you would be just below your knees," she said hurriedly. "Your instincts were spot on finding this house. That's one off the list. What's next?"

As they drove towards Chewton, a light drizzle settled in—not enough to dampen Eleanor's spirits.

Alexa parked outside the red brick Chewton Post Office, and Eleanor recognised the tiny town hall building that sat beside it. It really was the smallest town hall she'd ever seen. While Alexa was checking something on her phone, Eleanor pulled on her raincoat, grabbed the umbrella from the back seat, and darted to the driver's side door. She opened the umbrella and held the door ajar for Alexa. "All set?"

Alexa slid her phone back into her bag and gave Eleanor a smile that didn't really light up her face. In fact, she looked a little strained.

"Is something wrong?" Eleanor asked.

"The Town Hall isn't open today. I should have checked. We may have to return another time. I mean, that's if you are actually interested in trolling through the photographs and archives in their collection." This time, her smile reached her eyes. Eleanor smiled back; she wasn't opposed to a return trip with Alexa; in fact, she looked forward to it.

Alexa popped her head out of the car and quickly ducked back inside, as if only just noticing the drizzle. "Look at the colour of those clouds. It could be a spring storm on the way. Oh, what the *cuss*!"

Eleanor gave her a perplexed look.

"I know, sometimes I sound like my Granny," Alexa said. "And here you are gallantly holding the umbrella for me." She stepped out of her car and stood beside Eleanor. When she bent her head to shelter under the umbrella, her hair tickled Eleanor's ear. Eleanor had the urge to run her fingers through Alexa's soft wavy tresses, but she gripped the umbrella with both hands to stop herself.

Alexa gently squeezed her forearm as they stood side by side in front of the single-storeyed Town Hall. "This is where the Yang family were photographed—on these very steps."

Eleanor could easily picture the family standing here, as very little about the old building seemed to have changed since the photo was taken. She dared not retrieve the image from the box in the back seat for fear the rain that had now developed into a steady shower would damage it.

As far as Eleanor could tell, the slide locations had no connection to Helen. Eleanor felt a pang of disappointment, but maybe—as Alexa had surmised earlier—Helen knew Yang's relatives in China. It was a possibility. If anyone could help her get to the bottom of this mystery, Eleanor was hopeful it would be Alexa—she was as immersed in the exploration as Eleanor.

With Alexa's hand still resting in the crook of her arm, Eleanor was guided back to the car.

"If it rains heavily, my car springs a leak under the dashboard. I have to protect the wiper spindles, or it will affect the electrics," Alexa said.

"Maybe we should park Farina under cover?" Eleanor scanned up and down the street and shook her head. "Maybe not." There appeared to be nowhere in the street to park out of the rain.

Alexa removed her hand from Eleanor's forearm and strode to the rear of the car.

Eleanor briefly looked down, regretting the absence of Alexa's firm grip.

"It'll be okay if I cover the windshield." Alexa turned the lock and lifted the boot lid. Quickly extracting a small blue tarp, she shook open the roll of thick plastic. "Help me throw this over the front of the car."

"Sure." Eleanor moved closer to Alexa and waited for instructions.

Alexa looked up at the sky. "If that rain develops into a storm, we may have to hold up at my cottage for a while until it passes over."

Eleanor's excitement mounted at the prospect of seeing Alexa's cottage. "Whatever you think best. Hopefully it won't last too long." With her left hand, Eleanor held the umbrella over Alexa and helped secure the tarp over the leaky windscreen with her spare hand.

Alexa had obviously done this many times before, and a minute later, she surprised Eleanor by winding her arm around her shoulder. "All done, thank you. Are you prepared to risk the rain and take a stroll along Main Road?"

"Okay, why not?"

Eleanor smiled as Alexa linked arms with her, and they walked companionably away from the car.

"During the 1860s, this little place was a busy commercial township. It had a court, a mine's office, two banks, as well as a butcher, a bakery, and—"

"Let me guess." Eleanor pursed her lips. "A candlestick maker?"

Alexa glanced at Eleanor sharply, gave Eleanor's arm a squeeze, and said, "Probably. I was going to say fourteen pubs."

"Fourteen? I can only see one hotel." Eleanor looked around. A peculiar little wooden building was set back from the grassy verge. She pulled Alexa to a stop, intrigued. "What is that?"

"That's the portable lock-up, circa 1850s. When the jail was overflowing they'd hold prisoners in here before a court hearing. The lock-up was found in pretty bad shape in a rubbish tip decades ago and rescued."

"Let's take a closer look—"

A very loud thunderclap directly overhead had Eleanor nearly jumping out of her skin and Alexa grabbing hold of her even tighter. The old pine and elm trees that lined the street swayed, their branches bending in the gusty wind, and rain started to fall in great dollops, drenching everything around them.

"Maybe not," Eleanor yelled over the rainstorm.

Alexa yelled back, "We're out of here." She started to run, dragging Eleanor along with her.

Eleanor's shoes squelched on the wet pavement, and the umbrella all but collapsed as the wind whipped the rain into their faces.

Thankfully they quickly reached the car, separating to clamber inside.

"Oh no. We didn't take the tarp off." The damp air rang with Alexa's peals of laughter as she pushed her hand through her tangled hair. "I can't see a thing through the windscreen. How am I going to drive?"

Tiny raindrops beaded on Alexa's impossibly long eyelashes like little diamonds, accentuating the emerald hue in her eyes. Impulsively, Eleanor ran her thumb along Alexa's cheek and gently wiped away the moisture that ran down the silky, smooth skin of her face.

Cool fingers wrapped around her wrist, shocking Eleanor out of the moment, and Eleanor snatched her hand back in a panic. Had she gone too far?

Alexa blinked several times. "I guess in this downpour, very slowly."

Eleanor pulled the raincoat tightly around herself, jumped out of the car, and untangled the flapping tarpaulin, trying to calm her racing heart. She shook the tarpaulin before stowing it in the back seat with her raincoat and jumped back in the car. Even though she was now soaking wet, at least she'd had an opportunity to compose herself after nearly kissing Alexa.

Alexa grinned mischievously at her. "Look at you."

Eleanor lifted her shirt and attempted to mop her face and hair. "I'm dripping all over your car."

"The seat will be fine," Alexa said, staring wide-eyed at Eleanor's naked midriff. "The sooner you get out of those clothes, the better. You might catch a cold."

Eleanor hastily pulled down her shirt and turned to Alexa with a bright smile. "Didn't you tell me you make a wicked hot chocolate?"

"I did," Alexa said. "There's a towel somewhere on the back seat. Why don't you use it, then I'll wrap it around the wiper spindle?"

"That's a smart idea." Eleanor reached for the towel that was tucked behind a blue Esky cool box, dabbed at her face, and handed it to Alexa.

Alexa secured the rolled-up towel along the dashboard. She started the engine, checked her rear vision mirror, and pulled out onto the road. "You are a good sport, Eleanor. I am so sorry our day has been ruined. Honestly, I had no idea it was going to rain like this."

The weather app Alexa consulted must have given a rosier forecast than the one Eleanor and her father had checked this morning. What did it matter? Eleanor didn't mind. The day had already turned into quite an adventure, and it wasn't over yet.

By the time they drove under an ironwork archway, the sky was hung with a dark blanket of clouds and rain continued to bucket down. Rivulets of water lined the gently winding driveway, and the earth had turned a deep mahogany. The car headlights bounced off the wet stone walls of the cottage and swept across garden shrubs and a paved courtyard, finally reflecting off the rear corrugated iron wall of the carport into Eleanor's eyes.

Alexa switched off the engine and doused the headlights.

They sat there in the semi-darkness, for several seconds. Alexa was strangely quiet. Did she regret having to bring Eleanor to her hideaway? Or was she still worried about her car? "The towel trick seems to have worked." Eleanor checked for water along the interior lining of the dashboard. "It's still dry."

"Good. I'm just glad we're here," Alexa said with a sigh, dispelling Eleanor's fears.

Eleanor peered out of the windscreen. The wind had picked up and cast flickering shadows around them. She jumped at the sudden weight of Alexa's palm on her knee.

"You must be freezing," Alexa said in a concerned tone.

"Just a bit. It's a little eerie. Is that the wind whistling or something else?" Eleanor closed her eyes. The pressure of Alexa's hand had her nerves twitching.

"We're at the edge of the woodland, and the wind can howl through the box ironbark trees. It took me ages to get used to the noises of the forest when I first came here." Alexa briefly squeezed Eleanor's leg, opened the glove compartment, and extracted the set of old brass keys. "The path to the cottage is a little precarious, especially in this shadowy light," Alexa warned. "Please, watch your step."

"Thanks. I will." Eleanor helped gather some of their things from the back seat. She pushed the door open and almost on cue, the rain hit the garage's tin roof with a loud roar. She fell back into her seat. "Crikey."

"I know." Alexa exhaled loudly before managing a half-smile. "I'm afraid when it rains like this, it could be hours before it eases." Her tone was earnest, and a deep frown creased her usually smooth forehead.

"Okay." Eleanor raised her voice. "It definitely doesn't sound like it's easing up. What should we do?"

"We might have to stay the night," Alexa said tentatively before dropping her gaze to meet Eleanor's.

Eleanor rubbed the back of her neck. Normally, a change of plans wouldn't faze her, so why was she experiencing a bout of nerves at the thought of being alone in the cottage with Alexa, overnight?

"Will that cause a problem?" Alexa asked. "If you have to get home today, I can ring my friends Kelly and Louise. They could drive you to Castlemaine Station. If you made the 14.47 train, you'd could be home by half six."

"I have nowhere I'd rather be," Eleanor replied a little too quickly. Despite her nerves, it was the truth. "I have no plans for tonight, just lunch with the folks tomorrow. I'll ring Mum later and explain. Anyway, we can't expect your friends to come out in this weather."

"Kelly and Louise are really good sports," Alexa assured her. "They'd do it in a heartbeat."

As if giving her an excuse to decline the offer, there was a flash of lightening, a rumbling of thunder, and the rain pounded even louder. Still, she didn't want to leave.

"Honestly, I'd like to stay," Eleanor shouted. "As long as you don't mind the company?"

"Hey, the more the merrier," Alexa said brightly. "I'd like it if you stayed."

Alexa sounded genuine. Sitting alone in a train, during a storm, all the way back to Melbourne would be lonely, and Eleanor would only spend the whole time wondering what Alexa was doing anyway. She was itching to know more about Alexa and her cottage. The little internal buzz of excitement was a pretty good indication she wasn't ready to end their time together.

"It's lucky we picked up a few goodies in Castlemaine. At least we won't go hungry tonight." Alexa scrambled in the back for her jacket and the cool box. "Let's get this stuff inside. I'll start a fire while you change out of those wet clothes." She slid out of the car with the cool box in one hand and held her jacket over her head. "We'll have to make a run for it. Follow me," she squealed. "And watch your step."

"Hey, let me find the umbrella for you," Eleanor called, but Alexa had taken off up the garden path.

The umbrella would be useless in the gusty wind anyway. It would turn inside out and fly into the forest.

Eleanor patted the rucksack with a satisfied smile before hoisting it onto her back. She had travelled enough to know—always be prepared. Camera. Book. Her toothbrush, a change of underwear, and a few other essential items.

She made a dash after Alexa, startled as the cold rain splashed her face. A second later, a tug at her leather boot almost tripped her, and she stumbled on a bump in the path. "Damn it! *God*, I'm so clumsy. That was close," she murmured, hoping Alexa hadn't seen her.

"Are you okay?" Alexa shouted. "Hang on, I'll come back and show you the way."

"Don't worry, Alexa. I'm fine." Eleanor felt her cheeks flush with embarrassment. She blinked as another flash of lightening lit the sky. "Just a goanna crossing my path," she yelled.

"Sorry, I didn't warn you about them. It's only a little further," Alexa said, with a chuckle. "I'm up here."

Eleanor took the two steps up onto the covered verandah just as Alexa stopped suddenly, and she ploughed into Alexa's back. "I'm sorry," she squeaked, stepping backwards, almost falling off the verandah.

"My fault. I should have given you some warning," Alexa said, her voice tinkling over the heavy thrumming of rain. "Can you hold this, please?" She turned around, handed over the cool box, and reached into the bib pocket of her dungarees.

Eleanor shivered as the rain soaked through her clothes. It seemed to take forever for Alexa to insert the brass key into the lock. She was relieved to hear a metallic scraping sound and a loud click, before Alexa opened the door.

Alexa smoothly flicked a switch, bathing them in a soft pool of light. "Thank goodness we have electricity. Welcome to Gold-Dust Cottage," she said. "Let me turn on more lights so you don't trip over the hall rug."

Eleanor glanced at her feet. "Good idea, because that's a definite chance around you," she blurted. Eleanor looked up to meet Alexa's amused smile. In fact, Eleanor had stumbled over her own tongue.

Eleanor yanked the screen door closed behind her. She pushed against the wooden door and heard the latch close, shutting out the wailing wind. Leaning against the door, she watched water droplets fall from her coat, pooling on the tiled floor. There'd been so much going on with the storm and the leaky car, it only now dawned on Eleanor she'd agreed to *spend the night* with Alexa. A shiver travelled down her spine, and it had nothing to do with the cold.

"Sorry. The cottage is a bit chilly." Alexa bent over, untied her shoelaces, and pulled off her shoes.

Eleanor stood rooted to the spot as Alexa walked about, switching on a couple of rustic-looking wall lanterns and an overhead branched brass lamp. Everything glowed invitingly in warm, mellow light, including Alexa.

"Give me a minute. I'll be right back," Alexa said, heading down the narrow hallway.

"No worries." Eleanor laughed to herself. She needed to lighten up a bit.

A moment later, Alexa returned with a folded towel and placed it on the entrance table. "This might help. Get out of your wet gear. There are a couple more things I have to do."

Eleanor undid the buckles, kicked off her boots, and toed them into a neat row beside Alexa's. Easing the pack off her back, she placed it on the tiled floor and hung her raincoat on the coat rack. With a relieved sigh, she grabbed the towel and wrapped it around herself. "That's better," she said, stepping off the tiled entrance and into a timber-floored sitting room decorated with a large Persian rug.

Even without heating, the sitting room was welcoming with its duck-white lath and plaster walls and eclectic but comfortable furnishings. Visible through wood-framed glass sliding doors was a kitchen with sage green, painted brickwork. Someone had lovingly renovated the old miner's cottage, adding modern touches without diminishing its charm. Beyond the kitchen, at the back of the house, was a dining nook with an oblong table. A couple of wicker chairs sat in front of shuttered French doors.

Taking it all in, Eleanor sighed. It was cosy. A perfect place to wind down. She could imagine sitting here with Alexa, drinking a morning coffee in the sunshine. That is, if the rain ever stopped.

Would Alexa be bright and cheerful in the morning or slow to wake and not very talkative until she'd had breakfast? Most likely, Alexa would be cheerful and chatty. Ready to get going. She might even accompany Eleanor on a morning run, when the country air was crisp and clear.

"There you are."

Startled, Eleanor turned around to see Alexa walking towards her, carrying a rusted pail full of kindling. She was stunning, her cheeks brushed with pink, and her eyes sparkled playfully.

"Here, take this towel from around my neck and dry your hair," Alexa said.

Eleanor carefully lifted Alexa's damp, tousled hair and removed the towel. Tossing her head forward, vigorously rubbing the towel over her own hair, she tried not to dwell on Alexa's silky waves and how they'd moved sensuously through her fingers.

"You've had a haircut since I last saw you." Alexa's voice was soft.

Eleanor flicked back her shaggy strands, aware of the way Alexa's gaze roamed over her. "Yes, thank goodness I found a good hairdresser."

"Nice." Alexa placed the box down on the hearth, crouched down beside the free-standing wood burner, and reached for an old newspaper and box of matches. "So, what do you think of the cottage?"

"I love it. You're so lucky to have a getaway in the country," Eleanor said. "We have a cosy haven out of the storm."

"And I haven't even got the fire going yet." Alexa pushed up her sleeves and opened the steel firebox door. "I've turned on the gas bottles and put a change of clothes for you in the bathroom. Why don't you take a hot shower, then you can relax in front of the fire with that promised hot chocolate?" Alexa scrunched up the newspaper.

"You must have read my mind. I do need the bathroom. I presume it's inside?"

"Yes, it is. You'll just need to pump water up from the well. The pail's outside the back door."

"But it's raining." Eleanor deadpanned, looking up at the ceiling. "Pretty hard, actually. I hope you have spare gumboots."

Still crouched in front of the hearth, Alexa turned around, brandishing a length of kindling. She quirked an eyebrow and waved the stick in Eleanor's direction with an amused stare.

"You're winding me up." Eleanor chuckled.

"Lucky you brought a raincoat and *umbrella*." The corners of Alexa's mouth lifted in a teasing smile, and she tilted her head to one side. "We have all the mod cons here, Eleanor. Gas hot water, electric lights. The bathroom is down the corridor, past the two bedrooms. And the loo is the last door before the back door."

"Thank goodness." Eleanor shuddered. "I'd hate the thought of finding a redback on the toilet seat."

"Call me if you need help," Alexa said, almost keeping a straight face. "I was just in there, and I didn't see any spiders. I'll have the fire going in a few moments. It'll be toasty warm by the time you come back." Her smile was innocent, sweet.

Eleanor pulled the towel even tighter around her shoulders. Her clothes clung to her body like a second skin. "Thanks, that would be great, but what about you?"

"Oh, there's only room for one." Alexa grinned, tugging at the bib of her dungarees. "I'll grab a shower after you." She gestured towards the hallway with the stick of kindling. "Off you go."

Chapter 11

Four blessings hovering over the door

ALEXA STOOD BENEATH THE METAL shower head, savouring the steamy spray cascading over her. The water coursed over her body, swirled about her feet, and drained away in the base of the claw-footed cast-iron bath. In her wildest dreams, she hadn't expected to be spending tonight at the cottage with Eleanor. But here they were together, sheltering in the eye of the storm, and she was determined to make the most of it. *I didn't engineer this.* Alexa rinsed her hair quickly and turned off the taps. No point wasting time in the bathroom, alone.

She leaned across to grab a fresh bath sheet and smiled when she eyed Eleanor's wet, straight-cut jeans and long-sleeved T-shirt hanging on the rail. She'd looked good in those clothes, especially when they were wet, clinging to her body. Alexa shivered at the image.

Eleanor's reaction to their change of plans had been positive, and she'd traded suggestive looks with Alexa during the day. Just because they'd got physically close at times, though, Alexa shouldn't assume Eleanor wanted to sleep with her. Alexa didn't want to *sleep* with Eleanor either, but she wanted her in her bed.

Alexa pulled on her comfortable pale blue flannel pants and her *Save the Bees* sweatshirt. Not exactly sexy nightwear. Oh well; that wasn't her goal anyway. Was it? She ran a brush through her tangled hair and let it fall over her shoulders. On her way out, she gathered up the towels and their clothes to place on the rack by the wood stove.

Eleanor sat cross-legged on the handwoven Persian rug in front of the fire with her long fingers wrapped around a mug of hot chocolate. She was alluring in the soft glow of the flames, her face unguarded and just a little pensive. Alexa was curious to know what had Eleanor so deep in thought.

"I hope you had a nice shower." Eleanor looked up and smiled at Alexa over her shoulder. "This is one of the best hot chocolates I've had. So creamy and rich." She licked her lips. "What is that subtle flavour…I can't quite pick it?"

"Ahh…my secret," Alexa said. "Actually, it's Mum's recipe. A bouquet of native herbs including lily pilly and strawberry gum."

"No wonder it tastes so good."

Alexa was mesmerised by the way Eleanor's tongue once again brushed over her lips in a slow, savouring motion. "Good thing to chase away the rainy-day chills," she said. Unwilling to dwell on Eleanor's lips for a moment longer, Alexa busied herself arranging the damp items on the clothes rack in the corner of the room. Then she opened the firebox and put another log into the already well-stoked fire. "Are you comfortable?"

"Super snug." Eleanor placed the mug down on the blanket box beside her and rubbed her hands over the well-worn T-shirt. "Thanks for the loan of this T-shirt and your pyjama pants."

"No problem. You look right at home. Though the trousers are a bit long."

"A tiny bit." Eleanor uncrossed and crossed her legs again to show off the neatly rolled-up checked flannel drawstring pants. "Just perfect."

Alexa's breath hitched. Eleanor's movements were languid and graceful, and all she could do was stare. The sweep of Eleanor's lashes, her fine straight nose, and the fullness of her mouth. Her drying hair shimmered in the firelight. The curve of her breasts was visible under the T-shirt. It was impossible not to linger over Eleanor's enticing attributes.

"Apart from the steady rain on the roof, it's peaceful here," Eleanor said, as though she was oblivious to Alexa's blatant appraisal. "I guess it would have been very different in the gold-rush days when the streets were teeming with horse-driven coaches and hundreds of people."

Alexa half closed the damper on the firebox and took a couple of steps to the leather armchair, where she sat, tucking her bare feet up underneath her. "In 1851, gold was found on a sheep run not far away, and within months, thousands of prospectors from around the world arrived here." She gazed into the dancing flames. The history of the goldfields was safe territory, keeping Alexa's mind and hands off her undeniably attractive houseguest.

"I had a quick glance through the notes you wrote." Eleanor pointed to the archive box. "So much activity went on back then."

"At first, it was a city of tents. Then came traders and general stores, blacksmiths, churches, and pubs."

"I read that there were also opium dens, brothels, and gambling houses."

Alexa nodded. "Men outnumbered women six to one in the goldfields. You can imagine with those figures and the harsh conditions…"

"It wouldn't have been a great place for a woman," Eleanor finished the sentence.

"I wouldn't have wanted to live here during those dangerous times." Alexa shuddered at the thought.

"Do you have to be back early tomorrow?" Eleanor suddenly asked.

"Not really," Alexa replied. "Don't worry, we can head back soon after breakfast. I could have you home by lunchtime if you want."

Eleanor drew her knees to her chest and wrapped her arms around them, resting her chin on top. "If the rain clears, I was hoping we'd search for the sites of the other slides. And then, maybe, you could show me around The Mill, in Castlemaine?"

Alexa tilted her head to one side. She was surprised Eleanor remembered she loved rummaging around at the market. "Are you looking for something in particular? Old knitting patterns, model planes, or frilly petticoats? Last time I was there, I considered buying a three-person cane basket from an old hot-air balloon. I'd like to take you to the vintage bazaar. I'd like that a lot."

Eleanor's cheeks coloured. She grabbed the empty mug and stared into it. For a woman with her worldliness, Alexa couldn't fathom where her occasional bouts of shyness came from. Could it be that she was the cause of Eleanor's nervousness?

"Would you like some more hot chocolate?" Alexa asked brightly.

Eleanor smiled and shook her head.

"Actually, that's a relief. We have a limited supply of milk, and I hoped to save the rest for our breakfast." Alexa pushed herself out of the armchair and held out her hand to Eleanor. "Come on, help me in the kitchen."

Eleanor clasped Alexa's outstretched hand, and she pulled her gently to her feet, neither of them breaking eye contact. With a surge of confidence, Alexa tugged until their bodies were just inches apart. She ran her other hand along Eleanor's arm and tipped her chin up with her finger. Alexa brushed the faint smudge of chocolate from Eleanor's top lip with her thumb, and when the corner of her mouth turned up, Alexa was convinced that she'd never seen such perfectly shaped lips before. *It would be so easy to kiss her.*

Eleanor's eyes widened, and she gulped in obvious surprise.

"Chocolate," Alexa said, now embarrassed by her impetuous move. She released Eleanor's hand as if it had singed her palm and walked briskly towards the kitchen pantry. "How about a glass of wine? I have a bottle of local red—a rich peppery Syrah. Or I can offer you a beer or water?"

"A glass of red would be nice, thanks," Eleanor said, looking flustered.

Alexa handed her the wine bottle and a corkscrew. She pointed to her mother's well-stocked, antique, glass cabinet. "If you look after this, I'll rustle up something to eat."

As Eleanor collected the glasses, Alexa emptied the contents from the cool box onto the kitchen bench, taking stock of the food inside to distract her mind from other thoughts. A loaf of thick-crusted sourdough bread, a jar of apple and fennel chutney, vine-ripened plum tomatoes, prosciutto, and a flask of freshly made ricotta. She could work with that, and reign in her libido while she was at it.

"That's the food you bought to take back to the city," Eleanor said.

Alexa shrugged. "Aren't we lucky? Otherwise our supper would have been baked beans on Sao crackers."

Eleanor put her hand on her hip. "Have you been talking to my father? That's my signature dish."

Alexa laughed. "I take it cooking's not your strong point, then?"

"Definitely not."

While Alexa gathered a few utensils—a grill pan, chef's knife, and cutting board—out of the corner of her eye, she watched Eleanor twist the corkscrew firmly into the cork, wriggling it until it popped. She set the open bottle beside two glasses on the table and walked over to browse the bookshelf where Alexa displayed part of her mother's horde of books. Alexa wondered if this was something else they had in common—a love of books.

Eleanor ran her index finger over the spines of several titles, scanning the shelves from left to right. "You have a diverse selection in your library."

"Those are just some of the books Mum amassed on flora and fauna, gardening and floristry. Also a few on the goldfields and travel." Alexa began dicing the tomatoes. "Most of her collection is at my loft, where I've had room to catalogue and properly shelve them. I guess that is over the top, but I am a librarian after all."

"You're lucky to have so many books. That's something I've missed, living out of a backpack." Eleanor gasped and carefully lifted a hardback from the top shelf. "*The Healing Land*," she read, turning to the front page. "I discovered this book before embarking on my first ever African assignment. Was your mother interested in the Kalahari Desert?" She turned to Alexa, and a scrap of paper slipped out of the open book and drifted to the floor. Alexa followed it with her eyes, wondering what was written on it, and Eleanor scooped it up quickly.

"Yes, she went on holiday to a wilderness camp in Botswana." Alexa put down her knife and peered at the book over Eleanor's shoulder. "To the Selinda Reserve—"

"In the Great Plains Conservation Park."

"That's it." Alexa swiped the scrap of paper out of Eleanor's hand and took a closer look. "This is a really old article about the Melbourne Cup." She pointed to the fine print. "And the winner was Peter Pan."

"I wonder why she kept it. Did she follow horse racing?" Eleanor asked curiously.

"Her florist shop was always busy during the Spring Racing Carnival." Alexa turned over the yellowed press clipping and squinted at the tiny print. She held it out to Eleanor. "I don't have my glasses. Can you read what's on the back?"

Eleanor narrowed her eyes. "It's a list of births, engagements, and deaths from November 1934. A very old newspaper; I assume from before your mother was born?"

"Way before. Gran would have only been five years old. I don't know where Mum got it or why she kept an article from 1934." Alexa went back to the kitchen bench and resumed her task of preparing their meal while Eleanor continued to study the scrap of paper. "Mum was a bit of a collector of random information. You could barely see the door of her fridge, for all the snippets, notes, and drawings plastered over it." Alexa reached below the sink for the breadboard. "But some of her books were second hand, so it's also possible the clipping was left in there by its original owner."

"It could have been your mum's," Eleanor said. "Would you mind if I copy this? I'd be interested to know what newspaper it came from."

Alexa shrugged. "Sure. Go ahead."

"Thanks, I'll just grab my phone. Where did I leave my rucksack?" Eleanor looked around, grinned, and tapped the top of her head. "Oh, it's near the blanket box. I'll be right back." Wearing Alexa's overlarge felt slippers, she flip-flopped like a clown towards the sitting room.

Alexa's gaze followed Eleanor, and she sighed. Today, Eleanor had been so curious and enthusiastic about the goldfield's region and history that Alexa had found herself more drawn to Eleanor than she'd been to anyone in a long time. Despite her views on long-term relationships, Alexa had felt the desire to kiss Eleanor growing inside of her all day, and she probably would have done it if Eleanor hadn't looked so startled back in the sitting room.

Alexa knew she hadn't imagined Eleanor's subtle gazes that lasted a little longer than normal, or her flirtatious smiles. There was definitely a spark between them, and despite Eleanor's earlier reaction, Alexa was keen to explore the possibilities. Who could blame her?

A cosy log fire, a glass or two of red wine, a light supper. The pattering of rain like music on the tin roof. It was still early. Alexa felt the temperature rise in the kitchen just thinking of ways she could ignite those possibilities.

Eleanor returned and stood under the lamp by the kitchen window, using her phone to scan the newspaper clipping. Alexa blinked out of her distracted daze, shaking off all thoughts of what might happen between her and Eleanor tonight.

She placed the frying pan on the gas ring, added a slurp of oil, and tossed in the roughly chopped tomatoes with a little fresh garlic, salt, and pepper. She brushed both sides of thickly sliced sourdough with olive oil and placed them under the grill.

"Something smells delicious." Eleanor placed a glass of wine on the workbench beside Alexa. "I'm glad I got the chance to come here."

"Is that so?" Alexa laughed. "Even though it's raining cats and dogs, the wind is howling through the forest, and you're stuck overnight at the edge of the dark woods alone with me?"

"Are you Goldilocks, and where are the three bears?" Eleanor beamed, dismissing Alexa's ramble with a slight wave of her glass. "Yes, despite all that. Thank you, Alexa."

Alexa grinned, lifting her glass. "You're welcome, Eleanor. Cheers."

Their glasses clinked together, and Eleanor swirled the wine around and raised it to her nose. "Spicy berries," she said. "I gather the cottage belonged to your mother?"

Alexa swiped her brow with the back of her hand. "Yes. Mum bought the property five years ago, before she retired."

"She didn't have it long," Eleanor said softly.

"Only three years. She worked really hard restoring the cottage and creating the garden." Alexa blinked away the tears that pricked the corners of her eyes. "What do you think of this red?" she asked, abruptly changing the subject. Sometimes it hurt to talk about her mother.

Eleanor rested the rim of her glass on her lower lip and sipped tentatively. "Hmm…that *is* nice." She ran her tongue over her top lip. "Are there still traces of gold in these parts?"

"There must be. You still see people with their point and shoot detectors, but a lot of the land is privately owned or protected by Parks Victoria. The only digging I do here is weeding, cultivating, and planting."

"Even through the rain-streaked windows, I can see your garden has an abundance of plants and colours." Eleanor walked back to peer outside. "What's under that long shade-cloth structure?"

Alexa flipped the sourdough under the grill and dragged the pan off the stove. She joined Eleanor by the window and stood as close to her as she dared. Her body seemed to gravitate towards Eleanor's quite independently from her conscious thought. "A handful of heritage apples, plum trees, a peach, and two pears. The herbs, vegetables, and flowers closer to the cottage are protected inside a wire fence. Mum built the net enclosure to safeguard the fruit trees from the summer heat, and from the birds, rabbits, wallabies, and kangaroos."

"Wallabies and kangaroos?" Eleanor's voice lifted playfully.

"Yes, I often see them grazing and hopping inside the boundary of the property."

"We might see them tomorrow," Eleanor said. "Hopefully I'll get a proper look at the garden when it stops raining."

Alexa sighed wistfully. She gave Eleanor's shoulder a gentle nudge and returned to the kitchen bench. "Mum loved this place." She just wished her mother had had more time to enjoy the fruits of her labours.

"Do you come here often?" Eleanor took another sip of her wine and followed Alexa back to the bench.

"Whenever I can, but I have the loft in Abbotsford, and I don't like being away from Granny for too long. Working a nine-day fortnight gives me a bit of freedom. Louise and Kelly keep an eye on the place for me."

"You're lucky. You can enjoy all the benefits of city life as well as the peacefulness of the country." Eleanor's voice sounded a bit pensive.

"I thought I was a die-hard city girl, but the cottage has changed my mind," Alexa said. "What about you, Eleanor? You've led quite the nomadic life. Worked with notable magazines and organisations and received numerous accolades for your photographic work. What's next for you? You must want to have a bit of a good time before you jet off on your next assignment."

The moment the words were out, Alexa saw the 'door-slamming-closed' look on Eleanor's face. She pinched her lips together. *What did I say?*

Eleanor's eyes fluttered before opening wide to stare at Alexa. Alexa had seen that look of indecision and doubt flashing across Eleanor's face when she'd been reluctant to part with the slides the day she'd brought them to the Library. Alexa immediately regretted her words. She hadn't intended to trigger that response again.

"I'm sorry. You've only just come home, haven't you—to spend time with your father while he recuperates?"

Eleanor just nodded.

Alexa had conjured up a fun fling with Eleanor while they explored their shared interest in the slide collection, but Eleanor was more complicated than she'd first realised. It had been naïve of Alexa to even consider that this alluring, worldly woman would be a pushover. She walked across the room, picked up the wine bottle, and refilled Eleanor's empty glass. "I'll put together the bruschetta, and we can eat by the fire," she said, reaching for the rest of the ingredients.

"I'd like that. Want some help?"

"Thanks, but it's almost ready. Simple meal tonight." Alexa smiled. Food and wine always improved the mood.

"Considering the lunch we had, I can't believe I'm hungry. What is it?"

"Let's just call it 'stuff on toast.' Or 'a little imagination and whatever I had on hand on toast.'" Alexa was aware of Eleanor watching her, and her hand trembled as she piled the roasted tomato mixture onto toast with fresh ricotta and wafer-thin prosciutto before topping it with a little fresh rosemary.

Eleanor looked at her with a smile. "For someone who's travelled to places where they eat some strange ingredients, believe me, toast is my go-to food." She leaned in to have a closer look. "This, on the other hand looks like a scrummy supper."

Alexa gave a little bow. "Okay, grab the wine bottle. Let's eat."

Eleanor leaned back in the armchair and gazed at Alexa through half-closed eyes. She'd been entertained by Alexa's amusing stories about her work at the library and some of her unconventional colleagues. Eleanor looked forward to spending time with the Digital Imaging team and experiencing more of Alexa's world.

They'd stopped drinking halfway through the second bottle of wine, and now, reclined on the sofa, Alexa had her head supported on the padded armrest, and her fluffy red-socked feet were flung over the other end of the sofa. Her eyes were closed, but her fingers tapped against her thigh, as though she was preoccupied. Was Alexa feeling a little off balance? Even though they were two and a half metres apart, was she as unnerved by the almost sensuous intimacy of the softly lit scene, as Eleanor was?

Outside, the storm had eased to a gentle rain, and the sound of it was soothing. Eleanor had enjoyed Alexa's mild flirting, which had escalated since they'd arrived at the cottage; however, being the focus of Alexa's attention also made her skittish.

The fire crackled, a log popping loudly, and her eyes were drawn away from Alexa's reposed figure to stare meditatively into the swirling flames.

When she glanced back in Alexa's direction, she found her watching her closely. She smiled sheepishly.

"Do you want to go to bed?" Alexa asked in a gravelly voice and stretched lazily.

How should Eleanor interpret that? She didn't know what to say. She looked back at the flames for inspiration. "Ah—."

Alexa swung her legs off the sofa and sat up. "Are you tired?"

"Pleasantly tired," Eleanor croaked. She pushed herself out of the chair and rubbed the muscles at the back of her neck. "I'll just clean the glasses before..."

"Don't worry." Alexa got to her feet and stepped across the rug to stand alarmingly close to her.

Eleanor patted the sides of the pyjama pants, searching for pockets to bury her quivering hands in. No luck; no pockets.

As she started to cross her arms, Alexa's hand gently closed around her wrist. "The glasses can wait until morning." She lifted their joined hands and gently placed them on Eleanor's chest, over her heart. Her eyes had turned a darker shade of green, and her breath was warm against Eleanor's face.

Could Alexa feel the quickening thrum of her heartbeat? Eleanor took a calming breath. As though time had slowed, she watched Alexa lift one hand and place it lightly onto her shoulder.

"Eleanor," Alexa whispered, lengthening each syllable. She angled her head to one side, leaning forward until her soft lips caressed Eleanor's.

The tension between them had been building all day, and the gentle brush of Alexa's lips came as sweet relief, but it wasn't enough. With her cheeks flushing warm and getting hotter, Eleanor instinctively wound her arms around Alexa's neck, filling her hands with silky hair. She covered Alexa's mouth with hers, wanting to breathe her in, taste her, explore every inch of her mouth with her tongue. When Alexa stroked Eleanor's tongue with a maddeningly sensual lick, a husky, helpless moan of need escaped Eleanor.

Alexa slowly broke the kiss, giving them a chance to catch their breath. "Hmmm..."

Eleanor buried her face in Alexa's neck, and she moaned again when Alexa caught the lobe of her ear between her teeth.

Eleanor teetered backwards and grasped Alexa's shoulders.

Alexa's hands moved down to Eleanor's hips, to steady her. "Whoa that was nice…more than nice, actually," she murmured and asked softly, "Are you okay?"

"I'm good, thanks," Eleanor said. She was still reeling from her steamy response to Alexa's kiss.

Alexa's smile was inviting and playful. "As you know, I have a guest room, but I'd be happy for us to share my room."

Eleanor ran her hands through her hair. Their kiss had her light-headed. Longing sent a slow burn through her entire being. Once Alexa had drawn attention to the two bedrooms, Eleanor had assumed they'd be sleeping separately. What now? Had Alexa presumed all along they'd sleep together tonight?

Alexa whispered into her ear, "Eleanor, bed?"

Eleanor wanted to reach up, pull down Alexa's head, and kiss that self-assured smile off her face. Alexa was infuriatingly sure of herself.

Eleanor recalled Alexa's earlier words about her transient lifestyle; how she must want to have fun, live it up before heading back overseas on her next assignment. Eleanor hadn't corrected her. Did Alexa think that she was someone who regularly engaged in brief sexual liaisons? Or perhaps that was what Alexa wanted. Impermanence. It may have been true for Eleanor in the past, but she was tired of one-night stands and soulless connections.

"Well. Shall we?" Alexa turned her lips up in what could only be called a smirk.

Eleanor's uncertainty about what she wanted and what Alexa expected was all it took to change her mood. "I'm really tired. I'm afraid I wouldn't be great company." What a lame excuse. She took a deep breath and resisted her desire to grab Alexa's sweatshirt and to hang on to it.

Disappointed and irritated with herself, Eleanor gently pushed Alexa away, turned around, and took the few steps to the blanket box where she'd placed her rucksack. She picked up her bag and started walking towards the guest room. *Alexa must think I'm a complete twit—it's not as though I didn't kiss her back.* Eleanor stopped and turned back. She lifted her chin, forcing herself to meet Alexa's gaze. "Thank you."

Alexa had her arms crossed as she stood and watched Eleanor, a bemused look on her face. "What for?"

Eleanor involuntarily took a step closer. "Driving me all over Chewton and Castlemaine. For bringing me here, sharing your beautiful cottage, cooking me supper, my delicious hot chocolate—"

"Stop, please." Alexa uncrossed her arms and held up her hands. "Thank you for coming along. I—"

They both looked at the ceiling. The rain had returned, and what sounded like hail pounded against the side of the house.

Alexa hitched her shoulders. "So much for the abating storm. I should have brought you here in better weather."

"Even the weather bureau can't always make accurate predictions. How were you to know?"

"You're really sweet." Alexa leaned forward and pressed her lips to Eleanor's cheek.

With this small gesture, the tension melted from Eleanor's shoulders. Maybe she hadn't short-circuited their friendship.

"Why don't you go ahead and use the bathroom?" Alexa asked. "I'll batten down the hatches and turn off the lights."

"Thank you...if you're sure?"

"If *you're* sure?" Alexa gazed at her for a moment, then nodded towards the bathroom. "Go on."

She was at the door when Alexa called with a soft, mellow tone, "Oh, Eleanor?"

Eleanor gripped the rucksack handles; a tremor of indecision had her questioning what she'd do if Alexa asked her again. No. She wouldn't let Alexa sway her resolve. She turned around. "Yes?"

"I'll stack the fire, but it may get cold during the night. Do you need a hot water bottle?"

"Thank you. I'll be fine. I'm a warm sleeper." *That is if I actually get any sleep.*

Alexa's mouth tilted in a smile. "The cottage is stone, but these inner dividing walls are paper-thin. Give me a call if you change your mind." She hesitated before saying, "Goodnight, Eleanor."

Eleanor couldn't even hear her own voice, for the thumping in her chest when she whispered, "'Night, Alexa."

Chapter 12

Whispering motions

RAIN HAD PELTED ALL NIGHT long. The radio news reported that there were trees down, flooded roads, and hazardous conditions. Alexa knew there was absolutely no way they could drive home today in her precious car and risk a leak from the windscreen blowing a wiper fuse and turning Farina into a rust bucket.

The modern, bright carriage was almost empty when they boarded the train at the historic red-bricked Castlemaine Station. As they settled in at the back of the quiet carriage, Eleanor chose to sit by the window, and Alexa sat down in the seat diagonally across, not wanting to encroach on Eleanor's space this morning.

Alexa had left behind her frayed mood, not allowing herself to dwell too much on last night's anti-climax. She'd had a restless night, kept awake by the total silence from the adjacent bedroom. Her guest obviously had no trouble falling asleep, while Alexa lay awake itemising the events of the day.

Mild flirtation had taken place. The chocolate incident—she'd *almost* kissed Eleanor, then. Romantic setting with candlelight, pattering rain and log fire. A nice meal and easy conversation. Eleanor freshly showered, in pyjamas hanging loosely on her slender hips. The kiss. Delicious, tumbling, at first tentative, their kiss had turned into a full-on, open mouthed, almost sexual caress. Culminating in rejection. In bed, alone, feeling sorry for herself.

Had she made a mistake? Had she moved too fast? Whatever that meant. If Eleanor was going to take off on assignment, surely, they shouldn't waste time. Alexa licked her bottom lip, remembering the taste of Eleanor's mouth, the stroke of her tongue—the way her mouth fit perfectly against hers—like pieces of a puzzle. She groaned.

Eleanor tapped her lightly on her foot.

Alexa looked up and covered her mouth with her hand. Eleanor must have heard her. "Yes?"

"It was good of Louise and Kelly to drive us to the train station. You're lucky to have friends in Castlemaine."

"I am." Alexa smiled. "It's not the first time they've come to my rescue."

As soon as Alexa had explained the situation, they'd hopped into their dual-cab utility and, despite the hazardous weather, arrived at the cottage bearing fresh croissants, homemade strawberry jam, and milk.

Gradually, their barrage of questions and effusive compliments, all aimed at Eleanor, of course, had subsided, and the four of them got stuck into breakfast before the girls drove them to the station. In the back seat, Louise had surreptitiously nudged Alexa, glancing at Eleanor, raising her eyebrows in question. Alexa had adamantly shaken her head. She didn't even want to think about what had happened last night, let alone tell Louise about it.

Eleanor tapped her on the foot again to get her attention.

The rolling motion of the diesel locomotive train had the effect of lulling Alexa into a reflective mood. "Sorry."

"They were extremely curious. Tell me about Louise and Kelly." Eleanor angled her body towards Alexa and gazed at her intently. "Have you known them long?"

"Louise and I went to school together," Alexa began. "They've been a couple for over ten years."

They chatted for a while, then fell into a comfortable silence until the train lurched out of Woodend Station halfway through their journey.

Alexa browsed through the latest copy of Archivist Magazine while trying not to listen to Eleanor's phone conversation. When she'd taken the call from her mother a few minutes ago, Eleanor had plugged her ear with a wireless headphone, positioned herself as close as she could to the window, and lowered her head.

"I sent you a text last night, Mother," she said in a loud whisper. "So, you knew I wouldn't be back for lunch. I gave you plenty of notice. Even sent you another text this morning." She sighed heavily.

The carriage filled with new passengers from the last stop, forcing Alexa to give up the aisle seat and shuffle over to the window, opposite Eleanor. She carefully arranged her feet in between Eleanor's parted legs, trying not to disturb her while she was having a heated conversation with her mother.

Alexa turned to a random page and stared. She wasn't reading anything, but she couldn't watch Eleanor's distress. Hearing the one-sided conversation was bad enough. Even the muffled sound from the large over-ear headphones worn by the teenager sitting beside her wasn't enough of a distraction.

"No. You misunderstood. I messaged you this morning that we couldn't take an earlier train. Didn't you get the storm in Melbourne? There are trees down in Castlemaine causing traffic chaos. We had to wait for Alexa's friends to give us a ride to the station."

After a moment of silence, Eleanor glanced Alexa's way, held up her phone, and rolled her eyes. *Sorry*, she mouthed, and Alexa gave her a warm smile. "Well, please apologise to the Wrights for me. Anyway, Leo is there." Eleanor glanced at her watch. "Yes. Are you sure Leo doesn't mind? We're running on time, I think. If it's any consolation, I'll be there for afternoon tea. Yes. Around 1.30 at Southern Cross. In the public car park near the bus terminal. Thank you. Bye."

She yanked the earpiece out of her ear and tucked it with her phone into the outer compartment of her rucksack. "Fuck." Eleanor leaned back against the seat and closed her eyes.

That one word summed up the tone of the conversation. Hopefully it didn't encapsulate the entirety of Eleanor's relationship with her mother. She couldn't bear to think how painful it must be to have a fractious relationship with your mother.

Alexa removed her glasses, placing them on top of the magazine. She gazed at Eleanor for a few seconds. "Trouble?"

"No more than usual." Eleanor sighed, opening her eyes.

"I couldn't help but hear. It's a bummer we didn't get you back in time for lunch. I guess your mum was really keen to have you there."

"You could say that. My mother doesn't like to admit she's wrong."

Alexa placed her chin in her hand and considered the situation for a moment before saying, "I suppose it was confusing. Our plans did change."

"That's the whole point! I kept her informed. She's so intent on controlling me." Eleanor's eyes narrowed. "Even when I try and do the right thing, it's wrong."

"She's just disappointed." Alexa tried to calm Eleanor's indignation.

"Ha, you've got that part right. I'm a constant disappointment to her." Eleanor scoffed. "As far as she's concerned, my career is too unstructured. I take photos. That's not good enough. She wanted me to follow in her footsteps and become a lawyer. She doesn't understand what I'm doing with my life, and that's an ongoing point of tension."

"I'm so sorry you feel that way. It's a shame you two don't get along." Alexa soothed. "I never experienced that with Mum. Of course, she was strict when she had to be, but I always felt it was out of love. Things were tough when my father took off, and Mum had to work really long hours to make ends meet."

Eleanor leaned forward, reached for Alexa's hand, and gave it a gentle squeeze. "God, I'm sorry, Alexa," she said. "You lost your mum only two years ago."

"It still seems like yesterday." Alexa took Eleanor's hand in both of hers, relishing the comfort. Eleanor didn't appear to object; she didn't pull away.

How could two years have passed already? The memory was still so raw she could feel the pain welling up inside of her. When Alexa had received the call about her mother's death, everything had changed in the flash of a second. How could she explain to Eleanor the million things she would never experience in the same way again? She and her mother would never sit at the movies with a huge bag of popcorn between them; spend all day in the cottage garden and then rustle up a meal just for two with produce they'd freshly harvested; or play Scrabble with Gran, turning a blind eye to her made-up words, often letting her win.

Alexa let go of Eleanor's hand and stared blankly out the train window. The three weeks before her mother died Alexa had been juggling her PhD studies and work commitments, choosing to spend what little free time she had in the arms of her former post grad professor. They'd re-connected at an art history conference in Melbourne, flirted over cocktails at the seminar dinner, and the rest was history. It was three weeks she hadn't spent with her mother. Three weeks she'd always regret.

She turned away from the window to find Eleanor still focussed on her. "Mum always called us the three musketeers. Gran, her, and me," Alexa whispered. "I have no right to say this, but please don't take the moments with your mother for granted. When she's gone, you'll wish you'd tried harder to understand her."

Alexa squeezed her eyes shut. She would not cry. Why on earth was she giving Eleanor advice? Half expecting to be told to mind her own business, Alexa glanced up shyly and was heartened by the look of understanding in Eleanor's eyes.

"My mother and I don't always see eye to eye, but I do love her," Eleanor said softly. "Thanks, Alexa."

The train slowed, and the loudspeaker announced they were approaching Southern Cross Station. "Please collect all belongings and disembark from the right side of the train. Watch your step."

"Mind the gap," Eleanor said.

Alexa smiled and tucked her glasses and magazine back into her satchel.

Eleanor's phone beeped with an incoming text, and she checked the screen. "Leo's here already."

"I can grab a taxi, Eleanor, so I don't delay you any longer," Alexa said, not wanting Eleanor to be in any more trouble. In a lighter tone, she added, "You promised your mum you'd be at the Heysen home in time for afternoon tea."

"It's not Downton Abbey, you know." Eleanor snickered. "There's no fixed time."

"Is that so, Lady Eleanor?" Alexa laughed. For all she knew, the Heysens did live in a mansion. Hawthorn was a ritzy suburb, after all.

"We'll take you home," Eleanor insisted.

"Are you sure about dropping me in Abbotsford? It's out of your way."

"Hardly." Eleanor nudged Alexa with her shoulder. "Anyway, you'll get to meet my favourite brother."

"Your older brother?"

"Actually, Leo is my only sibling. And yes, he's five years older than me."

They stepped out of the cosy carriage and onto the chilly platform, joining the stream of Sunday commuters. Eleanor transferred the folded umbrella to her right hand and linked her left arm through Alexa's as they made their way towards the exit. "I don't want to poke you with the umbrella or lose you in the crowd," Eleanor said in a raised voice, over the intercom announcements, the general hum of people, and the squeal of trains arriving and departing.

Alexa tugged Eleanor closer, blushing at the realisation that Eleanor had initiated the physical contact. At the Bus Terminal sign, they stepped onto the moving escalator and continued to walk as it rode upwards.

"Sorry to rush you. It's only a drop-off, pick-up point, so Leo can't park there long."

"No problem."

At the top, Eleanor slid her arm free and headed directly towards a nice-looking man with an affable smile who was leaning against a compact black hatchback. He was fashionably dressed in a fitting checked polo shirt, narrow dark trousers, and leather loafers. A bit preppy. His hair was a little darker than Eleanor's, and like his sister, he was agreeably well-proportioned.

Alexa stood back as Eleanor went to her brother and he slipped an arm around her shoulder, hugging her tightly. Considering Eleanor's troubled relationship with her mother, it was reassuring to see the siblings' obvious affection for each other.

He shifted his attention to Alexa, let go of Eleanor, and held out his hand. "Hello, Alexa, it's a pleasure to meet you."

Eleanor turned. "Excuse my manners. Alexa, this is Leo."

Alexa gave his hand a firm shake. "Nice to meet you, too. Thanks for picking us up. I'm sure you had better things to do on your Sunday afternoon."

Leo shrugged, and when he looked directly at her, his blue eyes were kind. "Believe me, I was more than happy to escape Mum's luncheon for an hour or so," he said. "We'd better get moving, though, before I get a parking fine."

Leo opened the front passenger door, leaned down, and tilted the seat forward. "Eleanor, squeeze in back here and watch your head. Alexa will be more comfortable up front with me."

Before Alexa could protest, Eleanor stooped and clambered into the back seat with her rucksack and umbrella, then pulled the rear door closed.

Without further hesitation, Alexa climbed into the passenger seat. Leo gently closed the door and jogged to the driver's side, sliding in. It would have been cosier to sit in the back with Eleanor, but that would have been rude.

Eleanor lightly bopped Leo's headrest. "Drive on, chauffeur."

He glanced at his sister in the rear vision mirror, winked, then backed out of the car space.

Alexa turned around to Eleanor and gave her a big smile, and Eleanor grinned back. It was clear she and her brother were close.

As an only child herself, Alexa's mother had encouraged her to bring schoolfriends home and mix with the neighbourhood children. She'd never lacked for company, but watching Eleanor and Leo, she couldn't help but feel a slight pang of envy. It would have been amazing to have a built-in support system. Especially after her mother died—when the pain was unbearable for her and Gran, and Alexa had longed for someone with a shared life story, experiences, and memories.

"Fasten your seat belts, ladies. We're off," Leo said. "Alexa, I guess you'd better give me directions."

"What a great location. This is where you live?" Eleanor looked up at the solid brick building, its factory-styled windows and pencil-thin black steel frames. "I love how the elm tree's green canopy and twisted branches reflect in those huge windows. It must be bright inside. How lucky you are to have such a place, just a stone's throw away from the city." Eleanor longed to have something like this for herself. One day.

Alexa spread her arms wide and smiled. "Home sweet home."

"You're so close to the park and walking trails along the river. What was this building originally?"

"A shoe factory. My loft is one of two self-contained apartments. It has its own street entrance and a lock-up garage."

"Of course." Eleanor glanced along the narrow semi-residential street. She couldn't imagine Alexa leaving her cherished car parked on this road. She would have to have undercover parking for Farina.

Leo raced around to the passenger side and opened Alexa's door. Eleanor liked that her brother was old fashioned and gallant in the nicest of ways. He opened the rear door, holding the front seat forward for Eleanor to climb out as well.

Once out of the car, Eleanor and Alexa stood there smiling at each other. Eleanor thrust her hands in her pockets, shifting her weight from one foot to the other. She knew she should say something instead of standing there like a fool, but she couldn't think of anything sensible to say.

Leo cleared his throat. "So, would you like me to walk Alexa to the door, or will you do the honours, Eleanor?"

Eleanor thumped him on the arm as Alexa turned to face him with an appreciative smile and held out her hand. "Leo, it was good meeting you. Thanks for the lift home."

They briefly shook hands. "You're welcome." Leo tilted his head towards Eleanor. "I'll be waiting right here."

Alexa opened a heavy iron entrance gate and walked through. "Come with me?" She looked invitingly over her shoulder at Eleanor.

Eleanor nodded, following her through the gateway. A wire-mesh fence covered in a tangle of colourful vines lined one side of the cobbled path, leading to an impressively large door, deep blue in colour.

Alexa pulled her satchel off her shoulder, placing it down on the bluestone step. She crouched, rummaging around in her bag. "Where are those keys?" She looked up apologetically as her hand continued searching. "I'm sorry the weekend didn't quite achieve what we'd hoped."

Well, that had a double meaning, didn't it? Eleanor wanted to run and hide; instead she ducked her head in agreement.

Jasmine laced the air, and Eleanor inhaled its fragrant scent, feeling a little giddy and unsettled. Here she was, outside Alexa's apartment. After putting the brakes on and not accepting Alexa's invitation to share her bed at the cottage, could Eleanor ever expect an invitation inside? Where would they go from here? If anywhere. She had to remind herself that it was sometimes best to focus on the moment and not get hung up about the future.

"You were great company, especially in the storm with your red umbrella." Alexa waved her keys in front of Eleanor. "Bingo," she said.

"Give me a buzz when you meet with the Image Tech team. We could have a coffee together."

"I will." Eleanor was relieved that her rebuff last night had not altered Alexa's good nature and readiness to spend time with her.

Alexa turned the key in the lock, pushed open the door, and dropped her satchel on the polished concrete floor inside. Eleanor peered into the cavernous space. It was inviting and spacious. An exposed brick wall lined the entranceway, and another wall was covered in floor to ceiling bookshelves.

"What day are you photographing Gran? Isn't that sometime this week as well?" Alexa stood in the doorway, watching Eleanor with interest.

"Err, Tuesday," Eleanor said. "I'm going to Grace's house on Tuesday morning and the library for part of Thursday and Friday. Luckily, Dad hasn't got many appointments this week."

"I'm off site on Thursday, but I'll be there most of Friday." Alexa tucked a strand of hair behind her ear. "So, maybe next time, you'll come inside." She leaned forward and planted a soft kiss on Eleanor's cheek.

Eleanor shivered. "I'd like that. See you sometime on Friday, then." She strolled towards Leo's car, trying not to skip a little in her excitement. Cupping her hand over her cheek, she could still feel the brush of Alexa's lips.

She didn't hear the door close; Alexa was probably still watching her. Eleanor looked down. She'd better concentrate. If she didn't watch her step on the uneven path, she'd likely trip over and make a complete clown of herself.

As soon as she'd fastened her seatbelt, Leo looked her up and down with one of his annoyingly smug expressions. "Well, that was a sweet, chaste kiss."

"What were you doing, perving at us?" She narrowed her eyes.

He started the car and pulled out into the street. "Just checking." He chuckled loudly. "Had an impromptu sleepover in the country, did you?"

"Uh-huh."

"Don't you think it's strange that Alexa took you on a road trip in a leaky vehicle when a rainstorm was predicted?"

"She didn't know there was going to be a storm," Eleanor said, defensiveness rising within her.

"Uh-huh," he repeated her words, shaking his head.

Eleanor gave him a withering stare. "Honestly, Leo. She wouldn't have endangered her prized Peugeot if she'd known."

"Handy, though. A cottage in the woods, log fire, nice and cosy during the storm. All night."

She placed both hands over her ears. "Enough," Eleanor said. "With three bloody lawyers in the family, I don't stand a chance."

"Okay, I get it. She does have dazzling green eyes," Leo said smoothly. "Captivating green eyes."

"Hmmm. Hazel-green eyes."

Alexa's eyes constantly appeared to change colour. One moment like the dappled hues of the Caribbean Sea. Sometimes, the lush yellow green of the Sri Lankan rice paddies. Just before they'd kissed at the cottage, her eyes had turned dark, like the gold-flecked amber sand of the Baltic seashore.

At a red light, Leo turned to Eleanor and stared fixedly at her. "Are you okay?"

"Yep, I am." Eleanor scrubbed at her forehead, as if to clear her vision of Alexa's eyes. "How was lunch with Mr and Mrs Wright?"

"The Honourable Judge Wright, Mrs Wright, and *Ms* Wright," Leo said with a hint of mischief in his eyes. "How could we go wrong?"

Eleanor laughed. "Ms Wright?"

"Yes." Leo nodded. "Stella Wright is a member of Counsel in commercial arbitration and dispute resolution."

"Impressive. I gathered Mum had an ulterior motive for the lunch," Eleanor said. "So, was she *right* for you?"

He laughed loudly and shook his head. "Oh, no. You've got it wrong. That's why Mum was so upset. Stella was there to meet you, the famed photographer, and you didn't show."

"What? No, Mum wouldn't be so blatant—"

They looked at each other knowingly and said simultaneously, "Yes, she would." Then burst out laughing.

Eleanor was still giggling and shaking her head thinking about her lucky escape when Leo drove down the tree-lined street where their parents lived, pulled into the paved driveway, and parked in front of the three-car garage.

Their mother had strange ideas about who would make suitable partners for her children. She uttered a groan of despair, remembering Alexa's lips on hers. What would their mother make of Alexa?

Leo switched off the car. "So, did you have a good time in the goldfields? Find what you were looking for?"

Eleanor shrugged. "We did find a few of the slides' locations. Not all of them though."

"Gives you a reason to go back, then?"

"Hmm…We'll see."

Of course, she wanted to go back, with Alexa as her guide. She'd had fun while they'd explored the goldfields and learnt heaps about the region. Alexa was beguiling, with her catalogue of facts and stories and her vivid imagination. Apart from a tendency to lose track of time, she was well-organised, and that was a definite plus for Eleanor. Alexa put Eleanor at ease. She was the perfect person to help Eleanor investigate into Helen's slides. Why, then, did the prospect of seeing her again on Friday both excite Eleanor and throw her into a panic?

Chapter 13

Bouquet of flowers

Eleanor arrived at the front gate of Grace's home with just her camera backpack and a bunch of coral peonies from her parents' garden. She hadn't had to cross a surging river or fight her way through a crowd of rioters for this photoshoot, but she was still excited at the prospect of photographing Alexa's grandmother. Eleanor was five minutes early for their ten-thirty appointment, and not wanting to be rude, she stopped at the gate to study the house. The two-storey terrace with its postage stamp sized front garden was as neat as a pin. Eleanor considered it to be a large rambling house for one person to live on their own.

Nana and Grandad Heysen's big old house in Melbourne was sold when Grandad died. Nana Marlies wouldn't listen to Eleanor's father, who encouraged her to stay, and instead re-located to a retirement village, where she lived in a tiny, two-bedroom unit. It had turned out to be a good move, because Nana enjoyed the company of the other residents and she still loved to travel. Eleanor applauded her nana for standing her ground.

Unlatching the gate, Eleanor traversed the short path and three steps onto the wide terracotta tiled porch. She hadn't noticed last time that there was a handrail but no ramp. Trust Grace to eschew modifications to the house. *Good on her.*

Grace met her at the front door attired in tailored slacks, a soft green argyle sweater, and a silk scarf draped around her neck. Bruce, the ginger cat, was held under her arm. Eleanor admired Grace's style and confidence.

"Good morning, dear. You are punctual." Giggling, Grace beckoned Eleanor inside and closed the door. "Not like my granddaughter."

"Not too early, I hope?"

"Of course not. Your timing is perfect."

"Good morning, Grace," Eleanor said. "Hello, Bruce."

"We love spring mornings, don't we, puss? He was up at the crack of dawn, itching to get outside and chase the lorikeets feeding on my tomato vines."

"Naughty boy…or is that a good thing?" Eleanor stroked his stripy fur, and he wriggled his torso in response, purring loudly. "I was up early for a jog around the neighbourhood before breakfast."

"Well, no wonder you're so radiant," Grace said so enthusiastically that Bruce leapt out of her arms and scurried down the hallway. "Where is all your camera gear? The lights and other paraphernalia you people use?"

Eleanor couldn't help but feel a tingle of anticipation as she held out her bag in front of her. "I've got everything I need in here. I'm going with a handheld camera today. We'll use natural light and our imaginations; it will just enhance your beauty." She handed Grace the flowers. "These are for you."

"You are a charmer." Grace accepted the peonies and took a deep breath. "Simply marvellous fragrance, Eleanor. Thank you." She covered her face with her free hand and peeked through her splayed fingers, her brown eyes challenging. "Where do we start?"

Grace stood near the leadlight panelled front door; prisms of light suffusing the entrance hall bathing her with soft colour. Eleanor gave a satisfied sigh. The gentle nature of the filtered light would make a flattering portrait shot.

"How about right here?" Eleanor opened her bag, pulled out her camera, and looped the leather strap around her neck. She focussed and snapped. "Perfect." Eleanor smiled. She had successfully captured the dreamy ethereal effect she'd been after.

"That was quick." Grace wriggled her slim shoulders. "Where to next? How about the living room? The light is just lovely at this time of day."

Grace perched on the edge of the chaise lounge while Eleanor took in the layout of the room, considering her options. When taking close-ups, she would use the 50mm lens to zoom in on Grace's facial expressions and textures. She'd take wide angle shots that would place Grace amongst her belongings—the ancient writing desk where she said she had penned her magazine column and the two bright semi-abstract watercolours on the wall above, painted by her daughter, Eloise—weaving together aspects of her life story.

"Sitting here, I have a perfect view of children playing in the street," Grace said. "When I finished school, I thought about teaching, but my mother was not taken with the idea. Father was much more of a forward thinker, though, and wanted me to have a career. He served in the First World War and was a keen sportsman, like many members of the Brown family. He was one of the first—" Grace stopped mid-sentence and shook her head. "He studied and played football for Melbourne University before he went to war."

"What did he study?" Eleanor asked. A spark of recognition had been triggered by the name. Alexa had mentioned her great-grandfather's name was William, but she'd never given a surname. So why did the name William Brown sound so familiar to Eleanor?

"Father was an engineer," Grace continued.

Eleanor examined the light meter in her hand, readjusting the dial. "And you married an engineer, too, didn't you?"

"Yes, I was working as a typist and just twenty-one when we met. He swept me off my feet, but Father insisted Gerald and I court for a year before we married." Her eyelids fluttered, and she placed her hand over her heart.

Eleanor pressed the shutter, capturing a series of shots. The angle of the light just grazing the skin surface, creating tiny shadows in the lines and pores of Grace's expressive hands. She wanted to draw attention to the details—bringing depth and emotion to the images, emphasising Grace's bony wrist that appeared too delicate for the oversized emerald ring she wore on the ring finger of her left hand.

"I was twenty-five years old when Gerald died. A widow with a two-year-old toddler. I don't know how we would have survived if Uncle Oswald hadn't offered me a job." Grace cupped her chin in her hand, perfectly framed, and Eleanor waited for the moment when she appeared to be between thoughts before she clicked the shutter again.

Grace seemed almost oblivious to Eleanor as she changed angles, checking the light meter and lifting the camera to her eye.

"I was suddenly a copy girl," she continued. "A newspaper career had never really been in my sights. It was not a particularly glamorous job in the 1950s."

Eleanor smiled as Grace leaned back in the chaise lounge, her hands folded in her lap. Bruce lay on the top of the backrest, paws tucked underneath his body, head erect like a sphinx.

Eleanor crouched and lifted her camera. *Click*. Grace was posed with the light through the sash window at a forty-five-degree angle, casting dramatic shadows. In this shot, Eleanor wanted to reveal Grace's sassy, independent soul. Fingers crossed she'd got it.

Studying Grace, it was clear where her granddaughter got some of her knockout features. "Alexa has your remarkable cheekbones," Eleanor said, her heart rate picking up a bit at the thought of Alexa.

"Must be in our genes." Grace smiled. "Although in this light, my wrinkles will look like the channels of a braided river plain."

Eleanor laughed. "Trust me. You've hardly got any lines, and the ones you do have just give you character."

"You know the right things to say to an old lady. My story is reflected in my face. And not all my stories are happy ones. A mother should never outlive her child." Grace sighed, and as if sensing her sadness, Bruce slinked off the headrest and crawled onto her lap. Lost in thought, Grace stroked the top of his head.

From a different perspective, Eleanor increased the aperture, using backlight to create a halo, isolating her subjects. Woman and her feline companion. The sublime qualities of both subjects were reflected in the image, showing the loving connection between these two kindred spirits.

Grace tickled the top of Bruce's head and drew herself upright. "I was desolate, on a downward spiral, so angry Eloise was taken from us. But I've had to be brave. Alexa needs me. She has no one but me."

On their train journey from Castlemaine, Alexa had encouraged Eleanor not to take her mother for granted. At the time, as Eleanor had been so irritated with her mother, she'd brushed the words aside. Later on, though, she'd recalled Alexa's advice with gratitude. Her immediate family was not large, but she had Leo, her parents, and both grandmothers. Alexa was right; she was lucky.

Eleanor put her camera on the coffee table and went to stand beside Grace, murmuring softly, "I'm so sorry for your loss." Alexa and her grandmother had suffered so much, and yet they were both courageous. Eleanor leaned across and gently clasped Grace's hand, hoping to give her some comfort.

Bruce stretched, resting his paw on Eleanor's shirtsleeve.

"Bruce is usually a fusspot," Grace said. "An anti-social fellow, but he seems to like you."

Eleanor scratched the puss under his chin, increasing the volume of his purr. She beamed. One of these days she hoped to have her own home, a girlfriend, and a cat or two.

"My granddaughter seems to have taken a shine to you, also," Grace added earnestly. "I'm glad you're spending time with her."

"Err…yes." Eleanor's cheeks flushed.

"When Alexa was here yesterday after work, she told me that your trip to the goldfields didn't turn out how she'd expected."

Eleanor rubbed her temples, feeling the heat rise in her cheeks again. What on earth had Alexa said?

"I worry about her driving that old jalopy." Grace shook her head. "And you two were stuck in the cottage overnight together in that terrible storm."

It was a sensitive subject Eleanor did not want to pursue right now. She stood and walked towards an antique bookcase in the corner of the room. "There's a great collection of Eloise's books at the cottage," she said, attempting to change the subject. "Quite a few travel books."

"Eloise worked terribly hard at that flower shop, but once Alexa was in high school, she took off for two or three weeks every year. Once, she went to Borneo to study rare plants. Alexa stayed with me."

"Yes, Alexa told me her mother went to the Kalahari Desert. I found a copy of *The Healing Land* on a bookshelf at the cottage. I love that book about the bushmen of the desert," Eleanor said. "Which reminds me, a newspaper article was tucked inside about the 1934 Melbourne Cup winner, Peter Pan."

"That no good ex-husband of hers was a gambler. My daughter wouldn't have known which end of a horse to place a bet on."

Eleanor laughed. "Okay."

"Did you say 1934? How strange." Grace frowned.

"On the other side of the newspaper clipping were the births, deaths, and golden-anniversary notices. Does that mean anything to you, Grace?" Eleanor couldn't even explain it to herself, but she had an inkling—call it second sense—that Alexa's mother had kept that clipping safe for a reason.

Grace gave a start, and the cat leapt off her lap. She clapped her hands together. "Now, before you pick up your camera again, let's have a cup of coffee. I had Patrick pick up some nibbles from the sandwich shop. He works ridiculously long hours driving that taxi car around but always finds time to run errands for me."

Though Eleanor welcomed the offer of coffee, she couldn't help but wonder why Grace had reacted to the newspaper clipping so strangely. What had elicited her response? Whatever the reason, it reinforced Eleanor's belief that there was something suspect about the clipping. It was unlikely to be Peter Pan, so, it must have been something to do with the notices on the other side. Eleanor resolved to look into them further when she got home.

She adjusted the settings on the Leica and took more photos while Grace brewed a pot of coffee on the gas cooker. She followed Grace's precise movements with her camera as she set out the fine bone china and silver cutlery on a damask tablecloth. In the middle of the black, lacquered table sat a crystal bowl filled with Eleanor's peonies, their scent filling the room. Eleanor wanted her images to evoke the extraordinary from what was probably an ordinary everyday ritual for Grace and she pressed the shutter button again, snapping more photos of Grace—when she used a pair of shiny tongs to arrange the delicate layered sandwiches on a two-tier platter.

"Are you sure I can't help?" Eleanor asked, looking through the viewfinder.

Grace looked up and grinned.

Snap.

"Surprise," Grace said, looking directly into the camera lens. Returning to her task, she poured the coffee, adding hot milk from a silver jug, and handed the tray over to Eleanor. "Could you place this on the table?"

Eleanor let the camera rest against her chest from its strap and took the oval tray from Grace's slightly shaky hands, waiting until she was seated before setting the tray on the table. She smiled warmly as she sat down across from Grace.

"Help yourself, dear."

Eleanor selected an egg and lettuce sandwich, placed it on the side plate, and reached for her coffee. "Thank you. This is a treat."

"And not a trace of gluten." Grace winked, lifting her own sandwich. "Ham and sweet mustard pickle," she said before taking a hearty bite.

After surprisingly strong coffee and filling treats, Grace allowed Eleanor to continue with the photoshoot for a short time before she shooed her out of the house. "You must have more important things to do than hang out with this old thing," she said with a wry chuckle.

In fact, Eleanor was in no hurry to leave, but it was time to go as Grace was obviously tired. She'd been inspiring company and an excellent subject. It was curious, how one moment Grace would be talking non-stop, the next she'd clam up, do an about turn, and head off into another train of thought. It was clear some subjects were off limits, or at least difficult territory, particularly where her father, William, and his side of the family were concerned. Eleanor couldn't help but wonder why.

With a spring in her step, Eleanor walked from Grace's house down Brunswick Street, and boarded the two-fifteen tram. Finding an empty seat, she tucked her pack snugly beside her, ensuring the twelve-thousand-dollar camera and lens kit was well hidden. She'd already transferred the images from the camera to her phone and sat browsing through them. Eleanor was sure she'd interacted with Grace and set up the scenes for maximum effect. She was pleased to see that, in many of the images, she'd captured a hint of Grace's spirit.

Eleanor paused at the series of black and white portraits of Grace sitting at her antique writing desk. She zoomed in on a picture taken just as Grace admitted to having four different suitors after Eloise had left home. She'd met Eleanor's look of surprise with a playful grin. Her eyes were sparkling and crinkled with laughter. Eleanor's heart warmed at the joy on Grace's face. She couldn't wait to show this image to Alexa.

She flicked through the images of Grace in her garden and then located the photos from last weekend. It wasn't the first time she'd looked at the pictures of Alexa, or the second, or the third. The ones of Alexa impersonating Mabel were so comical—pure Alexa. Mischievous and engaging.

The tram came to a screeching halt, and she lowered her phone. Eleanor looked up, but it wasn't her stop. Lifting her phone again, she found the picture of Peter Pan and then zoomed in on the next image. One of the obituary notices read, *Mrs Mei-Li Brown, nee Kwan, wife of Otto (deceased), mother of William.* She snapped her fingers. "That's where I've seen that name!" Her heart pounded in her chest. What was going on with Alexa's family? Why the secrecy about William? Eleanor had no idea, and although she knew it was none of her business, she couldn't ignore her desire to find out more.

She looked back at the images, searching for the one of Alexa holding the red umbrella in the rain. These photographs were conduits to mostly pleasurable memories. Memories of Alexa Bellamy. Alexa stirred something inside Eleanor that refused to settle, spreading through her like warm honey.

According to Gran, yesterday's photo shoot had taken place mostly indoors. Last night, she'd chattered away on the phone about Eleanor's visit with an excited edge to her voice, slightly raised and breathless. Her grandmother was clearly impressed with Eleanor's charming and respectful manner. Alexa admired Eleanor for the way she'd put Gran at ease.

Alexa couldn't wait to see if Eleanor had captured Granny's feisty personality and her air of mystery. She'd have loved to have been the proverbial fly on the wall, listening to their every word and watching Eleanor—catching a glimpse of her artistry and skill at work—but she'd been too busy debating archival principals with the Pictures Collection team at the library.

Gran had skipped their usual lunch date today because of a Mahjong tournament she was attending with Patrick, giving Alexa an excuse to go shopping during her break. Thankfully, he and her grandmother were *simpatico* especially when it came to Mahjong because, although Alexa had occasionally played with her mother and grandmother, she hadn't shared their passion for the game.

While her mother had been caught up with wedding bouquets and party floral arrangements, Alexa, aged six or seven, often accompanied her grandmother to her friends' home for a Saturday afternoon game of Mahjong. She remembered foreign languages being spoken and the clicking and clacking of the tiles being shuffled. When the adults had moved on to cups of tea, spring rolls, and colourful coconut cakes, Alexa would build towers with the tiles under the table.

Alexa joined the end of the cue at her regular coffee stop. The delectable aromas from the vegetarian noodle shop next door wafted in the air. Ginger, garlic, lemongrass. Yum. She'd never have time to pick up an order of steamed dumplings *and* race down the street to check out the funky jacket Jac had spotted in the arcade. She patted her stomach regrettably. Not today. Perhaps, another time, with Eleanor.

Pleased with her purchase from the second-hand shop, Alexa hummed quietly to herself as she stepped out of the Royal Arcade into brilliant sunshine. The pavements glistened like sealskin, and car tyres sizzled on the wet road surface. After the weekend's storm, followed by days of dreary weather, it was such a relief to see the sun again.

Alexa pushed through the doorway and took the back-of-house stairs two at a time. Her lunch break had gone on a smidgen longer than usual. She swung the brown paper bag in her hand, pleased with Jac's tip-off.

Apart from Chrissy, the rare books librarian having a solo lunch at her desk, the other workstations in the partitioned office space she shared with the Collections Team were empty. Alexa tucked away her bag and new purchase in the desk drawer and hung her coat over the chair. She didn't feel too guilty.

Chrissy glanced up and raised her hand, clutching a half-eaten sandwich. "Have you been shopping again?"

"You know me and second-hand bargains. It's Jac's fault. She found it."

Chrissy stared at Alexa while chewing on the remains of her sandwich. She swallowed. "Show me what you've got."

"I don't know when I'll ever get to wear it." Alexa laughed. "I couldn't help myself." She pulled the package out of the drawer and extracted the black velvet, thigh-length coat with high collar, upturned cuffs, and barely visible silver threads, holding it up.

"Ooh, look at those shiny metal buttons. I'd love to run my fingers over them, but not until I've washed my hands," Chrissy said. "You'll look like a time-travelling, steampunk model on the catwalk."

"Meow." Alexa raked her free hand through the air, fingers splayed like claws.

Chrissy giggled. "By the way, *Catwoman*, the West Team delivered the stuff you requested into Workroom A. I signed the delivery slip for you."

"Thanks." She picked up the slip of paper. It was Eleanor's bequest. "I'll go and work on this now, so that's where I'll be if anyone needs me."

"No problem." Chrissy smiled and turned back to her computer screen.

Alexa returned the new purchase to her desk. She grabbed her glasses, tucked them into the pocket of her tweed waistcoat, and headed for the lab down the hallway across the corridor, eager to get back to work. She clicked on the light switch and entered the room.

At the end of the long white table sat a thick A3 cardboard envelope and a dove grey box. Beside them, a larger polypropylene storage box held the rehoused glass plate negatives. It was labelled, Heysen: Handle with Care.

Alexa reached underneath into the table drawer and pulled out a pair of nitrile gloves. She blew into each glove before slipping it onto her fingers. "Hmm...Eleanor Heysen. Handle with care." She sighed heavily as her imagination ran riot with visions of handling Eleanor with care. After last weekend's rejection, she had no idea if she'd ever get a chance. She really hoped she would.

Alexa opened the envelope and peeked inside to check the contents. Alongside the six prints interleaved with acid-free tissue was the certificate of thanks from Katherine Kent. The Head of Collections, affectionately known as Kit Kat, had requested the images be printed on archival paper using inks of the highest quality. Alexa looked forward to presenting the library's gift to Eleanor on Friday. It was a big deal. The fact that Alexa was the first person to realise the significance of Helen Heysen's slides was totally awesome. Having completed the Lehmann Collection, Eleanor's donation secured the Library's resources as one of the largest nineteenth-century photographic archives in the Southern Hemisphere. This was definitely a highlight in Alexa's career.

Alexa twirled her black-rimmed glasses between her finger and thumb. She removed the small bundle from the envelope and carefully flicked through the images until she found the slide that fascinated her most and which had triggered such a puzzling response from her grandmother. Alexa scrutinised the image of the Chinese herbalist; the gentleman was graceful in his seated position, reed-like with a short wispy white beard. He was dressed in a long suit coat, loose striped trousers, shiny black shoes, and a narrow pot-like hat with just a bit of shirt and bow tie visible above his crossed arms. The herbalist was handsome with a serene expression—the face of a healer.

The camphor wood trunk was open, displaying urns and boxes covered in Chinese symbols. Small drawers revealed bottles of many colours with half-waxed seals. The details in the image were so clear Alexa could see pieces of bone and animal hide spilling out of the drawers. She shivered. It was a little creepy, but the image wasn't frightening, so what had spooked Gran? Alexa was curious about her grandmother's reaction; the difficulty was how to approach the subject and find a subtle way of bringing the herbalist's picture into a conversation.

Alexa slid the images back into the envelope along with the accompanying certificate, resealed it, and placed it on the table. She switched on the computer, typed in her password and prepared to complete the data entry for Eleanor's bequest. This was the last step before the items would enter the stable environmental conditions of closed-collection storage.

On Friday, she would give Eleanor the envelope and find out how she'd spent her time behind the scenes with Digital Imaging. *Seriously*, Friday was a long way away. Could she wait that long before seeing Eleanor again?

Alexa had never experienced the kind of affinity with any woman that she did with Eleanor. There was such a physical energy between them, a spark that could be electrifying if taken into the bedroom. Alexa was convinced Eleanor felt it too. She'd been surprised and a little hurt by Eleanor's rejection considering the way they'd flirted with each other all day. If Eleanor hadn't been flirting and Alexa completely misinterpreted her behaviour—then she was losing her mind, or losing her touch, or both.

Eleanor never spoke about her life in London, her flatmates, or a girlfriend. She seemed perfectly contented with being home in Melbourne, but she was a photographer. No doubt she would take up another assignment and be gone soon. So why not have some uncomplicated fun? She and Alexa could be friends with benefits. And when Eleanor left, neither of them would get hurt.

That was the theory anyway. If she faced facts, though, Alexa was already in deeper than she should be, even though she and Eleanor hadn't even slept together. Once Eleanor left—if she left—Alexa would have to shake off the loss and get on with her life, but her stomach churned at even the thought. It was the emptiness she feared, the void someone else may not be able to fill. So perhaps, after all, friendship was best for both of them.

Alexa's cheeks flushed. Could she do just friendship? Uh-huh. If that was her only option. Eleanor was worth it. She'd rather have Eleanor as a platonic friend than not in her life at all.

Chapter 14

Fishing hands

THE LAST TIME ELEANOR VISITED the Queen Street law offices of Miller Legal in the CBD would have been over a year ago, to meet her father for lunch. He'd always make time for her when she was in town, making her feel extra special—whisking her off to a little pizza place in Hardware Lane or enticing her to grab a sandwich and head to the Flagstaff Gardens for a bit of afternoon jazz, even though jazz wasn't really her thing. She smiled fondly at the memories.

Her mother had rarely joined them, occupied with business lunches or working through with a salad at her desk. She always worked so hard; it was surprising *she* hadn't been the one to have a heart attack.

As she approached the elevator, Eleanor felt prickles of trepidation. She should have checked if her mother was in the office before embarking on her impromptu visit. The doors closed tight, and she was swept to the third floor.

Since the photo session with Grace, Eleanor's imagination had run riot. Grace had hinted at skeletons in the family closet, and now Eleanor was like a dog with a bone, determined to explore further. She was sure the key lay with Grace's father, William, who'd attended Melbourne University during the same period as her own great-grandfather. With luck, she'd verify her suspicions that William was linked to one of the obituary notices in the newspaper clipping found at the cottage, and she'd find the missing piece of the puzzle here, within the tomes of the firm's law library. When Eleanor had chosen to follow her instinct, she'd debated the merits of telling Alexa straight away but had decided against it, just in case her search was a dead end. A twinge of guilt nagged at her, but curiosity won out.

The elevator dinged, and the doors opened onto the foyer. As a small child, she'd been intimidated by the movie-set-like entrance with its dark wood-panelled walls and plush carpeting. It was still a little stuffy and old-worldly, but she no longer felt that same sense of childlike awe. She walked over to the massive reception desk—which was, at this moment, oddly, unattended.

Eleanor peered through the glass doors of the conference room, which was also empty. Just as she was contemplating sneaking down the hallway to the library, hoping to avoid running in to her mother, a dapper-looking man exited one of the side offices and briskly walked towards the reception desk with a stack of files wedged under one arm and another pile held in his right hand.

He deposited the files onto the desktop's polished surface with a thump and looked up. "Good afternoon. I'm so sorry I didn't hear the elevator. How may I help you?" He smiled, flashing a set of pearly white teeth. "Do you have an appointment?"

"No, actually, I don't."

He cocked his head to one side, appraising her. Then, as if having a light-bulb moment, his eyes widened. "Oh, wow, you're the boss's daughter." He held out his hand. "It's a pleasure to meet you, Ms Heysen. I'm Trevor Henry, paralegal cum receptionist. General dogsbody, really."

"Hi, nice to meet you, Trevor." She accepted his hand, shaking it briefly. "Call me Eleanor, please."

"We miss Mr Heysen around here, Eleanor. I hope he's back soon."

"Thank you. Me too," Eleanor said.

Trevor placed his elbow on the desktop, resting his chin in his hand. "I just received my copy of the latest *Global Conscience*. It has your excellent article about the Somali villagers working with NGOs towards climate change adaptation."

She gave Trevor a cautious smile.

"Your photographs just blew me away." He gave a little shake of his head. "You really captured it, Eleanor."

Eleanor took a deep breath and swallowed. "Thank you so much."

Trevor didn't know the half of it, but he was right about the article; Eleanor and the journalist had worked hard to ensure it was of the highest quality. Her primary goal had been to catch the reality of the villagers' lives without sensationalising their situation for the sake of attracting aid money. She *was* proud of her work.

But what had happened next still made her sick to the stomach. She'd returned to London to discover that a tabloid freelancer had covered the same village. When his images appeared on the front page of the paper, the colourfully dressed women and children that Eleanor had grown to respect were depicted in filthy clothes, the children crying, with desperate faces. It was a set-up, unethical, and although she was furious, there was nothing Eleanor could do.

"Eleanor? Are you okay?"

She looked up to find not one but two concerned faces staring at her. She swallowed hard. "Yep," she said, pulling herself together. "I'm good." Eleanor glanced from Trevor to the fair-haired woman beside him wearing a dark pant suit, soft blue blouse, and low black heels. Where had *she* come from?

"Well, that's good, if you're sure." Trevor wiped his hand over his brow. "Eleanor, let me introduce Stella Wright, our mediation adviser, expert in disputes of all varieties and insolvency matters." He gestured towards the newcomer. "If you ever need a negotiator, Stella is the best."

"Is that so?" Stella winked at Trevor, a grin tugging her bright red lips. She turned to Eleanor and held out her hand. "Finally, I get to meet the roving photographer. It seems you were AWOL at lunch on the weekend."

"Well, this is a surprise." Eleanor took a startled step back and looked into Stella's steel grey eyes. "Hi, good to meet you." She put her hand in hers. "Judge Wright's daughter?"

Stella smirked, shook Eleanor's hand slowly, and held onto it. "Yes, that's me. It's a shame you stood me up. I'm familiar with your work and would love to discuss it with you over a drink sometime."

It wouldn't hurt to have a drink with Stella. It wouldn't hurt to make a new friend in Melbourne, either. Eleanor removed her hand from Stella's clasp. "I'd like that," she said tentatively.

The reception phone chimed, and Trevor picked up the handset. "I'm on it, sir, sending her right in." He put the phone down and picked up a bulging folder, handing it over. "Stella. Mr Fischer is waiting for you in his office. I'll buzz you through."

Stella leaned towards Eleanor. "Call me." She smiled sweetly and slipped a card into Eleanor's hand before disappearing down the hallway.

Eleanor placed the business card in her top pocket. Stella was attractive, smart, and obviously had a sense of humour, but being set up by her mother didn't go down well with Eleanor.

Trevor cleared his throat. "Pardon me. Now, where were we?"

She turned back to him. "I'd like to use the library to do some research, please. Is that possible?"

"Sure…I think." Trevor hesitated. "Do I need to check with anybody? Or do you have the password?"

"I do. It's not the first time, Trevor," Eleanor said. "I sometimes use the library when I'm in town."

"All right, then." He nodded, handed her a pen, and pushed over the visitor's sign-in book. "You seem like you know what you're doing."

"Thanks, I'll be fine. Just have a few leads I want to follow." Eleanor glanced at her watch. "Is Mum in her office?" She really didn't want to explain the purpose of her visit to her mother.

"No, sorry." He accepted back his pen. "Mrs Heysen won't be in 'till later this afternoon."

"Okay." A sigh of relief escaped Eleanor's lips. "Thanks for your help. I really appreciate it."

"You're welcome."

The décor of her great-grandfather's library hadn't changed at all since she was a child—probably not since her mother was a child either—with its floor to ceiling mahogany bookcases and olive felt-covered walls that gave it a solid, ageless quality. The shelves were filled with law reports and court judgements as well as rows of leather-bound tomes of precedents and practise guides.

She located her great-grandfather Reginald Miller's 1913 and 1914 university yearbooks and took them to the corner antique reading desk. Eleanor was convinced that he had attended Melbourne University at the same time as Alexa's great-grandfather William Brown. Grace had told her that he'd played football for the university team before he went to war, and so had Reginald. Eleanor hoped to find a photograph of the team in a yearbook to establish if Alexa's William Brown was the same man mentioned in the newspaper clipping. Even if Alexa chose to keep the information to herself and never spoke about it to her grandmother, surely she would want to know.

She leafed through the first book, finding numerous photographs of her own great-grandfather. He'd been a keen sportsman and certainly looked the part, wearing his baggy cricket whites, holding a shiny trophy. Eleanor glanced up at the oil painting portrait hanging on the wall in between the bookshelves. He was a formidable figure.

I recognise that look. That's where Mum gets it from. She folds her arms over her chest just like that. She and Leo called it her defence and attack pose. She remembered the tremor of fear that pose had incited in her when she was younger.

"Where are your football team photos, Great-Grandpop?" She carefully turned a few more pages before stumbling upon exactly what she was looking for. "Ah-ha, this is it."

She examined the grainy black and white photo. There was Reggie Miller sitting cross-legged on the grass in the first row, surrounded by the other team members in dark jerseys and long white shorts. Eleanor peered closer, searching the list of players' names. William Brown, five along in the second row. *Bingo.*

She scanned the photograph. One, two, three, four, five. There he sat on the wooden bench, muscled arms resting on his thighs and dark wavy hair swept across his forehead in a casual style. Just as she'd suspected, William Brown, the handsome man with a cheeky grin, was clearly Chinese, just like the William Brown in the newspaper clipping. Alexa's great-grandfather was Chinese. Eleanor lowered her head into her hands. She'd have to tell Alexa.

The thought of seeing her *friend,* Eleanor, had Alexa smiling at everyone and everything all Friday. She'd kept her mood bright and upbeat for the past few days while coming to terms with their friendship status. It was a good thing she'd been caught up in meetings most of today, though, because, if she'd been at her desk, she'd have stared out the window or glanced at the clock repeatedly. She'd had two missed calls from Eleanor and hadn't been able to reach her back. Alexa's shoulders drooped. What if Eleanor was ringing to change their plans to meet at 4 p.m. in the library's imaging studio? Alexa would soon find out…she entered the studio's outer office and closed the door behind her.

"Good afternoon, Alexa," called Sanjay, the studio supervisor. "Have I missed something?" He glanced at his computer screen. "Are you working with us this afternoon?"

She shook her head and smiled. "No. I'm just here to collect Eleanor." Alexa sometimes worked in the studio cataloguing and creating bibliographic records. Not today, though.

"Ah. The lovely Ms Heysen." He dipped his head. "She should be just about finished. They've been preparing the last of the images for *Bohemian Melbourne* before the exhibition goes up."

"Great, she's still here, then." Alexa exhaled quietly.

"We've enjoyed having Eleanor with us." Sanjay's face lit up with a shy grin. "We're chuffed to spend time with such an insightful photographer. At lunch, she let down her guard and entertained us with some of her adventures. I wonder where she's off to next. I don't suppose she stays still for long."

Alexa shrugged. "Shame I couldn't join you for lunch to hear the stories. Too many meetings."

Why hadn't Alexa used the opportunity to coax more out of Eleanor at the cottage? About what she did? About her ambitions, inspirations, and her plans for the future? She mentally kicked herself. She'd been too caught up in their little adventure in the goldfields and too lost in her attraction for Eleanor.

"Go on in," Sanjay said. "If you've got time to stick around, have a cup of tea with us."

"I'd love to, but Eleanor and I have a meeting with Kit Kat in ten minutes." She walked towards the swing doors. "I'd better find her."

"Off you go. Will I catch you at drinks? Jac asked Eleanor to join us, too. Maybe you can tram it together to the bar."

Halfway through the heavy swing door, Alexa stopped. "Jac asked her, did she?" What was Jac up to? Alexa had told her about the unplanned night at the cottage but not the details. It would be just like Jac to suspect *something* happened between Alexa and Eleanor. Well, it hadn't. The force of the door closing pushed her back into Sanjay's office.

"Careful," he said, grinning.

"Yes. Nearly landed on your desk," Alexa exclaimed. "Okay, see you later in Fitzroy." *Now try going through the door again without knocking yourself out.*

Alexa observed Eleanor lean over the large format digital camera that hung suspended above the light table and was surprised by a soft tug of longing. Eleanor's honey brown strands of hair gleamed gold under the studio lights. With her striped shirt, sleeves rolled up above her elbows, and black apron, she could have been mistaken for a nineteenth-century studio photographer. Minus the ubiquitous moustache.

As if she knew she was being watched, Eleanor turned around. Her dark eyes danced with joy.

"Is it that time already?" Eleanor's lips twitched in a delighted smile that in turn delighted Alexa. "I've been trying out the light table with a glass plate negative," Eleanor said. "Sanjay explained how they are converted into positives, adjusted for exposure, and saved to TIFF files."

"You're obviously learning lots and having fun. It's a shame to take you away, but Katherine is expecting us in her office," Alexa said.

"That's okay. I'm good to go." Eleanor lifted the negative from the light table with gloved hands, slotting it back into its storage box. "They asked me back, if I'm interested. Which I am, of course. How could I not be?"

Alexa answered with a gentle smile and took a step towards the door.

On their way out, Eleanor stopped to say farewell to Sanjay, and she and Alexa walked briskly towards the stairwell.

"It's a good thing you came to get me. These basement corridors would have me lost in a nanosecond."

Alexa slowed her pace. "It wouldn't do to have you roaming the labyrinth of passageways and disappearing in the catacombs for all eternity."

Eleanor grinned. "I can think of worse places to get lost. But eternity is a long, long time," she said as they approached the marble staircase.

"Well, even though the State Museum moved out of this building years ago, you might have roamed amongst the ghosts of stuffed kangaroos, lions, and mummies, breathing in the stench of formaldehyde. They were stored right down here."

Eleanor grabbed her forearm and squeezed. "Okay, did I mention I suffer from mild claustrophobia? It's definitely time for me to surface. Let's get out of here. I'll meet you at the top." She shot up the stairs as though a shadowy spirit was after her.

Alexa's phone beeped. She retrieved it from her jacket pocket and read Jac's message.

Meet me near the Guild Café. I'll travel with you to Fitzroy.

Before she could reply, there was another message.

Eleanor's coming to work drinks, too! I'm guessing you know that by now.

Trust Jac to convince Eleanor to join the gang at the bar, but then Jac could persuade a mouse out of a block of cheddar cheese. Excitement swirled through Alexa at the thought of a night out with Eleanor. Putting the phone back into her pocket, Alexa glanced up the stairwell; Eleanor was nowhere in sight.

Alexa ran up the steps two at a time, narrowly avoiding Eleanor at the stairwell doorway. "Here you are. I didn't think you'd get too far."

Eleanor lowered her head. "I just realised I don't know where Katherine's office is."

Alexa bumped Eleanor's shoulder lightly as she passed her. "Follow me."

Chapter 15

Heads and tails

THEY BRUSHED PAST A THICK curtain of potted palms and shrubs and entered the back bar through a half-hidden iron gate. Alexa wasn't in the least surprised when Jac charged in ahead, searching for their colleagues amongst the Friday after-work crowd who were scattered in groups around tables in the undercover beer garden. As usual, the place hummed with multiple conversations and laughter, competing with clinking glasses and the whir of a blender or two.

Eleanor came to a sudden stop in front of Alexa. Alexa put on the brakes, extended her arms, and rested her hands upon Eleanor's hips. Had Eleanor changed her mind about joining them, after all?

"Sorry. Are you all right?" Alexa asked as Eleanor turned to look at her.

Eleanor just nodded.

"I haven't had the chance to ask you why you rang me earlier." Alexa had chosen not to bring it up during their tram ride with Jac.

"It can wait." Eleanor slipped her hands into her pockets, her gaze darting from left to right. She seemed strangely tense, even nervous.

Hoping to put her at ease, Alexa lay a comforting hand on Eleanor's forearm. "I am happy you came along tonight." She nudged her forward, giving her an encouraging smile. "Come on. Let's check out the cocktail menu."

Eleanor blinked rapidly. "This is a groovy place. Kind of busy, though."

"You don't like crowds?" Alexa leaned in and, for a split second, had an urge to kiss Eleanor's sulky lips, but instead whispered in her ear, "They're a friendly mob, and you've met quite a few of them already." She looked over Eleanor's shoulder. "And there's Jac, waving her arms frantically at me, probably wondering why we are huddled in the shadows."

Eleanor smiled, and her face relaxed a bit. "Jac said this bar is famous for its boozy cocktails."

Alexa was close enough to Eleanor that, when she let out a slow breath, a shudder vibrated through Eleanor's body, and Alexa's entire being hummed in pleasure at her reaction. "Why don't we go get one of those famous cocktails and join the others?"

"Yes, I could use a drink."

"Good. We'll head to the bar, and you can choose something from the drinks menu."

Eleanor pursed her lips. "Hmmm…I'd rather you surprise me."

"No special flavours you prefer?" Alexa lowered her head and whispered, "Tastes you don't like?"

"Nothing too sweet, nothing too sour." Eleanor lifted her shoulder.

"You're trusting." Alexa gave Eleanor a gentle push. *Something fun that will help her chill.* "Okay, leave it to me. I have just the thing in mind," Alexa said with a cheeky grin. *Raspberry Blossom Blush.*

A little after six thirty, most of their group had scattered, and the downstairs garden bar was overflowing with standing customers. The live music volume had increased along with the conversation level. Alexa leaned forward. "Are you into this uptown jazz?" It was a shame the music downstairs tonight wasn't more melodious.

Laughing, Eleanor placed her hands over her ears. Obviously not. She had been quick to agree when Jac had suggested they move upstairs to a quieter space. The three of them had made a bee line for the vacant couch and chair near the old stone hearth with a cosy log burner and ordered a couple of Mediterranean sharing plates.

"This is sure to make you happy," Jac exclaimed, handing back Alexa's refilled cocktail glass. "What's in it?" She rested her head against the back of the couch and closed her eyes.

Alexa took a sip, licked her lips, tasting the flavours of the drink. "Absinthe, bitters, fresh lime, and muddled raspberries. Strained and poured on an ice cube of Blue Sapphire gin."

"Muddled raspberries? What will they think of next?" Eleanor shook her head and lifted her water glass.

Reclining in the armchair, she crossed her legs at the ankles, gazing at Alexa for what seemed like a long time, her eyebrows lifting fractionally, almost curiously.

Alexa's heart sped up under Eleanor's intense stare. Taking the last sip of her drink, she placed the glass on the table. She pulled at her shirt collar and loosened her tie, inclining her head towards Eleanor. "How are you doing?"

"I'm fine," Eleanor replied slowly, gazing unashamedly at Alexa.

Eleanor was giving her some seriously interested vibes; that was more than just a friendly look. It was getting hot, especially under Eleanor's visual caress. Or maybe it was just the alcohol Alexa had consumed? No, it was definitely the look on Eleanor's face that had her temperature rising.

"Hey, Eleanor. How did you enjoy being a minion, today?" Jac asked.

"So, the building manager took you up to the dome and out on the roof?" Alexa chimed in quickly, glad for Jac's timely distraction.

"Yes, it was awesome. She led me up a meandering stairway, along some rickety planks, and into the ceiling above the dome." Eleanor's eyes sparkled. "Do they do that for everybody? I'm glad I'm not scared of heights. The skylight they're restoring is huge, and the view of Melbourne from out on the roof: wow! Let's hope my photographs do it justice."

"Bet you gave Michelle a heart attack." Alexa laughed. "I can imagine her holding onto your ankles while you swung off the scaffolding to get the perfect shot."

"Correct. I was trying to recreate the legendary photo of the Manhattan skyline, *Men at Lunch*."

Jac shook her head. "Ha, health and safety regulations are a lot tougher now than when they built the Empire State Building."

"Actually, it was the Rockefeller Centre," Alexa said.

"You knew that." Eleanor grinned at her in a way that made Alexa feel appreciated, and Alexa's cheeks flushed.

"*God*, where has the time gone?" Jac stared at her watch wide-eyed. "I told the babysitter I'd be home by eight. Got to run." Jac collected her bag, pushed off the couch, and pulled on her coat. She blew them a hurried kiss.

"Don't be a stranger, Eleanor. Have a great weekend. Bye, Alexa. See you at work on Monday."

Eleanor waved goodbye to Jac before turning back to Alexa with an amused smile. "Is she always so exuberant?"

"Unquestionably. Jac's a single mother with adorable twins." Alexa shimmied to the other end of the couch, closer to Eleanor's chair. "So, we're finally alone." She crossed her hands in her lap.

It was cosy sitting by the fire in their private little nook. From the noise filtering up the stairs, the bar and restaurant were crazy busy. "Are you hungry? The restaurant has a fantastic selection of mains and desserts."

"No thank you. I had plenty from the platters you ordered earlier." Eleanor patted her stomach. "It's comfortable and snug here, not too noisy. I can actually hear myself speak."

"Haven't you lived in London for more than ten years? You must be used to noisy, crowded spaces?"

Eleanor stared up at the ceiling. "When I first arrived, I was into everything. Experiences, sights, sounds, culture, art—people. London has it all. When my photography changed direction and took me further afield, though, my eyes opened to other worlds," she said with a faraway look. "When I returned between assignments, the whole London scene was an overload. I sought peace and quiet. There were some pub nights and parties but less and less."

"What kind of things do you do between assignments?" She tilted her head towards Eleanor. She wanted to make the most of this time to ask questions and learn more about Eleanor's life.

"Well I never spent much time sitting around at the flat." Eleanor smiled. "My flatmates were transient beings. Cabin crew and a journalist. We were like passing ships in the night. I'd often take myself on runs through the suburban paths or long rambling walks in the countryside."

Alexa waved her finger in the air. "With your camera, of course."

"Never parted." Eleanor patted her rucksack. "Except when I'm running, but I always have my phone," she said. "Coming home has made me realise what I've been missing."

Alexa waited for Eleanor to say more, but she didn't. Maybe Eleanor was thinking of basing herself closer to home and her family. For a few moments, Alexa contemplated what that could mean for her and Eleanor.

Would they be able to develop something more than friendship if given more time together? "What have you been missing?" Alexa asked, eventually.

"My family, of course." Eleanor tapped her lip contemplatively. "A sense of belonging. Wide open spaces. Lots." She stared into the fireplace intently.

"You haven't told me why you rang this afternoon. Did you miss me?" Alexa grinned sheepishly. She had missed Eleanor.

"I did." Eleanor hesitated. She opened her mouth as if she wanted to say something else, then shook her head. The deep brown of her eyes seemed fathomless.

Giving Eleanor time to figure out what she wanted to say, Alexa reached for the water jug and topped up their glasses.

"Thanks." Eleanor took a sip of water and placed the glass on the table. "It was super nice of Katherine to give me the prints. I'm going to get them framed. I didn't expect such a lavish afternoon tea in your boss's office." She smiled.

Alexa stared at Eleanor for a moment, certain the afternoon tea was not the subject that had Eleanor tongue-tied just before. "The cheese scones and lamingtons were entirely Katherine's idea."

"Thanks for offering to keep the envelope locked in your office until I can collect it next week." Eleanor smiled again. "It's been an interesting time at the library."

"Just interesting?" Alexa asked dryly. "You're a girl who's travelled a lot, seen a lot of *interesting* things." She winked.

Eleanor's eyes widened. "You're joking, right? It was fascinating actually, for someone who spent quite a bit of time there as a student. I always wondered what went on behind the scenes and above the dome. Now, I've had a look behind the stacks."

"You're even picking up the jargon." Alexa reached across to Eleanor and rested her hand on her knee. "Even though you're not into crowded places, I am glad you came tonight," she said. "So, what have you been up to apart from your very interesting time at the library?"

"Well, that's why I was ringing you, but then I changed my mind and thought I should talk to you in person." Eleanor's voice had taken on a serious tone.

"Now, this sounds intriguing—go on, what did you want to tell me?"

"Would you mind if I got a coffee first?" Eleanor started to pull herself out of the armchair. "Would you like one?"

Alexa jumped to her feet. "I need to visit the bathroom. What else can I get you, while I'm downstairs? How about a shot of cognac?" Curiosity gnawed at Alexa as she took in Eleanor's apprehensive state, but clearly, Eleanor needed more time and a little incentive to open up about what was on her mind.

Eleanor shook her head, then just as quickly changed her mind. "Yes, please."

"I'll order them on the way back, and you..." Alexa placed a finger in the middle of Eleanor's chest. "Get ready to talk."

Eleanor sank back into the armchair, her eyes riveted to the shapely retreating figure of Alexa Bellamy. She'd never seen anyone look as good in a tweed business suit. Earlier she'd enjoyed watching the casual, confident way Alexa had shed her coat, then loosened her shirt collar and narrow necktie.

At the top of the stairwell, Alexa turned and smiled, her eyes dancing with mischief.

Caught. Embarrassed, Eleanor looked down at her shoes.

It was obvious that her attraction for Alexa was burning brighter than ever. It had not diminished one bit, and Alexa's playful, friendly mood tonight was making it impossible to focus on the task at hand, which was, first and foremost, to disclose the information about Alexa's family without upsetting her.

She made herself take a deep lungful of air, breathing in and out slowly. For Eleanor, pursuing the mystery of William's background was second nature. The newspaper clipping, Grace's reaction to the photograph of the herbalist and the way she'd skirted around the subject of her father, had tugged at Eleanor's inquisitive nature. Now, Eleanor had connected the subtle clues, confirmed her suspicions, and she mentally prepared herself to stop being a wuss and tell Alexa.

The background music didn't match Eleanor's edgy mood as she waited. It was the kind they played in lounge bars to keep you chilled-out, but it wasn't working for Eleanor. She reached for her bag, unzipped the front pocket, and pulled out her phone, tapping it on her knee.

Alexa was taking forever. Eleanor looked at the time and her phone fell out of her hands and onto the floor with a soft thud. She cursed. Alexa had only been gone for five and a half minutes. She needed to calm down.

She scooped the phone off the floor, opened her photo app, and found the folder marked 'Alexa.' With trembling hands, Eleanor began to swipe through the photos she'd scanned from her great-grandfather's university yearbook.

"Mystery solved?"

Eleanor jumped and dropped her phone again. Luckily, this time, it landed in her lap. Her stomach did a backflip. "You scared me half to death."

"That would never be my intention, believe me." Alexa sent her an amused look beneath her long, dark eyelashes. "It's just that you seemed so immersed in your phone, you probably didn't even notice I was gone for ages, waiting in a queue three deep to fetch these." She handed Eleanor a cognac snifter filled with a generous splash of toffee-coloured liquid. "I've ordered the coffees downstairs, but they might take a while."

Eleanor cupped her hands around the curved glass and lifted it under her nose. She sniffed and took a tentative sip. It was warm and smooth like honey. She licked her lips. "Tastes as good as it looks."

Alexa sank into the couch and held out her glass to Eleanor. "Here's to drinking French cognac in the attic of a good old Aussie pub."

Their glasses clinked.

Eleanor wasn't usually in favour of liquid courage, but she had to admit it might help. "I'll drink to that."

Alexa sat upright, one long leg crossed over the other. "So, I'm ready."

Eleanor shifted around in her chair, took a healthy mouthful, and swallowed. She placed her glass on the table, reached for her phone and took a steadying breath. "Grace was an excellent subject, totally at home in front of the camera. So keen to share stories of her colourful life," she said, stalling.

"Gran did mention you have the knack of coaxing information from your subjects," Alexa said with a smile. "I would love to see the pictures when you're ready."

"Yes, yes, of course. I want you to see them. If you come out to my place, I'll show you the sample prints." Eleanor scrolled back through the images and found what she was looking for. "This is not of Grace." She hesitated. "Do you remember the old newspaper clipping that fell out of your mother's book at the cottage? This one?" She enlarged the image on the phone and held it out to Alexa.

Alexa glanced at her questioningly, then stared at the screen. "Of course, I do. For some reason, you asked if you could take a copy of it. It was about the Melbourne Cup winner from way back when."

"Yes." Eleanor went to the next image. She had to get on with it before she lost her nerve again. "On the back was a list of births and deaths."

"I remember at the time you seemed fascinated with the clipping." Alexa leaned back and took another sip of her cognac. "Is there more to this? What does it have to do with Gran?"

"During our photoshoot, Grace talked a little about her father, William, and mentioned he attended Melbourne Uni."

"He studied engineering, just like Grandad." Alexa swirled the liquid around the base of the glass. "Gran's always said that's one of the things that attracted her to Gerald. That he reminded her of her father." She laughed, her voice a little husky from the alcohol. "Unfortunately, I never met my grandfather and know virtually nothing about my great-grandfather."

"Ah...but would you like to learn more?" Eleanor sat forward in the armchair.

Alexa's brow raised in question. "I think it's time you told me what this is about and also what it has to do with the newspaper article."

"Grace told me her father played football for Melbourne Uni."

"Eleanor, what are you talking about?" There was an unmistakable note of exasperation in Alexa's voice that made Eleanor cringe.

"William Brown played football for Melbourne University the same year my great-grandfather Reggie captained the reserve team. I found a picture in Reggie's Yearbook. A team photograph, Alexa. With both of them pictured." Eleanor rubbed her sweaty palms along the top of her trousers.

"What makes you think it's my great-grandfather William?" Alexa narrowed her eyes and gave Eleanor a glassy stare. "There must have been hundreds of William Browns, a name as common as John *Smith*."

Eleanor swallowed hard, distressed that Alexa sounded angry. "Let me explain," she said slowly. "Remember the notices on the back of the clipping? That's the important part. One of the death notices is of a Mei-Li Brown." She zoomed in on the notice and passed Alexa the phone again. "Please, take a look."

Alexa squinted at the screen and reached into her bag with her other hand. "I can't read it without my glasses."

"I'm sorry, it's not very clear," Eleanor said.

"What is all this about, Eleanor? I'm totally confused."

"It will make more sense when you read the notice." Eleanor continued to keep her voice as calm as she could.

Alexa's brow furrowed in obvious interest, and she began to read it slowly, "Mr and Mrs Henry Ball are proud to announce the birth of their eight-pound daughter—"

"Not that notice. The first *death* notice. Scroll down a little; it must have moved." Eleanor rubbed her forehead. This was not going well.

"All right. Here goes." Alexa sighed deeply. *"Hargraves Funeral Home. BROWN. March 24. Mrs Mei-Li Brown, nee KWAN. Wife of Otto (deceased), mother of William."* Alexa looked up at Eleanor, her eyes wide, and then back at the screen. She cleared her throat and kept reading, *"Funeral services at 2 o'clock. The remains will be taken to Castlemaine for internment."*

Eleanor waited patiently while Alexa continued to stare at the screen. She tried to read the look on Alexa's face. Perplexed came to mind. That wasn't exactly the right word, though. Discombobulated was more like it. Alexa's reaction told Eleanor she'd approached the whole thing badly. With a shaky hand, she grabbed her glass and gulped down the last of her drink.

Twisting a tendril of glossy hair around her index finger, Alexa appeared to be silently reading the death notice a few times over. It seemed as if ten minutes had gone by before her green eyes flashed, and she regarded Eleanor unwaveringly. "What did you do? How did you get this information?"

Eleanor rested her forehead in her hand. "I told you, it was in my great-grandfather's yearbook."

"Eleanor. What the hell were you doing using your investigative tendencies to poke around in Gran's family history? My family history." A vein pulsed in Alexa's temple.

"I just wanted to help." Eleanor pinched the bridge of her nose. She was worried the news might unsettle Alexa, but she hadn't been able to think of an alternative way of conveying the information.

"Remember, I told you I did not want to upset Gran. That I would eventually do the research myself." Alexa's lips tightened to a thin line. Although her voice was low and controlled, it was clipped and chilly.

Eleanor put her head in her hands and tugged her hair. "I'm so sorry; this must be quite a shock."

Alexa put the phone face down on the table with a clunk. "Which part?"

"I beg your pardon?" Eleanor wished the chair would open up and swallow her.

Alexa's gaze slowly scanned the room before darting back at Eleanor. "Which part?" she repeated. "Which part did you think I'd be shocked about? The fact that I've never known that my great-grandfather was Chinese?" Eleanor watched Alexa's shoulders slowly slump. She looked crestfallen. "Or the fact that my grandmother has never spoken about our Asian ancestry?" Covering her face with both hands, she mumbled through her fingers, "Did Mum even know?"

"Your mother must have at least suspected something," Eleanor said. "The article fell out of one of her books. She might have been searching—"

"You can't know that." Alexa sighed heavily. "Why did you go ahead with this investigation without asking permission from Gran or me? I thought you had ethics, Eleanor."

"Good evening, ladies. Apologies it took so long." The waiter set the coffees on the table. "Un café piccolo, un espresso."

"Thanks." Eleanor looked up in time to catch Alexa's brief nod to the waiter before he turned and strode off.

"I can understand why you're upset," Eleanor said despondently, crushed by Alexa's assessment of her.

Alexa pushed Eleanor's coffee towards her. "Can you? Can you, really? Just because you have time on your hands, there was no reason to meddle," she said loudly. "I wish you hadn't."

At the sound of Alexa's raised voice, the people nearby turned in their direction.

Eleanor reached for her coffee, downing it so fast, she singed her tongue. "Ouch."

Alexa ran one finger around the rim of her cup and stared at her coffee. "Just when I was starting to trust you." She stopped and shook her head, closing her eyes tightly. "Just when I thought..." Her words faded away.

"I made a mistake. You're right. I should have come to you first." Eleanor stared at her feet.

"Big mistake." Alexa's voice was low and filled with warning.

Eleanor's heart hammered in her chest, but she looked up to meet Alexa's gaze. She had to explain. "Grace seemed to be leaving hints, as though she had something she wanted to say, as if she really needed to unburden herself but couldn't. And then she told me her father played football for Melbourne Uni. My great-grandfather Reggie was the captain of the football team at the same time," Eleanor spoke quickly. "Alexa, it was too much of a coincidence. I couldn't help myself. When I discovered William was half Chinese, I had to tell you." She hesitated, then whispered, "I thought we were friends."

Alexa pushed away her unfinished coffee, grabbed her bag, slipped into her suit jacket, and stood up. "A friend doesn't go behind your back, Eleanor. Let's call it a night before one of us says something she'll really regret," she said in a tone that allowed no further discussion. "Are you ready? I'll walk you to the tram stop."

"That's not a good idea." Eleanor shook her head. She couldn't stand the idea of them walking downstairs, through the crowded bar, and all the way to the tram stop without Alexa talking to her. "I'm fine. You go ahead."

"If you're sure?"

"Are *you* sure?"

Alexa gave Eleanor an intense, long searching look, her eyes stormy green, before she shrugged, turned on her heel, and walked away.

Eleanor collapsed further into the armchair. Suddenly very alone. *Friends don't go behind your back.* Alexa's words stung, but Eleanor probably deserved them.

She pounded her fist against her thigh. It was her damn spirit of enquiry, her inability to let things go, that had got her in this mess. Alexa wasn't just a project that Eleanor could focus on with the curiosity of an explorer. Eleanor had never meant to upset Alexa or endanger their fledging friendship. After being away from Melbourne for so long, Alexa was her only friend. Eleanor's heart sank at the realisation that she'd probably ruined the chance to deepen their connection.

Eleanor couldn't believe her own stupidity. The words in her head were like an animated GIF, trapped in an infinite loop. *I shouldn't have done it. I shouldn't have done it. I shouldn't have done it.* She had to find the pause button, figure out what to do next, and make things right with Alexa.

Chapter 16

Green dragons

"What a scraggly mess." Alexa pulled her hair back off her face and squinted blearily at her reflection in the bathroom mirror. There were dark circles under her eyes. "Well, *fuck*." What did she expect after such a sleepless night?

She ran the tap, cupped her hands, and splashed her face with cold water. The sharp icy jolt reminded her of last night when Eleanor coaxed her into a warm, cosy place and then turned on the hose. Fire smothered—but damn, not entirely extinguished.

Alexa gathered her hair into a tight ponytail. Her hazel-green eyes stared back as she quickly did the maths. Six per cent Chinese. "Really?" She blinked rapidly. If Gran was one-quarter Chinese, that made her mother twelve per cent. So, yes, she was six per cent Chinese. Alexa smiled tentatively at her reflection. "Well, I'll be damned."

Why hadn't she ever wondered about her grandmother's widely spaced dark brown eyes and prominent cheek bones? Well, she supposed those features alone didn't make her particularly Asian. When she'd seen the grainy image of William Brown, she knew—his resemblance to Gran was indisputable.

There had to be a reason her grandmother kept their ancestry a secret from her family. She couldn't think of anything plausible; her grandmother wasn't at all racist, so why had she never said anything?

Alexa yanked off her pyjamas and tossed them across the bathroom, ready to feel the steady stream of hot water hitting her skin.

Five minutes later, she turned off the taps, stepped out of the shower, and enveloped herself in a towel. She'd been so irritated with Eleanor last night, she'd failed to ask for a copy of the yearbook picture. The team photo on Eleanor's phone was far from clear, but Alexa wanted to examine that image of her great-grandfather again. The things she most remembered were his smiling eyes and cheeky grin—so like her mother. And unlike Alexa, who took after her tall, slim father, William was compact and stocky.

She ran her hands over her face and sighed. What quirks or characteristics did she share with William? What were his parents like? Questions were mounting up, and there was only one way to get the answers.

Alexa broke into a cold sweat at the thought of confronting her grandmother with what she'd learnt from Eleanor.

At four thirty, Alexa hesitated for a moment at her grandmother's front door before she tapped softly and turned the key in the lock. She opened the door a fraction and peered around the corner. "Granny? It's me."

"Alexa, come in," Gran called, "I'm in the kitchen."

Alexa relocked the door and slowly walked in, carrying the small bag of items her grandmother had requested. The weight of her task sat heavily on her shoulders.

"Hi, Granny." Alexa leaned down and kissed her cheek. "Hope I remembered everything." She emptied the groceries onto the kitchen table. "Two bananas, a few mandarins, and a loaf of organic sourdough—gluten-free."

"Thank you." Gran reached for the bread, pulled on her glasses, and read the label. A small frown creased her forehead. "Alexa Bellamy, this is not from the supermarket. You've been at that fancy health food store again. Please, take what I owe you from the cookie jar."

Alexa dismissed her grandmother's request with a smile and pulled out the last item from the cloth bag.

Gran returned Alexa's smile, her eyes glinting with delight. "Oh my. Dark chocolate with sea salt and saffron. You shouldn't be wasting your money, Alexa. You're spoiling me."

Alexa wrapped her arms around her grandmother and squeezed gently. "Who else can I indulge? I'll put the kettle on and make us a cup of tea."

"That would be lovely."

"What do you fancy?" Alexa stood beside the wooden sideboard. The top shelf was lined with an array of colourful tins. She hoped her grandmother would choose one of the more relaxing varieties.

"Oolong, please."

"Good choice," Alexa said. The tea was known for its stress-relieving properties.

"Don't forget to rinse the leaves with a little hot water before you let it steep."

"I remember, Granny." Alexa playfully rolled her eyes, even though she was comforted by her grandmother's tea rituals. She was always very particular about its preparation and kept an eagle eye on Alexa to be sure she followed her directions.

"Did Patrick find this oolong tea for you? I haven't seen it before." Alexa held up the blue and white tin of Canton Jade.

"Yes. He got it from his cousin's shop—Cousin Jake, who owns the Dragon Pearl Restaurant."

"I remember. Your Mahjong group went there for Chinese New Year celebrations last February, didn't they?" Alexa placed the rinsed tea leaves into the clay pot and poured on a small amount of water.

Her grandmother nodded. "They do the best Sichuan-style roast duck." She chuckled.

Alexa loved the way her grandmother still enjoyed her food. Especially *authentic* Chinese food. She blinked. Another thing that, until yesterday, would have seemed quite ordinary.

"You must have seen Eleanor at the library this week," Gran said, pointing at the tea pot. "Now. That's been long enough. You've steeped the leaves for sixty seconds."

Alexa hesitated and steadied herself for a moment against the edge of the table before pouring the tea into two porcelain cups, placing one in front of her grandmother. "There you go." She sat down, picked up her cup, and held it in front of her face. "I saw her yesterday." She stared into the delicate cup filled with pale green tea, hoping it would be a panacea to her inner turmoil. Alexa sipped, breathing in the calming, floral bouquet, but it did nothing to quell her disappointment in Eleanor. No matter how many times she'd thought about it, Alexa was no closer to understanding Eleanor's motives. Was it her sense of entitlement that led her to meddle?

"She really is such a lovely young woman. Attentive and tender-hearted." Gran waved her cup in front of Alexa.

Alexa gulped. Gran was right about Eleanor; but her contradictory behaviour had Alexa's insides in a twist.

"Eleanor made me so relaxed in front of the camera," Gran said. "We were chatting like old friends. I hope to see her again soon. It's just not easy viewing things on the back of those digital screens. She promised to show me some of the pictures when she'd printed them."

"I'm sure she will, then."

"Did you know she has a darkroom? I thought film cameras were obsolete, but Eleanor says she likes to keep her hand in with film photography. It's part of her art process."

"She treasures her grandfather's old analogue camera," Alexa mumbled, growing weary of her grandmother's constant praising of Eleanor.

"So, she's into 'retro' just like you are, darling. Like that old jalopy you drive," Gran said with a satisfied smile.

The fact that her grandmother enjoyed Eleanor's company so much and was happy talking about her past with her briefly made Alexa wonder if she'd over-reacted to Eleanor's snooping. She didn't think so. It was time Alexa explained to Gran what Eleanor had done, and it was about time her grandmother started sharing the family secrets with Alexa. She put her cup down and closed her eyes.

"What's wrong, sweetie?" asked Gran, her soft hand gently closing around Alexa's wrist.

Alexa turned her palm upwards and held her grandmother's hand, taking comfort from their connection. "You and I have always been able to discuss almost everything, haven't we?"

"Of course, child. What on earth is worrying you?"

"Eleanor told me you two had quite a chat during the photo shoot," Alexa said, easing mindfully into the difficult subject.

Gran smiled. "She said it was an honour when people shared their lives with her, when they opened up about their past, and dreams, and all kinds of things."

Alexa frowned. "And you felt comfortable doing that?"

"Yes, completely. Why?" Her grandmother's eyes narrowed. "How are things between you and Eleanor? I thought you were getting along just fine. Maybe more?"

"I thought so, too." Alexa squeezed Gran's hand and let it go. "How about some more tea?"

"No, thank you. You sit here and tell me what's troubling you first. Are you upset with Eleanor over something?"

"I am." Alexa swirled her teacup three times clockwise and peered into it. Was that a hammer or an anchor on the rim of the cup? According to tassology, either way, it meant she had challenges to overcome. She gulped, dragging her finger through the tea leaves. She was here to learn the truth, so it was only fair that she was frank with her grandmother. "You told Eleanor that your father, William, played football for Melbourne University."

"I did?" Her grandmother looked at her strangely and rubbed her chin. "Oh, I may have mentioned Father was a keen sportsman. Yes. Yes, I did. He played football while studying engineering. He was quite good, Alexa. That's how he met my mother. He was introduced to Elizabeth Hampton at one of those parties organised by the club. Her brother, Oswald, was part of the team."

"Uncle Oswald who gave you a job at his magazine?"

"Yes, they were friends. My father was a good-natured young man, but I think he didn't make friends very easily."

"Why was that?" Alexa asked quickly, then continued on before Gran could answer, "Granny, why have I never seen any photos of William? I can't remember Mum talking about him, and you never mention your father's parents." Alexa shook her head. "It's strange."

"Eloise was not even four when William and Elizabeth moved to Far North Queensland to establish a lychee fruit orchard. Remember, their old Queenslander house burnt down."

Alexa nodded. "The photographs and documents were lost." She couldn't stall any longer. She had to cut to the chase for her grandmother's sake; she was already looking befuddled. Alexa pushed the empty cup away, linked her fingers together, and placed her hands on the table. "Gran, Eleanor took it upon herself to pry into our business. She found a picture of your father, William. My great-grandfather."

"What?" Gran asked in a squeaky voice. "Where on earth?"

"It seems that *her* great-grandfather, Reginald Miller, and our William played for the same university football team in 1913," Alexa said slowly. "Eleanor found a team photo in Reginald's university yearbook."

Gran was silent and went pale as a sheet.

Alexa reached for her grandmother's hands. "Why have you never told us that your father was Chinese?"

"Half Chinese."

"So, it's true," she said softly, relieved that Granny hadn't denied it.

Her grandmother held her head high, and her eyes fluttered. "It is the truth." She let go of Alexa's hand and, using a serviette from the table, dabbed at the corner of her eye. "I've had to live with the secret so very long, Alexa."

"Why, Granny?" Alexa looked hopefully at her grandmother, then asked the question she most feared. "Are you ashamed of your Chinese heritage?"

"Oh, my God, darling. No. Definitely not! How could you even think that?" Gran held her hand tightly to her chest. "I have spent most of my life carrying my family's shame. But please believe me, Alexa, it is not because of our ancestry."

"I couldn't imagine that it would be, but why have you hidden it from us? Surely, Mum had no idea. She would have told me."

Gran lifted her right hand to her neck and twirled the gold chain around her shaky fingers. From the chain hung a locket that held two tiny pictures of Eloise and Gerald. "She didn't know; at least I don't think so."

"Why did she have a newspaper clipping hidden in a book at the cottage? Eleanor pieced it together. It was your grandmother's death notice. Mei-Li Brown, née *something*. I don't remember."

"Her maiden name was Kwan."

Being told this information by Eleanor a few hours ago was one thing, but now Gran had confirmed it. "Mei-Li Kwan," Alexa said aloud, just to hear the name. She needed to piece together the facts now, but knew it might take her a long time to work through the emotional upheaval. The fact that *Eleanor* was the bearer of such a significant revelation, coupled with Alexa's regret for not making the discovery herself had her world spinning out of kilter. She tugged at her ponytail. "Your grandmother, Mei-Li Kwan, married a Mister Brown."

"Yes. Mei-Li was married to Otto Brown."

"Otto Brown," Alexa repeated. "William was their son. Were there any other children?"

"No, my father was an only child. He married Elizabeth Hampton, who as I told you was the sister of his friend, Oswald. The Hamptons did not approve of the boys' friendship. It got even worse when their daughter dared to fall in love with someone who was half Chinese. They threatened to cut her off."

"Oh, Granny." Alexa clutched at her chest. "That is horrible. Thank goodness the Hamptons' animosity didn't tear William and Elizabeth apart."

"The strength of their love for each other overcame her parents' disapproval." Gran put her head in her hands. "I'm sorry to say, the Hamptons of Toorak were racial bigots. Except for Oswald, who came to my rescue." Grace looked up and eyed Alexa steadily, as though she had more to say.

"Are you okay to continue? You look awfully tired," Alexa said gently. "Eleanor should have spoken to us first before going off and investigating on her own." Her hands clenched into fists. "I'm so angry with her for stirring all this up."

Her grandmother waved her hand briskly in front of Alexa. "I'll admit to being tired; however, I must finish this story now."

"If that's the case, Granny, I know what we both need." Alexa reached for the slab of chocolate. "A little boost of energy."

Gran's eyes softened. "Don't be angry with Eleanor. I don't believe she intended any harm."

"She had no right, sticking her nose into our business." Alexa pushed the broken pieces of chocolate across the table. She grabbed a large chunk, popped the whole thing into her mouth, and devoured it so quickly she couldn't taste it.

"I'm nearly ninety-two, Alexa. It's time."

There was a strength in her voice that made Alexa look straight into her grandmother's brown eyes. Eyes that were sharp and determined.

Alexa took a mouthful of tea to wash away the remains of the chocolate and gave her grandmother her full attention.

"I've been carrying this secret for far too long." Gran caressed Alexa's hand, shaking her head regretfully. "I wish I'd had the courage to have this conversation with your mother. She had the newspaper notice, so she must have suspected something." Gran's eyes sparked suddenly. "When Eleanor mentioned the clipping and I realised what it meant, I didn't want to believe it. My grandmother's death notice is filed away in a safe place along with—" She paused for a moment's reflection. "How did Eloise get it?"

Alexa looked down as Gran's grip tightened on her wrist. "What's the matter, Granny?"

"The box that Patrick has of mine with documents, letters, and Mei-Li's sketchbooks and poems. How did Eloise get hold of it?"

Alexa closed her eyes, trying to concentrate through her confusion. She rubbed her forehead. Her head felt heavy, as though full of cement. "What box?"

"Just a few things that were hidden away in the attic, inside a bolted cupboard. When I had that termite treatment done years ago, I asked Patrick if he'd keep my things in his storage unit."

"You did? Why didn't you ask Mum or me to look after them?"

"I didn't want to burden you both with my old things." Gran hunched forward, her chin resting on her chest. "I don't want to burden you now, but I have to tell you what happened to Mei-Li."

What on earth could have happened to Mei-Li that had her grandmother so distressed? Alexa squeezed her hands. They were shaking. She gently lifted Gran's chin with her finger. "Please, tell me," Alexa said soothingly. She couldn't bear to see her grandmother in such a state.

"In the 1920s, Mei-Li Brown practised as a Chinese herbalist in Castlemaine under her maiden name, Mei-Li Kwan."

"A herbalist...in Castlemaine?" Alexa tapped a finger against her chin. That was why Granny had reacted so strangely to the print of the Chinese herbalist Alexa and Eleanor showed her during lunch at the library.

"Yes. She was treating a young American woman, the wife of a hotelier. Tragically, the woman died, and Mei-Li was charged with manslaughter and imprisoned, awaiting trial."

"Oh my *God*, why? What went wrong?" Alexa bent forward and nearly fell off the chair.

"The prosecutor alleged it was the herbs she was prescribing that lead to the woman's death. After a short trial, it could not be proven. Mei-Li was released and the case was dismissed."

Alexa sat up straight, sucked in a deep breath, and exhaled slowly. "What a relief. She surely didn't poison her. How did the woman die?"

"Nothing was resolved, and suspicion remained with Mei-Li. She never practiced in public again. Her reputation, both as a herbalist, and a person, was in ruins." Gran sighed heavily. "The Brown family's standing in the community was destroyed. I'm sure racism played a part."

Alexa dug her fingernails into her palms. "It's absolutely detestable, but you're probably right. What did she do?"

"When Mei-Li was arrested, Otto lost his job as a junior accountant at the American hotel. The manager was the husband of the girl who died. Otto couldn't get another job even though Mei-Li was released, and his health deteriorated. He passed away soon after." Her voice had trailed off to a whisper.

"Oh, Granny. What a tragedy. I can't believe it." Alexa rose from her seat and knelt down on the floor beside Gran, resting her head on her shoulder. "Why was this kept a secret?"

"It was the Hamptons. They were a very influential banking family. My mother, Elizabeth, was the youngest and only daughter with four older brothers. Oswald was the only decent one, and they were all extremely protective of their baby sister. They didn't approve of her marriage. When William's mother was accused of manslaughter and the story emerged in the papers, they did everything possible to ensure their sister, and the Hampton name, was not embroiled in the scandal."

"It was hateful, Alexa. They threatened to destroy my father's career if he ever let on that Mei-Li was his mother. A blanket of denial was thrown over the entire business," Gran said with a muffled cry. "The whole family was sworn to secrecy."

Alexa was incredulous; she couldn't believe what she was hearing. She rubbed her grandmother's back in slow circles until her breathing returned to normal.

"I'm okay, darling." Gran stroked Alexa's cheek. "I want to tell you more. Where was I?"

"What happened to Mei-Li after Otto died?" Alexa asked. "How on earth did she survive? She must have been devastated."

"The Chinese community rallied around her when the house was confiscated by the bank. One of the market gardening families gave her a place to live and work. My parents helped secretly, as much as they could. I remember going by steam train to visit her with Mummy and Papa once. I'm sure my father visited her whenever he was able, but he had to be so careful. We were afraid of the Hamptons."

"How terrible to fear your own relatives," Alexa murmured. "But I'm still not clear as to why it had to be kept under wraps for all these years; after all, Mei-Li was not responsible for the American woman's death." She pulled herself up off the floor, and sagged back into her chair opposite Gran. She'd come here today hoping for answers, but what she was discovering was beyond her imagination. She was incensed that Mei-Li and her family had been treated so badly for no reason.

"Because the cause of death was never established, the shadow of doubt has always remained with my grandmother."

"I find it really hard to believe my direct ancestors were so heartless. They made life incredibly difficult for Mei-Li, who had already suffered so much. And her son, William."

"My mother suffered, too," Gran mumbled. She rocked back and forth, tipped her head back, and closed her eyes. "I was sworn to secrecy. I felt I had to protect Eloise. There are still Hamptons around who know Mei-Li's story."

Alexa sighed. "It's sad Mum never knew about Mei-Li."

"Eloise was very interested in the healing quality of herbs, just like her great-grandmother," Gran said thoughtfully. "When your mother was a child, I introduced her to Chinese culture, including Mahjong and the Chinese New Year celebrations. We cooked authentic food together."

Alexa nodded in realisation. "That was your way of helping Mum to experience some of her heritage."

"It wasn't enough." Gran sighed.

"Granny, look, Bruce is here." Alexa scooped the cat into her arms. Her grandmother was exhausted to the point of collapse. She didn't want to push her any further.

"My poor boy. We didn't even notice you come inside. You'll be wanting me to feed you, won't you?" Gran smiled, reaching out to pet him.

His tail swished, brushing Alexa's face. "I'm going to fetch his dinner, and then if you don't mind me foraging around in your fridge, I'll rustle us up something healthier than chocolate for an early supper."

"Are you sure you want to cook?" Gran supported her head with her hand and gave Alexa a slightly dazed look. "This must be distressing for you. I'm so sorry, Alexa."

"There's no need for you to be sorry for me, Gran. You're the one who's had to carry this around on your own for all these years."

Bruce meowed loudly, wriggling in Alexa's arms.

"We're both tired now, but we'll have lots of time to talk when you're ready, Gran." She lowered Bruce to the floor. "I'll feed him before he chews my hand off." Alexa was grateful she had something to keep herself from dwelling on everything that had been revealed tonight.

Alexa spooned diced meat and dry biscuits into the food bowl on the mat by the back door.

Bruce purred loudly and brushed against Alexa's leg before attacking the food ravenously.

After their light meal, Gran refused Alexa's offer to stay the night, telling her not to fuss. So, when her grandmother was propped up in bed with her latest novel and Bruce was curled up fast asleep at her feet, Alexa checked the back door was fastened and quietly let herself out the front.

As she walked briskly to her car, the spring air was cool and pleasant on her skin. A new moon hung almost directly overhead, and the clear sky was filled with stars. She loved that this inner-city suburb was a melting pot of people, and the aromas wafting from the open windows of the homes she passed told of diverse cultures and traditions. She'd like to think people with the Hamptons' narrow-mindedness would not be tolerated in this neighbourhood.

Alexa climbed into her car. She rested her head against the steering wheel and closed her eyes. Granny may have accepted that Eleanor was full of good intentions, but Alexa wasn't ready to forgive her. Even though her intent had not been to hurt anyone, Eleanor should have considered the consequences of her actions and come to Alexa with her suspicions. Alexa lifted her head and stared out into the darkness. Hadn't she made it clear enough that she didn't want Eleanor interfering?

Whether Eleanor had meant to or not, Alexa's family tree had been given an almighty shake, and the ghosts of her ancestors were cast to the four winds. There was no going back from here, only forward. "Pull yourself together," she muttered as approaching headlights lit the inside of her car. It wasn't just that the family secrets had been revealed. Alexa had been given a wake-up call. Determination stirred within her. She had to investigate the case against her great-great-grandmother—to learn the truth.

Chapter 17

Flowers and dragons

"OKAY, OKAY. I'M ON MY way. Stop banging down the door," Eleanor cried out. She sat on the edge of her bed, pulled on her track pants, and reached around for the hoodie she'd tossed on the floor last night. Who the hell was at the door so early on a Sunday morning? Whoever it was could damn well wait. She groaned and grabbed her watch off the nightstand. It was only eight o'clock, and Eleanor's bones were still heavy with sleep.

After a restless Friday night, she'd spent most of yesterday hiking. Just by herself, music through the headphones, and her camera ready. Physical exercise should have been the best way to push away thoughts of how she'd mishandled things with Alexa. Instead, every rock, every tree root, and every branch had seemed to be out to get her as images of her disastrous encounter with Alexa filled her mind. She had the scratches and scrapes to prove it. Of course Eleanor should have approached Alexa first about her hunch before playing amateur sleuth. *What a fool!*

The knocking at the door grew louder. Whoever it was wasn't going away. Eleanor groaned, cursing as she pushed herself off the bed.

Eleanor glanced at herself in the mirror and winced. What was that bird's nest doing on top of her head? She combed her fingers through her hair in an attempt to tame the tangles before descending the stairs.

"Hammering on the door is a really bad way to wake up a person." Eleanor scowled and swung open the door. "Leo? What on earth are you doing here?"

"At least it woke you up," he said with a smirk, walking past her and into the room. "Good morning, sunshine."

Eleanor pushed the door shut and followed him. "Thank goodness you're not Mum. I don't want to deal with her this morning," she said. "Anyway, why are you here in your running shorts and—"

"You asked me to go for a run with you this morning." Leo's eyes twinkled with amusement. He placed his hand on her shoulder, gently nudging her back until she sat down on the sofa. "You've forgotten. I've texted you several times. Where's your phone?"

"Turned it off last night." Eleanor leaned forward and put her head in her hands. "I remember now. Running date, 8 a.m." She looked up at Leo. "Are you staying for Sunday lunch?"

"Yes, Dad asked me to help him with some papers this morning."

"Good. Because I'm not in the mood to sit through an inquisition from Mum."

He walked over to the coffee machine, checked the water level, and switched it on. "I'll make you a coffee while you change into your gear, and then we can be off. We can take it easy, do the 5K along the Yarra River."

Eleanor moaned. "I couldn't, Leo. I'm totally wiped out after my trip to the You Yangs Park yesterday."

"That's not a long drive, an hour and a half tops."

"It wasn't the drive. I walked the East-West Trail and Flinders Peak. It's a decent hike with stunning views, and the wildflowers are amazing now." She gratefully accepted the cup from her brother. "Thanks. And then I spent a few hours back here messing about in the darkroom and updating my social media stuff." She sipped her coffee before continuing, "It was a late night. I don't feel like chasing behind you."

Leo sat down beside her and put his espresso glass on the table. "That would make a nice change, because you've been able to outrun me since you were about fourteen." He rubbed her shoulder. "Anyway, what's up? When I spoke to you on Friday afternoon, you were on cloud nine, swanning around the library and looking forward to seeing the gorgeous Ms Bellamy. What's put you in such a funk?"

Eleanor scrubbed her hands over her face and moaned again. "Don't even ask."

"What did you do?" He snickered and nudged her with his elbow.

"Something incredibly stupid." She grimaced.

"Okay, tell me what happened?"

Leo listened intently as Eleanor relayed the whole sorry story, waiting until she'd finished, then stroked his chin pensively. "I know you wanted to help, Eleanor, but you should have spoken to Alexa first before intruding."

She gulped her coffee and jumped up to pour another cup. "Don't you think I've told myself that about a hundred times?" she growled, stabbing the start button on the coffee machine. "I'm used to following my gut instincts, and it felt right at the time. *God*, you should have seen the way she stared at me before she left the bar on Friday night."

"With daggers?"

"More like a hurt, angry bear."

"I don't blame her. It must have been a bolt out of the blue to be shown a photograph of her relative for the first time when she had no idea of her Chinese ancestry."

"Agreed, I was a fool. But why the secrecy?" Eleanor narrowed her eyes at Leo. "Most of us are a mixture of cultures and ethnicities."

"Let's think about it. What reason could there be? What is Alexa's grandmother trying to hide?" Leo wore his burning-with-curiosity, lawyerly look.

Eleanor smiled, her foul mood starting to fall away at Leo's apparent interest in the mystery. "That's the big question. I need to know the answer."

Leo held up his hand. "No, Eleanor, you don't. My mistake for suggesting it. That's not for you to concern yourself about unless they ask for help."

"Why on earth would Alexa ask for my help after what I've done?" She sighed, deflated.

"I do think you should stay out of it unless she comes to you," he said. "You like the woman, don't you?"

Eleanor nodded in agreement, and her cheeks heated. Of course, she liked her. More than liked her.

"Then work on getting back into Alexa's good books. Work on your friendship and regain her trust."

Eleanor sighed deeply. That would be a challenge, only possible if Alexa was willing.

"Enough of those deep sighs and pouty looks." Leo jumped to his feet and pointed to the stairs. "Get in your gear. We're going for that run. I've got a good chance of beating you today. You'll probably trip over your long face."

Eleanor threw a cushion at her brother. "You can always try."

"What do you mean you'll be seeing Eleanor tomorrow?" Alexa nearly dropped the phone.

"I'll go," Jac whispered. If it wasn't for the creaky floorboards, Alexa wouldn't have noticed her tiptoe across the room and close the lab door silently behind her.

"Eleanor is accompanying me to the Merri Community Home on Tuesday, I mean tomorrow, to observe our Mahjong game," Gran said cheerfully, oblivious to Alexa's clipped tone. "She plans to photograph me and the group."

"What?" Alexa could hardly hear her grandmother's words over the alarm bells going off in her head. "Isn't your game usually on a Thursday?"

"Yes, Alexa. Didn't you hear me? It is especially arranged for this Tuesday. Patrick will pick me up, and we are meeting Eleanor for an early *yum cha* lunch at Tao Tao in Hawthorn before we make our way to the home. Patrick assures me there are plenty of gluten-free options," Gran talked rapidly. "I hope Eleanor likes *yum cha*."

Alexa stared at the screen, speechless.

"Alexa? Are you still there? Have we been cut off?"

"No, Gran. I'm here," Alexa said. "I'm just surprised. I don't like the way Eleanor went behind my back…I mean *our* backs and interfered. Don't you agree it was wrong? It was our concern." She couldn't believe her grandmother was taking Eleanor to the Mahjong game *and* out to lunch. It stung like salt in an open wound.

Gran was silent for a moment, then said, "I agree it was ill-considered. However, Eleanor's done us a favour. I feel a weight's been lifted off my shoulders. It was time."

"Are you saying the end justifies the means?"

Gran sighed. "Perhaps, in this case, yes."

What could she say to that? Nothing. Alexa's heart ached to know that her grandmother had been carrying the secret of Mei-Li and their ancestry almost her entire life. Eleanor had lifted the lid, exposed the past, and while

Alexa remained angry, she couldn't ignore the fact that her grandmother appeared genuinely relieved.

Alexa drew herself up tall. "What did you say about *yum cha*?"

"I said, I hope Eleanor likes it. Tao Tao serves excellent Cantonese food."

Alexa clenched her teeth, supressing the snort of dismay that threatened to escape. *I didn't get an invitation.*

As if reading her mind, her grandmother said, "I'm sorry it's not a day you can join us, Alexa. Even though you're not particularly fond of Mahjong, it would have been fun for you to tag along, maybe play the photographer's assistant."

This time, Alexa couldn't hold back that snort.

"Alexa, what did you say? My hearing must be failing."

She cleared her throat. "It's nothing, Gran. I'd better get back to work. I have phone calls to make. Love you," she said, ending the call.

Five minutes later, she was still pacing. She couldn't recall how many times she'd stopped, reached for her phone on the desk, stared at the screen, then placed it down again. It was absurd.

She rolled her shoulders, grabbed the phone, scrolled through her contacts, and finally called Eleanor's number.

Maybe she won't answer, Alexa thought when the line rang for the third time. On the fourth, she was sorry she'd even rung. On the fifth, she imagined Eleanor looking at the caller ID and choosing not to answer, in fear that Alexa would just have another go at her.

She stared at the picture she'd assigned to Eleanor's contact. It was taken at the cottage after dinner, once they were snugly ensconced by the wood fire. Eleanor's face was slightly flushed from the heat and the red wine they'd shared. Her hair was ruffled. Alexa knew the taste of her precisely shaped, far-too-perfect mouth and those soft pink, sensual lips. She moaned. Why was she being tormented? She refused to think about those lips for one more moment. Alexa shook her head and was about to hang up when, after the sixth ring, Eleanor answered.

"Hello?" Her voice was low but held a small note of trepidation.

"Hi, this is Alexa."

"Hi. How are you today?" Eleanor asked slowly, as if the words were chosen with the utmost care.

"Good morning. I'm fine, thank you." Alexa knew she must sound cool, almost curt.

She heard Eleanor's sharp intake of breath, as though she was bracing herself for another reprimand from Alexa. She wasn't wrong.

"Can I help you with something?" Eleanor asked in a quavery voice. "Oh, if it's about the folder I left in your office, I can come by the library and pick it up. It's just that my father has a series of check-ups and tests this week, and I promised to drive him to his appointments. Umm, would Thursday suit you?"

"That's fine. You can collect it anytime you like. I'll leave it at the librarian service desk in the Cowan Gallery." Alexa bit her lip. She could have said that with a little less sting.

There was an uncomfortable silence before Eleanor spoke. "Okay. I'll do that. Thank you. I was hoping that we could—"

"I'm sorry, I have a really busy—"

"Okay," Eleanor said abruptly, cutting Alexa off mid-sentence.

Another uncomfortable silence hung in the air, while Alexa figured out how to approach the real reason for phoning Eleanor.

Eventually, it was Eleanor who asked, "Was there another reason for your call?"

"Gran told me that you're going with her to the Mahjong game tomorrow," Alexa blurted out.

"That's right. She suggested I photograph her with some of her friends while they play, and I thought it was a great idea. I'm looking forward to it."

Alexa stared at the phone screen. "Is that so?" After what had happened, how could Eleanor think it was okay? "I don't have a say in who my grandmother chooses to socialise with, but I wish you wouldn't."

"You wish I wouldn't what? Grace asked me, Alexa. She rang this morning to confirm our arrangements, and I don't want to disappoint her. You know how sorry I am about what happened."

Alexa sensed the irritation in Eleanor's tone, and she tried resolutely to keep her own temper in check. "That may well be true. I just don't want you to upset my grandmother any more. It's not appropriate for you to spend time with her at the moment."

When Eleanor didn't respond, Alexa imagined her pushing her fingers through her honey-coloured hair, pulling on the strands, which she had a habit of doing. *Just stop*, she admonished herself. Eleanor had let her down. She couldn't think about her in that way right now.

"I'll think of a way of getting out of the photo session," Eleanor said flatly. "Grace will understand that I have to help Dad. Alexa, I don't want to upset you any further." She hesitated a moment before adding, "Can I just ask you one question before I go?"

Alexa couldn't believe Eleanor had surrendered so fast, but some of the tension drained out of her body. "Go ahead."

"Was the information I uncovered about William at all helpful to you and Grace?"

Alexa sighed. "Maybe, Eleanor. It's complicated." The lid of Pandora's Box had definitely been wrenched off, but Alexa hadn't yet got her head around her grandmother's revelations. She certainly wasn't ready to share any of it with Eleanor.

"I see. Goodbye, Alexa."

The phone screen went blank. Dammit, she'd ended the phone call without giving Alexa the opportunity to have the last word. Was it that, or did Alexa want to keep hearing her voice? The dulcet tones and her faintly British accent. *Dammit.*

Alexa's hand shook as she traced a line of the delicate ink-brush painting. "These are exquisite. If only I could read the Chinese calligraphy," she said, closing Mei-Li's small sketchbook with a deep sigh. She placed the fragile rice paper book on the kitchen table and looked up to see her grandmother smiling sweetly.

"Unfortunately, I couldn't read the poems either, so I asked Patrick to find someone who could translate the Cantonese characters. His cousin Lily typed this up for me." Gran waved a single sheet of paper in front of Alexa.

Alexa took the piece of paper from her hand and began to read out loud:

The earth heavy with spring rain.
Softening all things with little sound.
Furrows in the rich dark soil.

The sun's warmth is welcome, bringing new life.
A thousand green shoots.
Butterflies and the apple tree on the hill with soft pink blossom.

She wiped her eyes with her sleeve and cleared her throat. "This is lovely, Granny. Mei-Li was an artist and a poet." She glanced to the left, to where her mother's watercolour adorned the wall. It depicted the vegetable garden in Chewton. How sad that her mum never learnt about Mei-Li, the herbalist, gardener, poet, and artist.

"She truly was remarkable," Gran agreed. "You can read the other poems at home, Alexa. I have copies for you. Don't be sad. I believe Mei-Li led a meaningful, happy life working with the market gardeners in Castlemaine."

Alexa squeezed her grandmother's hand. "She couldn't have written these heartfelt words without having found peace. Thank you for sharing this with me."

"I always hoped to tell you about Mei-Li, darling. The paintings and poems prove our ancestor was a pure soul. It's impossible to believe she had any part in the American woman's death. She was a healer." Gran had a determined glint in her eye.

"I'll find out what really happened. I promise." Alexa didn't know exactly how she would accomplish that. For her grandmother's sake, though, she had to get to the bottom of the story.

Gran tilted her head to one side. "If anyone can discover the truth, it will be you, my expert historian. But, my dear, I suspect you'll need some help. Which brings me to the other reason I asked you to visit me this evening."

Alexa could only say, "Ah," and hang her head. She had a fairly good idea what was coming next.

"Eleanor phoned me earlier. She had to cancel our arrangements for tomorrow, apparently because she must drive her father to a doctor's appointment. I don't suppose you know anything about this?" Gran asked in the stern voice she rarely used with Alexa.

"My bad, Granny. I suggested Eleanor cancel. She did the wrong thing, and I'm not going to sit back and let her get away with it." Alexa tried to back herself out of the hole she'd dug. "She didn't want to cancel your date, but she finally accepted my point of view." *Albeit, reluctantly.*

"That may be so; however, it was wrong to punish Eleanor by having her tell me a fib."

"It was the wrong thing to do. I realise that now." Alexa removed her reading glasses and pinched the bridge of her nose. "I was beginning to trust her. Eleanor seemed such an honest and principled person, in her professional and private life. That's why it came as such a shock when she went behind our backs, treating our ancestors' lives like some kind of special investigation."

"Eleanor got a wee bit carried away, I'll give you that," her grandmother said. "But she only intended to help us. You know, dear, Eleanor is an intuitive woman. She sensed that I was holding something deep inside me, something painful that twisted and turned but couldn't escape, and she helped me free it. The pain hasn't entirely gone, but it's more bearable now."

"Granny, I'm so sorry." Alexa swallowed the lump in her throat.

"Well I'm sorry too. When you rang this morning, I knew you were upset with Eleanor. I should have been more thoughtful and not gone on about the *yum cha* lunch date. Especially since you couldn't join us."

Alexa met her grandmother's contrite gaze with her own. "Oh dear, I acted like a spoilt grandchild, didn't I?"

"We're a pair of silly duffers. I think we are both a tiny bit smitten with the photographer, aren't we?" Gran chuckled. "You more than me, perhaps?"

"Is it that obvious? I guess it is," Alexa said, surprised by her own admission.

"Your blush confirms it, darling."

Alexa covered her face with her hands. She had to face facts—her attraction to Eleanor had not diminished despite what had happened. She missed the sparks that flared between them when they touched and the easy connection when they talked. Alexa had to admit the information about William made a huge difference. Her eyes welled up with tears at the thought of Gran going to her grave bearing the secret. Maybe she needed to swallow her pride and admit it to Eleanor. Maybe Alexa owed Eleanor an apology.

Chapter 18

The wriggling snake

Eleanor sat at an outdoor table of the café adjacent to the library, staring into space, lost in the incredulousness of her predicament. Just a few weeks ago, this had been the very place she'd joined Alexa and Grace for lunch. In less than a month, they'd both become so important to Eleanor, each in their own ways. She tugged at her hair. Eleanor was trying not to lose all hope, but because of her giant lapse of judgement, she figured her chances for a deeper friendship with Alexa had been dashed.

Surely Alexa wouldn't be passing by the café at eleven o'clock in the morning, would she? The chance of Eleanor running into her on the way from the café to the pick-up point was slim, wasn't it? The corner table, shaded by a large striped umbrella, gave her a perfect vantage point to people watch, on the off chance that Alexa did walk by. And if she did, would she come over or would she ignore Eleanor?

Running her finger around the half-empty cup of lukewarm coffee, she watched the pigeons precariously stepping along the rooftop ledges like tightrope walkers. After the terse conversation with Alexa on Monday and then having to spin a story to Grace and make apologies for abandoning their arrangements on Tuesday, Eleanor felt as if she was on a tightrope doing her own balancing act.

Alexa's voice on the phone had been aloof. She sounded pissed off. Eleanor couldn't blame her. She reminded herself it was nothing compared to the look of disdain Alexa had cast her way when she'd left the bar last Friday night.

Eleanor should stop mooning around outside the library, get a grip on reality, pick up the envelope, and go home. She shoved the photographic journal she'd been pretending to read into her backpack and eased the pack onto her shoulders.

Eleanor slipped through the security check and into the Redmond Barry Reading Room. She gave a soulful sigh, recalling how she'd hurried through here for her appointment with Katherine Kent last month and ended up meeting Alexa instead. Eleanor took a moment to absorb the unique atmosphere of the grand high-ceilinged chamber. It reverberated with whispered echoes that seemed to chase each other between the wooden chairs, desks, and the rows of bookshelves.

At the far end of the reading room, she passed through a wide doorway that was flanked by two staircases leading up to the mezzanine floor. Eleanor took a left turn, arriving at the Ask-a-Librarian service point and joined the short queue in front of the information desk. She glanced around at the large portrait paintings that adorned the walls of the Cowan Gallery, thankful the place was not a hive of activity this morning so she wouldn't have long to wait before collecting her envelope.

She looked down, tapping her feet on the parquet flooring. Her leather ankle boots were a new purchase, incredibly comfortable and well matched with her straight-leg jeans, cobalt turtleneck, and narrow scarlet scarf. She'd even caught the approving nod from her mother when they'd briefly spoken outside her father's study earlier today. That made a pleasant change.

"Excuse me. How can I help you?"

Eleanor looked up with a start, realising she'd been lost in thought. She stared at the woman behind the librarian's desk and glanced at her name tag. "I'm so sorry, Mary. I was daydreaming."

"How can I help you?" Mary repeated with a smile.

Eleanor explained about the envelope, all the while furtively glancing around just in case Alexa should stroll by. Despite knowing Alexa wouldn't be happy to see her, Eleanor hoped she would at least get the chance to apologise one more time.

"Hmm." Mary scanned her computer screen. "One moment. I have it here somewhere." She bent down and rummaged through some cupboards.

Alexa had been definite about leaving it at *this* particular service point. No doubt the librarian would find it soon. Eleanor was like a sitting duck in the middle of the gallery with at least five access points. It was doing her head in. Alexa never indicated she would meet her here, and yet Eleanor couldn't help but look for her, everywhere.

"Here it is," Mary said. "You'll just have to sign for it."

Eleanor spun around to Mary. "Thank you." She signed the paperwork, handed back the pen, and accepted the package.

"I'll inform Ms. Bellamy that you've retrieved the package. Enjoy your day, Ms Heysen."

Having tucked the envelope safely into her backpack, Eleanor headed for one of the Library exits. *Job done. That's all I came here for.* She tried her best to ignore the tiny pang of disappointment in her chest.

In the reading room, she stopped at the base of one of the four identical staircases to admire the intricate detailed balustrade and contemplated how best she could photograph its aesthetic beauty and symmetry. A flicker of movement at the top of the stairs caught her eye and she spotted what looked to be a small foot. Eleanor's eyes widened. Yes, it was a foot, and it was moving.

"Robbie, Robbie." A child's voice caught Eleanor's attention. Tucked in the crook of the left arm of a tall man, a little girl with blonde curls pointed upwards.

The man was looking at his phone and pushing an empty stroller at the same time. To Eleanor's amazement, he seemed unconcerned with the wriggling child he held.

Eleanor's gaze snapped back to the staircase. *That must be Robbie's foot.* Now she could see two small hands gripped around the balustrade. *The kid must be stuck.* She darted to the staircase, weaving stealthily through groups of people and was already climbing the second flight when she heard a man's slightly panicked voice call from below.

"Robbie, stay put. Daddy's right here."

As she approached the boy, Eleanor's heart sank at the sound of his faint whimpering. Not wanting to scare the child, she dropped into a seated position just below him and slid sideways along to the railing where his foot was clearly jammed.

"Hi Robbie. My name is Eleanor."

He sniffed and squeezed his eyes shut. "I'm not supposed to be up here," he whispered. "I'm stuck."

"How did you manage that?" Without waiting for his answer, Eleanor stood up slowly, placed her hand on the rail, and leaned over the side. She quickly surveyed the situation. Robbie looked light enough that she could lift him with one arm and free his foot with her other hand. "Ah yes. Your leg is definitely jammed."

"That's what I said." He squirmed, wedging his leg further between the scrolled bars.

In a calm, steady voice, Eleanor said, "Robbie, I need you to keep still for a moment. Do you think you can do that?"

"Of course."

"That's great. Would you mind if I slipped my arm around you? Then I can scoop you up, and together we can free your leg."

"Sure," Robbie said in a shaky voice. "Are you Captain Marvel?"

"Why?" Eleanor smiled.

"You've got her suit on and you look pretty strong."

Eleanor chuckled and lifted Robbie upwards, supporting his weight with one arm. She clasped his foot and gently wriggled it free from the coiled ironwork. When he reached up and grabbed her jumper, Eleanor perched him onto her hip. He was heavier than he looked. "There, that wasn't so bad, was it?"

"No. It was cool." Robbie patted her face. His hands were hot and clammy. "It was like being in a superhero movie and you came to the rescue. You're pretty awesome." Robbie looked around. "Can you take me to my dad? He must be worried 'bout me." He gave a little sigh.

"I can do that," she said. "If I hold your hand, would you like to walk down the stairs with me, or do you want me to carry you?"

"Walk." Robbie gave her a toothy grin.

Eleanor lowered him to the step and held out her hand.

He reached up and clasped her fingers tightly, sending a warm, fuzzy feeling through her. They slowly descended the stairs, where the man with the stroller and the little girl waited.

"Robbie. Thank goodness you're okay," the man said.

Eleanor let go of Robbie's hand, and he raced into his father's arms. "Hey, Dad, look it's that superhero," he said, looking over his shoulder with a smile.

Robbie's dad turned to Eleanor. "Sorry I couldn't help you." He gestured towards the little girl in the stroller. "I couldn't leave Lucy," he said sheepishly. "Anyway, I'm so glad you got to him so quickly. Thanks."

Eleanor shrugged. "Glad I turned up just in time to help Robbie."

Lucy grabbed her brother's shirt sleeve. "Robbie, you're in trouble." She giggled.

"I'm going to tell Mum I've been with Captain Marvel," Robbie chimed in a raised voice.

His father just groaned and turned to Eleanor, shaking his head. "Come on, you two."

Eleanor waved goodbye as the family hastened towards the exit. She imagined that the parents of little children occasionally required superhero powers. She smiled fondly. Those two seemed quite a handful.

"And here she emerges in the face of danger. With powers including strength, resilience, and selflessness."

Eleanor looked up so fast, her heart pounding. "Alexa, what are you doing here?"

"You obviously made an impression," Alexa's voice was low. "Do you mind if we sit here for a moment?" She indicated to the nearest bench seat with a theatrical flourish of her arm.

Eleanor moved to the bench and sat with her hands tucked under her thighs. Her face flushed. "Where did you come from?" she asked as Alexa sat down beside her.

"I do work here." Alexa tipped her head to one side and stared at Eleanor. "In this particular outfit, I can see why the boy thought you were Captain Marvel."

"How did you… I mean, where were you?" Eleanor stammered.

Alexa placed her hands on her hips. "Believe it or not, I happened to be passing through, just in time to witness your dramatic rescue."

Eleanor winced at the slightly sardonic tone in her voice. "Hardly," she said.

A woman cleared her throat, and they both looked up. Mary the librarian stood in front of them with a security officer just behind.

Eleanor briefly closed her eyes. Had she done the wrong thing?

"Hi, Mary and Jeff," Alexa said, casually folding her arms.

"Ms Heysen, well done. I must thank you. You've probably saved me from having to fill out a lengthy incident report," Mary said, and Eleanor let out a relieved breath.

"Security glass was supposed to be installed last week, but there's been a delay," Jeff said gruffly.

"How on earth did you manage to see the child from so far away?" Mary asked.

"Eleanor is very observant." Alexa rose from the bench. "We're off to the Dome. I promised to show her our collection of chess resources," she said to her colleagues.

Eleanor glanced from Alexa to Mary to Jeff and back to Alexa. *What on earth is she talking about?*

"Have fun." Mary winked at Alexa before she and the security officer walked off.

Alexa turned to Eleanor. "Are you ready?"

"Ready for what?" Eleanor adjusted the backpack on her shoulders.

Alexa reached out and stroked Eleanor's forearm, causing her muscles to twitch. "We need to go somewhere private and talk."

"Really?" Eleanor raised her eyebrows in confusion. "Okay, shall we go to the café?"

"It will be too busy now," Alexa said. "It is lunchtime."

"Where to then?"

"The chess collection."

Eleanor eyed Alexa suspiciously, but when Alexa headed for the lifts, Eleanor followed. The lift arrived, and they stood back as a group of patrons exited and filed past them, as though in slow motion. A knot of tension prodded Eleanor between her shoulders.

They stepped into the lift and waited for the doors to close.

"Did you know we have the largest chess collection in the Southern Hemisphere? It includes 13,000 books on strategy, novels featuring chess, and the history of the game. There's even a leaf from a book published by Caxton in 1483 about the game of chess."

Why was Alexa rambling on about chess? Eleanor tapped her lightly on the arm. "What do you really want to talk about?"

Alexa replied with a shrug, "Not here, Eleanor. We need to go somewhere private."

As the doors began to slowly close, Eleanor bravely leaned into Alexa. "The last time we spoke on the phone, you were angry. What's going on?"

"Hold the lift, please," a woman called out. Eleanor moved forward with her arm extended and stopped the door from closing. She didn't have much choice, even though she was impatient to hear Alexa's answer.

As the woman on a red mobility scooter and her companion entered, Alexa and Eleanor were forced to separate and press themselves against opposite walls of the lift. The doors closed, and the lift soared upwards.

"Thank you," the woman said softly in a sweet, heavily accented voice. She and her friend smiled and nodded simultaneously, and Eleanor smiled back.

Alexa looked up at the ceiling and buried her hands deep in the pockets of her paprika-coloured jacket. The colour brought out a hint of chestnut in her hair. With her tall, nicely curved figure, Alexa could carry off any style, and Eleanor decided she carried off the chic retro look especially well. Why did she have to look so damned attractive all the time?

Desire flickered in Eleanor like a small flame. *Help.* Eleanor had to pull herself together. She and Alexa were sharing the lift with two strangers. Anyway, where was this little adventure of Alexa's going?

Eleanor wasn't the only one who appreciated Alexa. Their two lift companions were definitely checking her out. She didn't like it, but she didn't blame them.

The lift came to a sudden halt, and the doors slid smoothly open. Alexa announced in an officious voice, "The Dome, La Trobe Reading Room, and the MV Anderson Chess Collection, which is here for only one more week until it relocates to the Queen's Hall balcony."

This time, it was she who stepped forward and prevented the door from closing as the couple exited. Eleanor could have sworn the woman on the scooter smirked at her.

Alexa took her hand and began tugging her towards some mystery destination for the all-important talk she insisted they must have.

They scurried past lines of shiny silky oak desks and antique swivel chairs. The reading room was illuminated by beams of light from the skylights forming the dome above. It was such an awe-inspiring space that Eleanor would have been tempted to stop and remove her camera from her bag if not for the fact that she was desperate to know what the hell was going on with Alexa. Was she going to serve Eleanor with another lecture even though Eleanor had done as Alexa instructed and cancelled the appointment with Grace?

Alexa's behaviour was contradictory. Sardonic one minute, playful the next. She appeared to be on a mission, though, dragging Eleanor along in her wake. Anticipation had Eleanor's heart beating double-time.

When Alexa had caught sight of Eleanor darting up the reading room staircase, her first thought had been that she'd seen Alexa and was running away—and Alexa wanted to chase after her. Then she'd spotted the child with his foot stuck between the balustrade and had watched Eleanor free him and lift him safely into her arms. Her second thought was that Eleanor moved like a gazelle. She was loose-limbed, agile and so appealing. Alexa's third thought was that she'd treated Eleanor unfairly. She swallowed hard. It was imperative that she find somewhere to apologise. Right now.

Why hadn't she thought to get Eleanor signed in, so they could go to a quiet space, back of house? Her mind was churning through the options.

Small fellowship study rooms skirted the domed La Trobe Reading Room. With any luck, one of them would be empty. Alexa marched on. Her pass key would give them access, and they could talk there in private.

Luckily, it was lunchtime and thanks to the library's strict 'no food' policy in the reading rooms, it was almost free of students—their textbooks, laptops, and all their usual fidgeting and bag shuffling—allowing a relatively smooth passage through to their destination.

Just in time, Alexa jumped aside to avoid a briefcase that lay in her path. Two men with a large pile of books stacked between them looked up and shook their heads.

"Hey, no running in the library," one of them said in a loud whisper.

Alexa stopped to flash her Library ID. "Sorry," she said, using a contrite tone of voice. With a sharp twinge of guilt Alexa acknowledged she should have known better than to sprint through the reading room.

Eleanor came to a standstill behind her. "You seem to be in a bit of a hurry."

Alexa agreed; she couldn't leave things as they were between them and was determined to make amends. She'd been unable to concentrate all morning, knowing that Eleanor was coming to collect the envelope. Witnessing Eleanor's small act of heroism and her charming interaction with the troublesome child and his father, Alexa glimpsed another layer of her personality. It was impossible not to be impressed by the woman. Gran was right. Eleanor's heart always seemed to be in the right place.

"Do you actually know where you're going?" Eleanor murmured, tugging Alexa's sleeve.

"Right here." Alexa ducked between shelves labelled Political Biographies and the blue bound tomes of History Records, stopping in front of a door with an etched glass insert that read, *ENTER Without Knocking.*

When she peered through the glass window, Alexa sighed with relief. It was vacant. She patted her side pocket and extracted the key-card. "Here goes." She swiped the card, turned the shiny brass handle, then pushed open the door, leaning in to switch on the light.

Eleanor stood on her tippy toes and snuck a peek over Alexa's shoulder. "Oh goodie, more bookshelves," she said, walking into the eerily soundless room.

"And a couple of chairs and a desk. Why don't you take a seat?" Alexa pushed herself against the door, and the lock engaged with a click. She took a deep breath. They were finally alone.

Eleanor dropped her bag onto one of the chairs and stood beside it, regarding Alexa with an intense, curious look. She seemed to quiver with energy, a coiled spring ready to dash into the breach like a superhero. Superheroes had their antecedents in legends and myth, but Eleanor was no myth, and even though she was no superhero, she was courageous and compassionate in her chosen profession. The flash of vulnerability in her eyes, the tiny faint scar at the corner of her enticing parted lips made Alexa's knees wobble. She leaned heavily against the door. Eleanor was all human, a maddeningly appealing one.

Eleanor strode towards Alexa, determination flaring in her eyes.

Alexa held up her hand and swallowed the lump in her throat. "Stop, Eleanor. Even though I was mad with you, I was wrong, and I need to apologise. I had no right to keep you from going to the Mahjong game. Last night, Gran gave me a serve about my behaviour. She was right. I shouldn't have channelled my shock about your discovery into anger against you. I'm really sorry."

"You were trying to protect your grandmother. You were so upset about what I'd discovered; I should have given you time to absorb the information and let things settle between you and Grace," Eleanor said. "I'm sorry. Agreeing to go to the Mahjong game was stupid of me."

"Thank you, Eleanor." Alexa smiled, appreciating Eleanor's sincere apology.

Eleanor continued, "As a documentarian, it was automatic that I checked my facts about William before coming to you, but I shouldn't have gone behind your back and delved into your family history. That stuff is personal, and I had no right to violate you or your grandmother's privacy. I really am sorry."

"I really appreciate you telling me that." Alexa's heart warmed. Eleanor's explanation reinstated Alexa's belief that she was the kind of person who was generally careful not to hurt others, and someone who took responsibility for her actions.

Eleanor rested her hip against the edge of the desk; her pent-up energy seemed to have dissipated. "Are we okay then?" she asked.

Alexa nodded, wanting to kiss the worried frown from Eleanor's forehead.

"Why did you have to drag me all the way here to apologise? You could have just rung me. I do have a phone." Eleanor had a cheeky glint in her eye.

Alexa couldn't explain her actions. When Mary had rung to tell her Eleanor was in the library picking up the package, she'd dropped everything—not literally, of course—and sped to the Cowan Gallery desperately hoping to find Eleanor before she left the building. Now that they'd resolved their differences, with Eleanor so close—now coming even closer—it was impossible to resist her.

Eleanor might have said something, but Alexa didn't hear it. All she could focus on were Eleanor's lips curved in a sensual smile and her hands that clasped Alexa's hips possessively.

"We shouldn't be doing this here." Alexa didn't really mean it. Her body buzzed with anticipation, caught up in her unstoppable gravitational attraction to Eleanor. Her heart pounded in her ears.

"And yet, here we are." Eleanor's words came out in a breathy rush. Her chest rose and fell rapidly.

Alexa grasped Eleanor's shoulders tightly, stared into wide brown eyes, then squeezed her own eyes shut, afraid of falling into those hauntingly dark pools of swirling emotions.

It was no surprise when Eleanor's lips collided with hers. They were luscious and hungry, and when her mouth was urged apart, Alexa instinctively curled her lips around Eleanor's silky tongue relishing the sweet, fiery taste of her.

A little murmur that sounded from the back of Alexa's throat seemed to urge Eleanor on. Her hands were first in Alexa's hair, then like butterfly wings at the nape of her neck. The gentle touch of Eleanor's fingers sent tremors through Alexa's body.

The door handle prodded into her lower back. It was uncomfortable, but Alexa wasn't going to move now. She had her hands locked around Eleanor's neck, and Eleanor's body was pressed securely into hers.

The urgency of Eleanor's kiss overwhelmed her, yet made her feel safe. This was impossible. This was scary. Alexa wasn't ready for this. It was like careening down the middle of a single lane highway at a hundred miles an hour and taking your hands off the wheel. Dangerous.

Eleanor's hands were everywhere. Caressing, stroking, moving across Alexa's body. Eleanor traced her fingers up to the swell of Alexa's breasts and Alexa gasped, breaking the kiss. Their gazes met and held for a few heart thumping moments, and the air seemed to crackle.

"Eleanor. *Damn.*" Alexa dropped her arms to her sides.

Eleanor's eyes fluttered in surprise, and their breaths mingled in raspy sighs.

"That's a hell-of-a-way to apologise," Eleanor whispered in her ear. "I believe more of an apology is required."

Alexa turned her face to bring their mouths closer. She was giddy, craving more, and wanted to hold onto that feeling a little longer. She pushed away reason—Eleanor had already obliterated her ability to think clearly.

Lowering her head, she sought Eleanor's mouth again. She ran her hand through the short hair at the back of Eleanor's neck, tugging her forward. She couldn't get close enough. Eleanor's muscles tensed under Alexa's touch, and their mouths met in a frantic knee-trembling kiss that had Alexa's own body awakening in the nicest possible ways.

Eleanor reached under Alexa's jacket and loosened her shirt, her hand strayed to Alexa's stomach, and she began undoing Alexa's trouser buttons.

Oh my God, where was this leading? Alexa groaned in frustration and grabbed Eleanor's hand. "Hey, stop. We can't do this in here."

"Hell." Eleanor sighed. "Do we have to? You're a…wow…*superb* kisser." She trailed her lips to Alexa's ear, biting the lobe gently.

Alexa moaned. Her heart was beating at triple time, and she was light-headed. She slumped back against the door. "We can't."

"Why not?" Eleanor looked down and pointed to Alexa's pocket. "What's that noise?"

Alexa tried to ignore the annoying buzzing sound of the reminder alert on her phone. "Blast, Eleanor, I couldn't stop myself from kissing you."

"Actually, I kissed you." Eleanor placed her hand on Alexa's forearm. "I couldn't help it either."

Alexa stared down at Eleanor's beautifully shaped, slender hand and thought for a second about where that hand would have been if they hadn't stopped. She shuddered. There'd never been any doubt that Eleanor would be such a fierce and decidedly intense kisser. The reminder buzzed again. She shoved her hand in her pocket and reached for the phone. *Fuck. The workshop.*

Her senses were still reeling from Eleanor's kiss, and she had to leave for a bloody meeting, still warm and breathless—achingly incomplete and wanting.

Alexa sighed deeply. She had to be responsible. "We have to stop, Eleanor. This is where I work," she said, cringing at the pleading tone of her own voice. "I forgot I'm supposed to be at a workshop this afternoon, and I'm already running late."

Eleanor stared back at her. "Looks like I'd better go, then," she said a little sulkily. She shrugged, turned around, and walked across the room to collect her bag.

Alexa tucked in her shirt and straightened her jacket. "Will you be okay to find your way out?"

The phone pinged, and she glanced at the screen. It was a text from Jac. Alexa huffed in annoyance. She already knew she was late for the workshop. With an irritated shake of her head, she strode straight for the door.

"Yes, no problem." Eleanor swung her pack onto her back, hesitating before she joined Alexa. "Can I see you again soon? How about tonight?"

Alexa shook her head, again. "I'm so sorry. I can't. Louise is bringing the car back, having dinner with me, and staying the night." Alexa couldn't let her friend down. But still, continuing what she and Eleanor had just started was so tempting.

"How about tomorrow night?"

"That would work… Oh no, tomorrow is Friday," Alexa said through clenched teeth. "There's an official work event I must attend." The wary look in Eleanor's eyes told her she wasn't convinced by Alexa's excuses. Alexa covered her eyes with a hand and rubbed her temples. Why would she be making excuses? Of course, she wanted to see Eleanor.

They stared at each other.

"I'll ring you—" Eleanor said.

"Ring me—" Alexa said at the same time.

Alexa forced a smile, pulled the door open, and waited for Eleanor to pass through. As she walked into the reading room, Eleanor's chin was low, and her hands were buried deep in her pockets. Alexa couldn't let Eleanor leave looking so despondent.

"Eleanor?" Alexa called.

Eleanor stopped and looked back over her shoulder—her eyes narrowed, cautious like a cat.

"See you soon?"

"Sure, Alexa. You know where to find me." Eleanor's half-smile didn't reach her eyes or light up her face like it usually did. She turned on her heels and walked towards the exit.

Alexa smacked her hand against her forehead and swore. She pulled the door shut and walked as fast as she could without actually running towards the staff stairwell. Late again.

She couldn't change her plans with Louise; after all, Louise was making a special trip to Melbourne—and she'd probably already left Castlemaine. But what about tomorrow night? No way. Alexa and Katherine were representing the library at the Historical Society Auction charity event at Government House. Alexa wouldn't leave Katherine in the lurch.

Maybe it was wise to slow things down with Eleanor and not get entangled like Pooh Bear searching for the honey pot and getting stuck in the rabbit hole.

Chapter 19

Catching the moon from the bottom of the sea

"You did what?" Louise's eyes widened in disbelief. "No way." She launched herself onto Alexa's sofa in a flurry of giggles.

Alexa lifted her chin and glared at her friend.

When Louise calmed down and was able to speak again, she said, "You've had many adventurous trysts in the past, done some wicked things, but I've never known you to *make out* in your workplace. Not in the library, of all places."

"It wasn't planned, believe me." Alexa handed Louise a squat tumbler of whiskey and slid into the retro lounge chair across from her friend, tossing her leg over the low-slung arm. She held up her own glass. "Cheers."

Louise waved her glass in the air. "Cheers, to you too."

Alexa stared into her glass. "I messaged and rang Eleanor after the workshop, but she hasn't answered. What do you think that means?" She wished she could find the answer within the deep amber liquid.

"You told her you were with me tonight, and she knows you've got that posh event tomorrow evening. She's just giving you space."

"How much time does it take to reply to one little message?" Alexa whined. "Lou, I'm regretting the way I handled things." She grabbed the cushion from behind her back and tossed it across the room. "It was stupid hurrying her away without making a definite plan to see her again. That damn *Professionalism in the Workplace* workshop had already started. I wasn't thinking straight; I had to run."

Louise spluttered and hastily put down her glass. "I hope you learnt something useful at the workshop. Was 'How to lure a woman into a study room and seduce her,' one of the topics?" She waved her index finger at Alexa.

"I honestly didn't expect to see her. Especially catching her in action, rescuing that little boy from the stairwell."

Louise rolled her eyes. "So, you just happened to be in the same place at the same time?"

Alexa crossed her arms defiantly. "Purely coincidental. She literally pouted when she walked away from me, with her shoulders slumped." Alexa massaged her temples. "Do you think she's annoyed with me? Why hasn't she replied?"

"Don't you think you're over-reacting?" Louise pointed at the cuckoo clock on the wall. "It's only seven fifteen."

"It's hours since I messaged her. Something could have happened. It could be her father; he's had heart surgery not long ago." Alexa twisted her fingers in her hair until her scalp hurt.

"Alexa, it's not like you to let a woman get under your skin like this." Louise raised her eyebrows. "It must have been some kiss."

Alexa rubbed her forehead. "Hell, yeah." It wasn't just the whiskey making her face flush.

Louise slid back on the sofa and crossed her legs. "You could have invited her over tonight. I wouldn't have minded."

"Sure." Alexa shook her head. She didn't want to think about what may have happened if Eleanor *had* come over. Actually, she did want to think about it. But now wouldn't be appropriate.

Louise smirked. "Well, two is company, and three's just a drag."

"Stop it. Come on, you're helping me choose my outfit for tomorrow evening." Alexa pulled her friend off the sofa, spinning her around and marching her to the stairs. "It has to be something semi-formal, but I'm wearing low heels—it could be a long night."

They climbed the staircase into Alexa's bedroom, and she headed straight for the walk-in wardrobe, hoping to push the topic of Eleanor from her mind for a while. She gestured to the clothes she'd earlier selected for consideration.

"Are you leaning towards a dress or suit?" Louise perched on the three-legged stool in the corner.

"A jumpsuit or wide leg pants will be more comfortable."

Louise rifled through the garments. "Hmm... No. Maybe," she said, sliding the coat hangers across the rack.

"Hey, why have you rejected that floral jacquard blazer?" she asked with an exaggerated pout.

Louise put her hands on her hips. "Is it a 60s Motown party at the Governor's residence?"

Alexa placed her own hands on her hips, mirroring Louise's stance. "Nope."

Louise picked out a couple of items and lay them across the bed. "This might do it." She held up the black velvet jacket Alexa had bought at the second-hand shop. "Nice. Very dashing and elegant, with just a hint of steampunk. You can wear it without a shirt over this sleeveless silk crop. These super fine wool suit pants will go nicely." She tugged at the hem of the trouser leg. "I like how they just flare. They'll show off your long legs," she said, waving the trousers in the air. "You'll just need a bit of extra bling."

"Okay, good choice. I could wear Mum's peridot drop earrings." Alexa raced to the far end of the wardrobe to extract them from her jewellery box. It was an important event, and wearing her mother's earrings made her feel warm inside. Standing in front of the dresser mirror, she tucked her hair behind her ears and slipped in a single earring. "What do you think?"

"Perfect." Louise stroked the matching ring on Alexa's index finger. "It's a set. They bring out the green in your eyes."

"That's it then. Thanks for your help. Problem solved." She headed back to the wardrobe to put away the earrings. She ran her fingers lightly over the jewellery box, her chest tightening as she thought of her mother.

Louise called, "How are you dealing with the news about your Chinese heritage?"

Alexa plonked down on the edge of the bed, grateful for the distraction. "You know me, Lou; you're my oldest friend. I believe we should embrace our heritage." She hesitated, remembering how appallingly the Hamptons had treated Mei-Li and her family. "Obviously, there are some situations when you might not be proud of your ancestors. Gran is a quarter Chinese, and I am one-sixteenth. How could I have not known that? I'm a historian for crying out loud." Alexa curled her fingers into her upturned palms. "I'm different now, and yet I'm the same. Of course, I want to find out more about my great-great-grandmother's life and everything that happened."

"There's a lot to take in," Louise said wide-eyed. "First, Eleanor told you what she'd discovered, and then Grace revealed the family's long-kept secret. You poor thing; a double shock."

"It sure was." Alexa nodded. "It also set off a raft of unanswered questions in my head. How did Mei-Li become a herbalist? Who were her parents? What were their lives like? Why did they come to Australia?" She looked up at Louise. "They must have endured so much racism. I have to find out more, but what if—I mean, as a historian, I'm supposed to welcome the truth and the facts—but what if there are even more secrets? Things Gran doesn't even know about. Horrible things."

"It's a challenge. There are risks," Louise said. "But you're right. You'd never shrink from the truth." She squeezed Alexa's hand. "Eleanor set things in motion by digging up the information, which in turn finally gave Grace the courage to speak. You must be itching to do more research. Where on earth are you going to start?"

"Phyllis from the Historical Society in Castlemaine is going to suss out whatever information she can about the Kwan family." Alexa returned the clothes they'd rejected back to the wardrobe, using the private space to pull the phone from her pocket and check for messages from Eleanor. Nothing.

Alexa rested her elbow on the top of the dresser and said, "The Castlemaine court records about Mei-Li's case should be relatively easy to find. It's going to be harder to discover details about the woman who died though, especially if her family had requested the findings from the coroner's inquest be closed. That is, if there was a coroner's investigation at all."

Louise hung the coat hangers with Alexa's outfit for tomorrow on a hook on the back of the bedroom door. "You need someone with legal knowledge."

Alexa sighed. "Hopefully, that will be Eleanor."

"Hopefully," Louise repeated. "At least Grace has shed her burden. The poor woman had been carrying the secret for so long, and now it's up to you to find out what actually happened. Kelly and I will help however we can. But Eleanor's your best bet with the legal stuff." She winked.

"Hmm, maybe." Alexa checked her phone again. "Nothing," she said despondently. "Why hasn't she replied?"

Louise offered no answers, just shrugged her shoulders.

"What the hell." Alexa kicked the corner of the dresser with her bare toe. "Ouch." She winced and rubbed her foot. "I can't sit around here waiting for Eleanor to call or message. Didn't you say you were in the mood for *pho* and spring rolls?"

Louise grinned. "Yes, please. Aren't we lucky you live within a stone's throw of some of the best Vietnamese food outside Hanoi?"

Alexa grabbed her bag and threw the phone inside. "Come on, I know just the place. No point sitting around moping. Let's go get some food and chill with a cold beer. It's my shout. I can't thank you enough for bringing my car safely back to the city."

The irritating jangling of her phone alarm woke Eleanor with a start. She yawned, rolled over, and took a deep breath. The rich fragrance of frangipani and jacaranda blossoms wafted through the air, and of course, Alexa came to mind. "Where am I? That's right, I'm in Queensland."

The editor of *Global Conscience* had called late yesterday afternoon with an amazing offer of work, and Eleanor had eagerly accepted. She'd had barely enough time to talk to her father about the out of the blue request and seek his blessing, gather her camera gear, laptop, and a few clothes, before the Uber driver arrived.

She'd been at Melbourne Airport ready to board the flight to Far North Queensland when Alexa's brief message came through.

All it said was, *Are you free this weekend?*

The perfunctory text put Eleanor in a grumpy mood, and she hadn't known how to respond. So, she hadn't. Alexa could wait.

By the time she'd disembarked in Cairns and checked into her hotel, it was nearly midnight. Too late to return the message or missed calls. Or at least that's the reason she'd given herself.

She should call Alexa now but instead came up with a handful of excuses why she shouldn't. Alexa could have her hands full with Louise. Or she might use that sharp straightforward tone that turned Eleanor inside out. She wouldn't call, just yet.

Putting aside thoughts of Alexa, Eleanor shook herself out of her funk, which gave way to a rush of excitement. She was on assignment in the tropics.

With a hastily prepared plate of vegemite on toast, slices of pineapple and mango, and a pot of strong coffee, she sat out on her balcony shaded by palms. A pang of guilt nudged at Eleanor's conscience, and she finally gave replying to Alexa's text serious consideration.

Recalling the way Alexa had hurried her out of the study room after their meltingly sensual tryst, even faster than she'd dragged Eleanor in there, Eleanor crushed the piece of toast in her hand. Alexa hadn't made time in her busy schedule to meet up with Eleanor again after that—until now. *Are you free this weekend?* Eleanor gritted her teeth. What did that even mean? Did Alexa assume Eleanor would be available at *her* convenience?

Alexa either surmised Eleanor would head back to the UK when her father fully recovered, or she thought their fledgling connection was destined to be a fling. Was a fleeting connection all Alexa wanted?

Eleanor grabbed a slice of mango and popped it into her mouth. She licked the sticky yellow juice from her lips and slurped the sweet fibrous pulp from her fingers. For now, a fling would be better than nothing, but that's not what Eleanor hoped for or wanted. So, what did she want?

Despite her annoyance, Eleanor wanted Alexa in her life. That was a no-brainer. She replied to Alexa's message, explaining where she was and why, adding she'd be back mid-week, and asked if they could catch up the *following* weekend.

Her phone rang. *Alexa?*

Eleanor reached for the tea towel, wiped her hands, and with a tingle of anticipation picked up the phone. She looked at the caller ID. It was Max, *Global Conscience's* editor. She sighed.

"Good morning, Max."

"Good. I presume you've arrived safely," he said. "Is everything to your satisfaction, Eleanor?"

Eleanor stood up and stretched lazily in the warm air. She glanced out across the palm fringed foreshore and the crystal-clear swimming pool sparkling in the bright sunshine. "Yes, thank you, Max. It's perfect, but I can't wait for the next leg of the journey."

The JetRanger helicopter skirted above miles of golden sandy beaches, pockets of lush rainforest, and rocky headlands before heading away from the city of Cairns and the mainland and entering another universe. Eleanor's stomach lurched as the pilot suddenly manoeuvred lower, levelled out and the ocean went from mottled turquoise, then cerulean, to a paler blue. A thrill ripped through her at the spectacular sight. They hovered above a group of islands, fringing reefs and keys, gliding over varied hues, shades, and shapes that were like sparkling jewels in the vast sea.

Eleanor stared out of the window trying to grasp the sheer magnitude and the exquisite beauty of the Reef. It was breathtaking and hard to believe that what she could see below was only a small part of the entire coral reef system that stretched for two thousand, three hundred kilometres. Eleanor couldn't believe the magazine was paying her to be here—even if she did plan to donate most of her earnings to the Reef campaign.

Over the long weekend, one of her assignments would be to photograph the Save the Reef campaign's celebrity guests and their activities on the island during the filming of a documentary. On the final day, she would accompany the journalist interviewing the Traditional Owners who held the rights and interests of the Great Barrier Reef World Heritage Area. She was especially looking forward to that.

Eleanor peered out of the chopper window. Having a bird's eye view on the flight to the island was definitely a bonus.

Raising her camera, she clicked off a series of shots. She bit the inside of her cheek in concentration, wanting to do this natural wonder justice. The structure of the aircraft limited her view, so she positioned the Leica carefully, avoiding reflections from the cabin's rear window.

"Sorry we had to fly you out here in such a rush. Thanks for making yourself available on crazy short notice," Dylan, the event co-ordinator, shouted above the noise of the rotor blades. He scratched at his clean-shaven chin. "Our main photographer severely sprained his ankle yesterday afternoon, and there is absolutely no way we'd be able to cover the event kicking off today without you. We have celebrities who've given up their time and money to be part of the doco. *Global Conscience* has to maximise its coverage."

Eleanor knew this already. "I'm so sorry he injured himself," she said, turning back to stare out of the window. She couldn't stop the prickles of excitement that ran up her spine at the prospect of working again.

Lifting her camera back up to her eye, she zoomed in. The most magnificent water with almost opal-like colours spread out beneath her—emerald green in the sunlight, like Alexa's eyes—showing their palest, purest tints. She sighed heavily, her breath fogging the camera display.

As the helicopter tilted to the left, Eleanor clutched her seatbelt, steadying herself. Her response to Alexa had been vague, but for the next few days, the job had to be her focus. In any case, she'd been warned there was no mobile signal on the island, so they wouldn't be able to communicate. She supposed there might be some benefits to staying in the present moment; it would certainly keep her mind from wandering to starry-eyed thoughts of Alexa too often.

Dylan tapped her on the forearm. "Look ahead, we'll be on the island in a few minutes. Serina, our journo, is already there, and she'll brief you. You've worked with us before; you know the drill."

Eleanor gave him the thumbs-up. She was no Jacques Cousteau. Her role was to record the filming of the documentary, sponsored by *Global Conscience*, and the activists who were campaigning to save the reef due to the Australian Government's failure to respond to climate change. How devastating it would be if humanity allowed this unique coral ecosystem to be lost forever. Eleanor was fortunate to be involved in this campaign.

"You can see the ecoresort now," Dylan said in a raised voice. "It's located along the west side. The rest of the island is protected national park with a university research station."

Eleanor caught sight of a blinding expanse of white sand and a sprinkling of people dotted along a narrow wooden jetty. A meandering row of thatched roofs was just visible through the palm grove canopy. At the top end of the resort, Eleanor glimpsed a larger crescent-shaped building with wide decks perched right on the beach. An ample swimming pool was surrounded by lush greenery. *Nice.*

The helicopter lowered onto the heli pad, and even before the rotor blades calmed, Dylan threw open the cockpit door. Pointing to the hut where a dark-haired woman in brightly coloured pants and a flowing white shirt stood waving her arm, he shouted, "Serina is here...she'll show you to your accommodation etcetera. Nice having you with us, Eleanor. Enjoy your stay. I've got to run." He grabbed his bag and straw hat, leapt out of the helicopter, and sprinted in the opposite direction.

"Do you need a hand with your gear?" the chopper pilot asked.

"Thanks." Eleanor stashed her camera into her backpack, collected her jacket, and hopped out of the cabin. Lifting her face to the welcoming salty sea breeze, she inhaled deeply.

The pilot reached in behind the seat in the rear and extracted Eleanor's compact travel bag. The adventure was about to begin.

After Serina and Eleanor made hasty introductions, the journalist walked her to a thatched-roof bungalow at the far end of the resort. "Most of the media crews are on and off the island today, but as sponsors of the event, we've scored these digs. Lucky us. I hope you don't mind bunking in with me," Serina said, opening the door to reveal a decent-sized room with two double beds, a couple of armchairs, bar fridge, and coffee-making facilities. "As you can tell from the mess on my side, your bed's on the right. Not bad, huh?"

Eleanor did a full circle and grinned. "I think this will do nicely." She placed her gear on the luggage table beside what was to be her bed. Sharing a bungalow with a stranger was not expected, but no problem. They'd both be busy doing their jobs, and the accommodation was more than adequate. A place to shower, dress, and crash for the next couple of nights.

"I'd better get myself going. I'm buzzing." Serina handed Eleanor a manila folder and a set of keys. "Everything you need to know is in here."

Eleanor narrowed her eyes. "You're from Manchester? You've come a long way."

"Yep, I'm a proper Manc." She winked. "I was following a story in Indonesia when the call came through. It's mint scoring this assignment." Serina walked over to the mirror, tousled her hair with both hands, and straightened her shirt collar. "You're an Aussie, but you don't sound it."

"I flatted in London for over a decade."

"But you're home now?"

"Yes, for now, based in Melbourne. My family is there," Eleanor said.

"That's nice, love. Oh well, with the magazine spreading its wings all over the globe and with your experience, there'll be plenty of opportunities here if you want them."

Eleanor nodded. Maybe Serina had a point. The guilt Eleanor had suffered after her aunt's death had set her on a quest to tell stories about things that mattered all over the planet. Serina's assertion that Eleanor *could* base herself in Melbourne was quite a gear shift, though not an entirely unwelcome one.

Serina pointed to the folder in Eleanor's hands. "We both need to read through the guidelines and protocols for our interview with the Indigenous communities."

"Thanks. I'll definitely make time to do that."

"I'll leave you to sort yourself out, then." Serina grabbed her leather notebook and recording device from the coffee table. "Oh, I nearly forgot to mention, your ex is on the island. I interviewed her earlier today."

Eleanor did a double take. The keys slid off the top of the folder, onto the wooden floor. *Clang.* "What?" She scooped them up. "Who did you interview?"

"Mia Conti. Hey, I know, right? Mia was surprised as well when I told her you were here replacing the scheduled shutterbug." Her thin pencil-line eyebrows furrowed. "It won't be an issue, will it? I mean, she seemed thrilled about the chance to catch up."

Not an issue, no. Maybe a little awkward that Eleanor hadn't known Mia would be here, but she smiled at the thought of seeing her again. It would be fun. Mia's presence shouldn't surprise Eleanor. Her ex-girlfriend was a fierce campaigner on environmental issues. With her roots in Far North Queensland, of course she'd want to be part of saving the reef. "No, not at all. Do you know where I can find her?"

"Yeah. She's staying in a luxurious beachfront bungalow. Garden terrace with maximum privacy," Serina said. "Dylan organised your ID card. It's in the folder. You'll need it to get past the security guards near the celebs' sleeping quarters. See you later." She raced out the door.

Eleanor blinked, slightly baffled at Serina's sudden exit. Serina seemed pretty laid-back, though. She'd be easy to get on with.

After quickly reading over the brief, Eleanor's curiosity got the better of her, and she decided to visit her ex-girlfriend before her appointment with the director. She peered at her reflection in the bathroom mirror, deciding a quick wash and tidy up was in order. She washed her face, brushed her teeth and changed into a clean shirt.

Eleanor fastened the ID to her shirt collar, slung the Leica over her shoulder, picked up her camera bag, and stepped into the sunshine. After just thirty minutes in the relative cool of the bungalow, the sultry heat outside enveloped her like a heavy blanket. Keeping in the shade beneath the palm grove canopy, she strolled along the shale pathway flanked on the right by the seashore. Half a dozen black nodding terns nested in the sea grass and some kind of egret—Helen would have identified it in a heartbeat—sunbathed nearby.

Nobody was paying her to take photos of the local bird life, but what the heck? The egret's snowy white plumage made a dramatic silhouette against the intense blue of the calm sea, drawing Eleanor's hands straight to her camera. The egret turned to face her, and Eleanor snapped. The bird stared back, unfazed by Eleanor as she crept closer.

"Excuse me, Miss, I'll need to see your identification."

Eleanor looked up with a start.

The security officer stood over her, his huge bulk providing much needed shade, and glanced at the card on her collar. "You're good to go, *Ms* Heysen. But sorry, no cameras." He held out his hand.

She smiled and flipped over the ID card. "That's going to make life difficult. I am an official photographer for the event."

He grinned. "I see your point. Where are you heading?"

"I'm looking for Mia Conti's accommodation."

"I don't know why you're bothering with these feathered birds if you're on your way to visit Ms Conti," he said with a smirk. "Her bungalow is right on the beach, just behind those trees. I spotted her on the terrace."

"Thanks for your help."

"No problem," he called after her. "Have a good day, *Miss*."

Eleanor tread warily into the private garden, hoping Mia wouldn't object to an unannounced visitor. She set her camera bag on the wooden deck and glanced around, looking for Mia. Ahh. She'd recognise that very shapely behind anywhere. "Security told me you were out on the terrace. They failed to mention I'd find you on your hands and knees, crawling in the dirt under a bush."

"Shush…it's a *diplodactylus vittatus*." Mia glanced sideways at Eleanor, and her smile widened. Scrambling to her feet, she said, "It's you! I wondered how long it would take 'till you came looking." She grasped Eleanor's hands and pulled her into a fierce hug.

"Making friends with the wildlife, are you?" Eleanor could only mumble with her face squashed against Mia's shoulder, enveloped in her warm, familiar scent.

Mia held her at arm's length. "Imagine my delight when Serina told me you were here. You're a sight for sore eyes." She caressed Eleanor's cheek with the back of her hand. "God, you look well. Tremendous in fact."

Eleanor covered Mia's hand with hers and smiled. Mia was always such a charmer. "Yes, the surprise was mutual," she said. "You look...what can I say...pretty fantastic. Even with mud and grass stains on your white trousers." Eleanor picked out a sticky purply-blue flower that was caught in Mia's auburn hair, tossing it over her shoulder.

"Oh, *shadup*." Mia laughed heartily, combing her fingers through her stylish bob. "I spotted a couple of wood gecko scurrying under the native plumbago and was trying to get a quick look-see. One of the little darlings is still there if you want to take a peek."

Eleanor took a couple of hasty steps backwards. "I'll pass on that, thanks."

"How could I forget? You are not fond of amphibians and creepy crawlies." Mia clutched Eleanor's hand and pulled her onto the deck. "You'll stay for a few minutes to chat, won't you? I know we'll be around each other for the next couple of days, but there'll be lots of other people. It would be sweet to catch up privately. Or are you working now?"

"I am here to work, as you know." Eleanor pointed to her camera bag. "There's time for a quick chat, though, if you don't mind me taking a few pictures. My brief for the rest of this morning is to check in with the director and get lots of shots of guests *interacting naturally*." She made quotation marks in the air. "Pity I didn't get a shot of you crawling about in the dirt."

Mia lightly thumped Eleanor's shoulder, pushing her into a cane armchair and taking the one opposite. "Sit. You. I don't think a picture of my butt would aid the cause, do you? And yes, you can take a few shots. That's why we're here after all, for the publicity. Anyway, you've always made me look super."

"Not like that's a difficult task." It was true. Not only was Mia attractive, she was extremely driven, intelligent, and surprisingly humble. It was a shame she and Eleanor hadn't worked out, but after two years of juggling timetables and demanding careers, what had broken the camel's back, though, was Mia's big break in Hollywood.

Mia shrugged and gave her a genuine smile. "Thank you. You're so endearing, Eleanor. Not to mention all your other qualities." She winked mischievously. "Has anyone lassoed you yet?"

Eleanor met Mia's amused gaze. "No. You're the one who's been snagged—by a Californian farmer, no less. Sorry I couldn't make it to your wedding. Congratulations." She briefly closed her eyes, recalling the stab of regret that surfaced when she'd received the invitation, and she'd wished for a moment that she and Mia had tried harder to make their relationship work. The moment had passed quickly, though, replaced by happiness that Mia had been able to move on with someone else.

"Thank you. Stephanie manages a community garden in the Hollywood Hills. She loves getting her hands dirty, supplying the local restaurants with fresh organic produce." Mia sat back, looking thoughtful. "As far as being captured…it's true… I am blissfully happy. Steph keeps me grounded."

And that's what had been missing in Mia and Eleanor's relationship. Back then, neither of them had been ready to settle. They'd never even shared a home or been able to find enough time for each other. But now Eleanor's circumstances had changed, and she too wanted someone special in her life. Out of the blue, she recalled the hunger in Alexa's eyes just before she'd kissed Eleanor in the library study-room and nearly brought her to her knees.

Mia sat forward in her chair. "It's early days yet, but I have to tell you. Steph is pregnant. We're expecting the stork to arrive in five and a half months." Her voice bubbled with excitement.

"Motherhood," Eleanor exclaimed. "That's a big step, Mia. Congratulations."

A warm glow of contentment radiated from Mia, and Eleanor wondered if she would ever find the same happiness.

"It sure is." Mia squeezed her knee. "I heard about Harold. I'm so sorry, but it's grand he's on the mend. Having you there must be a blessing. Coming home seems to be good for you, too." She frowned. "I caught you on the Ian Sinclair Show last month. You looked exhausted, El. Now that you're back in Oz, are you planning to stay?"

Eleanor raised her shoulders in a half shrug. Mia wasn't the only person to tell her how well she looked since her return to Australia, and she did feel re-energized. "I really don't know. I have to admit though, I'm tired of the constant travel."

"Tell me about it."

"Yeah." Eleanor tilted her head to one side. "I know this may sound crazy, but I could stay in Melbourne, if there were enough projects that interested me."

"Like this one. There are plenty of causes to support in the region."

"I need to start giving it some thought. Mum would be keen for me to stick around; Dad, too." Eleanor pushed her hands through her hair. "Actually, if it was possible, I could handle basing myself closer to home." Her mind sparked with possibilities as realisation washed over her.

"Lots to think about." Mia's neatly shaped eyebrows lifted. "How is dear Sarah?"

Eleanor couldn't stop herself from rolling her eyes. "Working harder than ever since Dad's illness, as you can imagine."

"Don't be hard on her. The firm is her family legacy, isn't it? Her responsibility. It can't be easy," Mia said in a calm voice.

Those were almost the same words Alexa had used on the train. "Someone else told me that lately." Eleanor was unable to hide her silly grin.

"Oh? What kind of someone?" Mia gazed at her quizzically. "Have you met someone of interest?" Her eyes twinkled.

"What makes you think that?" Eleanor stared into the sky-blue eyes that were boring into hers, although it must have been obvious from the blush that went right to her ears.

"I knew it," Mia said with a chuckle. "I'm an actor and very good at reading people…especially you. Who is she?"

"A new friend." Eleanor licked her lips, recalling the feel of Alexa's mouth against hers. She gave her head a little shake, not wanting to dwell on sexy thoughts of Alexa now. "But I can't just sit here all day." Reaching for her camera bag, she pulled out the Leica M10 and looped the strap over her neck, pushing all thoughts of Alexa from her mind. She primed the 50

Lux, which was her perfect in-between wide angle and portrait lens. "I have to record lots of behind the scenes action during the filming. You're not the only famous name on the island you know, and I have a lot to cover."

Mia pointed her finger at Eleanor. "Don't think you can hide behind your camera. A new friend, huh? Eleanor Heysen, your cheeks are bright red."

"It's true; she is a friend." Eleanor squirmed at the accusation. She didn't want to tell anyone about what was going on between her and Alexa until she'd figured it out for herself.

"You're going to have to tell me more. I'm not leaving the island until you do." Mia winked.

Eleanor laughed. "Come on, Mia. Showtime," she said, firing off a series of playful portraits. With hands on hips, Mia struck a provocative pose, looking incongruous in her grass-stained pants and smoothly tanned bare feet.

Mia pursed her lips. "Hey. These photos aren't going to be featured in the magazine, are they?"

"Nope. Don't worry. Consider these my warm-up shots," Eleanor said, pointing the camera in Mia's direction again.

Mia scrunched her nose and stuck out her tongue.

Eleanor pressed and held the shutter button in burst mode. "Yep. They'll be on the front page, I expect." She peeked over the camera, caught Mia's eye, and they both started to giggle.

"Now, stop goofing around and let me do my work." Eleanor glanced around and pointed to the patch of grass. "I want to change the angle of my next shot. Why don't you sit cross-legged right here, so I can photograph you with the palm grove leading down to the golden sand and the stunning colours of the coral reef behind you?"

Mia gave her a blinding smile and said, "Now that we've re-connected, you must promise to stay in touch."

"I will, Mia. I'd really like that." Eleanor returned her smile.

Chapter 20

Plucking the plum blossom from the roof

THAT KISS IN THE LIBRARY. *Damn.* It was all Alexa could think of lately. She knew if they'd been somewhere more appropriate and she'd had time, things would have escalated, fast.

Recalling the power of the kiss still made her knees wobble. Everything had got hot and steamy until Alexa came to her senses. What had she been thinking—making out in her workplace?

A quick glance around the open plan office confirmed that Alexa's colleagues had left for their lunch break. She signed into her Instagram account.

With an exasperated sigh, she located the *Save the Reef* campaign that had been all over the news for days. She was still slightly amazed that photographs of Eleanor were on social media, and that she had even appeared fleetingly on the *Current Affairs* program last night.

Alexa peered at her computer screen. Why did Eleanor have to be standing practically on top of her ex-girlfriend in every frame? Eleanor's shoulders and finely muscled arms were bare, and her sun-kissed skin glowed as she stood intimately close to Mia Conti on the deck of the Ecotourism catamaran. Eleanor's figure-hugging black tank top and the loose white shorts sitting low on her hips were unnecessarily revealing, according to Alexa. "Humph," she snorted, digging her nails into her palm. *Fuck.* They did make a stunning couple. Wasn't Eleanor there to *work*?

Mia was gorgeous, of course, in a summery, mini orange playsuit with a plunging V-neckline. At the next image, Alexa winced, wishing she hadn't already seen this publicity group shot where Mia had her arm proprietorially around Eleanor's midriff, but she'd managed to come across it at least ten times already. Mia's wide smile displayed her perfectly even, pearly white teeth. She and Eleanor were having way too much fun together.

Alexa and Eleanor weren't even dating, and yet here Alexa was, incensed because the woman she'd kissed twice was spending time with her ex-girlfriend in a sultry, tropical paradise. Why had Alexa allowed Eleanor to get under her skin? Was there something going on between Eleanor and Mia? *Is this ugly feeling jealousy?*

Alexa enjoyed light and casual dalliances, steering clear of women who had expectations she couldn't fulfil. Pinching her lips together, she drummed her fingers on the desk. Let's face it, she already had expectations of Eleanor, which was hardly fair. Alexa twirled a lock of hair around her finger and glared at the damn picture again. Eleanor may not even want to continue what they'd only just started when she returned from *Love* Island.

With a squeak and a clunk, Jac rolled an office chair to Alexa's desk and plopped down beside her before Alexa had a chance to toggle away from the Ecotourism page. *Blast.* Jac was bound to ask questions, and Alexa didn't want to talk about Eleanor or the strange discontent that was gnawing at her insides.

"So, how are you this fine afternoon?" Jac asked in her usual chirpy voice. She craned her neck to look at the screen. "What are you looking at? That looks heavenly. Are you planning a holiday?"

Alexa removed her reading glasses, spun her chair around, and scowled. "I wish."

"Looks like the sunny coast of Queensland and the Great Barrier Reef." Jac nudged Alexa aside. "Hey, that's the documentary they're making about the destruction of the reef, isn't it? Good on them. Those celebrities are really pushing the government to make changes."

"Uh-huh, it's time the political parties stopped fighting each other," Alexa agreed, hoping Jac hadn't noticed Eleanor in the pictures.

"And listened to what we want. It's such an important—" Jac hesitated as she scrolled down the page. "Well, well, well, that's Eleanor. What's she doing right there, amidst the action?" She shot a curious glance at Alexa. "Is she one of the famous, supporting the campaign?"

Bloody eagle-eyed Jac. Now she'd want details. Alexa shook her head. "Well, I'm sure she supports saving the reef, but I believe she's there to work."

"Is she part of the film crew?"

"No. She's on assignment for some environmental magazine covering the event, I think."

"Lucky her. Nice place to be on assignment."

"Hmm. Fantastic." Alexa pursed her lips. *Especially when your ex happens to be there—all over you.* Had she mis-read the situation between herself and Eleanor? It was after all just a kiss or two. Maybe she was a fool to think that Eleanor too had experienced the electrifying sparks between them.

Jac waved her hand between Alexa and the computer. "You aren't listening to me, Alexa. You're distracted."

Alexa blinked out of her daze and lifted her chin to meet Jac's questioning stare. "What did you say?"

"You're distracted. I asked if you've learnt any more about your ancestry since Eleanor presented you with the startling news?"

"No, not yet. I've made an appointment with a historian in Castlemaine who specialises in Chinese settlement. Hopefully, she'll direct me to ship passenger records or anything relevant to the case against my great-great-grandmother." Alexa sat back in her chair and crossed her arms tightly. "I'm going to the cottage this weekend."

"Is Eleanor back from Queensland? Is she going to Chewton with you?"

"I haven't asked her yet." Alexa's brows furrowed, and her eyes were drawn back to the monitor screen. She hoped Eleanor would take part in the research, but after her whirlwind trip to Queensland, would she really want to bother with a trip to Chewton?

"What are you looking at now?" Jac asked with a frown. "It's Eleanor, isn't it? You can't keep your eyes off her. I bet you're green with envy because she's there in that amazing location."

Alexa pointed to the picture of Eleanor and Mia standing knee-deep in crystal-clear water at the turtle rehabilitation centre. "Just look at them."

"Isn't Mia gorgeous? I think it's fab that she's flown home to support such a worthy cause. Don't you?"

"Did you know she's Eleanor's ex?" Alexa didn't mean to raise her voice, but she couldn't hold back her annoyance.

"No. I didn't know that." Jac jerked in surprise. "I haven't seen you like this before. You really do have a thing for Eleanor." Her eyes widened in realisation. "Are you pissed off because they're there together?"

"They're not there *together*, Jac. Eleanor's supposed to be working. But it doesn't look much like work to me. And that ridiculous man from Channel 10 was stupid enough to ask if they were back together again."

Jac gave Alexa a look of sympathy. "Eleanor does have her camera around her neck. She's obviously working. They do look cute together in this picture. It's nice they're still on friendly terms. That's all it is."

"Hmph..." was all Alexa could say. Why did they have to look *so* friendly? Alexa tossed the mouse onto the desk in frustration and leaned back. It looked as if Eleanor was having a hell of a time with Mia. Well, good for her.

"What's going on in that brain of yours? I can literally see the cogs grinding," Jac said, picking up a folder from her desk and fanning Alexa's face. "A little smoke puffing out of your ears."

Alexa waved her hand away. "I'm not angry. Just a little..."

"Disappointed," Jac finished her sentence.

That was it. Alexa was disappointed. She wanted Eleanor. She tried to quell the surge of longing that swept through her. What if Eleanor wanted to rekindle things with her ex?

"You have to admit Eleanor has a certain allure." Alexa laughed, shutting down the computer. "Women," she said, feigning nonchalance. She reached for the folder just as Jac pulled it away. Alexa frowned. "Give it to me."

"I'll hold onto this." Jac stood up and held it behind her back. "In your current state of mind, you'll certainly leave it behind," she said with a mock stern look.

Alexa raised her eyebrows. "I'm ready. Let's go to that meeting."

Just in time, Eleanor pulled a tissue from the pocket of her backpack. She sneezed. What on earth had triggered her allergy? She scanned Alexa's tiny front garden for the source.

Ah, there it was. She sneezed again and stared at the ceramic tub overflowing with purple asters. The bright gold pollen was the culprit. What would Alexa think if she arrived home and found Eleanor sitting on her doorstep with red eyes, a runny nose, and her roll-on bag and backpack? *God, no.* That wouldn't make a good impression at all.

Eleanor quickly rummaged through her bag, located an antihistamine, popped it in her mouth, and drained the last drop from her water bottle. Hopefully, it would work really soon, and when Alexa got home Eleanor would present a laid-back image, calm and totally together. No problem.

As the boat had docked in Cairns this morning, she'd messaged Alexa telling her she would be back today. She assumed Alexa would want to see her on the weekend or sooner and had anticipated an enthusiastic reply. Unfortunately, the message she received back from Alexa threw her for a loop.

She'd responded, *Oh okay, cool.*

Is that how Alexa felt? As though Eleanor was nothing special? That was not the answer Eleanor had hoped for. Far from it. She had no idea what was going on in Alexa's mind based on the cursory message, so rather than worry about it, she thought the logical thing to do was to come and find out in person.

Squinting in the sunlight, Eleanor looked at her watch again. It was six fifteen, ten minutes later than the last time she'd checked. She'd already worn a path from circling the tiny patch of grass so many times. Where was Alexa? She could be anywhere. It was Eleanor's fault for arriving at the loft without checking when Alexa would be home. What an idiot.

Eleanor slapped her forehead. She'd come straight here from the airport without a second thought. Her luggage was even sitting on the doorstep. It would look like she was ready to move in, and that was sure to scare off Alexa. She scanned the enclosed yard for a place to stash her bags. Behind the lavender bush? No, not tall enough. What about the big planter with the apple blossom? That wouldn't work either. Definitely not anywhere near those aster pollen bombs. She shoved the two pieces of luggage together, hoping they'd appear more compact. Nope, it didn't really work, but it would have to do.

Eleanor plonked down on the hard-as-iron bluestone step and put her head in her hands. Maybe she shouldn't have come here, but she hadn't been able to stop herself at the thought of seeing Alexa again. Even thinking of Alexa did funny things to Eleanor's insides.

A loud chirping caught her attention. Above the loft window, a pair of pretty brown house sparrows were busy cramming twigs and leaves into a high crevice. She smiled, watching them work, and reaching into her jacket pocket, pulled out her phone and snapped a string of pictures.

During one of her photographic jaunts around the English countryside with her aunt, Helen, an avid birdwatcher, had pointed out a nest tucked in the rooftop beams of a crumbling mansion. She'd explained that birds nesting was a lucky symbol representing growth, beauty, and fortune. Eleanor crossed her fingers, deciding fortune favoured the brave. Alexa would turn up soon, and she would be glad to see Eleanor.

Leaning her back against the solid blue door, Eleanor closed her eyes and ruffled her hands through her hair. Alexa was a fiery spirit, and the fact that they'd kissed in the hallowed halls of the library—was hot. Her heartbeat quickened at the memory of Alexa's sensual mouth. She wanted to kiss Alexa so badly right now.

Eleanor tugged the neckline of her T-shirt. The blue sky, bright with late afternoon sun, still bore plenty of heat. She licked her lips, wishing she'd topped up her water bottle at the airport.

"By the look on your face, you're still basking in the afterglow of tropical paradise."

Eleanor winced, surprised by the sarcasm and *something else* evident in Alexa's tone. She mustered her courage and peeked through half-closed eyelids, her gaze cautiously scaling Alexa's towering form, from her mid-calf buckle boots, up endlessly long legs encased in black tights, to the stylishly figure-hugging yellow pinafore.

"Hm… hmmm." Alexa cleared her throat.

Eleanor looked up guiltily. Alexa's face was mostly obscured by her Jackie Ohh sunglasses as she tossed her messy ponytail and curled her lips in a sardonic smile.

Was Eleanor's mouth open? Probably. Alexa was gorgeous. So sexy. It had definitely been worth sitting on the hard-stone step and getting a numb bum.

"Eleanor." Alexa pushed up her sunglasses, fixing her hazel eyes fully on Eleanor's.

"Hmm?"

Alexa had one hand resting on her hip and her head tilting to one side. "What are you doing here?"

Eleanor jumped to her feet, tottering like a toddler taking her first steps, and knocked her bags onto the grass. "I'm sorry to just turn up but—"

"You couldn't find your way home?" Alexa's voice was taunting, but her smile broadened, showing a flash of gleaming teeth.

"Um, no." Eleanor lifted her shoulders and let them fall. "It's just that I didn't know if you'd want a visitor," she stuttered nervously. It was as though she had a mouthful of marbles. "I really wanted to see you. Do you have time to talk?"

Alexa jiggled her key ring, and Eleanor stepped aside, allowing her access to her front door.

"Come on in." She turned the key in the lock, nudged the door open with the toe of her boot, and stepped inside. Eleanor didn't waste any time and already had one foot in the door when Alexa called out, "And, Eleanor, bring in your bags. This neighbourhood maintains a relatively low level of crime, but I wouldn't leave your fancy cameras outside."

Eleanor raised her eyes heavenward, scurrying to gather her gear like an anxious mouse. At least, this time, she'd been invited inside.

Balancing a bag under each arm, Eleanor narrowly avoided the satchel that was tossed on the wooden floorboards inside the door. Her eyes widened as she scanned the high-ceilinged loft, her gaze taking in the eclectic furniture that popped with colour, contemporary wall art, and large leafy wonders, including a giant palm. Alexa had maintained the apartment's modernist features, and Eleanor wasn't surprised that the ambience reflected Alexa's quirkiness and charm. She'd caught a glimpse of the loft through the front door the day she and Leo brought Alexa home. Now that she was actually inside, she could fully appreciate it.

She drew a deep breath. Alexa's subtle fragrance lingered in the air along with… What was that odour, burnt toast?

Where did she go? "Hey, this is a great apartment," Eleanor called out, tucking her bags behind the chrome coat rack.

The door slammed closed behind her with a thud. Before Eleanor could move, Alexa put her hands on her shoulders and eased her hips against

Eleanor's. The air between them was full of crackling intensity that made the hair on Eleanor's arms stand up.

"I've been crazy for the last few days." A low growl escaped from Alexa's lips. "Crazy for you." She gently cupped Eleanor's face, pressing their foreheads together. Her breath tickled Eleanor's cheeks. "Imagining you... you with Mia. All those pictures of you together in Queensland drove me insane."

It sounded as if Alexa was jealous. That was absurd. Eleanor tightened her grip around Alexa's waist. "We were working. The media focussed on us for a while, trying to drum up gossip."

Alexa scowled. "It didn't look like that to me."

"Mia is married," Eleanor said emphatically. She loosened her grip, running her hands over Alexa's hips. "Happily married. She and her wife are expecting their first child."

Alexa looked sheepish. "Okay, but you two were pretty chummy. Having a lot of fun, *together*." She curled her fingers through Eleanor's hair and tugged. "Did I mis-read the situation?"

"Believe me, you did. Mia and I are friends, that's all." Eleanor drew her hands across Alexa's abdomen up to her breasts, and her own stomach fluttered.

Alexa nibbled the sensitive skin below Eleanor's ear. "That's reassuring. No need for me to be jealous, then?" she whispered.

Eleanor was barely able to catch her breath before Alexa's mouth descended on hers. There was a determination in Alexa's kiss, and Eleanor answered with equal exuberance, just as hungry to taste her again. Alexa's mouth was luscious and sweet. Dazed with pleasure, Eleanor's world seemed to shift beneath her feet. A moan escaped her.

Alexa's lips left a fiery trail from Eleanor's chin to her ear. "God, how can you drive me crazy with just a kiss?" she hissed, tracing the outer edge of Eleanor's lobe with her tongue.

Tingling heat rushed through Eleanor's body, her response showing just how much she wanted Alexa. She'd never realised until that moment her ears were such an erogenous zone.

Alexa pulled back and held Eleanor's gaze. "Is this okay, Eleanor? You're here, and I can't keep my hands off you. I'm sorry. You wanted to talk." She raised an eyebrow. "Now?"

Eleanor shook her head and smiled. "Not now. I want you, too. I couldn't form a coherent sentence if I tried. Talking will have to wait." She curled one hand at the base of Alexa's neck and pulled her in, sweeping her tongue boldly across Alexa's, searching her mouth. Then she grabbed Alexa by the waist, spinning them around until they'd reversed positions and Alexa was pressed against the door. If she didn't slow things down a little, her knees would buckle, her bones would melt, and she'd be at Alexa's feet, a useless puddle of longing.

Alexa's green eyes widened in surprise, and her dark lashes fluttered. There was a sharp intake of breath as Eleanor skimmed her hands down the curve of her hips to the hem of the pinafore and stroked the tops of Alexa's silk-covered thighs with her thumbs. Alexa moaned loudly, the back of her head striking the door with a thump.

Eleanor swallowed. Her whole being began to tremble with an overwhelming desire to touch, to feel, to breathe in everything Alexa. "I've wanted you from the minute I met you."

"Really. What happened at the cottage, then?" Alexa quirked an eyebrow.

Eleanor wished she didn't have to revisit that moment, but she owed Alexa an explanation. She hesitated before answering, "I wasn't ready. We hardly knew each other, and I was confused. You made a point of telling me there were two bedrooms when you showed me around."

Alexa tucked a strand of her hair behind an ear. "I didn't want you to think I'd lured you there, Eleanor. Planned the whole rainstorm—"

"But you kissed me."

"And you kissed me back." Alexa took hold of her hand. "Well, there's only one bedroom here. I'm asking you again, would you like to share my bed?"

"Yes." Eleanor's voice croaked. "Please."

Alexa pulled her through the apartment. At the top of the stairs, she nudged her into the spacious bedroom diffused by early evening light. She clasped a fistful of Eleanor's shirt and pressed her against the wall, licking Eleanor's bottom lip with a quick sweep. "Does the bedroom meet with your approval?"

Eleanor glanced around and fixed her gaze on the large, sleek low-line bed adorned with a moss green quilt. She nodded. "Looks inviting," she said in a raspy whisper. She'd fantasised about this moment many times and here she was. Her heart pounded, and her stomach fluttered. She was more than ready this time.

"One moment." Alexa walked across the room, unzipped her calf-high boots and kicked them into an open doorway. She pulled the door closed. "You don't want to see my messy wardrobe." She pointed to the adjacent door with her thumb. "Here's the en suite if you need it."

"Thanks."

Alexa strode towards her, hunger in her smouldering emerald eyes holding Eleanor captive. She tugged Eleanor's shirt from her jeans, her fingers gliding over Eleanor's stomach muscles, causing them to tense.

A flush of heat from Alexa's hands rushed all along Eleanor's skin like a wildfire. "I want you, Alexa," she moistened her lips with her tongue.

With the tips of her fingers, Alexa lightly brushed Eleanor's lips. "Believe me, the want is mutual," she said, tracing Eleanor's jawline with her knuckles. "I'd really like to see all of you."

Alexa fumbled with Eleanor's shirt buttons, clutched the collar, and pulled the linen shirt over Eleanor's head. Her singlet followed, and both garments were flung somewhere on the floor. Goosebumps rose on Eleanor's skin as the cold air hit her.

"God, you are amazing," Alexa said, brushing her palms over Eleanor's bare shoulders and down her arms, leaving tingles in her wake. She hooked a finger into the top of Eleanor's pants, pulling her forward.

Eleanor sucked in a breath and met Alexa's gaze. She clasped Alexa's wrists, holding them to her chest with shaky hands. "No, it's you. You are incredibly beautiful."

Desire flickered in Alexa's eyes, and Eleanor couldn't wait anymore, reaching around Alexa's shoulders to grasp the zip on the back of the pinafore with one hand, smoothly unzipping it.

Alexa's laugh was a wondrous sound, rich and delicious. "Cheeky move," she said, sliding her tongue once again across Eleanor's bottom lip, causing another wave of heat to flush Eleanor's entire body.

Eleanor lifted Alexa's pinafore to her waist. "Let me," she whispered.

Alexa nodded her approval, and her eyes darkened.

Eleanor gripped the top of Alexa's tights, sliding them off. Alexa kicked them aside. Eleanor crouched, running her hands slowly from Alexa's slender ankles, up the graceful curve to her knees. The temptation to bury her face at the apex of Alexa's thighs made Eleanor's head spin. She stood shakily and, with trembling hands, lifted the pinafore over Alexa's head. Her smooth black camisole bra showed off the swell of generous breasts.

"Exquisite." Eleanor brushed the elastic of Alexa's matching briefs, leaving a trail of goosebumps below her abdomen.

Alexa's steady gaze was part invitation, part challenge.

Eleanor reverently caressed Alexa's breasts through the sheer fabric of her bra. She could barely stay on her feet as she took the hardening bud between her lips, pressing firmly with her tongue, and a whimpering sound escaped from deep within Alexa's throat. Eleanor felt her senses unfold, opening like petals in the sunshine.

Alexa pushed Eleanor backwards until her calves hit the side of the bed and she sat down. "Still too many clothes," Alexa said, kneeling at her feet, tugging off Eleanor's shoes.

Alexa effortlessly flicked open the silver belt buckle, loosened Eleanor's jeans, and pressed Eleanor back onto the bed, quickly peeling off her remaining clothes, tossing them in the air.

Eleanor laughed, amused by Alexa's playful assertiveness. She pushed herself up on her elbows and grinned up at Alexa.

Alexa licked her lips. "Oh my. This is how I imagined you. So perfect." She quickly shed her undergarments.

The sight of Alexa naked had Eleanor light-headed and reaching for her. "Come here." Her own voice was unrecognisable. "*Please*."

With a provocative smile, Alexa placed her hands on either side of Eleanor's thighs. Eleanor held her breath as tension coiled deep within her. Alexa's glazed eyes raked over Eleanor before she lowered her body. Eleanor instinctively opened her legs, and Alexa settled between them.

The air sizzled with the heat of their connection, and Eleanor gasped at the sensation overload. Too quick. She wanted to slow things down. With one hand on Alexa's shoulder, she rolled them both over until Alexa was flat on her back beneath her.

Alexa lifted her head. "You're good at that, but I can still do this." She covered Eleanor's breast with her mouth, and a warm tingling ache spread to her centre.

"Alexa." Eleanor huffed out a shallow breath.

"Yes, Eleanor?"

"Please…stop. I mean, don't…" Eleanor moaned with pleasure. "I can't think straight."

Alexa gave a husky laugh. "Considering what we're doing, I'm very lucky you feel that way." She cupped Eleanor's breast, kneading it lightly. "Do you want me to stop?"

Eleanor bit down on her lower lip. "No, please don't."

Alexa clasped Eleanor's hips and expeditiously reversed their positions again. "Good. I've only just started." Alexa crawled down, her lips and hands travelling along Eleanor's body. "You're so sweet. Warm…golden… like sunshine." The vibration of Alexa's lips against her skin made Eleanor squirm.

She pushed her head back into the pillows. "That feels so good. So damn good." How did Alexa already know all her sensitive spots? Eleanor's fingers curled desperately in the sheets as Alexa's mouth lingered so close to her centre. She didn't have long to wait before the first brush of Alexa's fingers set a perfect rhythm. Seconds later, when Alexa's tongue found her, swiping slowly through her heat, Eleanor's hips arched off the bed, and she tumbled into sweet oblivion.

Alexa grinned lazily and flopped across the bed. It was a complete shambles. The dove grey sheets were pulled from their moorings. Lots of pillows were strewn around the room, like the aftermath of a pillow fight. She peered over the edge of the mattress. The green comforter lay in a heap with their discarded clothes. Eleanor's girl-shorts hung off the edge of the dresser where Alexa had tossed them. Incredibly, Eleanor still lay naked in her bed. Alexa sighed with contentment.

She turned her head to face the sleeping woman beside her, curling her hand around Eleanor's bicep, relishing the incredible feeling of Eleanor's muscles beneath her fingers. Heat radiated along Alexa's arm, and her skin tingled.

Recalling her wondrous response to Eleanor's touch, while they'd pleasured each other for hours, Alexa shuddered. Eleanor's boundless energy could have lit up the entire suburb. With the taste of Eleanor still on her lips, sweet and heady, Alexa inched closer to feel the length of her warm body, and desire flared. Alexa was ready to experience all of that magic again.

Usually, when Alexa dated someone, she had the urge to get up and run home to her own bed after sex. When she shared her own bed, she'd end up edgy and uncomfortable. Not now. Not with Eleanor. Alexa wanted Eleanor to stay.

Eleanor was lying on her side, one hand tucked under her chin. Alexa reached out and combed her fingers through the silky strands of Eleanor's hair. It couldn't hurt to lay here for a few minutes…or five. Eleanor looked so at peace and youthful, with flushed skin, and long lashes fanned across her cheeks. Alexa succumbed to the soft tug of longing and tightened her hold around Eleanor's narrow waist.

She trailed a finger along Eleanor's lean shoulder, inching the sheet down to her slightly flared hip, where a tiny black outline of a camera was inked.

Eleanor's eyelashes fluttered open. "I was twenty-two and got very drunk with a few friends from the newspaper." Her voice was a little husky. "Thankfully, I wasn't crazy enough to get a tattoo I'd regret for the rest of my life."

Alexa tickled her side with a light caress. "Oh, you mean like a huge curling dragon spiralling your torso? Or your girlfriend's name around your bicep? I mean your girlfriend then." She leaned over and kissed the indelible design, the only visible marking on Eleanor's otherwise unblemished skin.

"That would have been Terpsichore." Eleanor chuckled.

Alexa searched her memory. "Ahh, I think that's the Greek muse of poetry and dance. Was her nickname Topsy Terpi?"

Eleanor giggled. "She really loved dramatics, just like her namesake."

Alexa cleared her throat. "Speaking of stagy women…did you enjoy your time in Queensland with the *beautiful people*?" Alexa knew her tone hung somewhere between amused and mocking.

"You're wicked." Eleanor pulled the tangled sheet from around Alexa's legs and nudged her onto her back. She cupped Alexa's face gently in her hands. "And *you* are beyond beautiful."

Alexa sighed, putting her arms around Eleanor's shoulders, and wrapped her legs around her tightly, squeezing Eleanor's hips with her thighs. Unlike earlier, when they'd devoured each other at a ravenous, frantic pace, this time Eleanor moved against Alexa in a deliberately slow, seductive dance.

She squeezed her eyes shut as Eleanor cupped her breast with her hand and gently rolled Alexa's nipple between her fingers. When Eleanor's mouth covered Alexa's breast, she buried her face into the crook of Eleanor's neck, trying to slow the moment and lower the pace of her escalating heartbeat.

Alexa arched her back in anticipation and instinctively pushed against Eleanor until she moved her hand between Alexa's thighs, and her fingers stroked Alexa's tender flesh and slid inside. Alexa's body responded in a flash to Eleanor's touch, and her breathing hitched. She clenched the sheet in her fist as her legs began to shake, and she writhed under the exquisite pressure for several incredible moments. Alexa moaned loudly as her orgasm engulfed her, and she finally surrendered to the waves of pleasure that exploded through her body.

After a few minutes, Eleanor gently dropped a kiss on her temple and Alexa's breathing slowed.

"Lucky me," Eleanor said. Her voice was little more than a whisper.

Alexa wrapped an arm around Eleanor. *Lucky me.* The scent of Eleanor's hair, her warm breath fluttering against Alexa's neck and Eleanor's hand curled in the centre of Alexa's chest—felt natural. Alexa was contented and for now, just being here together, was all she needed.

After a while, Eleanor dozed off again, and Alexa eased herself out of her arms and snuck off to use the bathroom. When her bare feet hit the chilly tiles, she realised she'd forgotten to switch on the central heating. She grabbed her robe and headed downstairs to turn it on making sure to collect a jug of water on her way back through the kitchen so she could refill their glasses.

When she returned, Alexa smiled at the sight of the still-sleeping woman, bathed in a hint of early morning light. She topped up the glasses on the side table, pulled the sheet back, and slid back into bed. Wrapping her arms around Eleanor, she snuggled in once again and pressed her chilled feet against Eleanor's warm calf.

Eleanor shifted in her arms, trailed her hand over Alexa's silk robe, and asked in a croaky voice, "Are you cold?"

"A little. It cools off in this cavernous space overnight. I forgot to switch the heater on."

"Hey, I can warm you up." Eleanor wrapped her arms around Alexa and pressed a delicate kiss on her lips. "Are you okay?" she asked, blinking those amazingly broody dark eyes.

Alexa nodded. "Hmm…I am." She squeezed her eyes shut. There would be time later to examine the tender emotions that had surfaced each time Eleanor had brought her to an earth-moving orgasm. And the overwhelming joy and protectiveness that washed over her when Eleanor had shuddered in pleasure under her touch.

Alexa wasn't just wildly attracted to Eleanor; she cared about her, and that was okay. But the increasing desire to be around Eleanor, to include her in her plans, was dangerous and left Alexa exposed.

"I won't be able to see you for the next couple of days," Eleanor said.

Could Eleanor read her mind? Alexa slowly opened her eyes. No. She saw the flicker of disappointment on Eleanor's face. The longing in her eyes. It was probably a good idea to put a bit of distance between them. "I'll be busy at work the rest of the week, anyway."

"Of course." Eleanor sat up against the pillows and was quiet for a moment, then tugged the sheet up over her breasts. "Mum's in Sydney for work, and I promised to hang around at home to take Dad to rehab and keep him company in the evenings. You mentioned about doing something on the weekend?"

Alexa regretted sounding snappy earlier. In a soothing voice, she said, "I did. Can you come to Chewton with me on Saturday? Actually, through to Monday? I've made an appointment with a historian in Castlemaine and, on Saturday night, there's a friend's gig. The girls are coming, too." She pushed Eleanor's hair back from her face. "We haven't found all the locations of Helen's slides yet. What do you think?"

"Okay," Eleanor said quietly. "I'd love to. Count me in." Her stomach rumbled loudly, and her face flushed. "I hate airplane food. It's a long time since I ate."

"And we skipped dinner altogether." Alexa wiggled her eyebrows. "What can I make you?"

"I'd be happy with toast. I'd even eat it burnt."

Alexa looked at her quizzically. Eleanor must have a good sense of smell to know that she'd burnt her breakfast in her haste to catch the tram and get to work on time. "I'm sure we can do better than that. How about leftover lasagne?"

Eleanor moaned. "Yum, yes please."

"There's also lots of fruit and a tub of Bush Honey ice cream in the freezer." Alexa poked Eleanor gently in the ribs.

Eleanor's eyes widened, and she licked her lips.

Alexa grabbed Eleanor's hand. "Come with me. I can't have you fainting."

Chapter 21

Heavenly gates

A CAR HORN TOOTED, PULLING Alexa out of her trance-like state. She hadn't been able to get Eleanor out of her mind—not that she wanted to—and found herself constantly reliving their amazing time together at the loft. When had the lights changed to green? She waved her hand out of the window in apology. "Sorry," she called, telling herself to keep her eyes on the road and concentrate.

Alexa had never known three days to pass so slowly. The nights were worse. When she had slipped into bed, the essence of Eleanor lingered between the sheets, tormenting her. She had to bury her face in her pillow to get any sleep.

Eleanor had left the loft on Wednesday morning around seven thirty, insisting she travel home in an Uber so Alexa wouldn't be late for work. They'd polished off a rather unconventional breakfast and fed each other spoonfuls of wickedly delicious honey ice cream.

Alexa shivered, recalling the way Eleanor had licked the melted ice cream that had dribbled on her chin and between her breasts, starting another bout of love making, with Alexa on the kitchen table. Eleanor was certainly creative. Alexa wound down the window and fanned herself with her hand.

Crossing the Yarra River at Bridge Road was like entering a different world. Wide leafy streets with some classy homes on huge lots with impressively landscaped gardens. Hawthorn was one of the suburbs where Melbourne's well-to-do had retreated in the wake of the gold rush.

Alexa had always lived in inner-city higher density neighbourhoods, where weekend markets, cafes, and restaurants were all within walking distance. The houses here were so far apart, you could imagine not meeting a neighbour for a week. How lonely that would be. Not like her own community where it was impossible to avoid running into neighbours and stopping for a chat.

Did it matter that Eleanor's privileged upbringing was different from Alexa's own? Alexa hoped not.

She parked alongside the two-metre high stone fence outside number eighty-three Oxford Avenue and peered curiously through the open iron gates and down a tree-lined driveway. Eleanor's parents were partners in a prominent Melbourne law firm established by Eleanor's maternal great-grandfather. Alexa wondered if the double storey Victorian mansion had been passed along the generations. Old money. Alexa tapped the leather steering wheel. Not that it mattered. Eleanor was down to earth and altruistic. She didn't seem affected by the wealth she'd apparently grown up with.

Alexa checked herself in the rear-view mirror and nervously tucked a strand of hair behind her ear. Taking a few deep breaths, she pushed open the car door. She was eager to see Eleanor again, but now that she was here, outside her parents' house, she felt queasy.

Inside the gate lay a generously spread-out garden, one corner shaded by a large elm tree. Had Eleanor scaled those majestic branches as a child? She was lucky to have grown up surrounded by flowers, shrubs, and trees. Her own parkland.

As a child, Alexa would meet her friends in the local public gardens, and of course, there were mountains of blooms to enjoy at her mother's florist shop. Maybe Alexa would have enjoyed a private adventure playground like this, but not at the expense of the freedom to roam with the gang of local kids.

The Heysens' garden was already rich with the colour and the perfume of spring—the flower beds a riot of varying hues. A rhythmic chopping and a slightly off-tune humming drew her attention to a neatly trimmed English box hedge.

Spotting a wide-brimmed straw hat bobbing up and down, Alexa peeked around the hedge. The gumboot-wearing gardener had her back to

Alexa as she scooped up a pile of cuttings, dumping them into an already overflowing wheelbarrow.

Alexa nearly jumped out of her skin when a gloved hand reached backwards, and a women's voice demanded, "Don't sneak up on me, Eleanor. Pass me my water bottle."

Alexa picked up the bottle that lay on the lawn by her feet. "Here you are."

The woman pushed back on her heels and turned her head. Her eyes widened in surprise. "You're not Eleanor."

"I'm sorry." Alexa stood to attention and held out the bottle. "The gate was open, and Eleanor told me to come straight to the studio, but I was distracted by this gorgeous garden."

The woman stood gracefully, pulling off her gloves. She flung them into the wheelbarrow and removed her hat, releasing a tumble of tawny brown curls. "Ah, you must be Alexa." She smiled, reached for her bottle, tucked it under her arm, and held out her hand. "I'm Sarah Heysen. The studio has its own street entrance off the lane on the right side of the gate."

Alexa took Sarah's hand and shook it firmly. "I am Alexa. Yes, Eleanor told me about the lane, but I was drawn into your garden. It is lovely to meet you, Mrs Heysen."

Sarah gave her an appraising look. "Katherine was right. You are a very pretty woman." She put her head to one side. "Actually, you're rather beautiful."

Alexa lowered her eyes as a flush crept across her cheeks. She couldn't tell from Sarah's expression if the comment was meant as a compliment or not.

Eleanor's mother was attractive. She wore little makeup and her light-olive skin, like her daughter's, had a vibrant, healthy glow. Eleanor was taller and more slender, but her straight nose and her eyes—those intense deep brown eyes—were definitely inherited from her mother.

The toot of a horn drew their attention and thankfully broke the awkward moment. Alexa turned to see a Triumph Spitfire glide down the driveway.

"Here's Harold," Sarah said. "He nicked down to the shops. I believe we were out of coffee."

The car was a brilliant, British racing-green.

The driver waved. At a quick glance, his thick grey hair and wide grin reminded Alexa of a younger version of that Australian actor who played 007 in the sixties. Eleanor had told her the two of them were taking her father's car away for the weekend. Surely not this car?

"Come and meet Harold. He finds any excuse to escape from his minders." Just for a second, Sarah's mask was gone, and affection for her husband shone clearly in her eyes. She brushed the soil from her apron and wiped her brow with the back of her hand.

Although Sarah Heysen didn't appear to be the formidable matriarch that Eleanor had described, Alexa would be careful what she said and how she behaved around her, especially when Eleanor turned up.

"I gather your car is parked on the street," Sarah said in a sonorous voice. "There will be room for your vehicle in the garage once Harold manoeuvres things about and brings out the SUV for your trip."

Well, that answered Alexa's question. Her shoulders dropped. They wouldn't be driving the Spitfire this weekend. If Eleanor's father was anything at all like Alexa, he'd trust very few people with his classic car.

Harold walked towards them. "Alexa, I presume." He offered his hand. "It's a pleasure to meet you. Eleanor's told me all about you."

Alexa gulped. Not *everything,* she hoped. She pulled herself to her full height, smiled, and clasped his hand. "A pleasure to meet you, too, Mr Heysen. You have an awesome car."

A brown paper bag was tucked in the crook of his arm, and the faint aroma of dark roasted coffee wafted through the air. "Thank you. Please, call me Harold," he said. "I spied your 404 coupé out front. Very nice. Yours is French, mine is British, but they're both styled by the Italians."

"Is it a Mark II?" Alexa appreciated designers who used flowing lines and elegant shapes—classic cars were the best.

"Yes. Spitfire 1965. Painstakingly restored. Wired wheels and twin exhausts. She can still reach ninety-six miles per hour." He quickly glanced at his wife. "Not that I have ever pushed that speed, of course," he said with a charming grin. "Give me a minute, and we'll park your little beauty safely in the garage." He looked up at the blue sky and shrugged. "The weather can be unpredictable in spring. As you know."

Alexa tapped the toe of her high-top sneaker in the lush lawn. She already liked Harold; after all, they had things in common. They both appreciated classic cars and good coffee. And he had a sense of humour.

Sarah removed her apron and folded it across the wheelbarrow handle. "Darling, don't forget I have to duck into the office this afternoon."

"I'll move the BMW forward and park Alexa's firecracker in the back." He wriggled his eyebrows. "It will be great for Eleanor to get away and to spend time with friends. Lovely spot, the goldfields region."

"When will you and Eleanor return?" Sarah squinted, glancing briefly towards an iron gate and paved pathway that most likely led to Eleanor's studio. "Anyway, where is that girl?"

"If all goes well, around dinner time Monday," Alexa replied to the first question. As for where Eleanor was, she didn't have an answer.

"Good, I'll make sure to be home from the office. You'll be able to join us for supper. At least the SUV isn't likely to spring a leak." Sarah's dark eyebrows slanted in a frown.

Alexa covered her embarrassment by meeting Sarah's gaze with a bright one of her own. "Yes, indeed."

Harold said, "I'm fascinated to hear what else you two discover about those negatives."

"Me too—"

Out of the corner of her eye, Alexa glimpsed Eleanor striding across the lawn, and suddenly she was there beside her.

Alexa grinned; she couldn't help herself.

Eleanor looked relaxed, wearing low-riding loose cargo pants and a cropped, white long-sleeved T-shirt revealing an alluring smidgen of midriff. She was bouncing up and down on her toes like a spring.

Alexa bit her bottom lip, but a soft sigh escaped anyway.

"Don't wait on us for dinner on Monday, Mum." Eleanor turned to Alexa for confirmation. "I don't know what the traffic will be like, and I'm not used to driving the Skoda on country roads. Best to take it easy, I guess." She turned back and gave her father a half shrug.

"An excellent idea, sweetheart." He smiled at Eleanor affectionately. "It's a lot more powerful than my old Triumph."

"I'd certainly like a drive in the Spitfire someday." Alexa glanced quickly at Eleanor who winked at her.

Harold chuckled at Alexa. "I'd be happy for you to visit us again, and we can take it for a run." He squeezed Eleanor's shoulder. "The Skoda is watertight, much more reliable, very comfortable, and has plenty of safety features. A necessity if my darling daughter is driving." He walked over to his wife and linked his arm through hers. "Sarah, let's not delay the girls' departure any longer. They have places to be and things to uncover."

Sarah pursed her lips and raised an eyebrow. "Of course, the negatives." She looked directly at Alexa. "A lot of time has been spent on those *negatives* already."

"Oh, darling, if you had the time, you'd love to be getting away for the weekend, unravelling a puzzle or two." He patted Sarah's hand and grinned at Alexa. "Anyway, thank you for your expertise, helping us learn more about the contents of Helen's trunk."

"You're welcome," Alexa replied. "I'm glad to assist."

She really did want to help Eleanor learn why Helen was in possession of the negatives, why they'd been separated from the collection and how they'd ended up in China. But that wasn't the only reason she was excited about the weekend. The thought of private time with Eleanor had Alexa's body thrumming with energy. She almost gave in to an urge to take Eleanor's hand. Instead she shoved her hands in her pockets.

"Nell, Alexa and I will shuffle the cars and park the coupé out of the weather while you grab your gear," Harold said.

"Thanks, Dad." Eleanor took a step beside Alexa, brushing Alexa's arm with her hand. "Do you want to get going now, or would you like to see the studio first?" The warmth of her voice echoed in her smile.

Alexa didn't think that was a good idea. Who knew how long they'd be waylaid? If she was alone with Eleanor, she'd want to tear off her clothes and take her to bed. She gulped. But she'd definitely like to see Eleanor's studio another time. "Actually, we should probably head out," she said. "We have an appointment with the historian at the Chewton Town Hall. She's making a special effort to meet us."

Eleanor smiled acquiescence. "That's great. I'll be right back."

"Alexa, I hope you two have an enjoyable weekend. Be safe. Be careful." Sarah gave Alexa a pointed stare and set off in Eleanor's direction.

What instructions would Sarah have for her daughter? Alexa rubbed the back of her neck. She'd probably be pointing out all the dangers of having a fling with someone like Alexa.

Harold gave Alexa a quick tour of the Skoda's features. His friendly, easy going nature put Alexa at ease immediately. Under his guidance, she carefully drove the Skoda out of the garage, and Harold indicated where to park with a sweeping hand motion. He tapped on the window, and she lowered it. "I'll go inside and check what's keeping Nell," he said. "Not like her to take so long. I'm sure she's been ready and waiting for hours. I'll bet her mother is giving her last-minute instructions." He chuckled and shook his head. "Enjoy yourselves. And another thing; do keep an eye on her speed."

She watched Eleanor's father trudge towards the house. Despite his joviality, he looked tired.

Alexa ran her hands over the smooth curves and lines of the dashboard, recalling that Harold called this the cockpit. There was plenty of room for Alexa to stretch out her long legs. She scratched her forehead. What did he mean by keep an eye on Eleanor's speed? Her throat went dry at the thought of Eleanor being unsafe on the road. If Alexa stayed put in the driver's seat, would Eleanor agree to be the passenger? Not likely.

There was so much Alexa *didn't* know about Eleanor. They'd slept together, and now Alexa had met the parents. These were big developments, yet Alexa still didn't know what Eleanor's plans were for the future, after her father recovered. An entire weekend together would be a test of their growing connection and where it may lead. Alexa needed to be *cautiously* excited. There was some truth to what Sarah had said.

It seemed their paths were destined to cross. How bizarre that their families' pasts were entangled. But was this strange connection reason enough for Alexa to let down her defences? Not entirely.

The back door on the driver's side popped open, and Alexa swivelled around. "You're back."

"Sorry to keep you waiting," Eleanor huffed. "It was my mother with last-minute orders. You'd hardly think I'm thirty-six and have lived overseas for more than ten years."

Obviously, Eleanor had been given a talking to by her mother. Alexa could only hope that Sarah Heysen had *something* favourable to say about her.

Eleanor dumped her overnight bag and fancy leather camera pack onto the back seat beside Alexa's stuff. Looking up, she stared at Alexa with wide eyes. "Hey, why are you sitting there? I'm the driver today. I need the practice."

Recalling Harold's warning, Alexa laughed uncertainly. "Just keeping the seat warm." She jumped out, leaning her hip against the open door. "Hop in then, driver."

Eleanor climbed in. "That's better."

Alexa raced around the back of the SUV, and when she reached the passenger door, Eleanor had already opened it for her.

"Thanks," Alexa said, sliding in. She glanced up at the house warily to ensure they weren't being watched before she leaned towards Eleanor.

Eleanor tilted her head to one side. "Ready to go?" Her eyes bore into Alexa's, expectant and tender.

"Give me a second." Alexa cupped a hand gently around Eleanor's neck and pulled her close. "Let me say hello properly," she murmured against her lips.

Brushing her fingers along Alexa's jaw, Eleanor answered with a smile. "I've missed you."

Alexa clasped her hands on either side of Eleanor's face. She watched as Eleanor's dark eyes fluttered and her pupils dilated. Alexa leaned in, and time seemed to stand still when their mouths met and Eleanor parted her lips. She was warm, sweet, and delicious. At the taste of her, Alexa's heart sped up and her senses began to unfurl like a flower bud at the touch of the morning sun.

"Damn, Eleanor. Now I wish you *had* taken me to the studio," Alexa said when they finally parted, and she found herself gazing into Eleanor's dreamy eyes.

"You do realise there are cameras fixed to the front of the garage." Eleanor grinned wickedly.

"You're joking, right?" Alexa nudged her in the ribs.

Eleanor laughed, rubbing her side. "Don't worry. They're not turned on, I think. Anyway, it wouldn't be the first time I've been caught making out with a girlfriend in the driveway."

Alexa squeezed her eyes shut.

"I'm sorry. Forget I said that." Eleanor covered her mouth with her hand.

What was she sorry about? Mentioning girlfriends or implying that she and Alexa were girlfriends—then retracting her words? Alexa was unexpectedly deflated on both counts.

Eleanor adjusted her seat belt. "Are you ready for take-off?" She stared at the fancy instrument panel.

"Are you doing a flight check?" Alexa kept her tone light. "You have driven this car before, haven't you? Your father said you've been chauffeuring him around town."

"Uh-huh, just to his follow-up appointments and rehab."

Exhaling loudly, Alexa swallowed her concern. "Okay, you should know your way around it, then."

"I drove Dad across town to St Kilda last week, and he said I handled it like a rally driver." Eleanor flicked an imaginary speck of dust from her shoulder.

Alexa gulped and tugged her seat belt to check it would engage if necessary.

"Relax, don't worry." Eleanor pulled out of the driveway with a rapid look to the left and then to the right.

Alexa attempted to loosen up, stretching out her legs and resting back in the comfy car seat. She glanced over to Eleanor, who looked confident enough in her aviator sunglasses with her gaze fixed on the road. She wished she could at least get a hint at what Eleanor was thinking, but the dark lenses of her sunglasses hid her expressive eyes.

A lot of things had changed since they were at the cottage the first time. What were Eleanor's expectations of *this* weekend? Alexa smiled to herself. One thing was certain: they wouldn't be sleeping in separate bedrooms.

"So, we're off to the cottage again," Eleanor stated the obvious, glancing quickly over to Alexa.

The SUV swerved as she changed lanes and came to an abrupt stop at the red light.

Alexa reached out, bracing against the dashboard. Yep, off to the cottage. That was if they made it to Chewton in one piece. "I guess you've driven in many countries, different situations all over the world?" she asked, at least comforted by that thought.

"Oh no, not much. It's better to have a local driver who knows the conditions," Eleanor declared.

When the lights changed, she accelerated in jerky bursts and moved out onto the freeway. Then the open road stretched out before them, and Eleanor eased her grip on the steering wheel. The speedometer needle levelled to a more even hundred kilometres per hour, and Alexa relaxed her shoulders.

"Is it okay to ask you about William?"

"Ah, *that* can of worms." Alexa sighed.

"We don't have to talk about it, if you'd rather not."

"I do want to tell you. It's quite a story," Alexa said. After all that had happened between them, she was ready to share the details with Eleanor. Alexa conceded that if it hadn't been for Eleanor's actions, she and her grandmother may never have started the conversation, and Alexa wouldn't have learnt about her ancestors. She owed Eleanor a debt of gratitude.

"Well, thanks to your revelation, I had fascinating talk with Gran. Actually, what she told me nearly blew me away."

Eleanor sat upright, her knuckles white against the steering wheel. "I'm sorry, Alexa. I didn't mean to upset either of you." Her voice was strained.

"I know you didn't." Alexa squeezed Eleanor's leg, quickly withdrawing her hand as Eleanor's thigh muscles tensed. She glanced out the window. "You know, at first, I couldn't comprehend why Gran would keep something so important a secret. A million things went through my mind. I felt cheated and hurt."

"I shouldn't—"

"Shh… It's not that," Alexa said. "I was upset with my grandmother. Can you believe I thought that Gran was embarrassed she was a quarter Chinese? Thank goodness I was wrong." She pressed her palms to her eyes. "Gran and her parents were blackmailed by her mother's family. She was forced to keep the secret to protect her own family."

"Did you say she was blackmailed? How?" Eleanor put her foot on the brake, slowing the car to a crawl. "Oh, crap, I think we just took a wrong turn."

Alexa looked over her shoulder. "Yes, you did. And yes, Gran was," she said, turning back to Eleanor. "On second thoughts, I don't think we should talk about this while you're driving. I'll tell you the whole story when we stop for coffee in Woodend, now we are heading that way. No point turning back. We still have plenty of time before our meeting with Phyllis."

"Well, if you're sure. Anyway, I could use a coffee." Eleanor glanced quickly at Alexa and then back to the road. "Can I convince you I totally planned to take the wrong turn?"

Alexa grinned. "I'll drive if you want me to."

"No, I'm fine, really. It's fun driving the SUV." Eleanor accelerated, and the Skoda took off, nudging over the one-hundred-kilometre speed limit again. "I'm glad we have this for the weekend. Dad was right; the diesel turbo thingy has loads of power."

As they whizzed along the road, Alexa took a calming breath. Eleanor wasn't driving overly fast, but just in case, she hoped there weren't any hidden speed cameras. *Dad* would not be over the moon when a hefty fine arrived in the mail.

Half an hour later, at the Woodend café, Alexa drained the last of her coffee and pushed aside the glass.

Eleanor had her arms stretched across the outdoor table and her hands clenched together, exposing a spattering of pale freckles across her knuckles. She splayed her fingers, gave them a little shake, rolled her shoulders, and reached for Alexa's hand.

Alexa gave her a lopsided smile.

Gazing at her with a serious expression, Eleanor gently squeezed Alexa's fingers. "*God*, what a story; thank you for sharing it with me. So that's why Grace had to keep your Chinese heritage a secret. It was about the accusation against Mei-Li and the Hamptons' insistence that it was buried. You must be desperate to know the full story about your great-great grandmother."

"Yes, I am." Now that Alexa had told Eleanor everything Gran had revealed, the tension in her shoulders released. She curled her fingers around Eleanor's hand. She trusted her.

"I'm here for you." Eleanor smiled reassuringly. "What next?"

"Phyllis, the specialist in Chinese settlement, has a couple of leads about Mei-Li's trial. You don't mind, do you?"

Eleanor's big brown eyes were wide with interest. "Of course not. Are you okay?"

Alexa shrugged. "On one hand, I'm bursting with curiosity to explore my heritage, but I'm also reluctant. Finding out that Mei-Li was accused of murder, well, it is a big deal. Shocking. And what if we find out she *was* responsible for that women's death? I would have to tell Gran. I don't know if I can do that."

"You said the case was dismissed for lack of evidence." Eleanor tilted her head and spoke softly, "There may be a positive outcome, and you'd help Grace feel at peace."

"Let's hope so." Alexa smiled.

She squeezed Eleanor's hand, gazing into her eyes as they shared a moment of intimacy, before Eleanor let go of Alexa's hand and swung her legs over the bench seat, jumping to her feet. "I'll be right back," she said, heading inside the café.

Alexa smiled. Eleanor was just the right blend of shy and sweet. Caring and considerate. Seemingly unaware of her attractiveness, though not entirely lacking in self-confidence. She was definitely more comfortable with expressing her feelings than Alexa herself was.

Alexa propped her head on her hand. She should have thought this through a little more. *Girlfriend.* Perhaps just a slip of the tongue, but was that how Eleanor thought of them? After Tuesday night, there was no doubt they were more than friends. But had it been a rash decision to invite Eleanor away for the entire weekend, three days and two nights?

Alexa gathered her hair away from her face and let it fall back on her shoulders. Why hadn't she asked Eleanor about her future plans? Probably because she didn't want to appear needy. She was ashamed that, in the past, any sign of neediness in her girlfriends had triggered her flight response. Really, she'd have no one else to blame if Eleanor was biding her time with Alexa and took off on assignment or returned to London where she'd based her career for many years. Alexa had plenty of time to talk to her about it this weekend.

The moment of self-derision was broken by the jingling of car keys.

"Hey, ready to get on the road?" Eleanor's bright eyes and warm smile chased away the cloud of doubt for the time being.

Alexa smiled back. "Yep. But this time, my eyes will be on the road signs, so you don't take any more wrong turns." Alexa sprung to her feet. She tapped Eleanor's fancy watch. "Can't be late for our first appointment, the one with the historian."

"And what is our second appointment?" Eleanor exchanged a knowing look with Alexa.

Alexa arched an eyebrow. "I have plans for you."

"I hope they fit in with my plans for you."

Chapter 22

Chinese odds

"When you uncover secrets from the past, the revelations are not always pleasant." Phyllis reached inside her embroidered tote bag and pulled out a portfolio.

Eleanor cast a quick glance towards Alexa to gauge her reaction to the historian's statement. Alexa was sitting on the edge of her chair, her hands tightly clasped together on the table.

Phyllis continued, "We've found newspaper articles relating to the proceedings of the 1926 Castlemaine Court case that shed some light on the mystery surrounding your great-great-grandmother Mei-Li Brown, née Kwan." She tapped her freshly polished plum-coloured fingernails on the portfolio. "It's not a great deal, Alexa, but it's a start on that journey to seek the truth for you and your family." She slid into a chair across the table, pulled a sheet of paper from the portfolio, and laid it in front of them. "Let's see what we have here."

Eleanor reached under the table to lay her hand reassuringly on Alexa's leg.

Alexa squeezed her hand tightly. Her other hand swept up to her chest, and she pressed there as though to calm herself. "I'm grateful for your help, Phyllis."

"That's what we're here for." Phyllis nodded, pointing at the photocopied page. "This is a newspaper clipping from The Forrest Creek Mail, dated 10 June, 1926."

Phyllis presented the information methodically and spoke in a slow, rather ponderous manner. Eleanor realised the meeting may take a while, but it would be worth it for Alexa to find out more about her ancestors.

Alexa put on her glasses and began reading,

Mrs Mei-Li Brown, a Chinese herbalist practising under the name of Mei-Li Kwan, was arrested today under suspicion for the manslaughter of Mrs Edith Foster. Mrs Foster is said to have died from an accumulative allergic reaction to a mixture of herbs and potions prescribed by the Chinese quack—

Alexa lifted her head. "Typical." She continued,

...over a course of three weeks' treatment.

Eleanor scowled. "Talk about racist," she whispered under her breath.

Mrs Foster was the young wife of prominent Castlemaine hotelier Perceval Foster, who is now left with the burden of caring for their three-year-old daughter with no family assistance in Australia.

Alexa cleared her throat.

The grieving husband pleads with the community to support him and put the charlatan behind bars.

"Charlatan. Really?" Eleanor clenched her fists at the biased tone of the article.

"Indeed, racism ran rampant at the time," Phyllis said. "Chinese traditional medicine has been part of our Australian heritage since the gold-rush era, and on the whole, Chinese herbalists were still well respected in the 1920s, especially in Victoria."

"Clearly not by everyone." Alexa rolled her shoulders. "What happened to Perceval Foster and his daughter?"

Phyllis's forehead creased into a frown. "Unfortunately, I can't help you with that; however, I have summarised the main points of the trial as recorded in the articles."

With a flash of concern about what might be revealed, Eleanor stroked Alexa's knee and shuffled her chair closer until their thighs touched.

"Please, go ahead, Phyllis," Alexa said.

"Right-ho, then. According to Foster's recorded testimony, he and his wife came by ship to Victoria where he managed an American-financed hotel just outside Castlemaine."

"Did he mention any signs of illness before they travelled?" Eleanor asked curiously.

"It doesn't say. But after leaving America, Edith worked at home caring for their young daughter and keeping the books for her husband."

"I see," Alexa said quietly.

Phyllis continued, "When Edith first visited Mei-Li Kwan, she complained of sore teeth and gums with abscesses forming in her mouth, a sore throat, and aching limbs."

Eleanor wondered if they could be symptoms of a virus. She watched Alexa silently drum her fingers on the table as they waited while Phyllis extracted another page from the portfolio.

"Mei-Li prescribed *Dang Gui*," Phyllis said. "It's a common herb known as Angelica, and was added to a bone stock of beef or lamb to treat her patient's anaemia. She believed, at first, that Edith suffered from internal disharmony involving the kidneys and stomach, so she prepared a herbal mixture to be boiled up with water and used as a mouth wash every day."

"Angelica." Alexa rubbed her forehead.

Phyllis nodded. "Yes, otherwise known as female ginseng."

"I'm sure there is some growing near the compost heap at the cottage. Mum wrote something about it in her notebook," Alexa said to Eleanor. "A fragrant plant with small white flowers. It doesn't sound dangerous, does it?" Alexa tilted her head to one side, as if struggling with the information.

Phyllis shook her head. "Mei-Li states firmly that when Edith returned to the dispensary three days later, she was upset because her husband wouldn't allow her to prepare the remedy at home. He said the odour was repulsive. So, she suggested Edith visit her dispensary each day for the remedy. Despite daily visits, the woman's health continued to decline. She became frailer. Although by now Mei-Li was sure the illness was caused by some kind of poison, but she could not determine the exact one."

"What about the husband? Isn't the husband often the first suspect?" Eleanor shook her head, heart aching at what she was hearing. "Did the newspapers cast any suspicion on him?"

Alexa huffed. "I doubt it. Of course, the courts would have sided with the grieving husband, now with a motherless child to care for." She tossed her hair out of her eyes.

"This newspaper article says that Foster visited Mei-Li and was furious," Phyllis explained, turning to the next page she'd marked. "He said that Edith had fallen, broken her hip and leg, and was in hospital. He'd found out about the secret visits to take the 'foreign muck' and blamed the Chinese charlatan for the fall. He prohibited Mei-Li from visiting his wife in hospital. Edith died a few days later from pneumonia." She looked up from the paper with a sad expression. "Mei-Li was arrested, accused of poisoning Edith Foster, and charged with manslaughter."

"Sounds like they were too ready to blame my great-great-grandmother," Alexa said picking up a small glass paperweight from the table and turning it repeatedly in her fingers. "By the 1920s, Melbourne had a substantial Chinese population and their businesses were thriving, but it was still rare for Chinese women to be allowed into the country. Can you believe it was to prevent their children from being born in Australia? How difficult it must have been for Mei-Li to practise as a herbalist in country Victoria." She placed the paperweight heavily on the table. "I don't believe the court would have treated her fairly at all."

Eleanor gently squeezed Alexa's knee.

"I know it's hardly a consolation, but many of Mei-Li's patients testified to her honesty and the positive effects of her treatments."

"Unfortunately, by then her reputation had been destroyed. She lost everything." Alexa raised her voice and thumped the table. "Even after she was released, the scandal continued to take its toll. Her husband, her home, her business. Her good name. Gone!"

Seeing Alexa's anxious expression and her hunched shoulders, Eleanor took her hand and covered it with her own, wanting to give comfort.

"I'm so sorry, Alexa, for what your great-great-grandmother suffered." Phyllis settled back in her chair. "In those days, especially in small townships, there was a lot of anti-Chinese sentiment."

"Can you tell us any more about Mei-Li's family?" Eleanor was anxious for Alexa to learn everything she could. "About her parents? Whether she had any siblings?"

"How did Mei-Li get here?" Alexa rubbed her forehead.

Phyllis reached inside the portfolio again. "Those are interesting questions. More information has come to light. I've researched the photograph of the gentleman you weren't able to identify from the Lehmann Collection. You labelled him, Unidentified Chinese Herbalist." She placed the image Alexa had e-mailed in front of her. "The genealogical company we use for facial recognition uploaded his picture into their database and came up with a probable match." Phyllis extracted two sheets of paper and placed them next to the photo of the herbalist.

Eleanor's head collided with Alexa's as they both leaned over the table for a closer look.

Alexa rubbed Eleanor's forehead and mouthed, "Sorry."

Their eyes met, and Eleanor was lost in the tenderness of Alexa's gaze. Her heart swelled when Alexa pinched her on the arm and smiled at her fondly.

Phyllis cleared her throat. "It is good news."

"You've identified him?" Eleanor asked excitedly, turning her attention back to Phyllis.

"Yes. With the help of National Archives and the facial recognition software, it appears we do have a match."

"Oh, that's incredible." Alexa stood, pushed her chair back, and set her hands on the table. "Who was he?" Her eyebrows were narrowed, and she licked her bottom lip in concentration, studying the photos for a few moments before passing them to Eleanor. "Take a look."

Eleanor stared at a coloured copy of a faded yellowed image depicting columns of handwritten notes and figures in cursive script. "Ah… I've seen something like this before. Is it some sort of ship's ledger?"

"Well, sort of." Phyllis pointed to a spot in the middle of the list. "I apologise; it is not clearly visible on this copy, but it says here that the captain of the ship that had sailed from Amoy, China, paid the sum of ten pounds in December 1855 to allow his passenger, Guān Li-Shen, to disembark in Melbourne."

"The Chinese Immigration Act of Victoria passed in 1855," Alexa stated emphatically. "The government charged a tax for each passenger and restricted the number of Chinese on each ship."

Eleanor smiled to herself. Alexa was a genius at recalling facts and figures.

Alexa pressed her glasses to her nose. "'Guān Li-Shen from Guangzhou,'" she read. "Guangzhou was known by the British as Canton." She frowned. "How old would he have been then?"

"Maybe, around thirty years of age. This is where things get interesting," Phyllis said. "Travel to Australia was very expensive, and most of the Chinese paid for their passage using a 'credit-ticket' system. They borrowed money from merchants, and on arrival here, they had to pay back their debts with interest. Guān Li-Shen was a merchant."

Alexa pointed at the other document and motioned for Eleanor to come closer. "This looks like some sort of identification travel document."

Eleanor stood beside Alexa. "The man in the photograph is very smartly dressed, in a full suit. It says here he's a merchant." Eleanor picked up the image of the herbalist and compared it to the young man's picture, excitement building inside her. "Oh, my goodness. Look at this, Alexa. The man from the negative slide is older, and the image quality a lot better, but they are very similar. That's him."

"Yes. I believe so." Phyllis rapped her hand on the table. "It's Guān Li-Shen. The dated stamps on the document indicate that he travelled back and forth from China a number of times as a trader. His travel documents were issued before Chinese were allowed to apply for naturalisation, but they allowed merchants like Guān to move between countries relatively easily."

"It's bloody brilliant, Eleanor. They've discovered the identity of the herbalist." Alexa placed her arm around Eleanor's shoulder and pulled her close. "This could be the lead to why your aunt had the slides."

"It's fantastic we have a name," Eleanor said. "But there's still not an obvious connection to Helen." Had her aunt known Guān Li-Shen's relatives in China? This could be the link Eleanor was hoping for, but she was hesitant to believe anything without definitive proof.

Phyllis nodded sagely. "I'll tell you more about the image. Mr Guān is sitting in front of the now demolished Ball and Welch building, built in the 1860s. He practised from a small dispensary in the lane behind that building." She waved another page in front of them. "That address is here on the travel card and states his occupation as Merchant and Chinese Medical Herbalist."

Eleanor grinned. "Wow, you've discovered a lot."

"We're very grateful, Phyllis." Alexa nodded vigorously in agreement.

"Ah, but there's more." Phyllis gathered the scattered papers and placed them in her portfolio. "When you asked me to investigate your mysterious herbalist, I couldn't have imagined this outcome. Not in a million years." She motioned to their chairs. "I think you should both sit down."

Alexa gave Phyllis an incredulous stare. "What? What else did you find?"

Eleanor rubbed Alexa's back in a gentle circling motion. What more could Phyllis possibly reveal?

"Certificates for births, deaths, and marriages in Victoria date back to 1853, when the government began civil registration." Phyllis held a paper to her chest. "This Alexa, is your great-great-grandmother's birth certificate."

"What? It is?" Alexa dropped into her chair and leaned forward. "May I see it?"

"Of course; here." Phyllis handed it over.

Alexa scanned the page for a few moments, slowly shook her head, and gazed up at the ceiling. "I'll be damned. This is unbelievable."

Eleanor could hardly contain her excitement. "Show me, Alexa. What is it?" she asked, sitting down beside Alexa.

Alexa just shook her head again. "Eleanor, please read this out. I think I'm seeing things."

Eleanor took the page from her trembling hand and began reading, "'Mei-Li, Kwan. Female. Born Castlemaine, Victoria, 1870.' It says her mother was Guān Hei-Kim, born in Canton. Why is Mei-Li's surname different from her mother's?"

"That's because the Romanised version of Guān is Kwan, with a K," Alexa said.

"Really? It's the same surname as the herbalist. Guān." Eleanor frowned. "That is so weird and really confusing."

"Eleanor, keep reading." Alexa drummed her fingers on the desk.

Eleanor squinted, holding the page up to her eyes. "The print is faded. It's not easy to read. Okay, 'Father, Guān Li-Shen, Canton, 1825.' Oh, my *God.* Absolutely no way." She closed her eyes and leaned back, resting her head against the wall behind them.

Alexa's hand was shaking when she clutched Eleanor's thigh.

Eleanor opened her eyes and stared at Alexa, not knowing whether to laugh or cry. She handed the page back to Alexa and combed her fingers through her hair. "Is it really true?"

"This birth certificate says Guān Li-Shen was Mei-Li's father." Alexa's eyes were now glued to the paper. "How can that be possible? Why would *your* Aunt Helen have a slide of Mei-Li's father? My ancestor." She rubbed her face with her hands before meeting Eleanor's gaze again. "A photograph taken in *Castlemaine* and found in China. Brought into the library by you, Eleanor, and handed in to me. I can't believe the absurdity of it all."

Eleanor was speechless. She couldn't believe it either.

"Do you think there's a chance you two are related?" Phyllis asked in a high-pitched tone.

Turning sharply in Phyllis's direction, Eleanor's neck cracked. "No way."

"No way." Alexa laughed, reaching for Eleanor again, giving her an exuberant hug.

They both started giggling and couldn't stop until Phyllis began noisily stuffing photocopies into the portfolio, snapping it shut with a loud twang.

Eleanor's head was reeling. She still had no idea why Helen had the glass plate negative slides, but for now it didn't matter. She was just thrilled that, by some fluke of magic, Helen had played a role in unravelling the story of Alexa's ancestry.

"I'm sorry, Phyllis," Alexa said as she let go of Eleanor.

Eleanor reluctantly removed her arm from Alexa's waist and turned her attention back to Phyllis.

"Don't be sorry, girls. It's a lot of news to take in," Phyllis said with a bright smile and handed the portfolio to Alexa.

Alexa clutched it to her chest. "Thank you. This is gold."

Chapter 23

Buried treasure

"It would be funny if we're related," Alexa said, lowering her head to scrape her teeth over the sensitive peak of Eleanor's breast. She watched in awe as Eleanor's chest rose and fell with short breaths.

Eleanor gave a husky chuckle. "Totally hilarious. Not that it matters; it was such a long, long time ago. Haven't you heard of kissing cousins?"

"Ah-ha." Alexa flicked her thumbs across Eleanor's nipples. Watching them harden into perfect pebbles sent pleasurable sensations through her body.

"Please, you need to stop that. Give me a breather." Eleanor held Alexa's head gently in her hands. "You raced me back to the cottage and into your bedroom so fast, I didn't even have time to take my socks off."

"Yeah, well it's a wonder we got here alive. I could hardly concentrate on my driving, the way your hands were wandering over me. I could have driven us off the road."

Alexa had been giddy with excitement ever since she'd driven back to the cottage, when the slightest teasing touch of Eleanor's hand on her knee had made her press harder on the accelerator.

"Yes, and into the closest motel." Eleanor laughed wickedly.

"Ha. Lucky it's such a short drive."

Eleanor trailed a finger down her back, across her ribs, and all the way down to her thigh.

Alexa shivered. "Now *you* have to stop." She lifted Eleanor's hand and kissed the inside of her wrist, unable to control her silly grin. She gently traced her fingers over Eleanor's brow and brushed her hair back off her face. "I love how your eyes change. Sometimes they're a deep, earthy brown and sometimes bronzed and fiery."

It had been such an emotional day, with unexpected lows and astonishing highs. Eleanor's patience, encouragement, and frequent gentle touches during their meeting with Phyllis had been a balm to Alexa's soul. Apart from Gran and her mother, she'd never allowed herself to rely on someone else or put her trust in them, not like this.

Eleanor raised her head from the pillow and kissed Alexa softly, lightly sliding her tongue across Alexa's bottom lip. "Do we really have to put on clothes and drive back into Castlemaine? I'm not ready to face the world yet." Her smile was playful, cheeky, and damn tempting.

"It's been quite a day, hasn't it?" Alexa rolled onto her side facing Eleanor.

Eleanor stretched out on her back, pulling up the sheet to cover herself. "That was a hell of a lot of information to absorb in one hit. Are you sure you're okay?" she asked in a gentle tone.

Alexa reached out and took Eleanor's hand, wanting to maintain their close contact. "Uh-huh. It was a lot to take in." What they'd learnt today was mind-boggling, even though it didn't answer all the questions. Alexa was a mix of nerves and anticipation at the thought of discovering even more. "Phyllis was a really good sport, wasn't she?" Alexa snuggled into Eleanor, relishing the last few minutes before she would force herself to get out of bed.

"I don't know what she thought about the pair of us, especially after your giggling fit."

"My giggling fit. I think that should be plural. We were both in shock." Alexa poked Eleanor in the ribs. "Laughing lowers the body's stress hormones."

"So does exercise, and sex." Eleanor grinned. "Anyway, Phyllis seemed genuinely glad to help. You could tell she was getting a real kick out of parsing out the information in a tortoise-like trickle 'till she got to the punchline."

"True. She's a sweetie." Alexa made a note to herself to write Phyllis a letter of thanks, but tonight, keeping a promise to a friend was more important. Alexa was a woman who kept her word. "You don't mind coming out with me this evening, do you? We'll have the next two days to explore the district and each other."

"Yes, I'm in favour of a whole lot more exploring." Eleanor gave her a crooked grin that made Alexa's stomach flutter.

"Me, too."

"Remind me again, who is this band? You said they are friends of yours."

"Yes. The Orbweavers. Marita and Stuart are playing at The Bridge Hotel tonight. I promised we'd be there. Louise, Kelly, and some of Kelly's work mates from Parks Victoria are also going." Alexa ducked her head to meet Eleanor's gaze and was relieved to see she was still smiling. "I think you'll enjoy their music."

Eleanor nodded. "Sure, okay." She grabbed Alexa's finger as she slowly circled Eleanor's navel. "None of that, or we'll never leave the cottage." Her eyebrows rose as Alexa pulled the sheet away and hopped off the bed. "Hey, that's not fair."

Alexa dodged Eleanor's hands as she reached for her. "Time to get showered and dressed." It took all of Alexa's restraint not to dive right back into bed, especially with Eleanor, stretched out, gloriously, uncovered and so inviting—her lips begging to be kissed. Damn. Alexa couldn't help herself. She leaned forward, capturing Eleanor's lips one more time. "Until later." Alexa sighed, breaking the kiss.

Eleanor held up her finger, shaking it from side to side. She leapt out of bed. "I dib first shower," she squealed, heading for the bedroom door.

"Why waste the water when there's plenty of room for two?" Alexa chased after her.

They showered as quickly as possible, Alexa constantly reminding them both there was no time to linger, but even getting dressed was difficult, with Eleanor in such a frisky mood. Alexa would usually have been annoyed, but she couldn't find it in her to be annoyed with Eleanor tonight. She enjoyed having such a sensuous, playful lover.

Finally, they left the cottage, and Eleanor promised to behave and sit on her hands all the way to the pub while Alexa drove.

When Alexa and Eleanor arrived, Kelly and the gang beckoned them over to the group of tables they'd commandeered. Even though Alexa introduced Eleanor as her *friend*, she wasn't fooling anyone. They probably had 'we've been having hot sex for hours' written all over their flushed foreheads.

Louise winked at Alexa. "You made it just in time," she said as Marita stepped up to the microphone.

After the band's first set, Eleanor leaned forward until their shoulders touched. "You're right, I love the Orbweavers."

Alexa couldn't stop herself from nuzzling Eleanor's ear as she whispered, "Told you so. I knew you'd appreciate their music."

Eleanor's eyes darted towards the bar, as if she was suddenly shy. "It's my shout. What can I get you?" she asked hurriedly.

Alexa looked across the table and met Louise's knowing gaze. She raised an eyebrow and shrugged.

Ten minutes later, Eleanor was only halfway along a line of people queued at the bar. Why was that short woman with spiky blonde hair standing so close, staring up at Eleanor with wide eyes and a toothy grin? She was blatantly appraising Eleanor, who was nodding her head and pointing at their table. Alexa's stomach knotted. She didn't like the idea of someone else being into Eleanor.

The woman shoved her hands in her jean pockets, glared at Alexa across the room, then turned to speak to the person behind her.

Alexa narrowed her eyes. What had Eleanor said to the woman?

She swivelled sideways as someone walked in front of her, annoyingly blocking her view of Eleanor. When she caught sight of her again, Eleanor sent a big grin her way, and Alexa felt some of the tension in her muscles fade. She exhaled slowly and flopped back in her chair.

"Eleanor's having a good time." Louise tapped Alexa on the forearm. "Everyone seems to like her."

"Yeah." Alexa blinked and answered back quietly, "She's a very likeable person."

Louise looked at Alexa intently, as if she was waiting for more information.

Alexa pushed her empty glass back from the edge of the table. It was unnerving the way Louise stared at her, as if she could read her thoughts. As if she knew that Alexa's fondness for Eleanor was growing.

Kelly plonked down in the chair beside Alexa. "The joint is overflowing tonight. I'm really looking forward to the band's second set."

The old styled pub was filled with a noisy, eclectic mix of patrons, from greenies with dreadlocks to fashionably dressed town folk.

Alexa was relieved to see that Eleanor had finally reached the end of the queue and was waving to get the bartender's attention. Her dark jeans hugged her slim hips and thighs, and the grey sweater stretching snugly accentuated her trim muscular build and perfect breasts. Alexa's whole body vibrated at the sight of her. It was impossible to look away. And it was impossible to push away the images that rose up in her mind of the great sex they'd had this afternoon.

Eleanor caught Alexa's eye and flashed her another dazzling smile.

Alexa drew a deep breath. Eleanor could make her heart skip a beat with just a smile.

"There you are, Alexa." She heard her name called over the racket and turned to find Marita, dressed all in black from top to toe, walking across the room to where she sat.

Alexa jumped up to greet her. "So good to see you, Marita. The first set was sensational. All my favourites from your *Deep Leads* album."

"Thank you." Marita's clear dark eyes twinkled. "I'm so glad you and your friends could make it." She nodded, acknowledging the rest of the group. "All of you. Thanks for coming."

"We're looking forward to hearing your new single," Louise said.

Marita smiled sweetly. "Coming up straight after the break."

There was a murmur of interest from around the table, and Alexa smiled.

"Yay." Kelly held up her tall glass of beer. "I hope you'll sing one of my favourites, 'Spotswood.' I grew up in Hudsons Road near the railway station back in the 80s."

"I know that area well, close to the West Gate Bridge." Marita clasped her hands together. "I'm sure we can do that for you."

Marita glanced to her left, and Alexa turned to find Eleanor standing beside her. She resisted the urge to slip her arm around Eleanor's waist.

"I'm back." She set two wine glasses down on the table. "Hi, I'm Eleanor."

Marita stepped forward, her hand extended. "Hello, Eleanor. It's a pleasure to meet you. You're the photographer who's just returned to

Melbourne. Alexa told me you've recently had a book released. Where can I see it?"

"Nice to meet you, too, Marita," Eleanor said. "The book hasn't been distributed in Australia yet, but the publisher expects it to be here soon."

"If it doesn't get here soon, I'll be battering down the door of the publishing house." Alexa smiled at Eleanor's wide-eyed expression.

"Looks like you've got yourself an agent, Eleanor." Marita winked.

Eleanor fished inside her jacket pocket, clearly embarrassed by the attention. She pulled out a CD. "I just bought *Deep Leads*. Maybe you and Stuart could sign it for me? I'm fascinated with your story of recording and producing the album near the Merri Creek. It's not an area I'm very familiar with, but now I want to go there."

Alexa sat down and sipped on her Pinot Gris while Marita and Eleanor continued to chat about the album. Eleanor was bound to have a copy of her book, and Alexa was surprised she hadn't offered to show it to her. She was also surprised at how much she suddenly wanted to see it.

"It's spine tingling. What is the song about?" Eleanor asked Marita, bringing Alexa's focus back to their conversation.

"Radium Girls," Marita said, "is about American female factory workers in the 1920s and 1930s who were poisoned by the luminous radium paint they used on aircraft instrument panels and watch dials."

Eleanor's eyes widened. "That's terrible. What drew you to write the song?"

"Well, I was as an inventory officer at Scienceworks Museum, and we were working on military and aircraft collections that contained some of the radium-painted dials," Marita said. "Every day I would look at those dials and reflect about the women who painted them using the highly toxic, radioactive paint without knowing the dangers. Many of them died, Eleanor." She shook her head slowly. "I was so moved by the story that one day, I came home, sat down, and wrote 'Radium Girls.'"

A few chords from Stuart's guitar drew their attention. "I'm being summoned," Marita said. A faint smile lined her cherry lips. "We'll be happy to sign the CD for you after we finish. Will you both still be here?"

"Yes, of course," Alexa said. "Now, you'd better go and entertain us."

Alexa watched Marita smoothly glide through the crowd and back to the stage where she and Stuart prepared for the next set.

"I imagine you already knew the story behind the song?" Eleanor asked.

"I do, but it still makes me shiver." Alexa, eagerly waiting for the music to begin, took her seat and patted the chair beside her.

Eleanor sat down and inched her chair closer to Alexa's. She turned the CD case over in her hands and smiled. "Really glad we came here tonight. I'm enjoying everything. And apart from being here with you and your friends, the music's been the highlight of the evening." She rested her cheek on her hand and sighed. "I love how they weave together history and nature, allowing us to imagine Melbourne's past through their music."

Goosebumps pricked Alexa's skin. Eleanor's appreciation of her friends' work sent a rush of pleasure through Alexa, and she was tempted to lean across and kiss her. She resisted, though, unsure if either of them was ready for public displays of affection yet.

"Hey, you two," Kelly called from across the table. "We're all going back to Sue's after. Want to come?"

Alexa held Eleanor's gaze. She was sure neither of them wanted to change the plans they had for the evening. "I think we'll be ready to head back after the show, Kel. It's been a long day."

Kelly huffed. "Oh, come on, Alexa. The night is but young…"

"Leave it be, honey," Louise said softly. She smiled at Alexa with a gleam in her eyes. "Maybe next time."

Alexa ducked her head, silently thanking Louise.

As Marita's delicate voice lilted through the strumming of Stuart's guitar, Eleanor pressed against Alexa's side. Alexa slid her hand stealthily across to Eleanor's thigh, reaching for her hand and entwining their fingers together. Alexa exhaled a deep sigh while the haunting music swirled like a spinning silk thread around them.

"I thought you were pulling my leg about the hot-air balloon." Eleanor peered over the side of the wicker basket that sat plonked in the middle of the Castlemaine Mill Market. She waved her arms in the air. "There's room for two. Come and join me." Eleanor shook the basket, swaying dramatically from side to side. "This place is a treasure trove for lovers of the old and quirky. I can see why you spend so much time here."

Alexa put her hands on her hips and shook her head. "Lovers of old and quirky, eh? Enough clowning around. Come over to the clothes rack. I've found something perfect for you."

"Thanks. I don't need clothes." Eleanor clambered out of the basket, pointing to the other end of the shed. "I spotted some old camera gear and photo frames I'd be interested in—"

Alexa studied her from top to bottom with an intensity that made Eleanor's face flush.

"Humour me, please."

When Alexa gave Eleanor that sultry look, there was no way Eleanor could refuse her. "Okay. Lead on."

Twenty minutes and several wardrobe changes later, Eleanor stood in front of a full-length mirror critically examining herself. Loose charcoal camel-hair trousers held up with a plain leather belt, white shirt with contrasting collar, and a narrow herringbone tie. Her outfit resembled something worn by the character Annie Hall in the Woody Allen film. She frowned. Definitely not what she would choose for herself. Alexa had insisted Eleanor complete the costume with patterned oxford shoes and a slim-fit black vest, which only made her look even sillier.

Grinning at her reflection in the mirror, Eleanor clicked the heels of the shoes together. "It's not bad, if I was performing on the stage, which I'm not."

Alexa rested her chin on Eleanor's shoulder. "The outfit enhances your sexy tomboyish style. All we need to find is a Trilby hat...you know the felt one with a narrow brim, to complete the look."

Eleanor shook her head. *Even in this crazy outfit, Alexa thinks I'm sexy.* She cast Alexa a sideways glance. "Isn't it nearly time to eat? I could smell fresh bread from that little bakery near the car park, and you promised me lunch at the Viennese café before we hunt for the old schoolhouse."

Alexa stared at Eleanor while tapping her finger against her chin. "Only if you let me buy you these first."

Eleanor looked down at the Oxfords. "The shoes and the shirt are a definite no. I like the pants, but I won't wear pants made from camel hair. I mean, how do they get—?"

"I wouldn't suggest anything that involves cruelty to animals." Alexa frowned. "It's like getting wool from sheep. Camels shed, or moult, about seven kilos of inner fleece each spring."

"How do you even know that?" Eleanor scratched her head. Alexa would be a sure thing on one of those TV quiz shows.

Alexa shrugged. "Look at the label. Blended with cashmere and sooo soft."

Eleanor jumped as Alexa bent down and brushed her hand up the inside of her calf.

"So, the pants and the vest?" Alexa looked up with a lazy, slow, very sexy smile.

"I'll buy the pants and maybe the patterned tie," Eleanor said, hurrying towards the change room. "You wait right here."

"Of course. I like it when you're a *just-so* mixture of adorable and feisty."

Eleanor tugged the curtain across and stared at herself in the mirror again. Even though she looked like she'd travelled back in time, the outfit had something daring about it.

The women in the slides from the 1800s wore bell-shaped layers and loads of petticoats, giving them the appearance of being fragile and doll-like. She grimaced. But they must have been tough; how else would they have survived the harsh conditions of the goldfields?

Meeting with Phyllis yesterday and spending time with Alexa had Eleanor contemplating her own family tree. Even though her work was a constant reminder of just how fragile life could be, it was her father's illness that had brought everything to the fore. She should talk to her parents about all those relatives who contributed to her DNA before it was too late. Eleanor wanted to learn about her ancestors and their stories. Maybe there were mysteries and scandals to be uncovered in her own family's past as well.

"Do you need help in there?" Alexa gave a slightly giddy, happy laugh from the other side of the curtain.

"I'll be right out," Eleanor called, quickly undressing and folding her chosen items into a neat pile. She grabbed her own clothes from the hook, stepping into her faded blue jeans, hurriedly pulling on her Henley.

Alexa pushed aside the curtain. "Anyone else would think you were stalling."

Eleanor stepped out of the booth with the new items of clothing tucked under her arm. "Why would I do that?" she asked. "Lead me to the cash register."

"And then on to that promised lunch." Alexa's eyes sparkled as she linked their arms, and they strolled towards the checkout.

Eleanor was euphoric walking along clutching Alexa's arm. She wouldn't have been surprised to look down at her feet and find they weren't touching the ground.

They meandered through the market grounds, still arm in arm, arriving at the coffee house in just a few minutes. They were seated at a cosy table for two by a server wearing a traditional Viennese outfit. The aromas of toasted bread, savoury spices, cardamom, and honey wafted through the café, tickling Eleanor's nose. Luckily, the service was swift, their meals arrived quickly, and they tucked in gratefully.

Alexa pointed to the leftover cheese and bread dumpling on Eleanor's plate. "Aren't you going to finish that?"

Eleanor shook her head. "This really is like a true Viennese coffee house, but I can't eat another morsel of *Knödel,* or I'd curl up right there on that gold leather banquette under the tear drop chandelier and fall asleep." She placed a hand over her mouth and mimed an exaggerated yawn.

"Have you spent time in Austria? You sound like a native speaker, the way you said *Knödel.*"

Eleanor laughed. Coming from Alexa, it sounded like *canoodle.* "I spent a month in the Austrian Alps some time ago."

"On assignment?"

"No, with a friend."

"Were you high on a hill with some lonely goatherder?"

"I don't think Heidi had any goats. She was a skier." Eleanor laughed. "That holiday romance went downhill pretty quickly."

"Heidi, eh," Alexa said with a dramatic eye roll. "Sometimes I forget how *well-travelled* you are."

Alexa seemed to be implying that Eleanor was not only well-travelled but had slept around. Eleanor hesitated. She didn't really want to talk about that now, so she found a safer subject. "Dad would love it here. The aroma from the coffee roasters is heavenly." She patted her abdomen. "I'll probably regret it, but I'm going to order an *Apfelstrudel* and a *Kleiner* mokka," she said in her best German accent. "What would you like?"

"I'll have a slice of the Almond Cake with a nice dollop of farmhouse cream and an espresso." Alexa's smile widened. "Don't worry. I know just the thing for working off those carbs."

"Are we heading back to the cottage for a nap?" Eleanor asked, although a nap was the furthest thing from her mind.

Alexa tossed her hair back and laughed wickedly. "I'm happy to take you to bed later. I thought we'd take a town walk around historical Castlemaine first."

"Really?" Eleanor's shoulders drooped. "Okay. I suppose that *is* why we're here."

"Phyllis thought the schoolhouse in the slide looked like the main building of South School, which is just a short walk away." Alexa's face was alight with anticipation. "What do you say to a history lesson?"

"Coffee and dessert first, and then we can get going." Eleanor jumped to her feet, keen to check out the cake cabinet display. "And if we're lucky, we'll enjoy another kind of dessert at the cottage."

"Only if you pay attention to my history lesson." Alexa wagged her finger at Eleanor threateningly.

A few hours later, at Gold-Dust Cottage, Eleanor sat on the sofa with sagging shoulders and allowed Alexa to lift her throbbing right hand onto the pillow she'd placed on her lap.

"Good thing this is just a minor burn."

Eleanor winced, looking away. "Ouch, ouch, ouch…"

"Silly. I haven't even touched it yet." Alexa slit a large spear of Aloe Vera in half and bathed Eleanor's finger with the cooling gel. "This will heal the burn. It's not too bad. You won't need a bandage."

"That does feels better." Eleanor sighed. "I'm just glad it's not my dominant hand."

"Poor baby. Lucky it's not the finger you use to press the shutter button." Alexa snorted. "I warned you not to use a damp tea towel to lift the cornbread out of the grill. I have an oven mitt for that."

"I just wanted to help." Eleanor lowered her eyes.

"You did help," Alexa's voiced dipped. "It was our first attempt at cooking together."

"And look what happened. A small disaster." Eleanor fiddled with the row of green beads she wore around her wrist. "How long do I leave my hand in your lap?"

"As long as you like." Alexa ran her fingers over Eleanor's bracelet. "This is pretty. It looks like jade."

"I think it is. Aunt Helen sent it to me from China."

"It's gorgeous," Alexa said.

Eleanor caressed Alexa's cheek with her uninjured hand. "Sometimes your eyes are exactly the same colour."

"Why don't we stretch out so you can get more comfortable?" Alexa shuffled to the corner of the sofa, straightened her legs, and beckoned for Eleanor to join her.

For a moment, Eleanor stayed where she was, gazing into Alexa's eyes. She quickly shook off her trance-like state, wandering over to settle herself back against Alexa's chest, safely wrapped in her arms.

"That's better." Alexa nuzzled Eleanor's hair. "Maybe we should try and get some actual sleep tonight. Give you time to heal."

"Hey, I'm not injured that badly."

"This is nice," Alexa whispered in her ear, her arms tightening around Eleanor's midriff.

Eleanor inhaled deeply. "God, you smell so good." She tilted her chin, kissing Alexa softly. "I could get used to this."

"Do you mean kissing? I'm rather partial to that particular pursuit myself."

Eleanor was enjoying their physical connection, but it seemed as if Alexa wasn't ready to acknowledge what they had went deeper. She supposed that was okay for now, but she hoped Alexa would come to want something more between them soon.

Alexa dragged her fingernails up the inside of Eleanor's thighs—with purpose—distracting Eleanor from her thoughts about Alexa's headspace.

For a moment, Eleanor pushed against Alexa's hand, then changed her mind. She didn't want this to be a quickie on the sofa. Stilling Alexa's hand with hers, Eleanor turned in her arms, drew herself up onto her knees, and put some distance between them.

"Something the matter? Did I hurt your hand?" Alexa wore a worried frown.

"No, not at all."

"What then?" A half-smile tugged the corner of Alexa's mouth.

"I'd like for us to take our time. Go slowly," Eleanor said hesitantly, even though she'd have to use all her restraint, because, really, she wanted Alexa naked and in bed quicker than the fastest shutter speed. "Come to bed."

Alexa rose from the sofa. Her fingers grazed the bottom of Eleanor's chin, tilting her head up. "I have a hunch; we're not going to get much sleep, after all."

Alexa was right. Two hours later, Eleanor lay drowsily propped up against the pillows, gazing at the gorgeous woman who had just dropped off to sleep. One of Alexa's legs was still curled around Eleanor's calf, anchoring her. Bathed in the soft light streaming through the multi-paned windows, Alexa's face was serene and very beautiful.

Eleanor sighed contentedly, recalling each moment, imprinting on her mind each image and every sensation of their lovemaking. The way Alexa moved in her arms—below her, above her. How she responded to Eleanor's touch, the sound of her laboured breathing before she cried out Eleanor's name—then reversed their positions and began the exploration of Eleanor's body, her mouth blazing a trail of fire. The surge of emotions welling up inside Eleanor filled her heart to bursting.

Eleanor rested her chin on Alexa's shoulder. Even though she hadn't uttered the words out loud, in her heart, she knew it was true. *I love you.* Eleanor swallowed hard. She wanted more of this friendship. More of this connection. More intimacy beyond just physical release.

Last night, after coaxing Eleanor to another dizzying, breathtaking orgasm, Alexa had said, "You are incredible, Eleanor. You are so much fun to be with, and the sex is...well, there's no denying we have chemistry. I care about you very much."

They'd made love again, but Eleanor sensed that Alexa was holding back something of herself. She wasn't ready to let herself fall. Would she ever? Was Alexa scared because of her own past experiences? Or was it something about Eleanor? A small wave of panic surfaced.

Alexa stirred in her sleep and sighed softly. She extended her arm and pulled Eleanor down beside her. Her slow, even breath warmed Eleanor's skin.

Eleanor sighed. She wished she could tell Alexa how she felt, wished Alexa felt the same way, but she couldn't be sure of anything. She buried her face into Alexa's neck and whispered into the darkness, "I love you."

Chapter 24

A run, pung and a pair

The journey back to Melbourne had been rather quiet so far. In her half-awake, half-dreaming state last night, Alexa had just registered Eleanor's declaration. She was sure she wasn't supposed to hear her whisper, so she'd pretended to be asleep.

This morning, Alexa suddenly felt uncomfortable around Eleanor, unsure of what to say to her, and they'd moved around each other cautiously, like two people unaccustomed to sharing their space at the start of the day. While Eleanor had taken off on a chilly early morning run, Alexa pottered around in the cottage. Sarah had summoned them home earlier than planned for Eleanor to drive her father to an unscheduled medical appointment. Perhaps it was for the best.

The silence in the car now was a little unnerving. There were so many questions Alexa wanted to ask Eleanor. This would be a good time, if Eleanor was open to talk. She glanced over at the passenger seat, where Eleanor was gazing out the window. She looked lost in thought. Unease settled in Alexa's gut. Perhaps Eleanor was regretting what she'd said.

Alexa placed her hand on Eleanor's knee and smiled when Eleanor covered Alexa's hand with hers. "I'd love to see your book, *Treading Lightly*, sometime, Eleanor. Do you have a copy? Or do I have to contact the publisher?"

"No, I do have a couple at the studio," Eleanor said. "I'd love for you to see it."

"You must be so proud." Alexa smiled eagerly.

Eleanor adjusted the sun visor with her free hand. "The production values are excellent. The book turned out well. I'm just sorry Helen didn't get to see it," she said sadly. "My aunt's mantra was always, *tread lightly on our planet*. The book is dedicated to her."

"Of course. She was your mentor," Alexa said gently. "When you talk about Helen, there's a kind of a shadow hanging over you. Is it okay to ask you why?" Alexa turned her hand to entwine their fingers, subtly encouraging Eleanor to open up about Helen.

"You'd think after nearly twelve years…" Eleanor tapped her head against the car window. "In Helen's trunk, there were some notebooks. She was always writing things down. In one of them, she talks about wanting me to join her in Beijing. If I'd gone, I could have stopped her from going to Chengdu." Her voice faltered, and she cleared her throat. "I know it's been a long time, but the guilt still lives in here." She removed her hand from Alexa's and placed it on her chest.

"I understand why you regret not meeting your aunt in China, but there was absolutely no way you could have known what would happen." Alexa looked in the rear vision mirror and moved into the slow lane. She could hear the pain and frustration in Eleanor's voice. She wished there was some way she could help Eleanor come to terms with Helen's death and let go of her guilt.

"I know that, but the trunk arriving has triggered everything all over again."

"I'm sure your aunt would be proud of you and all you've accomplished," Alexa said to comfort Eleanor. "The fact that we're making such good progress with the slides is a definite plus and—"

"Hey, Alexa." Eleanor pointed. "What's going on ahead? There's a long line of cars crawling really slowly."

Alexa craned her neck to get a better view. "Oh, shit, I can just see something in the middle of the highway and a truck pulled off on the side of the road."

"There's a couple of blue lights flashing. I hope nobody's been hurt."

Alexa hit the brakes as the car in front of them came to a standstill. She looked over to Eleanor and put her hands in the air in frustration. "One lane is partly closed, and there's only a trickle of traffic coming this way," she said. "We're going to be late, but at least it's not my fault this time." She smiled apologetically.

After another five minutes, they moved forward about five car lengths and then stopped again. With a wave, a traffic policeman signalled the drivers to pull off near the grassy verge.

Alexa rolled down her window and peered out. Up ahead, a shipping container lay in the middle of the highway, and cardboard boxes of various sizes were strewn across the road. *Hell.* She thumped the steering wheel with her hands. "We're not going anywhere for a while. At this rate, you won't be able to take your father to his appointment."

Eleanor pulled out her phone. "Don't worry. I'll message Dad and let him know we've been delayed. He can always get a taxi."

"All right; good idea." Alexa rested her head against the headrest and closed her eyes. That was one thing she didn't have to worry about.

Did Eleanor really mean what she'd said last night? It would have been easy to say *I love you* in the aftermath of their sexual passion. Was that what drove Eleanor to say it? Alexa's father had married three times and told each one of his wives the same three words. When Alexa uttered those words to someone, she would be damn sure they were true.

Alexa couldn't avoid the conflicting emotions in her heart and head. She needed time and space to think through what was happening, away from the sound of Eleanor's infectious laughter, away from those big brown adoring eyes.

"Alexa, they're waving us on. You're daydreaming." Eleanor caressed Alexa's thigh. "Where were you?"

The touch of Eleanor's hand sent ripples of pleasure coursing through Alexa's body, reminding her how perfectly they fit together and what an enthusiastic, responsive lover Eleanor was. "Just thinking about our weekend," Alexa responded with a smile. Eleanor was not shy when it came to their physical intimacy.

Eleanor licked her lips and blew her a kiss. The hazy, dreamy look in her eyes spelt trouble. How on earth would Alexa resist her and take the time and space she needed?

Alexa sucked in a breath and turned the key in the ignition. She selected an upbeat driving playlist and turned the volume to loud.

Nearly an hour later, fairly resolved with her decision to put some distance between them and take a break for the week, Alexa pulled into the driveway at Oxford Avenue, Hawthorn. "You're home at last." She smiled wistfully.

"Unbelievable. Even with the delay, I'm here in time to take Dad to rehab. He's got Farina out of the garage for you. That will save time." Eleanor's face brightened. "When will I see you again?"

"I'll be in contact. Anyway, we're having lunch at Gran's house on Sunday," Alexa said as calmly as she could.

"It's only Monday. That's days away." Eleanor's tone dropped, a flash of disappointment on her face.

"I know—" Alexa leant over to kiss Eleanor on the cheek. Sunday was almost a week away, and although she regretted causing Eleanor's despondency, she really did need that time to sort herself out.

A loud rapping on the window made them spring apart.

Harold was standing there tapping his watch, which left no opportunity for Alexa to give Eleanor any explanations or offer an excuse for her decision.

Eleanor wound down the window. "Hi, Dad."

"Glad you're back safely, girls, but it's time to go, Eleanor."

Alexa resisted the urge and didn't ask Eleanor to meet her earlier in the week.

Eleanor stopped running, bent over, and placed her hands on her knees to catch her breath. Looking through her legs back down Fairview Park's oak-lined boulevard, Eleanor saw her brother scurrying along the pathway.

He fell onto the grass beside her. "Why on earth are you running like a bat out of hell?" Leo asked through laboured breaths. "We already know you're in much better condition than I am."

She laughed, leaning over to ruffle his hair. "It comes from you sitting behind a desk all day."

"Well, we don't all lead exciting lives like you." He mopped his forehead with the front of his T-shirt. "Speaking of work, how was the Queensland job? Nice for some."

Eleanor sprang to her feet and bounced on her toes. "It was amazing to be involved with the project. The magazine wants to use some of the other photos I shot up north for a side piece on ecotourism. I need to spend a couple of days in the studio putting things together in the digital darkroom."

"Terrific," Leo said with a wide grin. "I gather the media tried to make something of you and Mia being in the same place at the same time. Anything I should know?"

"Absolutely not. She's about to become a mother." Eleanor took a swig out of her water bottle and clipped it to the top of her running tights. "It was nice to catch up, though. By the way, Mia said hello."

"It seems she's doing well for herself in Hollywood, both professionally and personally. I'm glad to hear she's got her shit together," he said, sounding genuinely delighted. "What about you and the very attractive librarian? How is Alexa?" He raised his eyebrows. "You spent the whole weekend together, didn't you? Is it serious?"

Eleanor shrugged, trying to seem indifferent.

Leo extended his arm, and Eleanor took hold of his hand and pulled him off the grass.

She wished she could give Leo a positive answer. "You're full of questions this morning, aren't you?"

"Hey, I'm getting used to having you around. Even though you whip my ass every damn time we run together," Leo said with a hang dog look. "As you know, I'm on a flight to Canberra this afternoon. I want to know more about what you've been up to. Come on, let's walk back, and you can fill me in."

Twenty minutes later, they parked themselves on the bench seat in the courtyard garden that separated the studio from their parents' house. Eleanor leaned forward to unfasten her running shoes and peel off her sweaty socks, sighing contentedly at the pleasant burn in her muscles.

Leo tapped her bare foot. "What a remarkable coincidence that the Chinese herbalist turned out to be Alexa's ancestor. Astonishing. You two have forged quite a connection, wouldn't you say?"

"Yes. You'd think she'd be eager to see me again soon, wouldn't you?" Eleanor rubbed her forehead. "But yesterday, when she dropped me off and we said our good-byes, Alexa informed me we'd next see each other on Sunday, at her grandmother's house. I have to say, it threw me, considering how affectionate she'd been on the weekend."

"Well, crap," Leo said, shaking his head. "That was a quick change in direction after you'd shared an intense couple of days and nights. Must have come as a surprise. Can you even wait five days until you see her again?"

"Yeah, well, not like I have a choice." Eleanor blew a strand of hair out of her eyes. She wasn't pleased by it, but Alexa had made the decision for her.

"Hmm."

Eleanor trusted her brother's opinion and hoped he could give her some sort of advice on Alexa's puzzling behaviour. "What do you think, Leo?"

Leo gave her a probing stare. "Why didn't you suggest meeting earlier in the week if that's what you want?"

"It just didn't feel like she was giving me an option." Eleanor sighed. "Anyway, Dad was tapping at the car window as soon as we got back. We were running late."

"Did you say something to scare her off?"

"No, of course not." *At least not while Alexa was awake.*

"Who are you scaring off?" They both jumped at the sound of their father's voice.

"Jeez, Dad, what are you doing sneaking around?" Leo asked.

"It is my garden," their father replied, his eyes crinkling in the bright sunlight. "And you haven't answered my question, Nell." He smiled, pushing his hand through his thick silvery-grey hair, which was disarranged, as if he'd just woken from an afternoon nap.

"You might as well join us." Leo jumped to his feet and lifted one of the wooden chairs that were clustered around an outdoor table, placing it next to Eleanor. "Sit yourself down, Dad."

He perched beside her and crossed his legs. "What are we talking about?"

"Women problems," Leo blurted.

Eleanor shot him a glare. "Thanks, Leo."

"Do you need some advice from an old man?" Their father laughed softly.

"You might as well try, Dad. She won't take my advice." Leo huffed.

"I don't recall you giving me any advice," Eleanor said. "Besides, you're hardly the expert on matters of love."

"Ah-ha," her dad drew out the words. "Is this about Ms Bellamy?"

Leo rhythmically stamped his feet on the ground and tapped his bare knees. "Woohoo..."

Their father scratched his eyebrow. "When is your next date?"

Eleanor shifted around on the bench. It had been a long time since she'd discussed such sensitive issues with her family. "Our next *date* is Sunday lunch with Grandma and a cat named Bruce."

Both men laughed heartily.

Leo nearly tipped the bench backwards.

"It's not that funny," Eleanor said, although she was unable to keep herself from grinning, so infectious was their amusement. Maybe it was best to laugh and not take the whole thing too seriously.

"May I join in the merriment?" Her mother closed the side gate. She glanced from Leo to Eleanor and then her gaze rested on her husband. She blew him a kiss.

As far as Eleanor was concerned, they'd finished their conversation about Alexa just in time. She'd rather not have to suffer through her mother's viewpoint.

"Hello, darling," her father greeted her affectionately. "You're home from the office early. Glad you can join us."

Her mother nodded. "I have some work to take care of from home. What's going on out here, family?" She pushed up the sleeve of her well-cut navy suit jacket, glanced at her wristwatch and then down at Leo as if he was still a twelve-year-old schoolboy. "Leo, your ride to the airport should be here in fifteen minutes. Don't you need to shower?"

Leo stood and cleared his throat. "Suppose I'd better get a move on. Here, sit down and join the fun."

"Are you grabbing an Uber? Let me take you, Leo," Eleanor said, not wanting Leo to have to pay for an Uber when she had no plans.

"Thanks, sis, but it won't be necessary." He sauntered towards the main house as if he had all the time in the world. "I have a ride."

"Is one of your mates giving you a lift?"

"Err...yep," he said. "Car-pooling."

Her mother took a seat in the vacated chair, adjusted her skirt, and crossed her legs at the knee. "Stella offered to swing by here and pick up Leo on her way to the airport."

Stella?

Eleanor looked from one parent to the other with raised eyebrows. "Stella? Do you mean Stella Wright?"

Leo stopped at the patio doors, turned, and called, "Excellent arbitrator, Eleanor. If you should ever need one," he added with a quick wink before disappearing inside.

Her father nodded slyly and smiled at Eleanor. "She is excellent at her job, and rather charming too."

"It's the Law Forum held in Canberra every two years. Stella is one of the key speakers," her mother explained with a slight rise of her eyebrows. "Leo should have been ready. Why don't you stay here with your father and talk to her? She could arrive anytime. I have a phone conference; I must go and prepare."

Eleanor resisted the urge to roll her eyes. She wasn't in the mood to entertain Stella. She kissed her father's cheek and pushed herself off the bench. "Sorry, Stella is all yours. There's work in the darkroom that has to be finished. Deadlines to meet."

Her mother shook her head and walked off in the direction of the house.

Eleanor collected her runners and socks and hightailed it towards the studio.

He laughed. "Don't worry, you two. *I'll* be here."

Were they still trying to set her up with Judge Wright's daughter, even though it was obvious she was involved with Alexa? Eleanor couldn't believe it. Why hadn't Leo mentioned Stella was coming to the house? The rat.

"Hold up a minute, Eleanor," her mother called just as she reached the studio door.

Eleanor sighed and turned. "Yes, Mother?"

"Are you okay?" The tight note in her mother's voice hinted at concern.

Eleanor took a deep breath. "I'm fine. Why?" She dropped her runners into the shoe storage box near the front door and tucked her socks into her hip pocket.

Her mother gave her a long, questioning stare. "Are you sure? Your father mentioned things seemed a little strained between you and Alexa when you got home from the country."

"Really?" Eleanor lowered her gaze. "Everything's okay. We'd been delayed, and I was worried Dad would miss his appointment. That's all."

She punched the code into the access panel, pushed open her door, and stood facing her mother. “Anything else?” Eleanor crossed her arms in front of her chest. While she appreciated her mother’s concern, it made her feel exposed and uncomfortable.

“No, just checking on you.” Her mother leaned forward and kissed her forehead, gently placing her hand over Eleanor’s sternum. “Just tread carefully, Eleanor.”

Eleanor watched her mother’s retreating figure as she disappeared around the corner of the house. A prickle travelled up Eleanor’s spine as she absorbed her mum’s warning. Her mother was right; Eleanor should tread carefully, and that meant giving Alexa space. Her chest grew tight at the mere thought of spending five whole days apart from Alexa, but Alexa had laid down the terms, and Eleanor intended to respect them. Even so, she hoped Alexa would cave before Sunday. Eleanor knew she hadn’t imagined their connection—the invisible thread that drew them together.

“You don’t usually visit on a Tuesday evening. And why didn’t you bring Eleanor?” Alexa’s grandmother asked. “I would have liked to see her tonight, and she would have liked my sticky coconut cake.”

At the mention of Eleanor, Alexa took a deep breath, doing her best to display a casual air. “I wanted to check up on you, and I have some news.” She sipped her calming aromatic tea while Gran doled out a generous portion of coconut cake onto their plates. “Eleanor sends her love, Granny. I’m not sure what she’s doing tonight.” Alexa had been fairly noncommittal when they’d hurriedly parted yesterday, and today it took all of Alexa’s strength not to message her. But she’d succeeded. She was proud of herself.

“Okay, then. I’ll package up a couple of slices, and you can deliver them to her.”

“I won’t be seeing her until Sunday, when we both come here for lunch.”

Her grandmother’s eyebrows shot up in an incredulous stare. “You’ll see her before then, surely?”

When Alexa shook her head, Gran asked, “Is Eleanor off on assignment again?”

“No, I don’t think so,” Alexa mumbled, reaching for the napkin she’d dropped under the table.

Her grandmother sharply tapped the ornate cake server on the edge of the plate. "Don't mutter, darling; my hearing is not the best."

"Sorry, Granny. I said, *no,* she isn't going away." Why had she even told Granny that she wasn't seeing Eleanor until Sunday? Alexa folded the napkin, placed it neatly on the table, and gazed out the window at the garden, where plump lemons hung from the tree in the centre of a patch of lawn. "That reminds me. Can I pinch a couple of lemons before I go?"

Gran gave her a quick nod. "Don't change the subject, dear. You haven't had a quarrel, have you?"

"What?" Alexa blurted. "I mean, no." She wasn't sure how to answer truthfully. They hadn't quarrelled, but whatever had happened was her doing. She regretted that she'd disappointed Eleanor but didn't regret her decision.

"We had a really great weekend together. There's so much to tell you. You won't believe what we discovered," Alexa said. "Anyway, it's a good idea for Eleanor and me to take a break this week. We've both got a lot on."

Gran frowned. "Whose idea was that, Alexa?"

Alexa stared at her napkin. "I don't exactly have a good track record when it comes to dating and commitment. As you know, I run for the hills when a girl arrives on the doorstep with a toothbrush in hand."

Her grandmother slowly shook her head. "And why would you do that now? I recall it was you who invited Eleanor away for the weekend."

"I did." Alexa cleared her throat and poured herself another cup of tea. "Things seem to be moving a little too fast for me."

Her grandmother gave her a knowing look. "What are you afraid of, darling?"

Alexa pulled at her collar. "What do you think? People just end up getting hurt. Like Mum; she was devastated when my cowardly father left us and ran off with his personal assistant. Like you, left all alone when Grandad died. What if I'm just like Dad, incapable of maintaining a relationship? I could hurt Eleanor."

"Dear Alexa, I'm so sorry you feel that way." Gran clasped her hands together. "You are not like him."

"How can you be sure of that?"

"I'm sure because you're worrying about Eleanor. You're considering her feelings," she said. "Your father, well, he's onto his third wife now, isn't he? Same pattern, just a younger version. He hurt your mother so badly, it's true, and even though she had other men in her life she never fully trusted anyone enough to marry again." Gran sighed.

Gran made it all seem quite simple. Alexa didn't have to act like her father or make the same mistakes. She didn't want to hurt anyone, especially not Eleanor. But she also didn't want Eleanor to hurt her. "I'm scared to ask Eleanor about her plans for the future. I'm scared of being hurt too," she said quietly. "I need a few days to think things through."

"Don't take too long, Alexa. Just talk to her. Communicate."

"I'll try." Alexa knew deep inside she shouldn't allow the demon of doubt to lead her down a negative path. She should message Eleanor to reassure her that she was very much looking forward to Sunday. The thought brought the first genuine smile to her face since she'd seen Eleanor yesterday.

"Good. You have to begin somewhere," Gran said firmly. "I was unlucky to lose the love of my life so soon, but you know, the time I had with Gerald gave me an abundance of love that has lasted a lifetime. It also gave me the two greatest gifts. Eloise, and you."

Tears blurred Alexa's eyes, and she wiped them with her sleeve.

Gran took her hands and squeezed them firmly between her own. "Your parents' relationship wasn't a good example for you. Mahjong teaches us it's not the tiles you start with but the decisions you make that define your life. Love never works perfectly all the time, but that doesn't mean it's not worth the risk. Everyone is afraid of getting hurt."

"Everything seems to be moving too fast, Granny. I'm not used to feeling so much..." Alexa bit her lip and exhaled shakily. "So much, so soon. I don't like feeling out of control."

"Ahh, yes. That's a scary feeling indeed." Gran smiled. "But unless you have strong beliefs about the benefits of a single life, you are going to have to change. You've enjoyed being single, but do you want to be alone forever?"

Alexa shook her head. For the most part, she did enjoy the single life. After a string of unfulfilling liaisons, she'd come to believe the right woman for her didn't exist. Because Eleanor had come along and chipped away at her defences, Alexa was having second thoughts. She couldn't even think of Eleanor without a pleasurable warmth spreading through her. Was this just lust, or was it different? Was this love? Was she prepared to make a commitment to Eleanor?

Bruce appeared from nowhere, jumped up onto Alexa's lap, and bumped the top of his head against her chin, his rumbling purr rising to a crescendo of joy.

"You understand me, don't you, Bruce?"

Her grandmother reached across and ruffled his ginger coat. "Yes, my Bruce is a confirmed bachelor, and even though being neutered curbs his roaming, he has plenty of girlfriends in the neighbourhood."

"And you to come home to." Alexa laughed. "Off you go, Bruce, and find one of your other girlfriends." Alexa lifted the cat off her lap and onto the floor.

He turned in circles a few times, scratched his claws on the kitchen rug, and bolted outside, the clatter of the cat flap echoing in his wake.

"That's my boy." Gran chuckled.

"Now, Granny, I've got so much to tell you." Alexa reached for her satchel and extracted Phyllis's portfolio. She cleared a space on the kitchen table and spread out several sheets of paper. Reverently, she placed the photocopy of the Chinese herbalist in front of her grandmother. Alexa's pulse quickened as she pointed to the picture and asked, "Do you remember this?"

"Why yes, I believe you showed it to me recently. Why? Who is he?" Gran looked thoroughly perplexed; she obviously didn't know the man's identity.

Alexa pulled down her reading glasses to the bridge of her nose. "Where do I start?" Gran's eyes began to widen as Alexa carefully explained about Mei-Li's birth certificate, the ship's records, and the travel documents. As she shared the good news about their family, all the tension of the day drained from her body bit by bit.

"This man is Guān Li-Shen." She put her arm around her grandmother and gave her a gentle squeeze. "He is your great-grandfather."

Gran picked up the photocopy of Guān and quietly stared at it for a long time. She closed her eyes briefly, as though saying a silent prayer. "Mei-Li's father. Oh, my goodness, this is remarkable. Isn't he handsome?" She held the image to her chest. "Low and behold, the universe has conspired to lead us to our ancestors," Gran said, in awe.

Later that evening, back at the loft, and spurred on by Gran's enthusiasm, Alexa sat at the desk in front of her laptop. Since their meeting on Saturday, she'd had no time to read through the articles Phyllis had given her. She furrowed her brows in concentration as she finally pulled up the first one and began to read. As far as Mei-Li's case went, Alexa was now more determined than ever to find the answers.

Alexa had been careful not to divulge too many unpleasant details to her grandmother about Edith Foster's illness and death. The newspapers had reported that Edith had died in hospital from pneumonia, but there had been other complications. Alexa opened the Google search engine and typed in Edith's symptoms as described in the court transcripts.

Sore teeth and gums. Mouth ulcers. Sore throat. Aching limbs. Brittle bones.

Alexa scanned through the first few pages of the eight hundred and fifty-six thousand search engine results before sitting back in frustration. This wasn't going to get her anywhere. She needed to rethink her approach. There were so many possibilities. Autoimmune disease? Cancer? Poisoning couldn't be discounted—Mei-Li had mentioned poisoning.

Marita's name flashed in the corner of the laptop screen, and Alexa clicked on the text message:

Hi Alexa. It was great to meet your Eleanor! Heartfelt thanks for bringing so many friends to the Bridge on Saturday.

Alexa grinned and tapped a quick reply:

The show was excellent. Always such a thoughtful, rewarding performance. You made a new fan in Eleanor. Catch up soon. X

Alexa returned to the main screen and skimmed over the webpages for a few minutes before shaking her head and closing her laptop. This was a waste of time.

Standing, Alexa elongated her spine in a full stretch. She gazed out of the high, loft window at the night sky and its hazy blanket of stars. Tired, her body pleasantly achy, she wrapped her arms around herself and was suddenly overcome with the memory of Eleanor's hands on her body and the feel of Eleanor's lithe form stretched out over hers.

Marita had written *your Eleanor*. Did Alexa's friends really see them as a couple now?

Alexa sank into the corner of the cushioned couch and folded her legs beneath her. Why had she said Sunday? Five days away. Gran was right; Alexa *was* deliberately keeping Eleanor at a distance, for now. By convincing herself that she was incapable of experiencing true love, Alexa had been repeating the same patterns. Meeting someone. Getting closer. Panicking. Calling it quits and justifying her retreat. If she didn't change, she was going to end up alone for the rest of her life.

She had inherited Steven Bellamy's genes, but she did not have to follow in her father's footsteps. And she could do something about it. Maybe Gran was right. Maybe it was time for Alexa to stop being so damn afraid all the time.

Chapter 25

The game of sparrows

Alexa woke up and automatically reached for Eleanor. She wasn't there. Damn, it was just a dream. A dream so real, so tangible, she could have sworn Eleanor was beside her. God, she could even smell her. She buried her head under the pillow and groaned piteously. Alexa ran her tongue around her lips; she could almost taste Eleanor. It was entirely Alexa's decision they wouldn't see each other until Sunday, and now she was being tortured by an unbearable mix of longing and frustration.

Rolling onto her back, she threw a hand over her eyes. When did the alarm go off, and how did it get so bright in her bedroom? The light filtering through the blinds wasn't doing much for her foggy head. Coffee. She needed coffee. With a heavy sigh, she flung off the covers and crawled out of bed. *Shit.* Was it really only Thursday morning? Three and a half days until she laid eyes on Eleanor again. At least she had a couple of intense workdays to focus on. She reached for the water bottle on her bedside table and took a large gulp.

Alexa stared at the bedside clock, grimacing at the late hour. "I'm going to have skip the caffeine until I get to work," she mumbled, rousing herself from her bed and heading straight to the shower. She could at least make an effort to get to work on time.

The ground-floor galleries were a buzz of activity and as lively as Flinders Street Station during peak hour when Alexa arrived. It was just over a month to Christmas, and after major refurbishments, the library would soon be opening its redeveloped spaces in a flurry of exhibitions and special events. As exhibition installers scurried to and fro through the restored heritage space, each concentrating on their specific tasks, Alexa caught up with Katherine Kent, who was observing the placement of the last new showcases.

"Right on time, Alexa. What do you think?" Katherine tapped her index finger on her rather prominent chin.

"The space is beginning to take shape, just how we planned. It's going to be fabulous. Crowds will pour through here all summer with the Ashes Urn in the gallery next door. This exhibition, *Recent Acquisitions and Highlights of the Lehmann Collection*—it's a bit of a mouthful, isn't it?—will get plenty of exposure."

"Yes," Katherine agreed with a chuckle. "It is perfectly timed, especially with the extra events organised for our grand re-opening. I've approved the mock-ups and will leave you and the curator to sort out the final design. Double check those thematic text panels. We had a problem in the Victoria Gallery with the printer. The text was too pale." She narrowed her eyes. "I could hardly read a thing."

The devil is in the detail. Alexa nodded, remembering one of her grandmother's favourite sayings. "Everything's set up in the workroom, so we can tweak the final layout."

"Excellent." Katherine checked her watch. "Let's leave the installation team to get on with it, and we can check back later. Unless you have any concerns, Alexa?"

"No concerns at the moment. If you don't need me, I'll head back upstairs now."

"Good. I'll walk with you." Katherine fell into step with Alexa, and they strode towards the staircase. "I'm having supper with the Heysens tonight. I expect Eleanor will be there."

Alexa gulped. She had almost forgotten her boss was Eleanor's mother's best friend. "That's nice. I expect she will," she said in a restrained tone.

Katherine gave her a sideways glance and lightly tapped Alexa's forearm. "I'm happy you and Eleanor are friends. It can be lonely coming home after such a long absence. Sarah worries that her daughter is having difficulty settling back in Melbourne—I don't think Eleanor kept in touch with many university friends after she left for London."

Had Eleanor really settled back, or was she just biding her time before traipsing off to some far away destination? The fact that she didn't know Eleanor's plans for the future sparked a bit of worry in Alexa.

"Are you still working together on finding the locations of Helen Heysen's slides?"

"Nearly done," Alexa replied.

Katherine stopped with one foot on the step above. She gave her head a small shake, and her tawny coloured hair, pinned to the side of her head with a large Art Deco hair comb, barely moved. "I know I've already expressed my amazement, Alexa, but the news about your ancestor's connection to the Lehmann slide collection—well, I am gobsmacked."

Alexa answered in a quiet voice, "Me, too."

"Considering Helen Heysen's contribution to the Lehmann Collection and your family connection, we could expand on the link. We should involve Eleanor. Her talent is a real asset," Katherine said. "Talk to her. I have faith that the two of you could come up with something unique that would work hand in hand with the Lehmann exhibition. Despite our time constraints and the extra work involved, there is scope in our budget to develop this further."

Alexa stared at Katherine. That was an inspired idea. A blossom of hope unfurled in her chest. Could Eleanor be persuaded to come on board and work with Alexa?

Katherine squeezed her forearm. "As I said, think about it. Just don't leave it too long."

Alexa could have hugged Katherine but restrained herself and just nodded. It would be a perfect excuse to contact Eleanor today.

At the top of the stairs, Sanjay Kumar ambled towards them, carrying a stack of flat document folders. "Good afternoon, ladies," he said, flashing a shy grin. "Alexa, you probably already know this, but Eleanor's agreed to work with us in Image Capture sometime next week. We're totally swamped and would really appreciate her help."

"Oh, that's great." Alexa stared at Sanjay who bowed his head at Katherine, then kept moving in the opposite direction down the corridor. No, she didn't know that about Eleanor. She also didn't know why everyone felt the need to mention Eleanor's name the moment they saw Alexa today.

Katherine raised an eyebrow but said nothing and kept on walking.

"I'm still trying to get my head around it." Alexa caught up to Katherine. "I mean that I'm related to Guān Li-Shen, *our* Chinese herbalist." The fact that she hadn't heard a whisper about Eleanor working at the library next week was another thing she had to get her head around.

"Remarkable," agreed Katherine. "Well, keep me informed about the installation and any ideas you come up with about expanding it."

They passed a workroom just as Jac appeared at the door, wheeling a small two-tiered cart.

"Good afternoon, Katherine. Alexa."

"Afternoon, Jacqueline," Katherine said. "Alexa and I have just returned from checking on the progress downstairs."

"That's good. Everything's coming along well, isn't it?" Jac tapped the top of the white tote box on her cart. "I'm transferring Eleanor's glass plate negative slide boxes to Exhibition Prep to measure up for display. I have it on my to-do list to ring Eleanor about the photograph of her aunt that's to be included in the exhibition catalogue."

Good grief! Was Eleanor going to haunt her all day?

Jac tilted her head at Alexa questioningly. "Or would you rather do it?"

"I guess I could," Alexa answered. "We'll need to know the proper dimensions, format, and all that stuff." Now she had another excuse to ring Eleanor today.

"Okay, you'll handle Eleanor then." Jac smirked. "I'd better be off."

Alexa looked down at her feet, hoping she hadn't flushed bright red.

Katherine paused at the office doorway and turned, folding her arms in front of her chest. "Eleanor seems to have made a number of friends at the library," she said with a gleam in her eyes. "Isn't it extraordinary how the stars have aligned to bring everything together? It's destiny." Katherine gave Alexa a sweet but knowing smile. "I'll catch up with you later."

Alexa stood with her mouth half open, watching her boss stride briskly away. Why did the stars have to align and bring Eleanor into every conversation with *everyone* she met? Alexa took a deep calming breath. It was true. If the stars hadn't aligned, the extraordinary discovery about her ancestors may never have come to light. She and Eleanor wouldn't have met, and Alexa would never have caught a glimpse of opportunities previously unimagined. Alexa reached for her phone. For the last few days, during her period of introspection, Alexa had tried to convince herself that she could manage without Eleanor, but she was tired of pretending. She unlocked her phone and began to type out a text.

Eleanor guided Grace to a worn leather armchair beside an elderly gentleman who'd introduced himself as Roberto. He'd insisted he was an *inmate* there, at the Merri Community Home, and Eleanor had laughed at his good spirit.

"Oh, thank you, Eleanor." Grace puffed a breath and sank into the armchair, resting her head back against the padded cover. "You finally got here without interference from my granddaughter."

"Yes, I am very glad to be here at last," Eleanor said. She was relieved that she and Alexa seemed to be back on good terms again.

"The players and the residents are happy for you to take their photos, although I suspect some needed a little cajoling. Wrinkles and vanity and all that." Grace shrugged her shoulders.

"You've been a great help setting things up for me, Grace. I think they'd do anything for you." Eleanor crouched down beside her and lightly held her hand. "Are you sure you're okay? Can I get you a glass of water?" She glanced at the long table laid out with a beverage station and dishes filled with interesting goodies, cooked by the residents in the home's central kitchen. "I don't think the hot drinks are ready."

"No, not yet. I'll be fine in a jiffy. I just need to sit here and rest for five minutes." She patted Eleanor's hand.

Grace had remarked that, thankfully, the home was not administered by one of those unscrupulous mining companies and the manager and staff were respectful of the residents' needs. Considering the horrors being revealed through the Royal Commission into Aged Care Quality and Safety, Eleanor was relieved places such as this existed.

"Roberto will look after me. Now, off you go to create some magic with your camera. Covertly, if necessary," Grace insisted with a wink. "When the games are over, the gang will make a beeline for the afternoon tea table like a horde of hungry mice."

"I'm not sure how much help Roberto will be. He's taking a nap."

He hadn't moved in his rocking chair for some time but startled to attention at the sound of his name. "What? What did you say, dear?" he boomed, "I'm awake."

"Off you go." Grace gently tugged the camera strap that hung around Eleanor's neck.

It wasn't at all surprising that Grace needed a rest. Eleanor was amazed that, even though Grace was ninety-one, a lot older than many of the residents, she'd been rushing around organising the tournament like a headmistress mustering her students at assembly. With two younger volunteers, they supervised the twenty-four participants, meandering between the square Mahjong tables of four, keeping scores, ensuring everyone was adequately hydrated, and resolving minor disputes before they erupted into something more serious. Hopefully, Grace wasn't totally worn out by all that rushing about.

The Merri Community Home's Annual Report would feature the tournament and participants, and Eleanor was tasked with the photoshoot. Her heart warmed at being able to help out the residents, and this was a great opportunity for her to gain more experience photographing elderly people. She'd already been introduced to an array of colourful characters, and many had allowed her to get up close. Eleanor smiled as she checked the photographs she'd taken so far. She'd been able to capture the fine details and expressions of these amazing individuals who'd laughed, cried, and loved for a very long time.

A fashionably dressed woman—her makeup perfectly applied—entered the recreation room, brandishing a long white stick, and carefully manoeuvred past the players towards Eleanor. "They tell me you're the shutterbug today. My name is Josie. Would you like to photograph me?" she invited sweetly.

Eleanor's eyes lit up. This petite, well-poised lady in her violet pantsuit would make a fantastic subject. "I'd love to. Would you like to sit down, or are you comfortable right here?"

"Here will do nicely," she stated with enthusiasm. "I'm legally blind, so I can't play anymore, but I want to be close to the action. Even though I'm a nonagenarian, there's nothing wrong with my hearing. I love the music of the Mahjong tiles being shuffled. All the players put their hands in and make as much noise as possible. The clacking of the tiles is like the twittering of sparrows. Do you know how to play, Eleanor?"

"Not really, but I can see why it could become quite addictive," Eleanor said. "Grace has explained the basics. After the twittering, they rebuild the walls and then they throw the dice to determine who gets to be East Wind and start the round."

"Yes." Josie turned to Eleanor with a bright smile. "It is a game of chance and strategy in equal measure, just like life."

"That's food for thought," Eleanor said. When it came to Alexa, she figured a bit more strategy was required—and less reliance on chance. She shook her head. Somehow, her thoughts always returned to Alexa.

"I'm ready, Eleanor. Are you going to take my photograph?"

Eleanor lifted her camera to quickly capture the alertness and determination in Josie's upright posture and strong jawline. How did Josie navigate life through a haze, through a foggy lens? Eleanor couldn't imagine losing her eyesight, and yet this woman seemed perfectly aware of everything around her, as though her other senses were more highly tuned to compensate. Eleanor knew she had gained more from this short time with Josie than a few photographs. Josie's resilience was inspiring.

Josie ran her finger over the raised dot face of her watch, and Eleanor quickly seized the moment. She grinned at the photo of Josie embracing the latest wearable technology.

"Afternoon tea will be in precisely ten minutes. You must try a slice of my poppy seed and walnut torte," Josie said.

"Definitely. Thank you for letting me photograph you. Please, excuse me. It's time to photograph the players on Table Three."

Eleanor leaned with her hip against the windowsill, her back against the light. She raised her camera and focussed on her next subject, snapping a close-up. Holding her breath, she shot another as the man's face suddenly reflected the utter triumph and joy of winning, raising his hands in the air. Glancing at the screen, Eleanor sighed happily. She'd managed to capture his exhilaration in one crystal-clear and heart-warming image.

The phone in her trouser pocket vibrated against her leg, and Eleanor silently moved to the corner of the room. She slipped it out to check the sender. Eleanor was pleasantly surprised to see it was from Alexa. A sigh escaped her and she grinned.

How are things going? Have they served afternoon tea yet?

Skimming her fingers over the screen, Eleanor typed out a reply:

They sure put up a good spread. This place is one of a kind. Truly lovely and everyone is bending over backwards to make my task easy.

In a flash, Alexa replied:

I'm sure you've charmed them all. How is Granny?

Eleanor glanced over to where she'd last seen Grace resting in the chair. But Grace wasn't there now. Eleanor paused, thinking about her reply. She didn't want Alexa to worry about her grandmother.

Grace has everything under control. Running around orchestrating the entire event. She's a little tired but I finally convinced her to take a break.

A few seconds later, the three bouncing dots appeared, indicating that Alexa was typing:

Typical of Gran. She can be a whirlwind. How are you doing?

Eleanor smiled and quickly typed back.

Fantastic. The residents are keeping me on my toes. Lots to do.

Eleanor would definitely feel more relaxed once she'd located Grace and made sure she was okay.

This time, Alexa's response was quicker:

Won't keep you any longer then. Just two things. Jac needs a photo. Details in my email to follow. I have a work proposition for you. Could be amazing. Discuss later.

Eleanor stared at the screen, stomach fluttering.

Okay.

What on earth could the proposition be?

Enjoy the rest of your day. Bye AX

Eleanor smiled and sent the thumbs-up emoji:

You too.

She hastily scanned the room and spotted Grace deep in conversation at Table Six. Her shoulders slumped in relief, and she shook her head at herself. Grace was fine. No need to worry.

Eleanor slipped her phone back into her pocket. Damn it, she missed Alexa. It turned her upside down. Since last night, she'd received two texts from her. They'd been short, light, and direct. Nothing overly personal. While Eleanor respected Alexa's obvious need to put the brakes on, she was frustrated and unsure what to expect from her next. Even though she didn't want to pressure Alexa, Eleanor wasn't prepared to hang back and wait for her to make all the moves. *Love,* like Mahjong, was a game of chance and strategy. "I mustn't let this push-pull dance get me down," she muttered.

"Did you mention dancing, young lady? The Christmas dance is not for a few weeks yet," a soft, quivery male voice said. "We'd be happy for you to join us. I'll put you on my dance card."

Eleanor tilted her head towards the gentleman who was seated on a small three-wheeler mobility scooter. Evidently, she'd spoken louder than she'd thought. "Good afternoon, sir."

"Teddy Kwong. *Kong* as in King Kong." He guffawed at his own joke.

"Nice to meet you, Mr Kwong." She lifted her camera and raised her eyebrows, asking permission to take a photograph.

Teddy nodded, lifted his tartan cap, and scratched his shiny bald skull. When he smiled for the camera, Eleanor noticed the gap in the top row of his slightly crooked teeth. His face was wrinkled beyond time itself, and yet his pale grey eyes were filled with humour.

Eleanor held the camera steady and filled the frame with Teddy's wise old face. She adjusted the focus. *Click.*

"I'm being impertinent, but can I take a look at my mug shot?" Teddy asked.

"Here you are." With a satisfied smile Eleanor flipped the screen to show him the photo. Years may wrinkle the skin, but they did not have to crush humour, self-confidence, and spirit.

"Oh, my word. You've performed magic." His face broke into a wide grin. "My late wife used to say this face told the story of my life. I didn't understand what she meant, but now I see it." He wiped a tear from the corner of his eye. "Grace failed to mention that you are a true artist."

"You are a flatterer, Mr Kwong. Thank you." Eleanor laughed.

He sneakily pressed the back button, bringing up a photo of Josie. "Ahh…that's our Ms Benko. She has an arresting face, doesn't she? …and your photo highlights her pluckiness. Did you know she was a trailblazer in women's fashion photography?"

"A photographer? She didn't mention that."

The dismay must have shown on her face because Teddy reached out and touched her arm. "She's had a stellar career and look at her now; she's happy—even though she never did marry," he said with a little smirk.

"Josie Benko. I'll have to look her up."

"There's a lot for you to discover behind the faces here," Teddy said.

Eleanor nodded. "I'm privileged to spend the afternoon with all of you, Mr Kwong."

A lot of time and attention was given to youth and beauty, pushing the older generation into the background. Today, though, Eleanor had met many talented people who refused to accept the *invisible* status expected of their age. So many stories just in this one room.

Eleanor was excited about some of the images she'd captured here, building on her growing body of work centred on the elderly. Perhaps an exhibition in the making.

Eleanor watched the players pack up their tiles in preparation for afternoon tea. She turned at the sound of a high-pitched ringing.

Grace stood by the buffet table waving a shiny brass bell in the air, a devilish grin on her face. Eleanor instinctively raised the camera. *Click.* Perfect shot. Sometimes it was best not to think too much.

She felt a sudden tug in her chest. Grace played a vital role in Alexa's life and was her most significant relative. Grace was gutsy and strong but not invincible, and Eleanor's heart ached for Alexa at the realisation that Grace couldn't stick around forever.

Reaching into her pocket, Eleanor placed her hand on the phone—as if creating a visceral connection to Alexa. How could she help Alexa unlock the secrets of her ancestors' past and set Grace free from her burden? They had to learn more about Mei-Li Kwan and clear her name. Eleanor's mind was a jumble of unanswered questions. Why did Edith Foster really die? What happened to the husband? Did he know more than he'd let on? Eleanor shook her head, pushing the questions away. She couldn't let her fact-finding, investigative nature get the better of her this time. She had to wait for Alexa to ask.

Teddy tapped her on the arm. "Would you be a dear and put aside a couple of pastries on a plate?" He wiggled his fingers and pointed to an old piano in the corner of the rec room. "I'm the entertainment this afternoon."

"Of course, Teddy. I look forward to hearing you play."

Eleanor was beginning to realise how she'd taken her own family for granted. Whenever she jetted in from overseas, she returned home to a safe, welcoming environment. As well as her mother, Dad, and Leo, she still had both her grandmothers. They were very different in appearance and personality, but both showered her with love. She looked forward to swapping travel stories with tall, sturdy Grandma Heysen when she returned from visiting relatives in the Netherlands. And now that her father was on the mend, she and her mother could take the four-hour road trip to visit Nan Miller, who lived with Uncle Will in Port Fairy. She smiled at the idea of sitting on the pier with Nan for a few hours, undoing knots in her fishing line and refusing to touch the wriggly worms she used for bait. Family. Eleanor sighed. How the hell had she got so lucky?

Chapter 26

All honour hands

"HERE'S TO FRIDAY NIGHT DRINKS at home in the *good room*." Leo passed his mother a tall glass of iced tea and handed Eleanor her gin and tonic. "It's been a while since we've been able to do this, together as a family."

Eleanor raised her glass and observed her family with fond affection. If she couldn't be with Alexa tonight, she was content to be at home.

"I left work as soon as I got the severe thunderstorm warning." Her mother glanced at the ornate carriage clock that graced the mantelpiece. "It's after six, and all we've had is heavy rain and lots of rumbles." Her parents clinked their glasses and wriggled closer to each other on the large sofa. "Cheers, Harold," she said.

"That wind is still pretty strong and the temperature's dropped, but I'm hoping the worst of it has passed over," Leo said, crossing to the French windows and peering out.

Eleanor plonked herself onto the lounge chair across from her parents, tucking one leg under her. "Thank God it's cooled down. It was unbearably warm and sticky this afternoon. Isn't it unusual for it to be this hot in November?"

Leo sat down and drummed his fingers on the arms of his chair. "And despite overwhelming scientific evidence, our government refuses to take meaningful steps to mitigate climate change."

"Hmm. Hopeless bunch." Her father took a tentative sip of his drink.

"Darling, how's your Dirty Martini Mocktail?" her mother asked.

He scrunched up his nose and winked at her. "I'd rather have the vodka version, but so be it," he said, squeezing her knee.

Eleanor met her brother's gaze, and they synchronised eye rolls.

"I'm a little peckish. I'll just grab us a snack. Something special for you, Harold?"

"I already have the olives." He swirled the stick in his glass. "Even though I'm not allowed to eat them. Cheese and crackers would be a treat."

"I won't be long."

Since Eleanor's father's heart attack, there were definitely more hugs and gushy shows of affection between her parents, or maybe she'd been away so long she'd forgotten their loving alliance. When she and Leo were young, she remembered a few arguments and some tension between her parents, and her mum was rarely home. Despite this, Leo had turned out to be a happy-go-lucky kid, always with a gang of school friends hanging around him. Eleanor, on the other hand, busied herself with solo pursuits like photography and exploring and had disappeared into her head reading about foreign lands. On reflection, she'd chosen to spend time alone and, as a result, had become a resilient and independent adult.

Eleanor swirled the ice cubes around in her glass. Watching her parents tonight, she wondered what kind of wife and partner she would be. What kind of mother? She took a large sip of her drink. Could Alexa imagine a future with Eleanor? Did she even want the same things Eleanor did?

"Nell, I watched you fishing leaves out of the pool earlier. Did you enjoy your swim?"

"I did, thanks, Dad. Keeping it clean so you'll have no excuse to dodge water therapy with your physio," Eleanor said. "Leo, I'll need your help to put up the shade sail over the pool."

He gave her a mock salute and glanced down at his phone again. "Sure, I'll be back here in a couple of days."

"That's about the fourth time you've checked your phone. What are you doing?" Eleanor asked curiously.

"Checking the weather forecast," Leo mumbled. "I'm meeting a friend for dinner." He cleared his throat and grinned at her.

Eleanor's eyes widened. "You have a date? With whom do you have a date?"

"If things turn out *right*, we might even go out dancing." He put his hands in the air and waved them from side to side.

"Seeing you've got two left feet, that hardly seems likely." Eleanor scoffed.

"Maybe I've never had the right partner."

"Leo, stop teasing your sister," their father said, lifting his empty glass. "A large G and T, please, son. Hold the gin."

Her mother re-entered the room and set a platter of cheeses, crackers, pâté, and cut fruit on the table. She sighed loudly. "At least with all the rain we won't have to water the garden." She placed side plates and napkins beside the nibbles, walked over to Leo, and perched on the arm of his chair. "You'd better hope the weather clears, Leo. What time did you plan to meet Stella?"

"Late," he replied. "She's been in court all day."

Eleanor stopped with the cracker halfway to her mouth as their words sunk in. "Stella?" The hard cheese rolled off the biscuit and bounced onto the wooden floor.

Leo raised an eyebrow. "What can I say?"

"*You* have a date with Stella Wright? You sneaky bastard."

"Language," their father said sternly.

Eleanor shook her head, scooped up the cheese, and pretended to toss it at Leo.

He ducked in surprise.

"What are you two up to?" Their mother glanced from Leo to Eleanor with a look of exasperation, as if to say: "Act your ages, children."

"Nothing, Mum. Just Eleanor's imagination running wild." Leo gave Eleanor another one of his cheeky grins.

Eleanor fixed him with a dagger stare. "My imagination? Just you wait."

Leo lounged back in his chair, legs crossed, nonchalantly waving his glass of gin and tonic in her direction.

She ignored him and peeked at her phone just in case she'd missed a message from Alexa. There'd been nothing from her at all today. With a resigned sigh, she placed her phone on the table and leaned back in her chair.

"What about your plans, Eleanor?" her mother asked. "I imagine Alexa's been busy preparing for the library's re-opening. Katherine mentioned that last night, didn't she? Also, she hinted about some exciting prospects ahead."

One of the prospects was likely the idea Alexa had outlined in her email late last night, about Eleanor working with them on an exhibition for the re-opening. She'd been blown away by the concept and couldn't wait to talk to Alexa about it in person. Even the thought of it had Eleanor jiggling her leg impatiently.

Her father helped himself to a *crostino* spread with a smidgen of pâté. Turning to Eleanor, he said, "You've been home every night this week. It's Friday. Why don't you give Alexa a call?"

Eleanor's phone rang, and she jumped to her feet, recognising Alexa's ringtone. Her pulse quickened. Did Alexa want to get together after all? Before she got to the table where her phone lay, Leo picked it up, his nose crinkling as he peered at the screen. Eleanor groaned. Leo could be such a pain sometimes.

"Speaking of Alexa. The woman must be psychic." Leo waved the phone high in the air, out of Eleanor's reach.

Eleanor knew Alexa wouldn't be able to wait until Sunday. She gave Leo a withering look, and he handed her the phone. Grabbing it out of his hand, she said, "Excuse me, I'll take this call in private." She walked towards the hallway, humming to herself.

Out of earshot, she answered the call with a chirpy hello on her lips, but a strangled sound greeted her.

"Eleanor. I'm so sorry to disturb you. I thought Gran was unconscious. She spoke to me, but it was garbled and made no sense at all. I don't know what's happened," Alexa's voice was frantic.

"Alexa, darling, slow down," Eleanor said as calmly as she could, even though her own heart was racing. "What's happened to Grace? Where are you now? I can hear traffic." Surely, Alexa wouldn't drive in such an agitated state.

"The ambulance has taken Gran to St. Vincent's. They wouldn't let me ride with her. I'm in a taxi on the way to the hospital now. There was no one else to call."

Eleanor heard a muffled voice in the background. "Alexa? What's that noise?"

"Hang on, we're at the hospital. I have to pay the driver." There was a rustling over the line and more mumbled voices. Sick with worry, Eleanor paced up and down the hallway, trying to take calming breaths, but it was no use at all.

"Eleanor, what's going on?" Her mother suddenly appeared beside her.

Eleanor stopped pacing and held a finger to her lips as Leo and her father gathered around. "Eleanor, they are going to admit Granny." Alexa's voice cracked. "I feel so helpless. I don't know what to do. Could you please meet me here?" she asked softly.

"Of course, I'm on my way. I'll be there as soon as possible, sweetheart."

"Thank you. I'm at reception now. I have to go," Alexa said. "See you soon. Thank you so much."

Eleanor's hands shook as she stared at the blank screen. "Dad, I need to borrow the car." She turned to her father.

"Yes, of course." He placed his arm around her shoulder.

"What's happened, sis? What can we do?" Leo asked.

Eleanor rubbed her forehead. "Grace has been taken to St. Vincent's. They don't know what's wrong, and Alexa is all alone. I have to go to her."

Her father gave her a squeeze and let go. "You'd better get going," he said. "Leo, grab the keys to the Skoda and bring it out front while Eleanor gets changed."

Eleanor looked down at her worn T-shirt, shorts, and bare feet. She looked as bedraggled as she felt. Taking off towards her studio, she yelled, "Thanks, Dad."

Thank God Alexa had called her. Eleanor's heart wouldn't stop pounding and fear made her clumsy as she desperately pulled on a pair of jeans and a not-too-crumpled shirt. Sprinting to the front of the house, she found, instead of the Skoda, her mother sitting in her BMW, the motor idling. Eleanor sighed with relief and smiled in deep appreciation.

The glass lowered on the driver's side. "Hop in, Eleanor," her mother said in a firm but gentle tone.

Placing her hand on the open window, Eleanor leaned in. "Are you sure, Mum? You've had a long day."

"Darling, you've had more than one drink. The traffic will be horrendous near the hospital, and you don't want to waste time trying to find a park. Alexa needs you," she said in a soothing voice.

Worried sick about Grace and Alexa, Eleanor was really in no state to drive. But Alexa had called her, and she sure as hell wanted to be with her. Right now.

Eleanor raced around to the passenger side and slid into the seat. Reaching for the safety belt, she pulled it across her lap and clicked it into place.

Her mother eased the car out of the driveway, manoeuvring slowly into the street.

"Mum."

"Yes, dear?"

"Could you go a little faster, please?"

"Of course." Switching lanes to bypass slower vehicles, Sarah soon had them ascending the on-ramp to the highway, where they merged into smooth flowing traffic heading into the city.

Eleanor leaned forward and pressed her foot down on an imaginary accelerator in a vain hope of speeding up their journey. "Mum, wouldn't it be faster to go through the back streets?"

"I'm avoiding the traffic lights. This way is faster."

"Good." Eleanor peered out of the window. "Thankfully the rain's not still bucketing down. The roads are slippery, though." Car lights glistened off the slick tarmac, making visibility difficult. "Thanks for driving me, Mum."

Alexa's anxious voice had scared her, and she would have driven like a maniac in these rotten conditions, trying to get to the hospital as soon as possible. She wanted to put her arms around Alexa, to comfort her and be there for her, no matter what. Eleanor let out a stifled sob as she thought of Alexa waiting there all alone.

"We'll be there soon, Eleanor," her mother said. "I hope Grace will come through this okay. I really do."

Eleanor stared straight ahead. "The heat must have been too much for her today. She could be suffering from exhaustion or dehydration..." Or was it something more serious?

Grace had moved around like a rocket at the tournament, hardly stopping, even though Eleanor had urged her, a number of times, to sit down and rest. Tears welled in Eleanor's eyes. She should have insisted more firmly.

"She has such tenacity for her age, Mum. She was tired yesterday, but that's hardly surprising," she said. "Having me there probably added to her stress. I should have helped her more."

Her mother patted her forearm. "Stop that, Eleanor. Grace asked you to take the photographs for the newsletter, didn't she? You were helping her out."

"I should have encouraged her to take a proper rest."

"You tried. From what you've told me about her, Grace is an independent soul. You're not responsible for other people's choices," her mother said.

They exchanged a brief look before Eleanor mumbled, "You mean Helen too?"

"Your aunt was fiercely independent. You've always blamed yourself for Helen being in Chengdu, but she was there on assignment. The earthquake that killed her had nothing to do with you not meeting her in Beijing." Eleanor's mother spoke slowly, and her voice rasped with emotion.

Eleanor hung her head. "You're right, Mum. Maybe I couldn't have stopped her from going to Chengdu." She was also beginning to recognise that her mother's evaluation of her career choice came from love and concern, not as she had always supposed—from her mother's resentment that Helen had enticed Eleanor to London.

"I'm glad you're starting to believe that," her mother said. "Helen would be so proud of you."

Eleanor squeezed her eyes shut. Those were the words she'd needed to hear from her mother for years. "Thank you, Mum. Helen taught me that it is our role is to observe, photograph, and make people stop and think. She was just doing what she loved to do."

"You're right, Eleanor." Her mother glanced over at her. "You're very fond of Grace, aren't you?"

Eleanor nodded. "At the tournament, Grace organised the group photos, and it was incredible the way she got everyone to smile and laugh. She has such a talent, Mum, just like her granddaughter." Eleanor pressed her fingers to her lips. *Alexa*, she sighed and willed herself not to cry.

"You're very fond of Alexa, too."

"I am," she answered quickly. "Quite a lot."

Her mother's smile gave Eleanor the courage to continue. "I know we haven't known each other for long, but it feels right. Alexa is..." She swallowed. "I've dated over the years, but Alexa is like no one before. When I'm with her, there's an indefinable sort of rightness. It's not just because she's beautiful and brilliant—I don't know exactly—I'm…"

"In love with her?" her mother asked tentatively.

"I think so. Yes." Eleanor looked down at her hands, surprised she felt safe enough to make that declaration to her mother even before she'd admitted it to Alexa. But it was the truth. The intense worry tearing apart her insides right now, not only for Grace but also for Alexa, was proof of that.

"How do you think Alexa feels about you?"

"I know she cares. She's honest and kind. I also think she's scared." Eleanor pushed her hand through her hair. "But she called me," she said as realisation sunk in. "When she needed someone, she called *me*."

"She did, darling."

"Grace and Alexa have a very special relationship. Apart from a father she doesn't see, Grace is her only close relative." Taking a deep breath, Eleanor closed her eyes for a moment. "I'm so lucky. Leo and I are lucky to have you and Dad. He's making a good recovery, don't you think? He really gave us a scare."

Her mother's hands clenched the steering wheel, but when she spoke, her voice was calm and steady. "And God willing, Grace will be okay, too."

"I hope so. She can't live forever, but Alexa is not ready to say goodbye yet. I don't want her to be all alone with no family." Eleanor's hands trembled, and a quiver of fear rippled through her body.

"She won't be alone, Eleanor. She has you." Her mother smiled warmly.

The car slowed near Carlton Gardens after the Nicholson Street turnoff. Thanks to her mother's skilful driving, they were already at the hospital. Eleanor pushed down the urge to jump out of the still-moving car.

"There's a space over there." Her mother pointed down the road. "I'm going to grab that park."

"You don't have to stay, Mum. Just pull off here. It's only a short walk to the main entrance." Eleanor quickly scanned the hospital map she'd pulled up on her phone.

"I'm coming in with you. I won't stay if you don't want me to, but let me come in and check on Grace's condition, just to make sure that she and Alexa will be all right."

"Are you sure, Mum? What about Dad?"

Her mother unfastened her seatbelt and opened the car door. "He'll be fine. Leo's still there for now, and I've asked Joel to stay on until I get home." She reached into the back seat for her purse. "Come on, then. Let's show Alexa that she's not alone; she's got us."

Eleanor grabbed her mother's hand. Tears filled her eyes, and she blinked them away, swallowing the lump in her throat.

"It's okay, darling." Her mother squeezed her shoulder. "You'd better text Alexa and see where she is in the hospital."

The automatic sliding doors opened with a whir.

Eleanor searched the emergency waiting room, checking out the people thrown together for whatever reasons. How on earth would she find Alexa in this crowd? Although, it was fairly orderly for a Friday evening in a city hospital. She screwed up her nose at the astringent smell of pine oil and sanitiser.

There were groups scattered throughout the large space. Parents with small pyjama-clad children hugging soft toys. An old man with a bloodied bandage around his head. A couple of white-coated staff strode past the nurses' station, drawing Eleanor's attention to a group of chairs, half hidden behind a potted palm. There Alexa was. A surge of love and a fierce desire to protect Alexa welled up inside Eleanor.

Alexa sat all alone in an upholstered tub chair between the nurses' station and a set of dark blue doors. Her fingers gripped the seat, and she sat bolt upright. Her eyes were focussed directly in front on those closed doors as if she would run towards them the moment they opened.

Eleanor hurried over to Alexa. Even before she reached her, Alexa must have sensed Eleanor's presence. She turned to face her, gasped, and flew out of the chair.

Eleanor wrapped her arms around Alexa. She seemed fragile as she clung to Eleanor. Swallowing the strangled sob that threatened to escape, Eleanor hugged her tightly.

"I'm so glad you're here." Alexa lowered her head, burying her face into Eleanor's shoulder. "I'm going crazy waiting on my own." She let out a muffled cry. "What if Granny's had a stroke?"

"I'm here, darling. You're not alone now." Eleanor comforted Alexa in the best way she knew. Holding her, stroking her hair, kissing her forehead over and over again as she cried. Grace had to be okay. It was impossible to imagine losing her.

Chapter 27

The gates of heaven

Alexa sank into the security of Eleanor's arms. "I'm so glad you're here," she repeated. "I don't know what I'll do if…" Just thinking about what might happen to Gran made her choke on her words and her heart thumped madly. "They wouldn't let me stay with her during their assessment. The waiting is excruciating. I'm so worried."

Eleanor gently lifted Alexa's chin and stroked her cheek. "I'm here now," she whispered soothingly. "We're here with you."

"We?" Alexa looked over Eleanor's shoulder and noticed Sarah Heysen a few feet away, a concerned frown on her face. "Mrs Heysen," she called out to Sarah. Alexa was heartened that Eleanor hadn't made the trip on her own.

Eleanor kept her arm firmly around Alexa's waist and turned to her mother.

With a nod and a warm smile, Sarah approached them. "Alexa, I'm so sorry. Has your grandmother been admitted yet? Have they explained what's happened?"

Alexa shook her head. "When I arrived at the hospital, they let me see Granny for a few minutes. Her speech was still slurred, and she seemed as confused as when I found her at home. She kept repeating, 'Where's Bruce?'"

"Has Bruce gone missing?" Eleanor asked.

"No. He was meowing like crazy and darting in and out of the cat door before I locked him in. I've spoken to Patrick, and he'll check on him and the house tonight. Of course, Patrick wanted to rush over to the hospital straight away, but I've promised to let him know of Gran's condition as soon as somebody tells me something." She stared at the blue doors, willing them to open. "I wish *someone* would tell me *something*." Alexa clenched her hands into fists.

Eleanor took hold of Alexa's hands, gently rubbing her thumbs over her knuckles, and Alexa leaned into her, thankful for her warmth and strength. Alexa was so grateful she was no longer alone. A little bit of the tension she'd been carrying for hours slipped away, and she could finally breathe again. "I can't pester the nurse manager again. He's already told me that the clinician on duty will speak to me as soon as possible, but they're taking so damn long."

"Why don't you two take a seat?" Sarah suggested. "I spotted a decent-looking coffee station near the entrance and some vending machines."

"I couldn't eat anything, but I'd love a herbal tea." Alexa's nerves were already rattled. Caffeine would probably make her throw up right now.

"How about you, Eleanor?"

"Thanks, Mum. Coffee for me, please." Eleanor glanced at Alexa with concern. "Maybe a muffin or protein bar in case you get hungry later?"

Alexa shook her head.

"I'll see what I can find. Won't be long," Sarah said calmly, before turning and briskly walking back towards the automatic glass doors.

They returned to the seats near the emergency room doors, where they sat close together. "I'm sorry, but Mum insisted she drive me," Eleanor said, squeezing Alexa's hand between hers.

"Don't be. I'm glad she came." Sarah's unflustered presence was an added comfort. Alexa smiled at the thought that Sarah, whom she'd only ever met once, would make the effort to come here just for her.

Eleanor's eyes widened. "Really?"

"Yes." Alexa shrugged her shoulders. "And I know I've said it already, but I'm so glad you're here." Biting her lip, she looked down at their joined hands, and guilt washed over her. When she needed support, Eleanor was the only person she'd thought of, and yet she'd kept her at arm's length all week. "I have to apologise for the way I spoke to you when we returned from the country. I'm sorry, Eleanor."

"It's fine. You don't need to apologise to me."

"I do, especially after being such an ice queen. We had an amazing weekend and then..." Alexa's voice faltered, and she took a moment, breathing deeply. "Eleanor, I like you a lot, more than—"

"Alexa Bellamy?" a voice chimed from the nurses' station.

Alexa felt the blood drain all the way down her body and into her toes. Knees trembling, she collapsed against Eleanor. After a moment, she allowed Eleanor to help her out of the chair. With Eleanor's steadying hand around her waist, she was guided towards the desk where a doctor wearing blue scrubs looked at her expectantly.

Alexa stared at the doctor. "Do you have news about my grandmother? How is she? Will I be able to see her now?"

"Hi, Alexa, I'm Doctor Cassell. I've been attending to your grandmother this evening. She's a spirited lady, I'll give her that." He looked down at the clipboard in his hand. "Mrs West insisted we let her go home," he said with a smile. "It took some work on my part to convince her it would be better for all concerned that she rests here overnight."

Alexa reached out and touched his arm. "Are you saying my grandmother is going to be all right?"

He nodded reassuringly. "I believe so."

With an enormous sigh of relief, Alexa turned to Eleanor and smiled. "Granny's going to be okay."

"That's wonderful news, Alexa." Eleanor turned back to the doctor. "What was wrong with Mrs West?"

Doctor Cassell raised his eyebrows.

"Sorry, Doctor. This is my girlfriend, Eleanor."

The pressure of Eleanor's arm around Alexa's back and the way their hips and shoulders connected kept Alexa grounded. She was tucked so comfortably beside Eleanor, it was as if she belonged there.

"Well, you'll both be pleased to know we have positive news." He removed his glasses and rubbed his eyes with the back of his hand. "Mrs West arrived suffering from heat stress and dehydration. Water and electrolyte replacement have done the trick, but we'll continue with that treatment and monitor her overnight as a precaution. She can go home tomorrow if all goes well."

"I'm surprised she agreed to stay," Alexa said to the doctor. She gave Eleanor a gentle bump with her hip. "Can you imagine the fuss she would have made? Gran would hate to stay in hospital overnight."

"As I said, it took a bit of convincing." Doctor Cassell chuckled. "She told me she lives by herself, and that's how she likes it. Someone will have to keep a close eye on your grandmother for the next few days, though. Give us half an hour, and you can visit her in the ward, for a short time only. Please excuse me, I must continue with my ward round. Good evening, ladies." He handed the clipboard to the nurse behind the desk.

Tears welled up in Alexa's eyes. "Thanks, Doctor," she called out as he strode briskly through the swinging doors.

"You must be so relieved." Eleanor pulled Alexa into a hug, and Alexa stood there with her face buried in Eleanor's neck, her heartbeat finally slowing to a more normal pace.

"Sorry to interrupt."

Alexa recognised Sarah's voice and reluctantly extracted herself from the safety of Eleanor's arms.

Sarah had joined them at the nurses' desk. She carried a cardboard tray loaded with three cups, a large muffin, and what looked like a couple of prepacked sandwiches.

Alexa's stomach rumbled and she rubbed her hands together. "That looks good, Sarah. I think I've got my appetite back."

"Really?" Sarah asked with wide eyes. "That sounds like encouraging news."

"Grace was suffering from heat exhaustion," Eleanor explained to her mother. "They're going to keep her overnight. Alexa will be allowed to visit in about half an hour."

"The doctor told us she's going to be all right," Alexa said, pressing her palms over her eyes.

"Oh, thank goodness. I'm so glad," Sarah said. "Now where should I put this tray?"

Alexa didn't want to be alone, but it wasn't fair to keep Eleanor and her mother waiting now that they knew her grandmother was out of the woods. "It could take longer than half an hour. I'm so grateful that you both raced over to be with me, but I'll be okay now."

"I'm not leaving," Eleanor said hastily. "I mean, if you don't mind, I'll stay with you. Mum, you should head home once you've had your tea."

"That's not necessary. I'll stay." Sarah shook her head. "Let's have our drinks and try to eat this sumptuous hospital fare." She wriggled her eyebrows. "There's plenty for me to read, and emails to send. I'm in no rush. After you've spent time with Grace, I'll take you both home to Hawthorn."

Eleanor didn't attempt to argue with Sarah, who walked to the line of chairs at the back of the waiting room and sat down.

Alexa turned to Eleanor to gauge her reaction to her mother's unexpected pronouncement.

Eleanor's eyebrows shot up, and her cheeks coloured. "I can't believe my mother just said that. You don't have to come back to Hawthorn if you don't want to. But I'd like it if you did, and then you wouldn't be alone tonight."

"Thank you. I'd really like that. You and your mum are very sweet." Actually, Eleanor was *incredibly* sweet and considerate. She'd stood fast, never pressuring Alexa when she had been cool and distant, keeping a lid on her emotions. Alexa had struck it lucky; Eleanor was an absolute gem. "Despite the doctor's assurances," Alexa said, "I'd be too wound up to sleep by myself at the loft." In Eleanor's arms, she'd feel safe...loved. She sighed contentedly at the thought.

Eleanor's beaming smile and the glint in her eyes told Alexa she'd made the right decision—not that it was a hard one to make.

Her grandmother had given Alexa a real scare. She couldn't bear the thought of anything happening to Gran before she was able to make good on her promise to clear Mei-Li's name. Alexa took a deep breath. Now was as good a time as any to ask Eleanor the question she'd been wanting to ask for days. She reached out and clasped Eleanor's hand. "Could you help me with something, something else?"

"Anything," Eleanor replied without a moment's hesitation.

"Anything?" Alexa smiled. A short strand of Eleanor's hair stuck out at a right angle over her ear. Alexa tugged it. "Maybe you should wait until I ask the question before you say yes."

"My hair's a mess, isn't it? I swam this afternoon and left the house in a hurry." Eleanor kissed Alexa's wrist. "And it would still be a yes."

"Your hair hardly looks any different from usual. I like it." Alexa held Eleanor's gaze. She took a deep breath. "Gran really frightened me today."

"It's been hard on you, Alexa. I was scared, too."

"That's why I've got to solve the mystery about Mei-Li." Alexa hesitated. "I know I don't have the right to ask for your help after I got mad at you for doing your own research—"

"We've moved on from that," Eleanor said firmly. "I want to help in any way, and if you need me, I'll spend time with Grace over the next few days. It would be no problem to work from her place if you can't take time off from the library. I know it's really busy at the moment." Eleanor patted her hair down self-consciously with her free hand, but it still stuck out at the sides adorably.

"Thank you. You are a darling." Warmth spread through Alexa at Eleanor's generosity. Alexa rubbed her forehead. "Aren't you helping out at the Image Studio next week?"

Eleanor nodded. "Yes, but not until the end of the week. Now, what can I do to assist you with the Mei-Li mystery?"

"There's a lot to research. Your knowledge of law would be really valuable," Alexa said, pressing into Eleanor's side.

"Of course, I'll help."

Alexa smiled. "I'd love to kiss you, but your mother's sitting across the room peeking at us over the top of her iPad. A cup of tea and a little muffin will have to do for now."

Eleanor planted a quick kiss on her cheek, followed by a satisfied grin. "Come on, let's go and join Mum."

Forty-five minutes later, they finally stood at her grandmother's bedside, and Alexa felt all the fear that had gripped her drain away at the sight of her grandmother's smiling face.

"I'm not ready to join my friends," Gran said with a wave of her hand, threatening to dislodge the cannula attached to the vein in her wrist.

Alexa swallowed. She and Eleanor stared at each other in horror.

"What do you mean, Granny? You're not going anywhere."

"Oh, not that." Gran giggled. "I'm not ready to move into the Merri Community Home just yet." She turned to Eleanor, smiling sweetly. "Alexa and I have discussed my wishes many times. She knows exactly what I want. Don't you, darling?"

"I do, Gran," Alexa said. "You've written down your instructions clearly. You're staying at home for as long as you are able to be independent. You're not ready for the Merri Community, and they sure as hell aren't ready for you." She winked at Eleanor, who had moved near the window.

Gran chuckled. "You've got it."

There, in the tiny hospital room, were the two people who meant the most to Alexa in the whole world. Growing up, family was always defined by her mother and grandmother. Two strong, trustworthy women. After her mother's death, her grandmother remained her rock. Alexa smiled as Eleanor helped adjust the pillows behind Gran's back, fussing and making her more comfortable.

It hadn't taken long before her gran had Eleanor wrapped around her little finger. In fact, she'd trusted Eleanor from the day they met, recognising her qualities. It had taken Alexa longer. She had two strong and dependable women in her life again, and that meant everything.

Eleanor laughed at something Gran said, and Alexa ticked off a box in her head. She loved that infectious laugh. Ticking off a few more boxes, there was also Eleanor's creativity and imagination and her eye for detail. People seemed comfortable in Eleanor's presence, and they trusted her with their stories—whether she was behind the camera or not.

Feeling her face flush, Alexa sighed. Why had she been putting up obstacles? Maybe it was because of her family history. It might have been her unwillingness to change safe patterns of behaviour. She knew, though, that the true reason for the walls she built around herself was fear. Fear of rejection; fear of being abandoned. Alexa was tired of being afraid.

She sat on the edge of her grandmother's bed, leaned over, and whispered conspiratorially in her ear, "So, was this all a ploy to make me come to my senses about Eleanor? Because if it was, it worked."

"I'm so glad it did, dear," Gran whispered back. "Haven't I been telling you your turn would come?" She smiled sweetly. "Love. Splendid, if you can find it."

Now, Alexa just had to find the courage to tell Eleanor how she felt. Maybe it was time to finally roll the dice and take a chance.

Chapter 28

Unique wonder

There was no way Eleanor would have let Alexa spend tonight alone. She would have suggested they go back to Alexa's loft together, rather than leave her side. Eleanor's limbs sagged with exhaustion after the intense emotion of the evening. Grace was being cared for, and it was good to be home with Alexa.

Eleanor pushed open the studio door and waited for Alexa to enter. "Welcome to my temporary bolt hole."

Alexa paused, one hand on the door frame, and shot her a questioning look. "What do you mean, temporary?" She toed off her shoes, leaving them just inside the door.

"You don't think I'm going to live at my parents' forever, do you? I'd like to eventually find my own place. Maybe somewhere closer to the city, with cobbled laneways and parkland, a strong sense of community—like where you and Grace live." Walking distance from Alexa's loft would be a bonus.

Alexa smiled widely, taking a few steps inside, checking out the studio apartment. "That's good to hear, but it looks like you'll be giving up a lot," she said, running her hands over the natural stone countertops. "Even a fully equipped galley kitchen."

"I don't use it much." Eleanor laughed, closing the door behind her. "If I do move out on my own, I may need to take cooking lessons." Eleanor walked over to join Alexa and watched, amused, as Alexa seemed to take in every detail of the kitchen appliances on display.

"That's right, you don't enjoy cooking, do you? But you have other talents that make up for it." Alexa poked Eleanor playfully in the ribs and spun around. "You have a rather tastefully furnished sitting room."

"Not my choice. I'm not into floral prints or French provincial furniture. I guess that's the deal when you're my age and lodging gratuitously with your parents." Eleanor lowered her head and shoved her hands into her pockets. "At least Mum's put some of my pictures on the walls."

Alexa stood in front of Eleanor's photograph depicting a tea plantation. "This is Sri Lanka, isn't it?"

"Yes, they're a Tamil community of tea-leaf pickers from the highlands."

"The colours of the women's saris look fantastic against the green of the tea bushes. It's one of my favourite images from your book," Alexa said, turning to Eleanor. "Finally, I got to see it. When I spotted it on your parents' coffee table, I couldn't resist, and your dad was proud to show it to me."

"Oh dear, I'm so sorry about that." Eleanor glanced at the ceiling. "You had to sit through his commentary about nearly every photo."

"Don't be sorry." Alexa squeezed Eleanor's forearm, immediately putting her at ease. "The book is extraordinary. That photograph of the volunteers splashing around in the river with an enormous puma is just crazy. Amazing."

"I had no idea what I was doing." Eleanor shook her head, remembering how naïve she'd been at the time. "The Bolivian jungle was so vivid, so supersaturated it was unreal. All around me, the trees were covered in orchids and dotted with monkeys and macaws. I was volunteering at the big cat refuge north of La Paz, and after a ten-minute briefing, we were sent to the river with two smaller jungle cats and a puma. Can you believe it?"

"Absolutely unbelievable." Alexa inclined her head towards Eleanor. "You travel a lot."

Although Alexa stated the obvious, there was a hint of a challenge in her frown. The transitory nature of Eleanor's job had been a stumbling block from the start, and now Eleanor was ready to address it by tossing that block into a deep mine shaft.

"I have," Eleanor countered in a determined voice. "But Melbourne is home now."

"Okay." Alexa's lips turned up in a half-smile.

Eleanor knew she'd given the right answer, not just to Alexa, but more importantly to herself. Melbourne really was home. Saying the words to Alexa made Eleanor's decision that much more real and definite.

Alexa pointed to the door leading off the galley kitchen. "Where does that go?"

"A half-bath, laundry, my darkroom, and it leads out to the courtyard and pool."

"I'd like to see your darkroom sometime," Alexa said. "You seem to have everything you need here. Except..." With her thumb, she indicated the stairway, asking with a cheeky grin, "I wonder what's up there?"

Eleanor yanked the fridge door and closed it again, suddenly unsure of her next move. She stalled. "Can I get you anything? A cold drink? Cup of tea? Ice cream?"

Alexa raised her eyebrows and offered a bemused smile. "No thanks. That supper Joel threw together for us was just right. It was kind of your father to share his favourite single malt, considering he can't drink at the moment." She ran her tongue over her bottom lip seductively.

Eleanor swallowed. "You've been through a lot today. What an emotional night." She moved slowly towards Alexa, stopping when the tops of her sneakers touched the tips of Alexa's toes.

"It has. Now, I'm here with you, where I want to be." Alexa reached for Eleanor's arm and gently tugged until their bodies pressed firmly together. She held her tight.

Eleanor hugged her back for a long time, until Alexa began relaxing into their embrace and Eleanor's own tension dissolved. "I know things between us were moving fast, and you needed a bit of space, but I'm glad you didn't hesitate to call me tonight."

When Eleanor looked up at her, Alexa's hazel eyes were piercing, unguarded, and full of need. "Four days apart from you was *way* too long. I was such an idiot," she said. "When they took Gran to hospital, you were the first person I thought of. The only one I wanted by my side."

"I couldn't get to you fast enough. It's a good thing Mum drove me, or I would have got more than one speeding ticket...or worse." Eleanor spoke quietly in Alexa's ear, "Did you mean it, when you introduced me to the doctor as your girlfriend?"

Alexa eyelids fluttered. "You are, aren't you?" She loosened her grip around Eleanor's waist, snaking her arms underneath her shirt.

Eleanor nodded. Her muscles twitched beneath the heat of Alexa's touch.

"We're okay then." Alexa inclined her head towards the stairs. "You never answered me before. Tell me, where do they lead?"

Eleanor spoke in the calmest voice she could muster, "My bedroom."

"I'd like to see it now, please," Alexa said in a raspy voice. She grazed her teeth along the sharp angles of Eleanor's collarbone and captured her mouth in a fierce, toe-curling kiss.

Eventually, they took a moment to catch their breaths and stared into each other's eyes. Eleanor was stirred by the intoxicating mix of vulnerability and desire in Alexa's gaze, igniting an equally powerful sense of protectiveness and longing. She closed her fingers around Alexa's hand, bringing it to her mouth and gently licking the inside of her wrist. "Didn't you want to see my bedroom?"

They navigated the narrow staircase entwined, stopping only once to kiss hungrily on the landing until Eleanor's knees began to shake and she hustled them as best she could to the top of the stairs.

Inside her bedroom door, Eleanor held up a finger. "Give me a minute." She clicked on a lamp and drew the blinds, gathering stray pieces of clothing along the way and tossing them into the open wardrobe, closing the door hurriedly. "I wasn't expecting company tonight," she said. "We left in a hurry. You'd never believe it from looking at this mess, but I'm usually quite organised and only have a limited selection of clothes." She kicked a stray boot under the dresser and turned to Alexa. "And not many shoes."

Still staring at Eleanor with a faintly amused smile, Alexa asked, "I gather you left London in a hurry, then?"

Eleanor nodded. "Yes, but over the years, essentially because of my work and constant travel, I learnt to do with less. I lived in a shared flat with a bedroom that was half the size of this."

Alexa's gaze wandered leisurely around the room. "You have plenty of space here. What about your photographic paraphernalia? Didn't you collect treasures travelling around the world? Where do you hide it all?"

"My camera gear fits into a backpack or two. I do have special things from my travels and a few books I couldn't part with…but not a lot. My flatmate is shipping the rest of my stuff home. It'll go into the garage here until I find a place of my own." Eleanor scanned her bedroom. Nothing was badly out of place, but she straightened the corner of the bedspread, just in case.

"Eleanor."

"Yes?"

"Are you nervous?" Alexa studied her with intense green eyes.

Eleanor raised her shoulders and let them drop. "Maybe…a little."

Alexa stretched out her hand. She clasped Eleanor's wrist and reeled her in until they connected with a soft *whoosh*. "Me too." She pressed their foreheads together and sighed. "You're so sweet and sexy. You needn't have bothered to tidy the bed. We're just going to mess it up again." Her tongue stroked Eleanor's bottom lip with a soft, sensual lick, and with one hand on Eleanor's chest, she propelled herself forward.

Eleanor gasped as she landed on her back on the bed—with Alexa's curves moulded to her. Their gazes met and held for a long moment. There was a mixture of rawness and tenderness in Alexa's eyes. "I want you so much, Eleanor." With a roll of her leg, she straddled Eleanor's hips.

Whatever concerns Eleanor had about Alexa's previous uncertainties fell away as tingling heat coursed through her body.

"From the very first time I touched you, it's been like this for me." Alexa leaned down and whispered against Eleanor's lips, "You light a fire in me. Feel how my heart beats like a hummingbird's wings." She pressed Eleanor's hand against her chest. "This has everything to do with you. It's like my first time…"

Eleanor slid her hands underneath Alexa's cotton sweater. She took a shuddering breath, intoxicated by the full, silky softness of Alexa's skin. "Let me show you how I feel."

Alexa's left brow lifted almost imperceptibly.

"Is everything all right?" Eleanor asked.

"Yes." Alexa stroked her fingers delicately across Eleanor's forehead, over her chin, and down her neck. "I want you, Eleanor—more than anything. I'm sorry it's taken so long for me to say it. But it's not just how my body reacts to you. I want you in my life. All of you. I love you, Eleanor, so much," Alexa whispered as a tear rolled down her cheek.

Eleanor struggled to keep her own tears at bay. "I love you, too."

"I know." Alexa squeezed her eyes shut, her long lashes dotted with tears.

Eleanor raised herself on her elbows and stared at Alexa with wide eyes. "You know? How do you know?"

"I heard you in the cottage that morning. You thought I was asleep."

"You heard me? Weren't you asleep?" Eleanor pulled her shirt collar up, covering her face to hide her embarrassment. "You've known all this time? Why didn't you say anything?" she mumbled through the cloth.

"I couldn't." Alexa tugged Eleanor's shirt down and gripped Eleanor's hand in hers. "I didn't say anything because I couldn't. You have every right to be confused and angry with me. When I heard you whisper those words, I was paralysed with fear." She sighed heavily. "I followed my usual pattern and backed off. I'm sorry."

"It's okay." Eleanor's finger caressed Alexa's chin, tilting her head up. "But I don't want you to be scared of my feelings for you."

"You're so sweet, Eleanor. I'm still terrified about how you make me feel." Alexa kissed Eleanor's fingers. "My reputation with relationships is appalling."

"I've heard that." Eleanor chuckled.

"Okay," Alexa said, eyes unblinking. "My family hasn't had much luck in love. So, the idea of a long-term relationship never seemed a possibility for me." After a brief hesitation, she continued, "But I want that to change. I want more. And if you're prepared to give a commitment-phobe a chance, I'm ready to stop running."

"Could you repeat that, please? In case I heard wrong." Eleanor grinned up at Alexa, a rush of happiness surging through her at the words.

"I'm ready to stop running," Alexa said, gripping Eleanor's shoulders and gently pushing her down on the bed. She nuzzled her ear. "I. Love. *You.* Eleanor Heysen."

With a sharp intake of breath, Eleanor buried her face in Alexa's hair. She'd never get sick of hearing those words. "Love you," she said softly.

Alexa's gaze pinned Eleanor in place as she skilfully unbuttoned Eleanor's shirt with one hand, easing it off her shoulders before slipping her fingers under the tank top and pulling it over Eleanor's head. Alexa rolled onto her side, and when she scratched her fingernails across Eleanor's back, Eleanor's abdominal muscles rippled with anticipation.

"So strong. You are amazing." Alexa urged Eleanor to lift her hips. She tugged Eleanor's jeans, sliding them over her thighs, and when she dragged a single finger over the front of Eleanor's briefs, Eleanor gasped.

She reached for Alexa's hand, but Alexa was persistent, adding a bit more pressure; she did it again. Eleanor let out a helpless giggle.

"You like that?" Alexa purred.

Shuddering under Alexa's touch and the intimacy in her tone, Eleanor said, "Let me show you just how much." She grabbed a fistful of Alexa's shirt and pulled Alexa down on top of her.

"More tests. Another hour or so to wait," Alexa said, sympathy for her grandmother tugging at her heart strings. "Her patience must be wearing thin. Especially since she's so much better this morning."

"How frustrating." Eleanor sighed and hit the elevator button for the ground floor. "Another wait for Grace just when she was all ready to leave, perched on the end of the bed with her overnight bag."

"What would you like to do to fill in the time? I know I need coffee." Alexa lifted her arms over her head and yawned. "Oh, sorry." She placed a hand over her mouth. "Didn't get much sleep last night, did we?"

"Nope," Eleanor said with a wide grin.

"I'm sorry I dragged you out of bed so early, but the hospital did say Gran would be ready at nine thirty."

"It was special waking up with my arms around you." Eleanor rubbed her thumb over her bottom lip.

As the lift doors closed, Alexa leaned into Eleanor, pinning her body against the lift wall. Sparks crackled between them. Alexa absolutely had to taste those lips again now. She dipped her head to give Eleanor a long, lingering kiss that awakened vivid memories of just a few hours ago.

When they came up for air, Alexa said, "You're a real snuggler." Opening her eyes this morning to Eleanor's loving gaze had sent a frisson of happiness rippling through her. At last, she'd found someone who didn't make her feel suffocated when she woke with their body draped around her.

"I am." Eleanor waved a hand at the security camera. When it failed to move in response, she took Alexa's face in her hands and they began the kissing all over again, heat beginning to build within Alexa.

They sprang apart when the elevator reached the ground floor, and the door opened with a loud ping.

"How about the Grub Café for breakfast? It's a short walk just around the corner in Fitzroy." Alexa reached for Eleanor's hand.

"The Grub Café? I haven't heard of that before." Eleanor swung their clasped hands together as they strolled along.

"I'm sure you'll like it." Alexa laughed, happiness bubbling inside her. "It has a great leafy courtyard with garden gnomes and a ping pong table. The coffee and food are damn good."

After placing their orders inside, Alexa chose a secluded table in the courtyard that allowed her to enjoy Eleanor all to herself.

Eleanor filled two glasses from the water carafe and handed one to Alexa. "How are you doing? You must be so relieved about your grandmother."

"She's always been the strongest woman I know." Alexa bit the inside of her cheek. "I am very relieved, but it makes you wonder…doesn't it? How long I have left with her?"

Eleanor squeezed her hand. "All the more reason to enjoy each moment."

"I cherish every moment with her." Alexa rubbed her forehead. "And to give Granny piece of mind I'd like to clear Mei-Li's name. As I've said, I must get back to the investigation."

"What's your plan?" Eleanor asked immediately.

"Gran's bound to kick up a fuss, but I have to stay with her for the next few nights. While she's resting, I'll take another look at the information we have and go on the hunt for more. With all that's been going on at work, I've put things on the back burner, but I need to do something now, and the Trove database will be a good start."

"Trove? I have heard of that. Isn't it the online search engine of the Australian National Library?"

Alexa nodded. "It is a brilliant resource. Virtually every page of every single newspaper is digitalized and available online for everyone to use. Unfortunately, that only applies to everything published before 1954 because that's when copyright laws changed."

"Perfect. We're in luck. Mei-Li's trial was in 1926." Eleanor tapped her chest. "What do you want me to do?"

"I'm really grateful you're willing to help. I'll show you how to access Trove." Alexa caressed Eleanor's forearm. "As you'd know, the Public Records

Office holds transcripts from Victorian court registers and can access trial briefs and correspondence. We should email them about the case."

"Good idea, but because Mei-Li's trial was eventually dismissed due to lack of evidence, there is a high probability the Public Records Office won't have kept anything." Eleanor drained the last of her coffee. "If there wasn't enough evidence against Mei-Li, the judge shouldn't have taken it to trial. There would have been no case, so why did he? The case should have been struck out."

Alexa frowned. "As we've said before, probably just because she was a middle-aged Chinese woman."

Eleanor scowled. "More than likely."

"I really do need you to interpret the legal jargon. That law degree of yours can be put to use." Alexa bit greedily at the corner of her gruyere-filled croissant, chewed, and licked her lips. She was hungrier than she'd realised.

"I'm glad to be of service," Eleanor said with a cheeky grin, handing Alexa a paper napkin.

"Why are you staring at me?" Alexa asked, taking hold of the napkin. "Oh. Have I got cheese dripping down my chin?"

"There's something so sexy about the way you eat." Eleanor reached under the table and ran her hand along Alexa's thigh.

Alexa dabbed her mouth. "Hmmm," she murmured as her cheeks flushed. "What about you? You haven't touched your breakfast. Not hungry?"

"Too busy watching you eat." With her hand still on Alexa's knee, Eleanor stuck her fork into the toasted brioche overflowing with creamy mushrooms. "I actually do have quite an appetite this morning." She loaded her fork and took a large bite. "How else can I help?" she asked after a few seconds. "What can I do, apart from interpret legal mumbo jumbo and start looking at Trove?"

Alexa smiled. "On the way to Gran's house, can we detour to my place so I can pick up some essentials? My laptop and the portfolio. Once Gran is settled, we can make a start. If you have time?"

"Yes, I do," Eleanor said warmly, squeezing Alexa's knee. "I'm free all day."

"To tell you the truth, I'd love your company." Alexa bit back a sigh and smiled. She reached for Eleanor's hand under the table, grabbing her wandering fingers. She wasn't ready to let Eleanor go.

Eleanor's lips parted in a dazzling smile. "What about tomorrow? Leo, Stella, and I are having brunch, but I can come over later if you need me."

"Stella Wright, *right*?" Alexa looked at Eleanor with a raised brow. "Weren't you in trouble for missing a lunch your mother organised so you could meet her?" A slight growl escaped her lips. "Sounds like she's still keen to meet you?"

Eleanor shook her head sharply. "No. Well she was, and she wasn't; it's a long story."

Alexa traced her fingers lightly over Eleanor's sun-warmed skin, feeling the little band of muscles in her forearm. She'd never thought of herself as a jealous person before, but when Eleanor even mentioned another woman, her kitty claws came out. Alexa swallowed the lump in her throat. "Tell me more."

"Well, she's apparently a fan of my work, but it's Leo who's taken her fancy."

"Leo?" Alexa tilted her head in question. "Ah…I see. And does Leo fancy Stella?"

"So, it seems." Eleanor gave a strained sigh and tucked her hands under her thighs. "That lug of a brother thought it was hilarious, letting me believe Stella was interested in dating *me*. I bet she was pretty amused by his joke, also."

A small chuckle escaped before Alexa could suppress it. "Leo's wicked. Your mum must have got the wrong idea. Unless Stella swings both ways?"

"Obviously Mum thinks so." Eleanor twitched an eyebrow.

Alexa let out a long, exaggerated exhalation of relief. "Anyway, thanks to Leo, I don't have to fight her off—*we* were meant to be."

Eleanor's eyes shone with pleasure. Inclining her head, she leaned across the table until her face hovered just a breath away.

"Her loss," Alexa whispered. She easily closed the distance and took advantage of Eleanor's open, smiling mouth. She slid the tip of her tongue along Eleanor's teeth and when Eleanor's lips parted further, she explored her warm, silken softness.

Before Alexa got totally lost in the wonders of their kiss, Eleanor pulled away, and Alexa opened her eyes with a start.

Eleanor shook her head and let out a shuddering breath. "You really shouldn't do that to me in public." She sat back in her seat.

Alexa's heart thrummed loudly at the tremor in Eleanor's voice. "I'm sorry. As far as I'm concerned, there's nobody here but you."

Eleanor squeezed her eyes shut. "That's the sweetest thing anyone has ever said to me."

"That's hard to believe," Alexa said with a grin. She lifted Eleanor's hand to glance at her watch.

"Is it time we headed back to the hospital?" Eleanor asked.

"Yes indeed," Alexa pushed aside her empty plate. "Granny will create a riot if they keep her there much longer. And we mustn't keep her waiting."

Just over an hour and a half later, Gran was fussing over Bruce, who meowed repeatedly, brushing against her trouser-clad leg. "I missed you too, my boy," she crooned. "Did Patrick feed you enough last night? Mind you, I'm sure you fared better than me, trapped in that sterile hospital room. At least you slept in your own bed." She huffed. "What a lot of fuss about nothing. I thought they'd never let me out."

"You are safely home now, Granny," Alexa said in a soothing voice. She heaved a sigh of relief. "And don't worry about Bruce. If anything, he's overfed."

Bruce lifted his big orange head and glared at Alexa as if she was his next meal.

Alexa glared back and shook a finger at him.

"You and Eleanor are my angels," Gran said, nudging Alexa aside. She placed three teacups and saucers on a tray. "But I'm going to be just fine from now on."

Alexa gently nudged her back. "I'm here for a few days. Get used to it. Even though you've been given a clean bill of health, I'm not going anywhere yet."

Gran batted her eyelids at Eleanor. "See how my granddaughter bosses me around?" She shuffled closer to Eleanor, who was methodically arranging a circle of gluten-free shortbread onto a serving plate. "Just be careful she doesn't try it with you."

Eleanor flashed Alexa a knowing grin. "Oh, don't worry, I will."

When Eleanor looked at her like that, her smile turning confident, slightly pleased with herself, Alexa wanted to drag her somewhere private and kiss her senseless.

Gran pulled out a chair and made herself comfortable at the kitchen table. "Ah…home sweet home." She sighed softly.

"This is just where you belong." Alexa gulped. Yesterday afternoon when Gran hadn't answered her phone, Alexa had immediately dropped everything and raced over to her house. What could have happened if she hadn't found her in time? Alexa's hands trembled at the thought of her grandmother collapsed on the floor all alone for hours. The china cups clinked on their saucers as she set the tray in the centre of the table and settled in a chair beside her grandmother.

Eleanor placed the biscuit plate beside the tea tray. "There's no place like home," she whispered, putting her hands on Alexa's shoulders.

Alexa almost whimpered as Eleanor's thumbs kneaded the knots between her shoulder blades. Her hands against Alexa's tight muscles were firm yet comforting, and Alexa soon relaxed into her soothing touch.

They sipped tea, snacked on biscuits, and chatted until Gran yawned and mumbled through her hand, "What are you two up to this afternoon?" She yawned again. "I do apologise. Maybe I'll take the doctor's advice and have a lie down. You can join me too, mister." She leaned down to caress Bruce, who stood next to her chair like a security guard with alert ears and flashing eyes. "Let us give the girls some time alone. The way they ogle each other, looks like they need some privacy."

Eleanor raised her dark lashes, gazing up at Alexa.

Alexa winked. "We have to do some research on my laptop."

Gran chuckled. "*Research*? Is that what they call it? Alexa, surely you have a fair idea of what to do by now?"

"Nice one," Eleanor whispered.

Alexa was relieved that her grandmother's sense of humour was unaffected by her visit to the hospital. She shook a playful finger at her. "Granny, you are naughty. We really do have work to do."

"Yes, we really do." Eleanor nodded to Gran and subtly nudged Alexa with her elbow. "Don't forget the sketchbook," she whispered.

"Thanks for reminding me," Alexa said, "With your permission Granny, I'd like to show Mei-Li's little book of poetry to Eleanor before she goes home later this afternoon."

"Oh, tosh. If *you* insist on staying with me, Alexa, then Eleanor can keep you company tonight. You know where the sketchbook is. I'd be delighted for Eleanor to see it."

Alexa glanced at Eleanor and lifted her shoulders in question.

Eleanor turned immediately to Gran and said, "Thank you, Grace. I'd love to stay."

Alexa flushed at the thought of sleeping with Eleanor in her grandmother's house. She did a calculation in her head. They'd had sex three times in three different locations: once at the cottage, once at Alexa's loft in Abbotsford, and once at Eleanor's studio. They'd also made out once at the library and kissed wherever and whenever possible.

This was completely different; a huge step. Alexa would never have brought any other woman to spend the night at her grandmother's home, and she still couldn't imagine making love with Eleanor for half the night, in the bedroom she'd used since she was a child—the bedroom directly above her grandmother's room. Then rolling out of bed in the morning, heading downstairs, and sitting at the breakfast table with Granny. Really? No.

Alexa rubbed the back of her neck. They'd have to practise some restraint tonight. Otherwise she'd be marching Eleanor down to sleep on the couch.

Eleanor cleared her throat, and Alexa looked up just in time to catch her lick biscuit crumbs from her lower lip.

Alexa ran a trembling hand over her face, swiping back a few strands of hair. *Damn.* Eleanor wasn't going to make this easy for her.

Chapter 29

Exposed hand

It didn't surprise Eleanor that Alexa was late. Grace had delighted in telling her that when her granddaughter was a schoolgirl, she and Eloise would set the house clocks several minutes fast, tricking Alexa into being on time. Eleanor always tried to be punctual, but that was just her thing—she wouldn't want to change the spontaneity that made Alexa, Alexa.

Eleanor found an empty desk, plonked down in one of the two chairs, and set her bag underneath. The Newspapers and Family History Reading Room where she'd been instructed to wait was as long as a basketball court and half the width. Even though all the white with its reflected bright light made it difficult to capture the finer details, she couldn't resist pulling out the Leica and taking photos of the grand, curved, pristine white ceiling with its recessed panels and skylights. It was an awesome room with state-of-the-art digital technology set inside a building with significant architectural heritage.

"I'm here at last. The email just arrived, and I rushed hotfoot to meet you." Alexa deposited her laptop on the desk and leaned forward to brush her lips chastely across Eleanor's cheek. Her mouth was firm and cool against Eleanor's skin. "Thanks for coming to meet me," she said quietly, squeezing Eleanor's shoulder affectionately. "We've got about twenty-five minutes before I'm back to the salt mines, stacking the shelves."

"Stacking shelves in a salt mine? That would make a curious photograph." Eleanor matched Alexa's low tone. She gazed at her appreciatively. "You in bubblegum-coloured trousers and retro-print shirt would be a fun subject against a stark white background."

"Prairie-print shirt." Alexa spun around in a circle before sitting down.

"Yeah, those. You look just like those sweet effervescent lolly bombs I bought after school that would explode deliciously in my mouth." Eleanor fanned herself with her hand. Had they turned the thermostat up a few notches, or was her flushed skin Alexa's fault? "Is the air-con working in here?" she asked sheepishly.

"Of course, the air-conditioning is on. I heard it's another scorcher outside but not as bad as last week. Thank goodness."

"How will Grace cope with the heat today? I would have called in to check on her before coming here, but I hitched a ride into the city with Mum."

"I left her with strict instructions to stay indoors." Alexa shrugged matter-of-factly and rolled her chair closer to Eleanor at the wide desk. "Before I left, Mrs Grasso from next door arrived bearing a large bowl of Italian vegetable and bread salad along with an esky of homemade granita and iced tea. I was almost tempted to stay home from work and have lunch with them." Alexa chuckled softly.

"She'll have some company, then. That's great," Eleanor said, flashing a smile. "Do you mind having to work through your lunch break? Should I have grabbed something for you to eat?"

"Thanks, but I had a sandwich before heading down here. Strictly no eating in these spaces, anyway."

"Of course. Only bottled water is permitted in this room." Eleanor cast her eyes to the ceiling. She should have remembered that.

Alexa opened her laptop and smiled at Eleanor over the rim of her glasses. "Shall we get to it, then? I'll open the email."

Eleanor nodded. "This is a lot different from the last time I was in the library, and you dragged me into that tiny room under the Dome. I recall there was just a couple of chairs and a table. And you got a little frisky."

"That won't be happening today, not in here—surrounded by all these other researchers and security cameras everywhere."

Eleanor met Alexa's resolute gaze with a pout. "You'd better behave then." She tapped her fingers on the desk, remembering how she'd sulked all the way home after Alexa had run off to a workshop just as things were getting steamy. "I gather you've had a response from the Public Records Office?"

"Yes, only just. I haven't had a chance to read it yet."

Alexa clicked the wireless mouse a couple of times, scrolling through her emails. "Since the state library doesn't hold records of historic cases that were dismissed unless they are of particular interest involving precedent, the PROV is our only option. Fingers crossed."

"Ah-ha. If a case ruling sets a new precedent, they would keep a record."

Alexa inclined her head towards Eleanor. "Yeah, you explained that to me on Saturday. And a whole lot of other legal stuff."

"Yes, you were a very attentive student." Eleanor grinned and gestured towards the computer screen. "Now, keep reading."

"Here we go." Alexa squinted. "They've got something."

"What?" Eleanor peered closely at the small screen in front of them.

"We're in luck," Alexa said. "They found records regarding the Foster versus Brown case because it created so much controversy at the time. That's probably because it involved a prominent American businessman and a female Chinese herbalist."

Eleanor leaned forward and pointed excitedly to the next paragraph. "Fantastic. Look at this. They've located an old address for Perceval Foster in Waterbury, Connecticut, in the US."

"Waterbury… I've heard of it." Alexa drummed her fingers distractedly on her knee.

Eleanor kept reading the email, "Foster and his daughter returned to Waterbury in 1926. The daughter's name was Betsy and she was three years old at the time." She stopped and read the last sentence to herself. Her shoulders drooped in disappointment. Eleanor slowly raised her chin and turned to Alexa. "That's it, Alexa. Unfortunately, they say that's all they've got."

"But it's a start." Alexa's tone was firm and encouraging. She typed Waterbury into the search engine. "It's seventy-seven miles from New York City," she read from the Wikipedia page. "It was known as Brass City and was famous for manufacturing brassware, clocks, and watches."

Eleanor scanned down the web page, searching for any relevant information. She refused to give up. "'The Waterbury Clock Company produced the Mickey Mouse watch, clocks, and watches for the military with glow-in-the-dark dials.' This is interesting, but I don't know how it helps us."

"Me either. Though I do remember those Mickey Mouse watches. I've seen something similar at the Mill Market."

"It says here that Walt Disney's Mickey Mouse watches kept the Waterbury Clock Company afloat during the Great Depression," Eleanor read. "It later became Timex watches."

Alexa turned to Eleanor resignedly. "So, we've only learnt two things. The Fosters came from Waterbury, a city famous for making brassware and glow-in-the-dark watches, and their daughter's name was Betsy. I think our next step is to find out more about Betsy Foster, right?"

Eleanor racked her brain, trying to think of some way to dig up more information. "Ahh, I've got it. We can use my account with Ancestry.com to search for Betsy," she said. "Can I borrow your laptop? I have an idea."

"Go for it." Alexa slid the computer and mouse over to Eleanor.

Eleanor typed in her username and password and pressed Enter. "Okay. Betsy Foster, Waterbury, Connecticut. Six hits." She scratched her forehead. "She'd be nearly a hundred if she was still alive, so we can disregard most of these women on the list."

Alexa waved her finger at the screen. "How about this 1940 census? Here's a Betsy aged eighteen years. Our Betsy would have been around that age in 1940. This Betsy lived at 56 Ridgeway Avenue, Waterbury. Hey, look at this; she lived with her father Perceval. *Bingo.*" She clapped Eleanor on the back, eyes gleaming with excitement. "Betsy lived with her father, Perceval Foster, her stepmother, and three siblings."

"Brilliant. Let's see if Ancestry has more about her." Eleanor typed in the name, birth year, and residence from the census and again hit Enter. Almost immediately, a match appeared on the screen, and Eleanor gave an involuntary squeal. "Here's the family tree. Betsy Jane Foster, deceased 2002, married to Frank Joseph Sabatini, and they had two daughters and a son."

"Her children would be in their sixties." Alexa stared at Eleanor with bright eyes. "God, I wonder if we could get in touch with them. Someone might be willing to talk with me."

"Let's go with the youngest daughter, Reyna. She is listed as unmarried." If Reyna subscribed to Ancestry, they could write her a carefully worded message and hope she would reply. She crossed her fingers, hoping Reyna used Ancestry.

Alexa grabbed Eleanor's wrist, making her jump. "How did it get so late? Damn, I've got a meeting, and Image Capture are expecting you now. What are you doing this afternoon?"

"Is it that time already?" Eleanor asked, glancing at her watch in surprise. They had both lost track of the time. "I'm rushing to get things done for the opening of our exhibition. Everything has to be ready for the framers by early next week." Eleanor's phone pinged, and she chose to ignore it.

"You're flat out, but aren't you at least curious to see the message?"

Eleanor shook her head. "Not really."

"Knowing you, I find that hard to believe." A whisper of a smile danced across Alexa's lips.

Eleanor's eyes lingered on Alexa's mouth before she blinked and met her gaze. "Okay." She lifted the phone from her pocket and glanced at the screen. She frowned. "That's unexpected. It's an email from the director of the Merri Community Home."

"Now I'm burning with curiosity." Alexa tapped Eleanor's hand. "Go ahead and read it."

Eleanor clicked the email app and scanned the screen, eyes widening as she read. "I'll be damned."

"Is it bad news?"

"On the contrary." Eleanor laughed out loud at Alexa's puzzled expression. "Listen to this. The Department of Healthcare and Ageing are very keen to include my images as part of a national education programme for their workers. They'd like me to expand the photo stories I did for the Merri Community and include new images of both elders living independently, and residents of other aged care facilities."

"Darling, that's fantastic." Alexa leaned out of her seat and folded Eleanor in her arms. "I know how important this is for you."

"It would be a substantial commission of work." Eleanor buried her face in the warmth of Alexa's neck. Her focus on celebrating the lives of older Australians had been validated. At the Mahjong tournament, she'd learnt if you didn't take a chance you could be stuck with a bad hand and indecision could lose you the game. Staying in Melbourne and expanding the focus of her work was a risk but one that was paying off. She snuggled in closer to Alexa. Definitely.

"I'm looking forward to sharing a celebratory drink with you tonight," Alexa whispered.

"Perfect, me too." Suddenly remembering where they were, and the fact they were both running late, Eleanor extracted herself from Alexa's embrace.

Alexa gently pushed Eleanor's hair off her forehead. "Meet me after closing? I have my car." She closed her laptop and tucked it into her bag.

"Shouldn't someone be home with Grace tonight?"

"Patrick and his daughter Amy are taking over a home-cooked meal. Amy is Gran's lawyer. They have legal stuff to discuss," Alexa said.

"Do you have to be there too?"

Alexa shook her head. "No. Matter of fact, Granny suggested I invite you on a proper date." She grinned broadly. "Eleanor? Would you like to have an early dinner with me?"

"I'd love to," Eleanor said eagerly. "We have two things to celebrate. We're making progress with the investigation and I may have some work." Actually, she had another thing to celebrate—Alexa just asked her on a proper date, even if her grandmother *had* suggested it—but Eleanor didn't say anything.

"We really do." Alexa stood up and planted a sweet kiss on the top of Eleanor's head. "Meet you near the Visitor's Centre just after five?"

Eleanor felt the blood rush to her face as she watched Alexa walk away, provokingly swinging her hips ever so slightly in her bubblegum trousers.

"Why have I never been to this place before?" Eleanor pressed her head back against the high-back chair, gazing around the restaurant's terrace while Alexa kept her gaze solely focussed on Eleanor.

"I mentioned the Abbotsford Convent to you ages ago, when we first met. You never took me up on my offer back then." Although Alexa didn't think the way she felt about Eleanor back then could possibly compare to the fullness of her heart right now.

"You did. I'm here now, and we'll have to come back during the day when the artists' studios are open, and we can properly explore all this medieval-styled architecture." Eleanor turned her camera over in her hands. She hadn't put it down since they'd arrived fifteen minutes ago, capturing a series of garden vistas as they walked to Lentil as Anything to have dinner. Being around Eleanor's simmering energy was addictive. She had a wide-eyed, insatiable thirst for anything new, and Alexa's pulse quickened in anticipation of taking Eleanor to all of her favourite places.

"Growing up, the convent was my playground. My friends and I spent hours scouting the six-point-eight hectares of historic buildings and gardens. It was awesome for a city kid. Magical." She smiled fondly. Despite being an only child with one parent who had to work a lot, she had many happy memories of those early days.

"Trust you to know the exact size of the property." Eleanor's mouth twitched with amusement before she took a healthy slurp of the restaurant's popular thirst quencher. "This mango lassi is so good." Eleanor licked her lower lip with a lazy swipe.

Alexa pressed an index finger to her own trembling lips. *She's totally kissable.*

"Did you scrape your knees and scratch your elbows climbing these giant trees?"

"Of course. Even though I wasn't exactly a tomboy, I was long and leggy, and my preferred outfit of overalls and Doc Martens gave me the freedom to get up to all kinds of mischief."

"What were you like at school?" Eleanor grinned.

Alexa put her chin in her hand and her elbow on the table. "High spirited, a dreamer, probably distracted—and a handful for the teachers. My favourite subjects were—"

"Let me guess."

"Sure. Go ahead."

Eleanor smiled, tapping her brow. "That's easy. History and English?"

"Would you believe, biology? I had a crazy crush on my teacher from the moment she stepped into our classroom. She made even dissecting frogs bearable." Alexa shuddered. "Literature, definitely. It was my way of connecting with faraway places and temporarily transporting myself to imaginary worlds."

Eleanor tilted her head to one side. "Books were my escape, too. Of course, photography as well," she added. "Where did you go to school?"

"Not far from here. I attended a Steiner School that's actually now re-located right here in the old convent building."

"This is a great location." Eleanor glanced around in amazement. "Pity it wasn't here back when you were at school."

Alexa prodded Eleanor's shoulder and huffed. "Back when I was in school? I'm not a whole lot older than you, you know." She cleared a space at their end of the communal table as the waitress placed down a generous platter of vegetarian sides and a mound of coconut rice.

"Yum. Thanks for bringing me. This is such a *heavenly* setting." Eleanor gave Alexa a cheeky grin.

Alexa handed over a ceramic bowl, cutlery, and napkin. "Help yourself." She sat back and watched, taking pleasure in the enthusiasm with which Eleanor attacked her meal.

The evening light diffused in pink-orange bathed Eleanor's face in the glow of the setting sun. Lovely. Alexa sipped her spiced tea and sighed. It was such a romantic setting and she was with the woman of her dreams. But was it just a dream? Was it all too perfect? Alexa had never done anything like this before.

Eleanor placed her fork down with a clatter. Her eyes narrowed. "Why aren't you eating?"

Alexa pushed the vegetables around in her bowl as she tried to find the right words. Finally, she squeezed out a breath and met Eleanor's questioning gaze. "I'm so happy to have found you. You are the first woman I've truly allowed into my world, my real world. So, this thing…" She waved a hand between them. "Is wonderful but terrifying at the same time."

Eleanor frowned. "Why terrifying?"

"You're a traveller, Eleanor, an international photographer, and even though you said you'd like to find your own place soon and live on this side of town, it's just hard to believe that you'll stay long-term in Melbourne." Alexa said it all rather fast, hoping not to sound needy. She couldn't help herself. "Are you going to stick around long enough to give us a go?"

"Yes, I am." Eleanor reached for Alexa's hand, and squeezed her fingers tightly. "This is home. Home is where the people you love are. If you're asking me if I want an *us*, I do. I want all of this, especially you."

"Are you sure?"

"Yes. One hundred and ten per cent."

Alexa laughed out loud at Eleanor's sheer confidence. A warmth stirred deep inside her. With just those few words, Eleanor had allayed her fears, and suddenly her appetite returned. She picked up her fork with renewed enthusiasm. "This food does smell amazing."

Alexa waited until Eleanor fastened her seatbelt before pulling out from the curb and turning right. "Next stop, the Heysen home, Hawthorn." She smiled wistfully.

"If you're anxious to see Grace, why don't you drop me at a tram stop?"

Alexa glanced at the clock on the dashboard. She couldn't help but worry about her grandmother, but it was only seven forty-five. Gran hated her to fuss. "Patrick messaged to reassure me that Gran is in good spirits. His wife is on night duty, so he's in no rush to get home." She pointed to her phone that she'd placed in the car console. "Sit back, relax, and listen to some music. It's connected to Bluetooth. You know how to push the right buttons."

"I do." Making herself comfortable, Eleanor patted the dashboard. "Your car has a retro looking music player, but I recall it has awesome sound." Eleanor hit play, and music streamed from the stereo speakers in the rear of the coupé.

"Yep, looks can deceive. Fits the classic vehicle but has all the mod cons." Alexa slowed the car, turning into Studley Park Road.

"Hey, it's the Orbweavers." Eleanor swivelled around in her seat to face Alexa. "We must be in sync. I've been listening to this at home, too."

Alexa smiled. "I'm glad you're enjoying their album."

"Very much. It pulls my emotions in all directions."

Halfway through Marita's poignant vocals on "Radium Girls", Alexa tapped Eleanor's forearm. "This one about radium poisoning is particularly intense." The haunting music and the sad lyrics gave her goosebumps.

Eleanor lowered the volume. "I'll fast forward if you'd prefer to listen to something a little less melancholy?"

"Please, don't. Marita has the sweetest voice, so tender." Humming the tune and listening carefully to the lyrics made Alexa's brain start processing the inspiration behind Marita's words. *By 1923. There were a hundred in the factory.* In a moment of sudden clarity, she turned to Eleanor. "Remember we read about the factory in Waterbury making watches for the military in the 1920s?"

"Yes. Yes, we did. What are you thinking?" Eleanor asked.

"On Saturday, we read that article in *The Argus* outlining Mei-Li's testimony. Mei-Li said Edith told her she'd worked in a factory, but Foster said in court that his wife *never* worked in a factory. Remember, he shouted, 'the *chink* is a liar?'" Furious at his words, Alexa banged her fist on the steering wheel.

"That's right, the bastard. You obviously think there's a link." Eleanor reached for the dial and turned up the volume.

They were silent as they listened to the rest of the song, Alexa a mix of anger and determination as she took the time to really process all the lyrics.

As the last strains of music faded away, Alexa reached out and pressed stop. "What if Edith did work in the clock factory?" She clenched the steering wheel. "I wouldn't be surprised if Foster was too ashamed to admit his wife was a factory worker. We *have* to find out if she actually worked there for sure."

"Let me check the city of Waterbury and see if we're right about the factory using radium paint." After a long, anxious minute, Eleanor waved her phone at Alexa eagerly. "*Eureka!* Listen to this. 'The Waterbury Clock Company employed women with keen eyesight and nimble fingers to paint the dials and numbers on watch faces.' It says here,

...to make the process faster, the assembly line of painters placed the paintbrushes into their mouths before dipping the brush into the radium-laced paint. It was a repetitive process that caused a build-up of radium in their mouths. They didn't know the risks and even painted it onto their nails and clothing, so they'd appear more attractive and glow in the dark.

Eleanor shook her head. "That is unbelievable."

"Totally unbelievable." Anger burnt in her stomach.

"*Exposure to radium led to the deaths of dozens of women,*" Eleanor continued to read. "And that's only the number reported. There could have been more."

"That's terrifying." Alexa shivered at the thought of it.

Eleanor clutched Alexa's thigh. "Edith may have been poisoned like the women in the Orbweavers song, who got horribly sick and died. Maybe she didn't have any symptoms until she got to Australia."

"How on earth can we prove that?" Alexa asked helplessly. It seemed impossible.

"We have to contact Edith Foster's granddaughter, Reyna." Eleanor rubbed a hand over her face. "At least we can try."

Alexa was in a daze. The possibility that they'd uncovered the cause of Edith Foster's illness had her head spinning.

Eleanor gently tapped her thigh to get her attention.

By the look of concern on Eleanor's face, Alexa knew she was driving erratically. She shoved the coupé into gear, turned left into the nearest street, and pulled over, taking deep breaths to calm herself down.

Eleanor put her hand on the back of Alexa's neck, rubbing gently.

"I just need a few minutes to digest this." Alexa rested her head on the steering wheel and sighed. "Eleanor, this could be the answer."

"It could be, Alexa. I feel jittery and excited."

"Me too," Alexa said, lifting her head.

Eleanor stared at Alexa, wide-eyed, for a long moment before she glanced at her watch. "What's the time difference in America? I'd like to email Reyna tonight. With your permission."

"Are you sure? It may still be a sensitive subject; we need to tread carefully. What will you say to her?"

Eleanor combed her hand through Alexa's hair. "I'll say that you work at the state library and that we're researching the American hotel in Castlemaine where her grandfather was the manager. And that we would be interested in any information about her grandparents' time in Australia."

"If you put it to her like that, Reyna shouldn't feel threatened by the questions and may be willing to share more," Alexa said, hope starting to mix in with her anxiety.

"Alexa, you may have solved the mystery. There's a chance that radium poisoning contributed to Edith Foster's death, and just as we suspected, it had nothing to do with Mei-Li's remedies at all. That's a brilliant discovery." A look of anticipation flashed in Eleanor's eyes. "I know we can't just yet, but I wish you had something to tell Grace right now."

"Let's not get ahead of ourselves, darling. We need to confirm it's the same Edith Foster and that she really was a Radium Girl," Alexa said as calmly as she could, but she could hardly contain the excitement bubbling up inside her.

Her body trembled as she grabbed a handful of Eleanor's shirt, pulling her forwards. Their lips came together hungrily. Just a few minutes, Alexa thought. They could afford just a few minutes of kissing like this before she drove Eleanor home. Eleanor's mouth was hot and fervent, pushing against hers. A barking dog and the sound of a gate creaking eventually drew them apart, reluctantly.

"Whoa..." Eleanor gasped, her brown eyes hazy, a little unfocussed. "Probably not the time or place for a make out session, huh? Especially when you have to get home to your grandmother," she said in a ragged voice. "But we'll have plenty of time for more. Let's make it soon." She smiled hopefully.

Alexa couldn't find her voice, nor could she wipe the big silly grin off her face. Reaching out to brush Eleanor's swollen lip with her thumb, she sighed. "Until then."

Chapter 30

The three philosophers

"WHAT A FINE SPRING DAY. The cottage looks as pretty as a picture," Grace said. "I'm so glad to be here."

Leaning against the open car door, Eleanor tugged at her T-shirt and smiled down at Grace. "It's a magical spot, isn't it?" The sun, sitting high in the rich blue sky, bathed the garden and surrounding fields in a golden-yellow glow. Eleanor filled her lungs with sweet, warm air and sighed, momentarily distracted by the big old red eucalyptus with its scarred trunk and crown of blue-green leaves casting interesting patterns on the grass below. "Picture perfect."

"It's been much too long between visits," Grace said, fluffing her hair with a cupped hand. "Alexa drove your father's car very competently. I assume you'll be the driver when we return home later today."

Eleanor chuckled. "I doubt it very much. Your granddaughter likes to be in the driver's seat." *Not always, luckily.* She took Grace's hand, helping her get out of the car. "I'm more than happy for Alexa to drive on these unfamiliar roads."

Grace glanced into the back seat. "Alexa's made quick work unpacking the car. She's taken the ornamental cherry tree out the back already."

"She gets an 'A' for efficiency." Eleanor smirked.

"That's my girl." Grace rested her hand lightly on Eleanor's shirtsleeve. "Can I lean on you for support? I seem to remember a few bumps and dips along this pathway."

"Certainly, Grace." Eleanor placed a firm but gentle grip under Grace's elbow.

"Alexa is very lucky to have found you, dear Eleanor."

Eleanor lifted her hand to her face as she felt a blush touch her cheeks. "Thank you for the compliment. I'm the lucky one."

"I've always loved coming to Gold-Dust Cottage," Grace said as they ambled towards the steps. "The garden is still as charming as ever." She tightened her grip on Eleanor's forearm. At the top of the landing, she hesitated, taking in a deep breath. "My old lungs need to take full advantage of the clear, country air."

Eleanor gestured to the table and two white wooden chairs in a partially shaded corner of the porch. "Why don't we stay out here for a while? There's a refreshing breeze blowing. We could sit for a few minutes while Alexa opens up the cottage."

She helped Grace settle into a chair, making sure she was sheltered from the harsh sunlight. Too jumpy to sit still, Eleanor propped herself against the porch's sturdy wooden railing. She couldn't wait for Grace to hear the news but feared some of it would be distressing for her.

"Thank you, dear." Grace picked one of the delicate flowers from the vine trailing along a trellis, holding it in the palm of her hand. "I remember the day Eloise planted this native sarsaparilla. She said it was vigorous and useful. Good qualities in humans, too." Her voice was laced with a hazy melancholy. "The leaves and stems can be used as a tonic. Eloise studied medicinal herbs and plants, and mixed herbal concoctions for neighbours and friends to relieve bronchitis or other minor ailments. Alexa has her book of drawings and notes. My darling daughter was a healer and a dreamer." Grace met Eleanor's gaze with a pensive look, as if her mind had briefly wandered someplace else. "Alexa has always been much more guarded. Careful. That's why it's so heartening to be an observer of what's developing between you two. I'm so glad she has you, Eleanor."

Eleanor took a deep breath, held it in her chest, and exhaled slowly. It meant a great deal that Alexa's grandmother was giving them her blessing.

A gentle breeze ruffled Grace's snowy white hair, the heat heightening the colour of her cheeks.

"Parents aren't supposed to outlive their children, it's just not the natural order of things. Not a day goes by that I don't think of my Eloise."

Grace closed her eyes for a moment, and when she opened them, she sat up straighter and lifted her chin. "Her spirit still lives on here, watching over the garden. She would be so proud of Alexa," she said with a sweet smile. "I have a feeling she would like you very much."

"Phew. The sun is beating down on the back patio mercilessly. You two have chosen the perfect spot to sit at this time of day."

Eleanor turned to see Alexa stepping towards them carrying a tray. She blinked. Alexa had changed into loose fitting shorts, tank top, and had bare feet. So relaxed and refreshed. Eleanor sighed. Breathtaking.

Alexa placed the tray laden with three glasses and an icy jug, already frosting, on the table. "Freshly squeezed minty lemonade." She winked at Eleanor. "What are you two chatting about?"

"You, of course." Grace regarded her granddaughter with an appraising look. "You were right to coax me along today. It's been too long since I was here."

Eleanor picked up the wicker rocking chair from the other end of the porch and placed it adjacent to Grace. "For you, Alexa." She held it steady for her to sit down, brushing Alexa's arm with her fingers. In an act of great bravery, she leaned over and planted a quick kiss on Alexa's lips.

"Hmmm." The flecks of gold in Alexa's eyes shone with affection.

Grace giggled. "Don't mind me."

Eleanor sat next to Alexa, quenching her thirst with a sip of the tangy, icy drink. "Grace was telling me about your mum's book of drawings and some of the medicinal plants and herbs she used."

Alexa arched an eyebrow and gave Eleanor a knowing look. "Perhaps an interest that was passed on from her ancestors?"

Grace sat to attention. "She inherited her passion from my grandmother, Mei-Li. It's such a shame that I couldn't tell Eloise the truth about our ancestry. I'll never forgive the Hamptons."

Eleanor handed her a napkin, and Grace wiped the moisture from her eyes. Hearing the love and anguish in her raspy voice, Eleanor's heart went out to her.

Alexa reached for Grace's hand. "Granny, we have some important news. We were going to tell you after lunch, but there's no point waiting now."

Grace's eyes widened. "What have you discovered?"

Alexa glanced at Eleanor as if needing assurance. Eleanor nodded, smiling encouragingly, and leaned over, running her fingers across the back of Alexa's forearm.

"We'll go through it step by step," Eleanor said. "Just so we don't leave anything out. Alexa, why don't you start?"

Alexa chewed her lip, contemplating where to begin. "It all started right here at Gold-Dust Cottage."

"What started?" her grandmother asked.

"On Eleanor's very first visit to the cottage, she found an old newspaper clipping that sparked her curiosity."

Gran looked sharply at Eleanor. "That day of the photoshoot. You asked me if I knew about the Melbourne Cup winner."

Eleanor nodded. "Yes. It was your reaction to the notices on the back—"

"That did freeze me in my tracks." Gran nodded her head vigorously.

"I'm sorry about that," Eleanor said sheepishly.

"And then, Eleanor's inquiring mind led us to the truth about William." Alexa placed a hand on Eleanor's knee to dispel any lingering fears that Eleanor may have had about what she'd done.

"And it was my turn to talk." Gran lowered her head. "To tell you about Mei-Li and the trial. To admit the family's hurt and shame I'd hidden for so many years."

With a shake of her head Alexa said, "You were just a child at the time, and the Hamptons put you under great pressure to keep silent."

"I know this already, girls. What exactly do you want to tell me?" Gran asked with a glint in her eyes. "I may be ancient, but I still have my marbles. Out with it."

Alexa's body vibrated with excitement, and she wrapped her arms around her grandmother, holding her tight, as if to anchor herself. "Granny, we have good news. It's not official, but what we've learnt will exonerate Mei-Li and clear our family name."

"What is it, Alexa?" Gran's voice was muffled against Alexa's clothing.

"After your trip to the hospital, we were determined to get to the truth," Alexa said. "It wouldn't have been possible without Eleanor's help." She moved back to her chair, still holding firmly onto one of her grandmother's hands—needing their physical connection.

"Through our research, we established that Edith Foster, the woman your grandmother was accused of poisoning, and her husband, Perceval, were originally from Waterbury, in Connecticut—"

"Yes, they were definitely American," Gran said. "He managed that American hotel where Grandfather Otto worked."

Alexa nodded, touching Eleanor's arm, motioning for her to continue and explain her part in the process.

"The Fosters had one daughter named Betsy. She was three when Edith died, and she returned with her father to Waterbury the same year," Eleanor said. "Through my genealogy account, our search led us to a 1940s census, which in turn gave us Betsy's address."

Gran wore an expression of earnest concentration on her face, clearly transfixed by the unfolding tale. Alexa gazed lovingly at her grandmother; she had always relished a good story.

"Do you need a break, Grace?" Eleanor refilled their glasses.

"No. Go on, Eleanor," Gran urged. "What happened next?"

Eleanor took a quick gulp of her lemonade. "I contacted Betsy's youngest daughter, Reyna, an economics professor at Berkeley. She confirmed that her grandmother had worked at the Waterbury Clock Company that produced instrument panels for warships, planes, and watches with glow-in-the-dark faces and dials."

"I remember seeing those watches," Gran chimed. "They were popular after the war ended, because the soldiers wore them."

"That's right," Alexa said. "And we know that, before her marriage, nineteen-year-old Edith had taken a summer vacation job at the factory. Even though her husband denied it during the trial, Reyna confirmed it. Foster lied in court." She lifted her grandmother's hand and gave it a little shake. "That was the amazing breakthrough, Granny."

After a startled look at Eleanor, Gran turned to Alexa, a frown wrinkling her forehead. "Apart from Mr Foster being a liar, what does this all mean?"

Alexa took a deep breath and exhaled slowly. "Edith and the other women at the factory used glow-in-the-dark paint containing radium. The young women were paid about eight cents for each dial they painted. They were instructed to sharpen the bristles with their lips and dip their brushes into the radium-laden paint to get the sharpest effect. It was called *lip point.*" Even saying the words made Alexa's stomach churn.

"The company never admitted full responsibility even though fifteen dial painters died." Stroking her throat, Eleanor grimaced. "More died later after years of suffering from crumbling bones, rotting jaws, cancerous tumours, and other complications, like pneumonia."

"Dear God. Those poor souls." Gran gripped Eleanor's arm, her eyes widening.

"Yes, Granny, and it's disgusting how the company tried to bury it," Alexa said, taking a deep breath to control her anger. "On returning to the United States, Foster filed a lawsuit against the company, but he was unsuccessful because Edith was already dead. The Clock Company never admitted that the women were poisoned by radium—they only compensated the remaining dial painters with free medical care."

Gran paled. "He would have known. That dreadful man would have known, and he never bothered to clear my grandmother's name."

"He was negligent. Foster would have known that, although Mei-Li was acquitted, her life would never be the same," Alexa said, her anger rising again. "Reyna was saddened to learn of Mei-Li's plight and that it had nearly ruined her life. She was truly sorry that her grandfather hadn't informed the Australian authorities."

"He *should* have done that!" Gran banged her hand on the armrest of her chair.

Alexa shook her head to dispel her dark mood. She didn't want her grandmother getting upset. She met Eleanor's soothing gaze before turning her attention back to Gran. "But isn't it wonderful that we've finally cleared Mei-Li's name, Gran? And the spirit of our ancestor can finally rest," Alexa said gently.

Gran bowed her head in a sage-like fashion and grasped the figurine that had hung with the locket on a chain around her neck for as long as Alexa could remember. "This was Mei-Li's."

Alexa reached out and closed her trembling fingers around the tiny pendant, unable to speak for the emotion welling up in her throat. From the look in her grandmother's eyes, Alexa knew without a doubt, this was one of her most precious possessions.

Eleanor got to her feet, walked to Alexa, and placed a reassuring hand on her shoulder. Alexa looked up, and their gazes locked. She'd never been surer of Eleanor. She'd never been more certain of their connection.

"Reyna is not responsible for her grandfather's deeds," Gran said. "It must have been devastating for her family to lose Edith under those circumstances." She stared at Alexa and sighed. "How on earth did you both figure it out?"

"It was your granddaughter who joined the dots," Eleanor said, winking at Alexa before turning to Gran.

"How? How did you do that, Alexa?"

Eager to tell her grandmother, Alexa moved to the edge of her chair. "Well, a friend of mine, Marita, was working at the Scienceworks Museum on an aircraft collection that had dials containing radioactive material. She learnt about the dial painters and wrote a song called 'Radium Girls' for her band, the Orbweavers," Alexa explained. "We listened to the album on our way to Eleanor's studio, and 'Radium Girls' started to play. Something just clicked, Granny, and everything fell into place."

"Well, I never. I can't begin to tell you what this means to me. It must have taken a lot of hard work and persistence on both your parts. You've made this old woman very happy." Gran was unable to choke back a sob. "I don't even have my hankie." She reached for the paper napkin and blew her nose.

Alexa knelt in front of her grandmother and hugged her as she wept openly. As each tear rolled down Gran's cheeks, Alexa imagined them carrying away the sorrow of all those years. Eleanor joined them, wrapping her arms around them both, and rested her cheek on the top of Alexa's head. Tears welled in Alexa's eyes, and it wasn't long before they were all crying.

All families had secrets. Her grandmother's grandparents and the Hamptons had entangled the young child in a web of shame, and she'd carried the burden alone for most of her life. But it was never too late to learn the truth. With Eleanor's arms firmly around Alexa, she knew it was never too late to put aside your fears and move forward.

Gran blotted her eyes and started to giggle.

Alexa met Eleanor's worried stare with one of her own. Maybe it had all been too much for her grandmother.

"Where is that ornamental cherry tree we brought to honour Mei-Li?" Gran asked.

Still puzzled by her grandmother's sudden change of mood, Alexa answered warily, "I put it out back in the shade, ready for us to transplant."

Gran started to push herself out of the chair. "Don't look at me like that, darlings. Do you remember, Alexa, your mother's favourite proverb?"

Alexa laughed and sprang to her feet, offering her grandmother a steadying hand. "I do. It is scrawled on the inside cover of Mum's notebook: *The best time to plant a tree was twenty years ago. The second-best time is now.*" Alexa had chosen the cherry tree because it would attract nectar-hungry birds, filling her mother's garden with birdsong.

"That's right." Gran swatted Alexa away and turned to Eleanor with a beaming smile. "You look like a strong young woman. Are you any good with a shovel?"

Chapter 31

Imperial treasures and happiness

The short preparation time for Eleanor's exhibition had been hectic and exhilarating, and now that opening night had arrived, Eleanor was a bundle of nerves. Fingers crossed everything ran smoothly. Her gaze was fixed on the stage when Alexa glided into view and stood at the lectern. The spotlight caught a flash of her white shirt under the aubergine coloured raw silk tux jacket and illuminated her face, giving her a bewitching aura.

Alexa tapped the microphone, silencing the room, and Eleanor took a steadying breath. The moment had arrived.

"On behalf of State Library Victoria, it is my great pleasure to welcome you to Queen's Hall, this resplendent historical space, to officially open not one, but two new exhibitions." Alexa's rich, warm voice resonated over the crowd, clearing their murmurs to total silence—turning Eleanor's insides to jelly. "*Acquisitions and Highlights of the Lehmann Collection* showcases a treasury of glass plate negatives documenting life in regional Victoria during the gold-rush period of the mid to late 1800s. Our other photographic exhibition is inextricably linked to the Lehmann Collection. *Stepping Between Frames: A Journey through Generations* is Eleanor Heysen's first show since returning home." Alexa smiled at the audience, her gaze scanning the entire room until it finally settled on Eleanor—who could have sworn Alexa winked at her. "Melbourne born Eleanor is an internationally renowned social documentary photographer. Due to a series of astounding circumstances, she and her late aunt, Helen Heysen, are responsible for the completion of the library's Lehmann Collection of historical images."

Eleanor pinched herself to check if she was dreaming. It still felt unreal that she and Helen had been the catalyst for what they were celebrating tonight at this event.

"As recently as 2012, one thousand seven hundred glass plate negatives were discovered in a garden shed in Ballarat." Alexa placed her hand in the pocket of her pinstriped trousers. "When the Library acquired and restored the negatives, we found just five were missing." Alexa paused, then removed her hand from her pocket, splaying her fingers. "Those five negatives were discovered in China by Helen Heysen and gifted to us by her family completing our rare photographic archive." All around Eleanor, there was a widespread murmur from the guests.

Eleanor's father touched her elbow and whispered, "Imagine how proud and amazed Helen would be."

"She would." Eleanor blinked and released a deep sigh. After carrying the burden for ten years about not meeting Helen in Beijing, after all the time she'd spent learning about the negatives and working on the exhibitions, her mother's words had finally sunk in. Eleanor was not responsible for her aunt's death.

"Today, we honour and celebrate Heinrich Lehmann, an immigrant German prospector, and his photographers who had a vision to record the cities, towns, and people of gold-rush Victoria," Alexa continued. "We extend our congratulations and gratitude to Eleanor Heysen, who pulled *her* exhibition together in just a few weeks. What a mammoth achievement." Finding Eleanor again in the crowd, this time Alexa's face lit up with a radiant smile, and Eleanor swooned. With a slash of red on her kissable lips, Alexa looked as if she'd stepped out of a 40s *Vogue* magazine.

"Congratulations, Eleanor. Well done," Patrick declared from where he stood on the other side of Grace.

Eleanor felt her cheeks flush at the attention drawn her way. She knew Alexa's speech almost by heart. But witnessing Alexa's professionalism and poise as she stood on the podium in Queen's Hall had Eleanor's pulse picking up speed.

"Hm-hmm." Eleanor bit the inside of her cheek.

Grace tugged the cuff of Eleanor's shirt. "Isn't she exquisite and smart? Her mother would have loved to see her up on the stage," she said. "You look rather dashing tonight yourself, Eleanor."

"Thank you, Grace. I made an effort for a special occasion." Eleanor looked down at her delicate flower-print shirt in crimson red and white, tucked loosely into the charcoal trousers Alexa had chosen for her in Castlemaine. When they'd briefly met before the event began, Alexa's gaze had roamed lazily over Eleanor, and the look she gave her had sent shivers up her spine.

"Imagine my disbelief when Eleanor Heysen appeared in my office," Alexa said, rolling her shoulders back in that self-assured manner Eleanor adored, "with an exquisitely carved Chinese dragon box, the contents of which were a revelation." She clasped her hands together on the lectern. "Carefully ensconced inside its red velvet lining were the Lehmann Collection's missing five glass plate negatives."

"*Imagine* her surprise when Eleanor turned out to be the missing piece of her heart," mumbled someone standing nearby.

Somebody else tittered, "Finally."

Eleanor recognised Louise's whispered tone. From their high spirits, she was positive Kelly and Louise had enjoyed more than a glass or two of bubbly. Eleanor shook her head with a smile.

The enticing, smoother-than-honey tone in Alexa's voice drew Eleanor's attention back to the stage. She had no need for alcohol right now. Eleanor was intoxicated enough by the sight and sound of Alexa.

"The coincidences and connections became even more extraordinary when we discovered that one of the new slides, depicting a Chinese gentleman sitting beside a herbalist box, was in fact my great-great-great-grandfather Guān Li-Shen." Alexa paused as a collective gasp reverberated through the room. "He had travelled from China to Australia in 1855 to fossick for gold."

Eleanor beamed with pride. The guests seemed to absorb every word and watch Alexa's every gesture as she cleverly wove the threads of the two stories together.

"Eleanor's exhibition in the Victorian Gallery skilfully showcases a ten-metre-long image that forms the backdrop to *Stepping Between Frames*. It is one of the photographer's landscapes from her travels in China. The muted scene, like a brush painting in greens and blues, explores the interconnection between photography, painting, Chinese calligraphy, and poetry."

Grace nudged Eleanor. "Thank you for sneaking me in for a private viewing before the speeches," she whispered.

Eleanor gently nudged her back. "I had to get your seal of approval before my exhibition opened to the public. It is about you and your family, after all."

"I'm just so happy you managed to incorporate one of Mei-Li's poems into the mural. You're so clever."

Eleanor squeezed Grace's hand. They'd both shed a few tears when she'd walked Grace through the exhibition.

Alexa placed her hand on her chest, over her heart. "Suspended to the forefront of Eleanor's mural, the viewer steps in between fifteen black and white portraits that trace the genealogy of *my* family—from Guān Li-Shen to his daughter Mei-Li, who also practised as a Chinese herbalist until the 1920s. Her son William played football for Melbourne University, became an engineer and a Queensland lychee farmer, and his daughter, my grandmother Grace West, was a magazine columnist in the 50s and 60s. Especially dear to me is Eleanor's photograph of the enchanting garden in the gold-rush town of Chewton that belonged to my late mother, Eloise Bellamy."

Grace leaned heavily into Eleanor's side, and Eleanor put a steadying arm around her small frame. Although Grace's eyelashes were moist, her face was alight with joy.

Alexa hesitated a moment, then smiled that dazzling smile that came from deep within and melted Eleanor's heart. "Imagine my amazement when, soon after my Chinese ancestry was disclosed, came the biggest shock of all—that the very same herbalist box belonging to Guān had been passed down through the generations to my grandmother, who kept it secure for all these years in the attic of her Fitzroy home."

Eleanor squeezed Grace's shoulder. Grace and Alexa had agreed not to disclose the reason why the box had been hidden away. Mei-Li's trial and the unjust way she and the family had been treated was the subject of a paper Alexa would present at the Immigration Museum Conference early next year. They saw no reason to complicate things just yet.

"The library is indebted to Museum Victoria for preparing this precious 150-year-old herbalist box at short notice. When you've had a chance to view the exhibition, you will see it on display. An exquisite medicine box that contains vials and potions that came from China and was then photographed with its owner in Castlemaine. We may never know why the five negatives were in Helen Heysen's possession, but now they rest here safely in the library." Alexa stared directly into the audience. "Each of the slides in the entire Lehmann Collection tells stories about families and places that quite likely touch on your ancestors also."

A gentle sob escaped from Grace, and Eleanor felt her own eyes mist.

"Eleanor," her mother whispered in her ear. "Your exhibition is phenomenal. I'm so proud of you. Sorry I gave you such a hard time about your visits to the library and the goldfields." She stepped closer, and their hips touched. "Alexa is an excellent public speaker. Half the room are reaching for a handkerchief. She's a sweetheart, too."

Ever since that night at the hospital, things had changed for Eleanor and her mother, and Eleanor was still getting used to it. Even now, her mother's praise of her work made her beam with pleasure. And her mother's approval of Alexa? That was just the icing on the cake.

In front of them, Leo stood with one arm around Stella's waist. He turned to Eleanor and winked.

Eleanor smirked in return.

The lighting in the hall dimmed, and Alexa stepped away from the lectern. "Sometimes family secrets are concealed over generations, for tens, even hundreds of years." Alexa's voice had lowered to a rich, melodious tone. "Imagine if the Lehmann Collection from the 1870s—almost as old as Australia's photographic history—had never been found. This time capsule of life during such a turbulent period in our history would have been lost forever."

Alexa turned around to face a 3D hologram that appeared like magic in the void. A photo Eleanor had taken of Grace and Alexa holding the herbalist box in Grace's home levitated metres above the stage. Grace grabbed Eleanor's arm and gasped. Eleanor grinned; clearly, she'd captured the moment perfectly. Alexa was smiling in disbelief, and the joy on Grace's face was indescribable. Slowly, the original images that Eleanor had transformed of Guān, Mei-Li, William, and Eloise also appeared.

Alexa raised her arms above her head, and a projector hidden somewhere in the room cast a sinewy shadow of her onto the wall, connecting the images. Eleanor had been at each rehearsal closely liaising with the multimedia hologram company and the event planner to make this happen. However, experiencing the whole thing tonight was out of this world, surreal.

"Part of my family tree." Alexa spun around to face them as the guests began to clap.

Wonderstruck, Eleanor stared, photographing Alexa with only her eyes.

At the mezzanine level, Alexa took a deep breath, pushed open the door, and guided Eleanor through into the dimly lit space that housed the library's chess collection. Amazingly, everything had gone like clockwork—even the holograms appeared on cue without a glitch—and tonight had been one of the highlights of Alexa's career. But now, Alexa wanted nothing more than to focus fully on Eleanor. She quickly closed the door behind them with a quiet click.

Alexa leaned against one of the huge fluted Corinthian columns, smiling at Eleanor's awed expression as she walked over to the balustrade and peered over. The melodic strains of the string quartet competing with muffled voices and the tinkling of glasses drifted up from the grand hall.

"Fantastic view from up here. What an unbelievable evening it's been." Eleanor turned to face Alexa with wide eyes. "Wow…"

Wow, indeed. That one simple word said it all. Alexa didn't want the feeling to end. The giddy, heady sensation that made her feel as if her feet weren't touching the ground. Really, it was all about Eleanor. The all-encompassing love she experienced just being around her.

"How long had Queen's Hall been closed?"

Alexa had to think for a moment. Sometimes Eleanor's enthusiasm and thirst for knowledge took her by surprise. "To the general public? Sixteen years."

"I remember there used to be amazing chandeliers. You could almost reach out and touch them." Eleanor leaned dangerously over the black metal balustrade with her arm outstretched.

Alexa dragged her back and wrapped her arms around Eleanor, pulling her close. "No superhero stunts for you tonight, darling." She smiled, remembering Eleanor's dash to rescue the boy caught on the library staircase. Alexa dipped her head, nuzzling the back of Eleanor's soft hair, breathing her in. Her heart was at bursting point, filled with passion and pride for Eleanor.

Eleanor turned a half circle in Alexa's arms. "Have you finished your official responsibilities for the evening, Ms Bellamy?" She moulded herself into the curves of Alexa's body. "Or are you still on duty?"

Alexa moaned in response, wishing she could stay in Eleanor's arms forever. "Ninety-nine-point-nine percent done. But we do have to go back down and mingle for a short while. Do you mind?" she asked.

"Not as long as you are in my sight." Eleanor raised her eyes to meet Alexa's gaze and grinned.

For a few seconds, Alexa was lost in the depths of Eleanor's eyes, and she sighed deeply.

Eleanor seized the opportunity and softly caressed the sensitive skin of Alexa's neck with her lips. "How private is this space?" she asked with a husky moan.

"I locked the door, but not at all private." Alexa choked back a gasp as Eleanor's fingers slipped under her jacket, along her stomach, and up to her breast. Alexa dropped her mouth to Eleanor's ear, taking the lobe between her teeth and biting down gently. "If you keep doing that, I won't care if those dancing beams of light bouncing around the room illuminate us or if three hundred people hear my cries."

"All the more tempting, don't you think? When we're together in the library, something magical happens," Eleanor whispered. She pressed her hip into the junction of Alexa's thighs, and a slow burn of desire curled through Alexa.

Alexa tugged Eleanor behind a column where the security cameras and the twinkling lights wouldn't reach them and pressed her lips to Eleanor's, unable to resist. When Eleanor whimpered, Alexa angled her mouth for a deeper kiss. Her phone pinged. *No way.* Alexa tightened her hold around Eleanor's waist, ignoring the interruption, and poured everything she had into their kiss.

The damn phone pinged again. Alexa groaned.

Eleanor gently eased away. "Go on, you'd better check it."

"Bugger. Sorry. I'd better." She pulled the phone from her jacket pocket. "Jac says we have fifteen minutes. The Mayor has asked to meet with you to have a copy of your book signed."

Eleanor's eyes widened. "What do you mean? Where did she get my book?"

Alexa leaned down to kiss her tenderly but briefly. "Silly me, I forgot to tell you. The copies arrived this morning. They're already on sale in the Library shop."

"Really? That's awesome." Eleanor's eyes shone. "Thanks to you and Katherine for slicing through the red tape and getting them here in time for the opening."

"Hey, they'll be walking off the shelves. There's been such a positive response to your exhibition already." Alexa's heart swelled with pride. "It's remarkable, darling, and I'm not just saying that because it's so incredibly personal to me."

"It wouldn't have happened without you." Eleanor laughed. "Obviously."

Alexa pressed a quick kiss to Eleanor's cheek before reluctantly pulling away. "We'd better not keep the Mayor waiting much longer. She wants to be introduced to the talented photographer."

"And her muse," Eleanor said cheekily. She lifted Alexa's hand to her lips, placing a single kiss on the inside of her palm. "You were amazing out there tonight. I am so proud of you."

"I'm glad my nerves didn't show." Alexa burrowed her face in the hollow of Eleanor's neck. "Every time I made eye contact with you..." Alexa took a couple of deep breaths and gazed at Eleanor. "I could feel your encouragement and your love."

Eleanor gave her the sweetest of smiles.

"You are absolutely stunning in this shirt. Bright colours really suit you." Alexa stroked the top of Eleanor's shoulders, brushing the crimson red and white shirt, allowing her fingers to linger on the stand-up collar. "I totally get why the President of the Chinese Historical Federation commented on your perfect choice of shirt *and* swooned over your exhibition."

Eleanor laughed out loud. "Did she? I bought this in London, but it does have a Mandarin collar." She held onto one of Alexa's fingers.

Alexa played with the button on the cuff of Eleanor's shirt. Something had been tugging at her mind for the past few days, and she figured now was as good a time as any to ask. "Would you consider something?"

"Definitely. I'd love you to take me home as soon as we finish here." Eleanor grinned.

"Well sweetheart, that goes without saying. It's been so busy, we've hardly seen each other for days." Alexa stroked Eleanor's cheek. "But that's not what I mean."

Eleanor looked at her earnestly. "What is it?"

Alexa blinked under her gaze. "Would you come to China? I'd love to have you with me when I trace the footsteps of my ancestors." She bit her lip, trying to keep her voice as casual as she could. "And now that the library has located some of the Yang family's descendants in Guangzhou, we have a clue to help us discover why Helen had the negatives."

Eleanor didn't hesitate. "Yes, I'd love to."

Grasping Eleanor's shoulders, Alexa managed a shaky breath. "If you're sure, let's go and buy the tickets right now."

Eleanor stared into Alexa's eyes and laughed.

"Are you sure you don't mind going on a big trip with me? China is a lot further than Chewton, and I do have a very slight tendency to run late." Alexa smiled sheepishly.

"You can't put me off that easily." Eleanor winked.

Alexa sighed contentedly. "Good."

Eleanor gave Alexa a self-assured and adoring smile. "I've travelled many roads...but the most important journey brought me home and led me to you. This is the beginning of our story, Alexa. Our life together. I love you."

Alexa felt a rush of love so strong. This was the first time she'd given her heart to someone and let go of her fears, and she was already reaping the rewards. Alexa slid her hands down Eleanor's arms, clutching her wrists. "You make me so happy, Eleanor. I love you too."

"I look forward to kissing you in hundreds of amazing places. Starting right here." Eleanor's mouth moved over Alexa's with exquisite tenderness, and she kissed her so passionately Alexa worried it might short circuit the library's lighting system.

The phone pinged again, and they slowly broke apart. "I could just toss it over the balcony," Alexa said, a little breathlessly.

Eleanor's eyes danced; they mirrored the great joy in Alexa's heart. "Lead the way, darling," she said, reaching for Alexa's hand.

Alexa intertwined their fingers. She knew she held the winning hand. Whether their ancestors had played a part, or it was pure destiny that brought them together—with Eleanor, Alexa had found love, hope, and a lifetime of infinite possibilities.

THE END

Other Books from Ylva Publishing

www.ylva-publishing.com

Food for Love

C. Fonseca

ISBN: 978-3-96324-082-9
Length: 276 pages (96,000 words)

When injured elite cyclist Jess flies to Australia to sort her late brother's estate, the last thing she wants is his stake in a rural eatery. She'd rather settle up, move on, and sidestep the restaurant's beautiful owner, Lili, and her child. Given her traumatic life, Jess isn't sure she'd survive letting her guard down. A lesbian romance about how nourishment is much more than the food we eat.

A Curious Woman

Jess Lea

ISBN: 978-3-96324-160-4
Length: 283 pages (100,000 words)

Bess has moved to a coastal town where she has a job at a hip gallery, some territorial chickens, and a lot of self-help books. She's also at war with Margaret, who runs the local museum with an iron fist. When they're both implicated in a senseless murder, can they work together to expose the truth?

A funny, fabulous, cozy mystery filled with quirkiness and a sweet serve of lesbian romance.

Requiem for Immortals

Lee Winter

ISBN: 978-3-95533-710-0
Length: 263 pages (86,000 words)

Requiem is a brilliant cellist with a secret. The dispassionate assassin has made an art form out of killing Australia's underworld figures without a thought. One day she's hired to kill a sweet and unassuming innocent. Requiem can't work out why anyone would want her dead—and why she should even care.

A Heart This Big

Cheyenne Blue

ISBN: 978-3-96324-202-1
Length: 253 pages (89,000 words)

Country girl Nina loves to offer city kids a taste of rural life at Banksia Farm. When a lawsuit threatens, she needs help to avoid losing the farm.

Enter lawyer Leigh, who doesn't have time for small, unpaid cases or rural visits that wreck her cool—and her clothes. Still, warm-hearted Nina and her challenging daughter are awfully hard to say no to.

A captivating opposites-attract lesbian romance.

About C. Fonseca

As a small child, C. Fonseca had imaginary friends. She told these friends stories and her family even set them places at the dinner table. When she grew up, she lost the imaginary friends, but she continued writing poetry and stories.

She lives in Australia, by the sea, with her Kiwi wife and their beloved Burmese cats. She is an expressionist landscape painter and can often be found at a cliff-top platform overlooking the Southern Ocean, daydreaming, plotting, and planning her creative adventures.

CONNECT WITH AUTHOR

Facebook: www.facebook.com/cfonseca1au

E-Mail: cfonseca1au@gmail.com

Tracing Invisible Threads

ISBN: 978-3-96324-481-0

Available in e-book and paperback formats.

Published by Ylva Publishing, legal entity of Ylva Verlag, e.Kfr.

Ylva Verlag, e.Kfr.
Owner: Astrid Ohletz
Am Kirschgarten 2
65830 Kriftel
Germany

www.ylva-publishing.com

First edition: 2021

Credits
Edited by Hayley Price and Sheena Billet
Cover Design and Print Layout by Streetlight Graphics
Copyright: Radium Girls by The Orbweavers from the album Deep Leads. Written by Marita Dyson and Stuart Flanagan
Mistletone Records 2017

Made in the USA
Coppell, TX
16 May 2021